THE RESIDENCY

LISE GOLD

MADELEINE TAYLOR

Lise Gold Books

And the day came when the risk to remain tight in a bud was more painful than the risk it took to blossom.

— ANAÏS NIN

1

ZARA

*P*eter's left eyebrow twitches when he's about to make us money. It's a tell I've observed over ten years of albums, tours, and deals—an involuntary facial tic that's become my personal fortune barometer. Right now, that eyebrow is practically dancing as he spreads glossy presentation folders across my kitchen island like a blackjack dealer with a winning hand.

"Vegas, Zara. The Olympus. Athena Stavros is offering exclusivity, creative control, and a number that makes your last tour look like a dive bar residency in comparison." He slides another page across the marble countertop, his finger tapping a figure that contains more zeros than seems reasonable.

I pull my silk kimono robe tighter around me. "Vegas," I repeat, trying to imagine myself there, planted in one spot instead of the perpetual motion that has defined my existence for the past decade. "For ten months?"

Peter brushes an invisible speck from his Paul Smith suit. At fifty-three, he still looks like he just stepped off a GQ cover shoot—salt and pepper stubble meticulously maintained, fitness-obsessed physique hidden beneath casually expensive clothing. His green tortoiseshell glasses have become his trademark.

"Ten months where you sleep in the same bed every night," he confirms, removing his glasses to clean them with a microfiber cloth he extracts from his breast pocket. "Where you can keep actual food in a refrigerator. Where you might—and I'm spitballing here—possibly make a friend who isn't on your payroll."

The jab lands with pinpoint accuracy. Besides Peter I have exactly one friend I would classify as genuine, and she dates back to my college days.

"The money is impressive," I concede. "But I'm not exactly hurting for cash."

Peter resumes his pacing. "It's not just about the money. It's about positioning. Every A-lister is securing a Vegas residency these days. It's no longer where careers go to die—it's where they evolve. You perform four to five nights a week in a venue tailored to your show. The rest of the time? All yours." He spreads his hands in a gesture that encompasses the theoretical expanse of my potential free time. "Write. Create. Rest. Live like a normal human being for once."

I'm aware that my kitchen, with its panoramic ocean views and designer appliances I rarely use, is about as far from normal as one can get. Sometimes I still catch myself thinking of the two-room apartment where I grew up, my mother stretching rice and beans for days, where luxury meant the electricity stayed on all month.

"Does this Athena person usually make these offers personally?" I ask.

"No." There's a hint of pride in Peter's voice. "She doesn't. The Olympus is rebranding as the premier arts venue on the Strip. I know the timeline feels tight, but we've been in preliminary talks with The Olympus for over a year. The Palestra, their theater, completed renovations and she wants you for the grand reopening. She wants their first major residency to make a statement."

I stand and move to the floor-to-ceiling windows that frame the Pacific like a screen. Three seagulls hover on the updraft, suspended in perfect equilibrium with the wind. I envy them—existing purely in the moment, without past or future to complicate the present.

"What's her angle?" I ask without turning around. "Casino owners don't just hand out creative control and astronomical paychecks without wanting something in return."

Peter's reflection appears beside mine in the glass. "She's building something," he says. "A legacy. Having you, Zara Nova, as her inaugural resident artist makes a statement to the entire industry."

I turn to face him. "So I'm a statement?"

"You're an investment," he corrects. "One that will pay dividends for both of you. Think about it—when was the last time you weren't exhausted?" He doesn't wait for my answer. "When was the last time you wrote something that wasn't on the back of a tour bus napkin between cities? When was the last time you dated someone?"

I flinch at that last one. My love life—or rather, the manufactured public version of it—has been a series of strategic relationships with appropriate men in appropriate industries for appropriate lengths of time. Entertainment lawyers. Film producers. Artists.

None of these arrangements have ever progressed beyond public appearances and the occasional goodnight kiss for the benefit of eager paparazzi. My team calls it "image management." I call it exhausting.

"The residency gives you stability," Peter continues, his voice softening. "It gives you space to figure out what's next without the pressure of globe-trotting and constant reinvention. Your friends and family could actually visit you instead of trying to intercept you somewhere between Tokyo and Berlin."

He has a point there. Jess, my friend from college, had her baby a few months ago. I've only seen my godson twice, both times jet-lagged and counting the hours until I needed to be somewhere else.

"I'm not sure Vegas is... me," I say, returning to the breakfast bar and the spreadsheet that outlines what my life could look like for the next year. I push a stray dark curl behind my ear. "I love the ocean. What if six months in, I'm climbing the walls of that suite?"

"Then you climb the walls in comfort until the contract ends," he says with a shrug. "But I don't think you will."

Peter has been with me since the beginning. He discovered me at a showcase in New York when I was twenty-one and too naive to realize how rare it was for someone of his caliber to take interest in an unknown. He's guided my career with a mixture of sharp business acumen and genuine care that transcends our professional relationship.

"The Olympus has a reputation for privacy and discretion," he continues. "They protect their VIP guests better than most venues."

"How soon would I need to decide?" I ask, reaching for the contract details Peter has brought.

"Stavros wants an answer within two weeks," he says. "She's got other artists interested, but you're her first choice." He hesitates, then adds, "I think this could be good for you, Zara. Not just professionally, but personally."

I flip through the pages, scanning the highlights—

performance schedule, compensation structure, accommodations. The Olympus would provide a multi-room suite customized to my preferences, a dedicated staff, security, and enough perks to make a royal family blush.

"The creative control is real?" I ask, focusing on the clause that matters most to me. "Full autonomy over the show design, setlist, band selection?"

"Everything," Peter confirms. "Stavros was adamant about that. She doesn't want a watered-down version of Zara Nova. She wants the full experience. Her exact words were 'I'm not paying for a sanitized casino act. I want the artist in her element, creating something Vegas has never seen before.'"

A reluctant smile tugs at my lips. "I like the sound of that."

"I thought you might." Peter drops the sales pitch persona. This is the Peter few people see—the one who sometimes remembers he's human before he's a manager. "Look, I know the idea of staying put is foreign territory for you. You've been running since we released your first single. But I'm watching you burn out, Z. The spark that made you special—it's still there, but it's flickering."

His honesty is painful. We don't usually do vulnerability, not like this.

"Tours are brutal," I admit. "Amazing but brutal. And the constant pressure to evolve, to stay relevant... sometimes I forget who I am beneath the Zara Nova everyone expects."

"Exactly," Peter says, leaning forward. "Vegas gives you something you haven't had in years—consistency. Same stage every night. Same bed. Same surroundings. Within that structure, you might find the space to remember."

"Remember what?"

"The girl who wrote songs because she couldn't not

write them. The one who performed because it was like breathing, not because seventeen thousand people paid three hundred dollars a ticket to see her."

The ocean breeze shifts, sending a wind chime on my deck into a chaotic melody. I close my eyes and listen to it, thinking about structure and chaos, about consistency and freedom.

"Ten months," I murmur, opening my eyes to meet Peter's gaze. "I could do ten months."

"Is that a yes?" he asks, unable to hide his excitement.

"It's a 'I want to meet Athena Stavros in person before I commit,'" I clarify. "Let's go to Vegas. I need to look her in the eye before I sign anything."

"No problem." Peter already pulls out his phone. "I can arrange that. When are you thinking?"

2

DIANE

*S*ilver clinks against bone china as my father works through his lamb. The Washington family dining room is a mahogany battlefield, my mother and father at opposite ends of the table, me positioned halfway between them.

"The Cunninghams are expecting you this Friday, Diane." My father doesn't look up from his food. Senator Richard Washington's statements have never required the weakness of eye contact to carry their weight. "Robert specifically mentioned how much Thomas is looking forward to seeing you again."

And there it is. I take a sip of Cabernet to mask my reaction. Thomas Cunningham. Second son of former FDA Commissioner Robert Cunningham. Harvard Law. Private practice specializing in pharmaceutical patents that his father conveniently oversees. Thirty-four, never married. Of course they're trying to set me up.

I set my glass down on its water ring. "Thomas Cunningham is looking forward to seeing me? That's interesting, considering we don't know each other."

"You were at the same fundraiser last spring," my mother interjects. Elizabeth Washington, née Spencer, raises her eyebrows a millimeter—her version of exasperation. "The Childhood Leukemia benefit at the Kennedy Center."

"I remember the event, Mom. I wrote the check. But I don't remember meeting Thomas."

"Well, he certainly noticed you." Her voice maintains the pleasant modulation she uses for junior league committees and congressional wives.

My father clears his throat, the sound echoing off the twenty-foot ceilings. The dining room, like everything in the Washington home, is designed to intimidate. Oil paintings of stern-faced ancestors judge us from gilt frames. The chandelier—crystal and brass, imported from somewhere impressive that my mother mentions to guests—hangs like a glittering guillotine. Even the table itself, which could comfortably seat eighteen, makes this dinner for three feel like a boardroom meeting with food service.

"The Cunninghams' dinner is not optional," he says. "It's a strategic gathering. Robert is positioning for the vacant seat on the Pharmaceutical Research Committee. Our foundation's education initiatives in STEM fields align with their interests."

I take another sip of wine. My father's never eaten a meal without a strategic objective in his life. His senate career spans three decades of calculated dinners and purposeful golf outings. The Washington Foundation—my daily professional home—exists primarily as an extension of his influence, neatly packaged with a tax deduction.

"I understand the strategic value," I reply, matching his businesslike tone. "I'm simply questioning why Thomas's interest in me is relevant to the foundation's STEM initiatives."

My mother sighs—a sound that conveys both disappointment and resignation. "Diane, darling, you've just turned thirty. Your biological clock—"

"Is a sexist construct designed to panic women into making life choices based on arbitrary timelines rather than personal readiness or desire." I finish for her, smiling pleasantly. It's an argument we've had since I turned twenty-five.

"Your father and I were married at twenty," she continues as if I hadn't spoken. "I had you at twenty-one. Our constituents—"

"They're Dad's constituents, not mine," I say, though I know it's futile. In the Washington family, everything belongs to everyone, especially political capital.

"The voters," my mother amends without missing a beat, "expect certain traditional values from the Washington family. Your perpetual singlehood is becoming... noticeable."

I resist the urge to roll my eyes. We've been having this same conversation for years, but its frequency has increased to nearly monthly now. The milestone of my thirtieth birthday has apparently transformed me from "career-focused" to "concerning spinster" in the eyes of Virginia's conservative voting base.

"I'm busy running our foundation," I say, setting down my fork. "A foundation that, I might add, raised twenty-three million dollars last year, implemented educational programs in twelve states, and garnered positive press coverage in every major publication. My marital status hasn't seemed to hinder our success."

"No one is questioning your professional competence," my father says.

The unspoken "but" hangs in the air.

"The point is," he continues, "that the foundation's work

and our family's position require a certain image. Stability. Continuity. Legacy."

The trinity of Washington family values. I've heard them invoked at every major decision point of my life—where I would attend school, what I would study, which job I would take after graduation. Always the family, never the individual.

"Thomas Cunningham comes from an excellent background," my mother adds. "His grandfather was Secretary of State under Nixon. His mother chairs three major charity boards. He's handsome and he'd make a wonderful partner for you."

Partner. As if marriage were a business merger, which, in my family, it essentially is. My mother and father's union was orchestrated by their parents, a combining of old Virginia money with political ambitions and New England connections.

"I have work commitments that weekend," I say, the lie forming instantaneously. "The foundation has potential donors in Las Vegas I need to meet with personally."

"Vegas?" My father's fork pauses halfway to his mouth. "Again? I thought you were there last month."

My mind races through our actual donor database. "The Meyerson Group. They're considering a significant contribution to our tech education initiative. Martin Meyerson made his fortune in hotel security systems before expanding into casino management software."

The details flow easily, plausible and specific enough to deflect suspicion. I've become adept at constructing these facades—lies that I can inhabit comfortably when needed.

"Surely someone else from the foundation can handle that meeting," my mother presses.

"They specifically requested me." Another improvised

detail to reinforce the structure. "Apparently, Martin's daughter attended my panel at the Education Innovation Summit last fall. She was impressed."

My father frowns. "How significant a contribution are we talking?" he asks finally.

"Potentially six figures," I reply, confident in my fabrication.

"I suppose I could tell the Cunninghams dinner could wait," my mother concedes reluctantly. "Though I do wish you'd mentioned this earlier. Thomas is quite the catch. Well-connected, Ivy League—"

"And as interesting as unseasoned grilled chicken," I finish for her, allowing a rare moment of honesty to slip through.

My father's eyebrows lift fractionally. "You *have* met him, then?"

"If you say so. He's clearly not that memorable."

My mother's lips press into a thin line while the grandfather clock in the hallway chimes eight times. The sound provides a welcome interruption to the tension.

"I should check on dessert," she says, rising. She never actually prepares the food—they have staff for that—but she maintains the fiction of domestic involvement, particularly when conversations turn uncomfortable.

Alone with my father, I brace for a more direct interrogation. He sets his napkin beside his plate and studies me.

"Is everything alright, Diane?" he asks, his tone calibrated to extract information rather than express genuine concern. "Your mother worries. She feels you've become increasingly... removed from the family."

What he means is that I've become increasingly resistant to their matchmaking efforts. What began as gentle nudges has evolved into a full-court press. The narrative they've crafted for me—brilliant daughter, dedicated to the family foundation, who eventually settles down with an appropriate man from a good family to produce the next generation of Washingtons—is running behind schedule.

"I'm committed to the foundation and to this family," I say, reciting my loyalty pledge. "That hasn't changed."

"But something has," he persists.

Has something changed? I consider the question more seriously than I intended to. There's been a restlessness in me lately, a dissatisfaction that my occasional escapes to Vegas temporarily soothe but never fully resolve. Each time I return to D.C., to this house, to the foundation offices, the feeling intensifies—like wearing clothes that no longer fit properly.

"I'm just tired," I offer finally. "Maybe I need a break."

3

ZARA

*S*he's ten minutes late. I sip my champagne and check my watch again, confirming what I already know. Athena Stavros, owner of the Olympus Casino, is officially keeping me waiting.

No one has kept me waiting since I shot to fame. Not promoters, not record executives, not even the President during that White House performance last year. Yet here I sit, alone in a private corner of the Pantheon, feeling oddly... ordinary.

Movement catches my eye as Athena Stavros finally approaches, dressed in an impeccable white suit and white fedora hat. She walks with the confidence of someone who knows exactly the space they occupy in the world. Her dark eyes scan the restaurant as she moves, missing nothing, acknowledging staff with subtle nods.

When she reaches my table, she smiles and extends her hand. "Ms. Nova. Thank you for coming." Her voice carries an accent.

"Please, call me Zara," I say, taking her offered hand.

"Call me Athena. I'm sorry for being late. I was held up in a meeting. I take it my staff have made you comfortable?"

"Very much." I return her smile. The woman is striking. "Thank you for meeting one-on-one," I continue. "My manager wanted to tag along, but these conversations get so bogged down in details when the suits are involved."

Athena takes her seat opposite me. "I prefer it this way too. It's easier to talk without being interrupted every other sentence."

Her directness is refreshing. In my industry, people typically approach me with rehearsed flattery and transparent agendas. Athena simply observes me, attentive but not fawning, as a server pours her champagne.

"I've gone through your checklist," she says, getting straight to it. "I don't see any issues with the points you've raised. The Palestra can be transformed to your specifications, and our sound and lighting systems are state-of-the-art. Do you have any concerns from your side?"

I nod, pushing aside the barely touched salad I ordered earlier. "I do, but my concerns are more personal than professional." I pause, unsure how to express my thoughts without insulting her city. "I need to understand what I'm actually committing to. Ten months in Vegas is..."

"A long time," she finishes for me. "Especially if you're not used to desert living."

"Exactly." I'm relieved she gets it. "I've done the weekend performances, the awards shows, but settling here? I'm not sure I can handle the constant noise, the tourists, the artificial everything. And I enjoy being outdoors. I'm afraid I'll get cabin fever."

"If you decide to live at the Olympus during your residency, you'll have a private entrance," Athena explains. "We have an excellent penthouse suite with a spacious terrace and a small private pool."

"That sounds promising," I admit, imagining a sanctuary above the chaos of the Strip. "But what about when I need to escape? I'm used to having options."

"The desert is beautiful if you need to get away," she says, her expression softening with genuine appreciation. "Most people who visit never see beyond the casinos, but there's something almost spiritual about the landscape once you leave the city behind." A smile plays at the corners of her lips. "I'd be happy to show you around. I love driving."

Something in her tone shifts—a subtle lowering of her voice, a slight pause before the offer. Her dark eyes meet mine with quiet intensity, charged with an energy I recognize instantly from years of carefully navigating these waters. My pulse quickens as I reconsider her.

It's rare that I meet women who aren't fawning fans or industry rivals. Even rarer to encounter one who exudes such self-possession and doesn't seem intimidated by my status. And rarest of all—one who might share my closely guarded secret.

I lean forward, matching her body language. "Oh? You want to be my tour guide?" I let a hint of flirtation color my voice, watching carefully for her reaction. "I might take you up on that."

She doesn't pull back or look uncomfortable. Instead, her eyes linger on mine, and I feel that familiar thrill of connection—the silent recognition between women who understand each other without needing explicit words.

"And do you live here too?" I ask. "I bet you have a badass suite. I'd love to see it sometime, if we're going to be neighbors."

Athena hesitates and I watch as understanding dawns in

her eyes. Suddenly I realize I've terribly misread the situation. The slight widening of her eyes, the almost imperceptible tensing of her shoulders—I recognize the signs of someone caught off guard.

"I..." she begins, but stops herself.

Heat rushes to my face as mortification sweeps through me. I've made a serious miscalculation, breaking my own cardinal rule of never revealing myself without absolute certainty. I force a laugh, though I feel like I might actually die of embarrassment.

"Oh God, I completely misread that, didn't I?" I bring a hand to my forehead, wishing the floor would open and swallow me whole. "I'm so sorry. I thought you were—" I stop myself before making this worse.

"No need to apologize," Athena says quickly. "And you're not wrong. It's just that there's... someone special in my life. I'm not sure where it's heading but..."

"Say no more." I hold up a hand. My usual poise abandons me entirely as I fumble for footing. "Professional boundaries restored. And can we please keep this awkward exchange between us? I think the champagne has gone to my head, and no one knows I'm... well, you know what I mean."

"Of course. Don't worry about it." Her manner is reassuringly unruffled. Then she surprises me. "But if you'd like to explore things other than the desert while you're here, I can help you with that. Discretion is my middle name, and I have a lot of successful and attractive single female friends who are equally discreet."

My eyebrows shoot up as I process what she's offering. This conversation has taken yet another unexpected turn.

"Wow," I say, trying to recover my composure. "The

mysterious Athena Stavros runs an underground queer dating service too?"

Athena reaches into her jacket pocket and pulls out a business card. She writes something on the back before sliding it across the table. "Not exactly, but I have connections." Her smile is enigmatic. "Anyway, the offer stands. That's my personal number. Please don't share it—I'm very private."

I take the card, turning it over in my fingers. It's surreal to be on the receiving end of this kind of discretion. "That's usually my line," I joke. "I'm supposed to be the one giving out my number with warnings about privacy."

We share a laugh, and Athena smoothly steers the conversation back to business, discussing rehearsal space and performance frequency. The blush on my cheeks still lingers; it's been a while since I've felt this embarrassed. I try to focus, but my mind keeps drifting to the implications of her offer. Who are these "discreet" women she knows? It's such a strange thing to say.

"What about the rehearsal schedule?" I ask, forcing myself to concentrate on what matters now. "I'll need at least three weeks of setup time before opening night."

"Not a problem," she assures me. "We can close the Palestra during the day for a full month before your premiere if needed. The space will be completely yours from nine to five."

Athena's phone vibrates on the table, and she glances at it. "I'm sorry," she says. "Would you mind if I quickly check this? It might be important."

"Of course. Go ahead," I reply, watching as she picks up her phone. She smiles as she reads whatever message has appeared on the screen.

"I take it that's good news?" I ask when she looks up again.

"Yes," she says, typing a quick response before setting the phone aside. "I'm sorry for the interruption. I'm all yours."

"Is that her? The special someone?" I ask, immediately kicking myself for being nosy. It's none of my business, but I can't help myself. I've only just met her, and I'm already way too fascinated with her personal life. Perhaps because I never met a woman who's more private than me. Someone who isn't fazed by me in the slightest.

Athena hesitates, then nods. "Yes."

"She's a lucky woman." I trace the rim of my champagne flute, contemplating. "I've always wondered what it would be like."

"What do you mean?"

"To explore that side of myself." I meet her gaze directly. "My whole life is decided for me down to who I'm dating."

"Have you had these feelings for a while?" she asks.

"Always." I pause, considering how much to reveal. "I kissed girls in college sometimes, but that was a long time ago. And then fame came knocking on my door. I'm grateful for that, but it also meant my days of experimenting were over, and I fantasize about dating women all the time." I study her for a moment before adding, "I wish I could be you for a day."

"Me?" She looks genuinely surprised by this. "I'm not sure I understand where you're coming from."

"There's this sexual confidence radiating from you," I explain. "I picked up the vibe immediately—that you're queer and completely comfortable with it. You own who you are."

Athena frowns and shakes her head. "Between you and me? I'm not as out and proud as you might think." Her confession catches me off guard. "I don't hide exactly, but I don't date in public either. The business pages feature me occasionally, and word travels. I've spent my life making sure my family in Greece doesn't find out, so I'm careful."

"You're not out to your family?"

"My sister knows now," she says. "Found out recently, actually. She's supportive, but my mother is traditional Greek Orthodox, so it's complicated." She takes a sip of champagne. "Sometimes I wonder what it would be like too. To walk through my casino with a woman on my arm."

"Huh." I tilt my head, reassessing her. "Who would have thought?"

"We all have our blind spots," she says with a small smile. "Areas where courage fails us, despite how strong we appear elsewhere." She leans back in her chair. "I think this residency could be good for you in more ways than one, and my offer stands on introducing you to some like-minded women. No pressure, no expectations, and certainly no headlines. Just... possibilities."

I smile as the idea of a real date settles over me like a new song taking shape—uncertain but thrilling, with melodies I haven't sung out loud yet.

"Possibilities," I repeat, savoring the word.

Athena's personal number burns like a dare against my palm as I slip the card into my purse.

4

DIANE

*T*he anticipation has been building since I boarded in D.C., a slow unfurling of something wild and honest inside me. It's close to midnight when I exit through the Cartwright Hotel's revolving doors. I'd much rather stay at The Olympus, but the Washington name carries expectations. A foundation director with family ties to Virginia politics can't afford to have her hotel receipts show a casino address—not when her father represents a state where many voters still consider gambling morally questionable. The Cartwright Hotel provides the perfect cover: upscale, respectable, and suitably removed from the neon excesses of the Vegas Strip.

A black limousine glides to the curb and the driver steps out, a new face—tall, clean-cut, with the bearing of former military.

"Ms. Washington?" he asks, opening the rear door.

I slide into the cool leather interior and the partition between us remains down as he returns to the driver's seat.

He catches my eyes in the rearview mirror. "Password?"

One word that separates my worlds. One word that unlocks everything I deny myself in Washington.

"Hedonism," I say.

He nods once, raises the partition, and pulls into traffic.

I power off my phone completely—not silent, not airplane mode, but fully off. The symbolic severing of my connection to Senator Washington's daughter.

Through tinted windows, I watch Las Vegas transform from the refined luxury of the Cartwright to the pulsing heart of the Strip. The limousine turns west and the landscape changes gradually—hotels giving way to upscale shopping plazas, then to the manicured developments that house Las Vegas' permanent residents.

We climb steadily as we approach The Ridges, exclusive even by Vegas standards. Massive homes perch on hills overlooking the valley, each property discreetly separated from its neighbors. The limousine slows as we reach a private gate, and we proceed up a driveway lined with date palms that leads to my friend Athena's house.

Robert—head of security—steps outside to greet me.

"Good evening, Ms. Washington," he says, opening the door for me. "Please come through."

I follow him inside, through the grand entryway and into the library—a space that would make my father envious with its leather-bound volumes and first editions displayed in custom cases. Robert opens the bookcase on the far end of the room, revealing a hidden doorway. Music rises to meet me as I descend the staircase that opens into an underground space. The walls are deep red, the furnishings plush and inviting—velvet sofas, intimate seating areas. The lighting is soft and flattering, creating an atmosphere of exclusivity and indulgence.

It's full of women. Women like me.

The club unfolds like a fever dream from another era—part Moroccan pleasure palace, part Victorian opium den, all reimagined through a lens of modern luxury. Divans in jewel tones cluster around low tables of inlaid brass. Against one wall, a black marble bar stretches beneath antique mirrors that reflect the room in dreamy, distorted fragments. The air carries notes of sandalwood and jasmine. This isn't the manufactured glitz of Vegas above us; this is something far more exclusive—a sanctuary that is both timeless and temporary, dissolved by dawn.

A circular stage holds a belly dancer, her body adorned with chains of gold that catch the light as she moves to the music's hypnotic rhythm. Deeper within the space, heavy velvet curtains hang in archways, occasionally parting to reveal glimpses of more intimate chambers beyond.

Waiters in tailored black move like shadows through the room, their presence barely registered until the exact moment a glass needs refilling. They operate with an impressive understanding of each guest's preferences—remembering not just favorite drinks but how strong, how sweet, at what temperature. In one corner, Marco holds court—the club's "facilitator" who can procure anything from last-minute opera tickets to private jets or top quality marijuana and cigars. His services are available to all members, his only limitations the boundaries of legality.

The rules here are few but absolute: No phones. No business discussions. No gambling. No illegal activities of any kind. Within those parameters, freedom reigns. It's a haven constructed with the understanding that power requires occasional release, that control sometimes demands its opposite.

The space radiates a sensual energy that an outsider might interpret as purely sexual. In shadowed corners, women embrace and kiss without reservation. Hands trace bare shoulders, fingers tangle in hair, whispers lead to knowing smiles and disappearances through velvet-curtained doorways. Many come here specifically for these encounters—the chance to express desire without judgment or consequence. But for me, the true seduction of this place lies in a different kind of intimacy. Here, I find the authentic connections that elude me everywhere else: friendships unburdened by strategic calculations, conversations free from political tripwires, laughter that doesn't need to be measured. The openness between us—the raw honesty— feels more intimate than any physical act. I've built a career on allegiances, but here, loyalty springs from shared vulner-ability rather than mutual benefit.

"Diane!" Elena waves from across the room. In Chicago, she runs one of the country's most prestigious neurosurgery departments, but here, with her silver-streaked hair loose around her shoulders and her scrubs replaced by a slinky black dress, she looks refreshingly unburdened. Beside her, Kira—the brilliant architect whose designs have trans-formed skylines from Shanghai to London—rests her head on Elena's shoulder, fingers intertwined. They've been meeting here for two years, their relationship existing only within these walls and occasional planned conferences that happen to align in the same cities. I make my way toward them, accepting embraces.

Then I spot Katherine and Jin-Ah, lost in each other. In public, Katherine is the reclusive hedge fund genius whose market predictions have earned her billions and a mythical status on Wall Street. Jin-Ah curates international art exhibitions, her impeccable taste and scholarly publications making her the darling of museums worldwide. Like me, Jin-Ah remains closeted due to family expectations—her parents are prominent figures in Seoul's conservative elite. Our conversations about navigating dual lives across different cultures are some of the few moments I feel truly understood. What makes our friendship particularly precious is how we've learned to find dark humor in our parallel predicaments—trading stories of disastrous setups and absurd excuses with laughter.

The women here aren't merely acquaintances—they're the only true friends I have. In Washington, I maintain countless professional relationships and political networks, but none qualify as genuine friendship. How could they? Those connections are built on the persona I present to the world. Only here do I exist without artifice. They've known me for two years, yet they understand parts of me my own family has never glimpsed. There have been a few casual hookups and I'm always up for a little flirtation, but what I cherish most is our sisterhood.

This is the paradox of my life: women I see six times a year know me more intimately than the people I've known since birth. Because true friendship requires honesty, and honesty is the one luxury I cannot afford in Washington.

"Hi, Diane. I didn't expect you tonight." Athena, friend, hostess, and owner of this place, joins me and places a hand on my arm.

"I was getting cabin fever," I say with a grin, turning to kiss her on each cheek.

A server appears with a glass of Barolo—my regular order. I accept it with a nod of thanks.

Athena watches me when I let out a long sigh. "Better?"

"Much," I admit.

"That's what I like to hear. Welcome back," she says, raising her Scotch.

I clink my drink against hers. "It's good to be home."

And in this moment, standing in an underground club beneath the desert, surrounded by women who live divided lives like me, that's exactly what it feels like. The only place where I'm truly free.

5

ZARA

I pour the deep red Cabernet into two glasses, enjoying the simple pleasure of sitting in Jess's kitchen without an entourage or a ridiculous outfit. Jess's modest but welcoming Silver Lake home feels like a refuge —mismatched furniture, walls decorated with candid photos instead of professional artwork, and a refrigerator plastered with magnets from places she's visited. It's everything my Malibu mansion isn't—lived-in and imperfect.

Outside, the Los Angeles evening settles in, pink and orange streaks fading from the sky. Through the open window, I hear neighbor children playing, their voices rising and falling with the breeze that carries the scent of someone's backyard barbecue. No paparazzi lurking in bushes, no fans pressing against security barriers, no handlers checking watches and murmuring about time constraints. Just an ordinary Tuesday evening in an ordinary neighborhood.

I should have probably headed home for an early night, knowing tomorrow brings another fourteen-hour marathon of obligations. My alarm will go off at 5:30 AM for a morning show segment, followed by a label meeting, two phone interviews, and a charity gala that will stretch well into the evening. Peter would certainly advise me to be in bed by now—"sleep is a career investment," he always says, but I need these small snippets of normalcy. I've missed my friend's unfiltered laughter more than any amount of sleep could compensate for. The exhaustion I'll feel tomorrow seems like a small price to pay for feeling human tonight.

"How was your day?" I ask, watching Jess sink onto one of the barstools.

She pushes a strand of blonde hair away from her face while her free hand absently massages the back of her neck where tension always settles after a long day hunched over spreadsheets.

"Client meetings while balancing a baby on my hip," she says finally. "You know, the glamorous life of a single mom CPA." She laughs, the exhaustion evident in the dark circles under her eyes. "Lucas decided today was the day for practicing his operatic screaming. I had to mute myself seventeen times during a Zoom call, and my client probably thinks I have some sort of neurological condition from all my bizarre facial expressions."

"Oh no," I laugh, picturing Jess's exaggerated grimaces. "Paint me a picture. What exactly does a 'please stop screaming during mommy's important meeting' face look like?"

Jess immediately contorts her features into a wide-eyed, teeth-clenched smile that has me nearly spitting out my wine.

"Somewhere between constipated Disney princess and serial killer trying to blend in at a networking event," she explains, returning to normal. "Then when he started flailing his arms and knocking things off my desk, I had to switch to this." She demonstrates another face—an apologetic wince combined with frantic eye movements meant to convey "everything is fine" while clearly nothing is fine.

"Where is the little dumpling? Sleeping?" I ask, glancing toward the hallway that leads to the bedrooms. The house is suspiciously quiet. "I really wanted to see him."

"He passed out early after fighting sleep for days like it was his mortal enemy." Jess takes another gulp of wine, then refills her glass without offering any apologies for the pace. "I know he'll be up all night, but honestly, I was just grateful when the crying stopped. I may have done a silent victory dance in his room."

I laugh, picturing Jess's signature awkward dance moves. "That I would pay to see," I say, raising my glass in a toast. "To silent victory dances."

"To small mercies," she counters, then stretches her legs out, wiggling her toes in mismatched socks. "My mom's coming for two weeks starting tomorrow," she continues, picking at the label on the wine bottle. "I've got a backlog of work I need to catch up on, and she's been dying to see her grandson."

"That's great," I say, genuinely happy for her. I know Jess's mother well—a warm, practical woman who shares her daughter's no-nonsense attitude. "She'll be good help."

"She will," Jess agrees. "But she'll also rearrange my kitchen, criticize my parenting choices, and make at least three comments about how I should move back to New York."

"The price of free childcare."

"Exactly," she says. "But beggars can't be choosers, and I'm definitely begging for help these days."

"You know," I begin carefully, knowing I'm stepping into well-worn territory, "I could easily get you a nanny. Even a part-time nanny would take some pressure off. Someone to help for a few hours each day while you work."

"No." Jess cuts me off with a smile that softens the rejection. "We've been through this."

"But it wouldn't be a big deal," I press gently. "Just a small thing I could do to help."

"Z, you already do plenty," she says firmly. "The stroller that's basically a mini-luxury car? The college fund you set up without telling me? The ridiculous baby clothes that cost more than my work wardrobe?" She gestures toward a tiny designer outfit draped over the back of a kitchen chair. "I draw the line at staff. I'm not going to become one of those friends who takes advantage."

"It's not taking advantage if I'm offering."

"It's a slippery slope," she insists. "Today it's a nanny, tomorrow it's private school tuition, then suddenly I'm living in your guest house and you're wondering how you ended up supporting your friend and her kid for the next eighteen years."

"Or," I counter, leaning forward, "you could work for me as my accountant. God knows Peter's team could use someone who doesn't treat my money like it's falling from the sky." I wiggle my eyebrows persuasively.

She rolls her eyes, but I catch the subtle lift at the corner of her mouth. "That answer too, remains no. I love you, Z, but I don't want to risk our friendship by working together. Besides," she adds with a wry smile, "you couldn't afford me."

This running joke between us never fails to make me laugh. It's Jess's way of maintaining the equilibrium between us, of reminding me that in her eyes, I'm still Zara from NYU who used to borrow her meal card when I was broke at the end of the month.

"Fair enough," I concede, raising my hands in surrender. "Just know the offer stands. Both offers."

"Noted," she says, her tone making it clear the subject is closed. "Anyway, how was your day? And don't give me the sanitized version you save for interviewers."

I wouldn't dare complain, not to Jess. Not when she's been raising Lucas alone for the past three months. Lucas' father selfishly took off right after Lucas was born, deciding fatherhood wasn't for him. Since then, she's been juggling a growing accounting firm with midnight feedings and diaper changes.

Jess is my lifeline to normalcy. We met as freshmen at NYU—both of us from working-class families on a full scholarship, both ambitious but in different ways. I was the theater major with music minor who spent weekends performing at any venue that would have me; she was the business major with no interest in anything creative. When I was discovered and suddenly catapulted into the spotlight, she remained steadfastly unimpressed by the glitz, treating me exactly the same unlike everyone else.

When love brought her to LA, I was selfishly grateful to have a piece of home nearby, even if it was for a relationship that ultimately failed. She stayed after the breakup, building her own small practice.

"It was fine," I say, shrugging. "Up at six for a photoshoot at eight, followed by an interview for the summer issue of Vanity Fair and some streaming platform's promotional thing."

I take a sip of wine, feeling the tension of the day begin to dissolve. "Then a meeting with the label about the Vegas announcement and costume fittings for a charity concert next month."

"So basically everything except actually making music or performing," Jess says.

"Exactly." I laugh, but there's an edge to it that I can't quite hide. "That seems to be my life lately—endless distractions from the one thing I actually love doing. It's like being a chef who spends all day reading recipes and shopping for ingredients but never actually cooks. I haven't written a new song in a year. Everything's been about post tour season and now planning the Vegas residency."

"Remember when you used to compose on that awful keyboard in our shared quarters?" Jess asks. "The one with the missing C key that would make that terrible buzzing sound whenever you hit it?"

"God, that thing was a nightmare." I laugh. "But I wrote some of my best early stuff on it."

"You did," she agrees. "You'd be up all night sometimes, headphones on, completely lost in whatever you were creating. I'd wake up for my first class and you'd still be sitting there, hair a mess, wearing the same clothes from the day before."

"I miss that," I admit.

Jess studies me with the kind of scrutiny only a close friend can get away with. "I'm sorry this has become your life—rushing from one obligation to another, always in transit, always on someone else's schedule."

"Don't feel sorry for me," I insist, waving her concern away. "First world problems."

"You're allowed to be tired, Z," she says. "Success doesn't invalidate exhaustion. And fame doesn't mean you signed away the right to have feelings about your life."

I look down at my wine glass, uncomfortable with her perception. Jess has always been able to see through my defenses, even when I try to hide behind humor or dismissiveness. It's one of the reasons I treasure her friendship, but also one of the reasons I sometimes avoid seeing her when I'm struggling—she makes it harder to lie to myself.

"When are you moving to Vegas?" she asks.

"In two months," I reply. "Prep, rehearsals... that kind of stuff." I spin my wine glass between my fingers, watching the liquid create a small vortex. "I'm getting a little nervous about it, to be honest. I haven't stayed in one place for that long since my career took off."

"It'll be good for you," Jess says. "Some stability, a routine."

"Those were Peter's words. I just don't know if I remember how to stay still anymore."

Jess chuckles. "Don't worry; it's like riding a bike. The boredom comes right back to you."

I laugh and shake my head. "Will you visit me? I'll arrange an on-site nanny and an office set up for you. And a chocolate fountain in every room. And trained dolphins bringing you drinks poolside. And a personal chef who makes those terrible kale brownies you pretend to enjoy. And—"

"Stop!" Jess laughs. "Of course I'll visit. Lucas and I both will. My son needs to see his godmother in her natural habitat—being extra."

"I'm not extra," I protest with mock indignation. "I'm appropriately proportioned to my circumstances."

"We'll come," she says, taking my hand and squeezing it. From the back of the house comes the unmistakable sound of a baby waking up. It starts as a whimper, then quickly escalates to a full-throated cry.

Jess sighs dramatically, her head dropping forward. "Here we go again. So much for my wine break."

"No, let me get him," I say, standing. "I need some quality time with my godson."

I walk down the hallway, push open the nursery door, and there he is—Lucas, red-faced and indignant in his crib, fists balled up in protest against the injustice of waking alone. When he sees me, his cries pause momentarily as he tries to place this vaguely familiar face.

"Hey there, little man," I say softly, approaching the crib. "Auntie Z is here."

His face crumples again, uncertain whether I'm an acceptable substitute for his mother, but I reach down and lift him, cradling him against my chest the way Jess taught me. He smells of baby shampoo and his tiny body is warm and solid, his heart beating fast against mine.

I begin to sway, humming a lullaby I remember from my own childhood.

6

DIANE

*T*en minutes. That's all I have between the Foundation's quarterly strategy meeting and my conference call with potential donors in Pittsburgh. Ten precious minutes to be something closer to myself.

I close my office door—a rare occurrence that my assistant knows signals "emergency calls only"—and settle into the leather chair behind my desk. The Washington Foundation headquarters occupies the top floor of a Georgetown brownstone, tastefully renovated to project the right balance of tradition and forward-thinking that appeals to our donors. My office faces the Potomac, and on clear days like today, the view is spectacular.

The walls are lined with photographs: my father shaking hands with three different presidents, my mother cutting ribbons at hospital wings and school buildings, me accepting awards and honorary degrees. A visual timeline of our family contributions to society. What's missing from these images is any hint of authentic joy. The kind I find myself increasingly desperate for.

I pull out my phone and open the dating app hidden in

a folder labeled "Productivity Tools." The small red notification bubble shows three new messages, and my pulse quickens. This is ridiculous. I'm running a multi-million dollar foundation, and I get butterflies over dating app messages. Messages sent to someone who doesn't actually exist.

Well, she exists. Parts of her do. Diana Peters is thirty, works in nonprofit management, lives in D.C., and loves hiking, animals, and obscure documentaries. She has my interests and my sense of humor. What she doesn't have is my last name, my family connections, or my photo. Instead, her profile pictures show artistic shots where you can't quite see her face: a woman (me) from behind looking over the Potomac, a silhouette against a sunset, hands cradling a coffee mug.

I created this profile eight months ago, after returning from a particularly liberating weekend at Athena's underground club. I'd felt an intoxicating rush of freedom during the trip which made returning to D.C. almost unbearable. Diana Peters emerged from that desperation—a compromise between the woman I am in Vegas and the woman I'm required to be everywhere else.

I tell myself it's not catfishing if most of it is true. If the point isn't to deceive but to protect. If I'm not trying to scam anyone but simply trying to experience some fragment of a normal dating life. The rationalizations are wearing thin, even to me.

I check my messages: one from a woman whose conversation fizzled out last month, suddenly resurfacing with a generic "hey stranger," and another from someone new whose profile shows more cleavage than face—an automatic pass. The dating pool for women seeking women in D.C. is smaller than most people realize, and smaller still when you eliminate anyone with potential professional connections to my world.

I tap on Eliza's message last, saving it like dessert. We've been chatting for just over a week, and unlike most conversations that fade out after two or three exchanges, ours has maintained a steady momentum. She's an environmental lawyer, thirty-three, with a dry wit that makes me laugh out loud—a rarity in my over-scheduled life.

Sorry for the late reply! Court ran long, then I had to talk a client down from a panic attack over a routine EPA filing. How's your Wednesday looking? Still buried in work?

I smile and tap out a response:

The avalanche continues. I'm actually stealing 10 minutes between meetings to check in here. If my assistant knocks on my door, I'll probably jump like I'm caught with contraband.

I hit send before I can overthink it. Eliza's response comes almost immediately:

A woman who takes dating app breaks instead of coffee breaks? I'm intrigued. Most people I match with take days to respond. Are you one of those mythical "good at messaging" people I've heard legends about?

I laugh and type back:

Only when I'm procrastinating something more important. What does it say about me that messaging a stranger feels more appealing than preparing for my next meeting?

Her reply pops up:

It says you're human. Also, "stranger" hurts a little after our deep dive on which Supreme Court justice would make the best dinner party guest. (Still can't believe you chose Roberts over Sotomayor, by the way. Bold and slightly concerning.)

The banter feels so easy, so natural. This is what normal people have, I think. This is what dating looks like when your last name isn't attached to a conservative political dynasty.

In my defense, I said *Roberts would be the most SURPRISING good dinner guest. Sotomayor is the obvious choice. I prefer the unexpected.*

Her response makes me smile:

Noted. You like to be surprised. I'm filing that away for future reference.

Future reference. The implication that there could be a future—even just a conversational one—sends a pleasant warmth through me. I check the time on my computer screen. Five minutes left.

Speaking of future references, Eliza writes, *I know we've only been chatting for a short time, but I've really enjoyed our conversations. Any chance you'd want to meet for coffee sometime? There's a great little place in Adams Morgan I think you'd like. Very quiet, off the beaten path.*

Fuck. It's happened. The inevitable moment when these digital connections attempt to breach the barrier into the real world. The moment I both crave and dread. My fingers hover over the keyboard as familiar excuses queue up in my mind. I've used them all before: *I'm traveling for work this week. I'm on deadline for a major project. Family emergency. Rain check?*

Each excuse buying time until the other person gets frustrated with my perpetual unavailability and moves on. It's a pattern I've repeated a dozen times. The first few rejections were easier—I told myself I was testing the waters, seeing what was out there. But with each woman who drifted away after my third or fourth rebuff, the reality of my situation grew clearer: this half-life, this digital flirtation without fulfillment, might be all I can ever have.

What would it be like, just once, to say yes? To sit across

from someone like Eliza in a quiet café, to see if her laugh matches the humor in her messages, to experience the simple pleasure of getting to know someone?

But what if someone recognizes me? What if she knows someone who knows me? What if she goes home and discovers exactly who I am? What if a photo appears online? What if word somehow gets back to my father?

A knot of tension forms between my shoulder blades. The truth—the truth I barely acknowledge even in my most honest moments—is that I'm a coward. I've constructed a life of half-measures: Vegas trips that sustain me like oxygen between dives, digital flirtations that offer the illusion of connection without risk, private thoughts hidden beneath appearances. I've become so accustomed to compartmentalizing that I sometimes wonder if I could integrate these fragments even if circumstances allowed it.

I take a deep breath and type:

I'm so flattered you asked, and I've enjoyed our conversations too. Unfortunately, I'm swamped with a major project launch this week. Rain check?

I hate myself a little as I hit send. The response is almost immediate:

Of course! I understand busy schedules better than most. The offer stands whenever you have time.

Her graciousness makes me feel worse. This is the third time in our brief acquaintance that I've alluded to my impossible schedule. How long before she notices the pattern? How long before she decides I'm not worth the effort?

I've watched it happen before. The initial understanding, the patient follow-ups, the increasingly direct questions about when we might actually meet, and finally the slow fading of messages until they stop entirely. A digital ghost story with no satisfying resolution. I type quickly, trying to salvage the connection:

Thank you for understanding. I promise I'm not usually this difficult to pin down. Tell me more about this coffee shop—what makes it special?

It's a weak deflection, but it's all I have. I glance at my computer—two minutes until my next meeting. My office phone blinks with a message from my assistant, probably reminding me of the same.

Eliza responds:

It's in an old row house, with mismatched furniture and local art on the walls. They roast their beans in-house, and the owner is this fascinating woman who used to be a cultural attaché in various embassies. She has stories for days. Plus, they make this lavender honey latte that might change your life.

It sounds lovely. It sounds like exactly the kind of place I would enjoy. In another life—a life where I could be both Diane Washington and a woman who casually meets other women for coffee—I would be there tomorrow.

7

ZARA

I stare at the mountain of designer clothing sprawled across my bedroom—a textile sea of silk, sequins, and leather that needs to be sent to Vegas over the next few weeks.

"We need to be strategic about this," Mei says, her iPad hovering over a particularly precarious pile of evening gowns. "The Olympus suite has substantial closet space, but nothing compared to what you have here."

Mei has been my personal assistant for nine years now —arriving in my life when the demands of fame became too unwieldy for me to manage alone. She's five-foot-nothing of terrifying efficiency, with sleek black hair perpetually pulled into a tight bun and the uncanny ability to anticipate problems before they materialize. Today she's dressed in her usual uniform: tailored black pants, a white T-shirt, and sensible shoes that allow her to keep up with my frequently chaotic schedule.

"I don't need to bring that much," I say, perhaps surprising both of us. "Also, this might be a good opportunity to get rid of some stuff."

Mei's eyebrows lift slightly—her version of profound shock. "You want to... cut down? That's new."

"Vegas is ten months, not forever," I remind her, though sometimes it feels like the same thing. "And it's not like I'll be attending the Met Gala from Nevada. The performance wardrobe will be separately stored anyway."

"True," she concedes, making a note. "So casual clothes, some day-to-night options, and perhaps a few special pieces for private or public events? We can always buy or order stuff when you're there."

"Yeah, that sounds good," I say. *Private events.* The phrase triggers a memory of Athena's business card, tucked safely in my purse.

"What about the Valentino?" I ask, trying to sound casual. "The black one."

"The jumpsuit?" Mei clarifies. "You've never worn it."

"I know. I've been saving it." I shrug. "Let's bring it. And the dark green Stella McCartney jumpsuit. The cashmere lounge sets. That black leather jacket from the Paris trip." I hesitate, then add: "And the red satin Dior."

"Sure." Mei's finger moves rapidly across her iPad, but I catch the subtle tilt of her head—she's cataloging these choices, noticing how they differ from my usual tour requests.

"Are you planning on dating in Vegas?" she asks with characteristic directness. "Lingerie?"

Heat rushes to my face. "I'm planning on having options."

"Makes sense," she says, mercifully moving on. "What about your instruments? The touring gear will go directly to the Olympus staging area, but what about your personal pieces? Guitars?"

"I want the Steinway," I say without hesitation.

Mei frowns, consulting her tablet. "The moving company estimates additional insurance and specialized transport would run close to thirty thousand dollars. It's a beautiful instrument, but... problematic to relocate for a temporary stay."

"It's not about its monetary value," I say, though that's substantial too—a rare 1920s Steinway upright in Brazilian rosewood that I found in Nashville years ago.

"The Olympus is providing a grand piano for the suite," Mei reminds me. "Brand new, concert quality."

"It's not the same," I insist. "Tell them I appreciate their efforts, but I prefer my own."

Mei nods. "No problem. I'll arrange it."

I wander to the window while she continues sorting through clothing categories. The ocean stretches to the horizon, unchanging yet never the same. I love the ocean view; it's the reason I bought this house. How am I going to cope with ten months in the desert? Ten months performing on the same stage, breathing the same recirculated casino air?

"How do you feel about Vegas, Mei?" I ask, turning to face her. "About being there for so long?"

She looks up from her cataloging. "My feelings aren't relevant to the logistics."

"They are to me."

Mei sets down her iPad, considering the question. "It's my job to go where you go," she says finally. "To make your life function smoothly wherever that happens to be."

"That's not what I asked."

"I know." A rare smile softens her features. "Vegas will be... different. The team will adjust."

"But seriously, what about you?" I press. "If you could be anywhere in the world right now, where would it be?"

Mei frowns and for a moment, the professional mask

slips. "Hawaii," she says softly. "With Jun." She blushes at the mention of her boyfriend, a concept so normal yet so foreign in my world. "Just the two of us on a beach with good food, a bottle of wine, and a blanket beneath the stars. I'll miss him when I'm in Vegas. But he can always come and visit me, right?"

"Of course. But you should take some time off," I say impulsively. "Once I've settled in Vegas, go to Hawaii with Jun. My treat."

"That's not necessary—"

"You haven't had time off in..." I stop myself as I try to remember when Mei last went on vacation. I'm ashamed to admit I don't remember. "I'm giving you paid leave, Mei. That's not a request." I shrug. "I can manage."

"Okay... Thank you." She studies me with a frown. "It must be hard for you. To date," she says. What she really means is, why in all the years I've worked for you have I never seen you genuinely smitten with someone?

But Mei would never actually say that out loud. She's never crossed a boundary, not once. She's delightfully professional, maintaining a balance between knowing everything about my life while never presuming familiarity.

Looking at Mei, I realize how strange my dating life—or lack thereof—must seem to someone who's witnessed my career up close. The photo ops with industry-appropriate men, the appearances at premieres and awards shows, the relationships that conveniently begin and end with album cycles. The men I'm seen with but never, ever bring home. Not once has she seen me truly interested in anyone, never witnessed the messy, beautiful chaos of actual attraction.

"Dating is complicated for me," I say quietly. If only she knew the whole truth—how I sometimes catch myself staring too long at a female backup dancer, how I wake up from dreams where soft lips press against mine. These aren't fleeting thoughts but persistent longings that have followed me since I was a teenager, shadows of desire that grow longer with each passing year.

It's not that it would be impossible. The industry has changed; there are successful queer artists now carving their own paths without apology. But they know who they are and they're comfortable with who they are. Me... well, I have no idea who I am, really.

Experimentation would be documented, dissected, headlines guaranteed. No one would stay quiet after dating me—it's currency too valuable to keep locked away. Every kiss would be a transaction, every touch potentially weaponized and sold to tabloids, armed with intimate details.

I pick up my NYU hoodie, the fabric worn thin from years of wear, and press it against my face. The scent of fabric softener can't erase the memories it holds. Sophomore year, music theory and composition, a tiny dorm room with posters covering water-stained walls. Emma Walters with her wild hair and wilder laugh, borrowing my hoodie one autumn night when the heating failed. The way she looked in it—drowning in fabric, sleeves covering her hands, the neckline slipping to reveal one freckled shoulder.

A bottle of cheap wine between us, Emma's guitar abandoned on the floor as a rainstorm tapped rhythms against the window. I remember the moment everything changed— her saying, "I bet you write love songs about someone," and me, tongue loosened by wine, admitting, "Maybe I write them about you." The shock in her eyes, not at the sentiment but at my honesty. The way she leaned forward, hesitant at first, then with unexpected certainty. Her lips tasting of wine, my heart thundering loudly.

We made out for hours that night, tangled together on my narrow dorm bed, discovering each other in the shadows. It never went further than kisses and cautious touches over clothes, both of us hovering at a threshold neither was brave enough to cross. When my roommate at the time returned from a party, Emma gathered her things, smiled awkwardly, and left. We never talked about it afterward— not during study sessions, not at parties, not even when we found ourselves alone again.

How simple it had been then, how uncomplicated by everything that came after. Sometimes I wonder if fame took more from me than it gave.

8

DIANE

I spot the ambush the moment I enter The Meridian. Mom stands near the hostess podium and she's not alone. Beside her, Barbara Cunningham—FDA Commissioner Robert Cunningham's wife—gestures animatedly as she speaks. And next to Barbara stands a tall man in his mid-thirties with the kind of bland good looks that grace banking advertisements: Thomas Cunningham.

I pause at the entrance, allowing myself three seconds of private frustration before stepping further into the lion's den. Mom's text this morning had been so innocent: "Lunch at The Meridian, 1pm. We need to discuss this month's calendar." A plausible excuse—our social obligations require coordination.

I should have known better. The setup is so transparent I almost laugh. Instead, I force my face into a pleasant mask.

"Diane, darling!" My mother spots me and waves, as though this encounter is completely coincidental. "Look who we ran into! You know Barbara, of course, and you've met her son, Thomas, too."

I approach, calculating my response. Confronting Mom

would create a scene. Best to save our disagreement for behind closed doors.

"What a surprise," I say, the lie smooth as silk as I extend my hand to Barbara. "Lovely to see you again."

"Diane, look at you." Barbara Cunningham's blonde hair is secured in a French twist, diamonds wink at her ears, and she's wearing a St. John knit suit in muted beige. She gives me a once-over, assessing everything from my shoe choice to my hairstyle in one sweeping glance. "Even more beautiful than the last time I saw you. Isn't she stunning, Thomas?"

Thomas steps forward and smiles awkwardly. At least I'm not the only one uncomfortable with this ambush. His eyes dart briefly to his mother with a flash of betrayal that tells me he wasn't informed about the setup either.

"Absolutely," he agrees. "It's nice to finally meet properly. I believe we were at the same benefit last spring, but there wasn't much opportunity to talk."

"I took the liberty of ordering champagne," Mom interrupts us as she ushers us to our table. "We're celebrating Barbara's wonderful news."

"Oh?" I inquire politely, sitting and placing my napkin in my lap.

Barbara beams. "We received approval for our new pharmaceutical research initiative. A joint venture with several major drug companies to accelerate development of rare disease treatments."

"How impressive," I say. "Congratulations."

"Thomas has been instrumental in structuring the legal framework," Barbara continues, patting her son's arm proudly. "Harvard Law training put to good use, wouldn't you say?"

Thomas adopts an expression of humble pride. "Just doing my part."

Our server arrives with champagne, pouring four flutes. Mom raises hers immediately. "To new ventures and new connections."

Its subtext is as clear as the crystal in my hand. And we're off—the parental auction begins in earnest. Back and forth they go, listing achievements and connections like competing auctioneers, their children reduced to résumés and potential assets. I meet Thomas's eyes and detect a flicker of shared discomfort.

I open my menu, though I hardly need to look. I've been to The Meridian so many times I could recite the entire food menu as well as the wine list from memory. The salmon will be beautifully poached, the steak medium-rare with four char lines, the salad artfully arranged topped with three asparagus tops—all as predictable as the conversations that take place over them.

The Meridian isn't just a restaurant; it's a Washington institution. Dark wood paneling lines the walls, adorned with portraits of founding members who all share the same stern expressions and privileged backgrounds.

"Barbara! Elizabeth!" A woman in her sixties approaches our table, A Washington board member and friend of Mom and Barbara. "How wonderful."

Mom and Barbara both light up, rising to greet her with air kisses. "Margaret, join us," my mother insists, pulling over a chair from a nearby table.

As the three women fall into conversation, Thomas leans toward me.

"I'm sorry about this," he says quietly, his voice low enough that our mothers can't hear. "I had no idea this was happening. I thought I was meeting my mother for a quick lunch."

I study him and decide he's telling the truth. "I didn't know either," I admit. "Seems we've both been tricked."

He laughs softly. "My mother has been not-so-subtly suggesting it's time I 'settle down' for about three years now."

"Try five years," I counter, smiling despite my irritation.

"Ouch. That's rough," he says. "For what it's worth, I've been trying to explain to my mother that I'm perfectly capable of finding my own dates." He glances at our mothers, still engaged with Margaret, and then back to me. "But you know what? Maybe we *should* go for a drink sometime. To get them off our backs."

I hesitate, torn between wanting to refuse on principle and not wanting to be rude to someone who seems equally trapped in this matchmaking scheme.

Thomas seems to sense my reluctance. "Look, I'm not suggesting a romantic date. Just two people with overly involved mothers venting over a drink."

"Well..." I pause. He doesn't seem so bad after all. At least he's not trying to flirt with me. "I guess I could do with a venting session, especially after today because I'm fuming," I whisper. "As long as it's not a date. No offense, but I'm not interested."

"Trust me, neither am I."

"Oh?" I raise a brow, pleasantly surprised. Not because I assumed he'd automatically want me—though I've grown accustomed to a certain evaluating gaze from men at these functions, the quick assessment that calculates my worth as a potential wife and political asset. I know that on paper, I'm quite the catch, but Thomas's eyes hold none of that calculation.

"Don't get me wrong," he adds with a self-deprecating smile, "you're impressive and obviously beautiful, but..." He lowers his voice even more. "I'm sort of seeing someone. I haven't told my family, which is why I'm still being paraded around."

I grin. "Let me guess... they wouldn't approve of her?" I hesitate. "Or him?"

Thomas blinks, momentarily surprised, then shakes his head with a wry smile. "No. Thank God. If I were gay, I might as well pack up and move to another continent. That's not even in the realm of possibilities my family would be willing to acknowledge."

I feel a little sting at his words, at how casually he can dismiss something I've built my entire life around hiding, but I paint on a smile, swirling the champagne in my glass.

"We shouldn't let them control us like this," I say, meeting his eyes. "We're adults, yet here we are, being arranged like it's the nineteenth century."

"Yeah." He shrugs. "I know I'm a pushover. I can't believe I'm letting Mom get away with this. She's listing my attributes like she's trying to sell a car."

"Washington's finest," I murmur. "Low mileage, only one previous owner—his mother."

"Premium model with built-in nodding feature," he adds. "Just don't check the trunk—that's where I hide all my actual opinions." He laughs, and I realize I'm warming to him. At least he has a sense of humor about the whole thing.

"So where should we have this non-date venting session?" I ask.

"How about The Rundown on 14th Street?"

I laugh. "Seriously? That place that occasionally makes the local news because of fights and drug raids?"

"You know it?"

"Only from the news. But I'm guaranteed never to run into my parents' friends there, so yeah... let's do it."

"Perfect." Thomas reaches for his wallet and pulls out a business card. "Here's my number. Text me if you want to grab that drink. No pressure."

Our mothers turn back to us as I take the card, and I don't miss the quick exchange of pleased glances between them. Mom looks so satisfied with herself, completely unaware she's just facilitated my first genuine social connection in years—one that has absolutely nothing to do with romance.

9

ZARA

"Welcome to your new home, Zara." Athena extends her hand. "I wanted to give you the tour personally." She adjusts the brim of her white fedora, a signature accessory, I've learned. The subtle movement draws attention to her confident posture and the quiet authority she carries so effortlessly.

I step into a foyer that feels more like the entrance to a luxury villa than a hotel suite. A crystal chandelier hangs from a domed ceiling adorned with a hand-painted scene of gods and goddesses lounging among the clouds. The walls are a soft cream color with subtle gold accents, giving the space a warm glow despite its grandeur.

"This is..." I pause, searching for the right words. "Quite spectacular."

"One of our four VIP Suites," she says, and leads me through an archway into a spacious living area with floor-to-ceiling windows.

The décor is both opulent and tasteful—plush cream sofas accented with deep blue pillows, marble-topped tables with brass legs, and strategic touches of gold throughout.

Abstract art in complementary colors adorns the walls, and a collection of leather-bound books fills built-in shelves flanking a gas fireplace.

"I lived here myself for a while," Athena says, gesturing around us. "So I know it's comfortable."

"I love it," I say honestly, running my fingers along the smooth surface of a blue agate side table. My beloved grand piano is positioned against the back wall, looking a little out of place in its new quarters.

"Thank you for accommodating my Steinway. I know it was a bit excessive."

"Some things are worth the trouble," she says. "Let me show you the master bedroom?"

I follow her into the next room where a king-sized bed faces those same spectacular windows. The bedding looks plush, in shades of cream and pale gold. There's a beautiful seating area with a wall mounted magazine and newspaper rack, and an antique Greek amphora, transformed into an elegant lamp, sits next to the chaise.

"The lighting can be adjusted to any intensity or color," Athena explains, demonstrating with a small touch panel near the door. The room shifts through various moods— from warm amber to cool blue to a soft rose glow.

Then she leads me to the en-suite bathroom that features a sunken marble tub large enough for three people, a separate rainfall shower, and double vanities with gold fixtures. Small inlaid mosaics depict ocean scenes and add splashes of blue to the otherwise cream and gold space.

"The bath has jets, of course," Athena continues, "and can be programmed to fill automatically at certain times of day, at your preferred temperature. The shower has six different pressure settings."

I laugh, shaking my head. "I might need a manual just for the bathroom. This is beyond what I have at home."

"Don't worry, everything is also voice operated." She cracks a smile. "Use the word 'Olympus' before your command."

We both laugh when a woman's voice sounds through hidden speakers. "Athena, what can I do for you?"

"Olympus, nothing for now," Athena says, shooting me a wink. "She knows my voice, but we fed her your latest album so she'll know your voice too."

The next bedroom has several of my guitars mounted on the wall. In one corner sits a comfortable reading chair with a small side table, and there's a desk next to the terrace doors.

"This is your guest bedroom. We took the liberty of storing your guitars here," Athena explains. "I've been told this room has good acoustics." She leads me back to the living area and shows me the kitchen. A wine refrigerator is built into one wall, already stocked with an impressive selection.

"I doubt you'll do much cooking," she says, following my gaze, "but the team has stocked the pantry with essentials and the refrigerator with your preferences."

We head through a set of glass doors that open onto a private terrace. The space is larger than most Manhattan apartments, with a small infinity pool glittering in the afternoon sun. Comfortable loungers and a dining table create distinct zones for relaxation and entertaining, and potted olive trees and Mediterranean plants provide touches of greenery.

"The pool temperature can be adjusted," Athena says. "Simply ask the system."

I walk to the edge of the terrace, taking in the sprawling

view of Las Vegas. From this height, the city looks almost delicate—a glittering mosaic of lights and structures against the stark desert landscape beyond. The contrast is striking —nature's minimalism against human excess.

"Anything you need at all, let the VIP concierge on duty know," Athena says, coming to stand beside me. "You can reach them through the golden buzzers in each room, or through the system. Don't hesitate to ask even if you feel it's an impossible or silly request. This is Vegas. Nothing is too much."

"I'm incredibly impressed," I say, turning to her. "You've gone out of your way, but I promise I'm not that demanding."

Athena shrugs, hands in her pockets. "Be as demanding as you like. That's what we're here for." She squints as she stares out over the city. "Vegas may take some time to get used to. Comfort goes beyond luxury, it's about feeling like yourself in a space. But I'm here if you need a friend."

I nod and shoot her a sweet smile. "How are *you* doing?" I ask, turning the conversation away from me. "How have you been since last time we spoke?"

Athena meets my eyes. "I'm good. Really good, actually."

"The woman you mentioned?"

"Yeah." I notice a slight flush on her cheeks. "It's going well. I'm happy."

"I'm happy for you."

"Thank you." She straightens slightly, as if realizing she's shared more than intended. "And on that note, don't forget what I mentioned about introductions. If you're ever interested in meeting someone..."

I nod and take a deep breath. I've been thinking about this nonstop—rehearsing what I might say, how I might approach the subject. Now that the moment has arrived, my heart is racing.

"Actually," I begin, trying to sound casual, "I'd like that. If you can promise it really will be discreet, I'd love to go on a date. Nothing serious, though," I add quickly. "I just want to have a bit of fun. Test the waters, you know?"

"Of course. I understand completely. Do you have a type?"

I laugh nervously, feeling heat rush to my face. "I honestly have no idea. This is all so new to me."

My embarrassment at my own reaction only makes me blush even harder. I've performed in front of hundreds of thousands of people, met presidents and royalty, yet here I am, flustered at the prospect of a date.

"I'm sorry." I cover my face with my hands. "I must seem ridiculous."

"Not at all. It's perfectly normal to feel nervous about exploring new territory."

"The truth is," I say, "I never thought it would actually get to this point—actually going on a date with a woman. I've been thinking about it so much, it's hard to believe it might be happening, and I'm freaking out a little."

Athena places a hand on my arm. "There's no pressure. If you decide it's not what you want after all, that's completely fine."

The kindness in her voice helps calm my racing thoughts. "Will you tell me who she is? Will you tell her who I am?"

Athena shakes her head. "No. My friends are very private, as are you. It's best if you meet and take it from there. No strings. If you don't click, I can arrange another date. No one will be offended, I promise. And noted— nothing serious, just a bit of fun."

I nod, mildly relieved, even though the conversation has skyrocketed my anxiety. A real date. With a woman. "And where would the date take place?"

"I'll arrange it on neutral grounds. That means not here in your suite and not in her hotel. I don't think either of you would be comfortable with that." Athena purses her lips as she contemplates. "I'll create a safe space for you," she finally says. "But you'll have to be flexible with time as my friends are very busy people too. Would sometime next week work? Peter mentioned you had some time off before your rehearsal schedule begins?"

"Yes, I'll make it work." I glance around the suite again, still trying to process that this is my life now, and that I finally have a chance to maybe be entirely myself for a while.

"Excellent. And don't be nervous. Look at it as meeting new friends. With or without benefits." Athena pats my arm and heads toward the door. "I'll leave you to settle in. I'll be in touch."

10

DIANE

*T*he Rundown is scruffy and gloriously different from my usual haunts. The wooden floors are sticky beneath my boots, neon beer signs cast a blue-red glow across the dim interior, and decades of graffiti cover the bathroom doors visible from the bar I'm seated at. The speaker blares something with heavy bass that I vaguely recognize.

I take a sip of my whiskey sour, savoring both the tart liquid and the delicious anonymity. I've dressed down in jeans, a faded Georgetown sweatshirt with the logo nearly washed away, and minimal makeup, and my hair is pulled back in a ponytail.

The door swings open, letting in a gust of cool evening air. I almost don't recognize Thomas as he scans the bar. Gone is the tailored suit and the styled hair. Instead, he's wearing a vintage band T-shirt under a leather jacket, jeans that have actually been worn rather than artificially distressed, and his hair is slightly tousled. He looks like an entirely different person—relaxed, younger.

When he spots me, his face breaks into a genuine smile.

He weaves through the crowd and slides into the barstool next to me.

"I almost walked right past you," he says, shrugging off his jacket. "Senator Washington's daughter is nowhere to be found."

"That's the idea," I reply, gesturing to his outfit. "What happened to the Republican Ken doll? I have to say, the transformation is impressive."

Thomas laughs, running a hand through his hair. "This is actually the real me. That other guy? He only exists between the hours of eight and six, Monday through Friday, and for special family appearances."

"So I'm meeting the after-hours Thomas Cunningham?"

"The authentic edition," he confirms, eyeing the female bartender. He orders a draft beer and shoots her a wink. "What?" he asks when I laugh.

"Imagine our mothers' faces if they could see us now. This is an interesting venue you picked. Don't get me wrong; I like it, but it's nothing like The Meridian."

He grimaces. "My mother would need smelling salts if she knew I was in a place that doesn't serve wine in crystal glasses."

"Here you go, honey." The bartender slides his beer toward him, and I impulsively decide to down the rest of my cocktail and switch. "I'll have what he's having," I tell her, handing over my glass.

Thomas blows the bartender a kiss, then raises an eyebrow at me. "A Washington drinking beer from a tap? Scandalous."

"I contain multitudes," I say dryly. "So, your girlfriend doesn't mind you meeting up with me? You could have brought her along, you know."

A voice cuts in from behind the bar. "Thank you, I appreciate that."

I turn to the bartender with dark hair, multiple ear piercings, and an intricate tattoo sleeve on her left arm. Her eyes are fixed on us with amused interest.

Thomas chuckles. "That's her. That's my girl."

The woman waves, and I laugh in surprise as I understand the situation.

"Diane, this is Jamie. Jamie, this is Diane," Thomas introduces.

"Nice to meet you," I say.

Jamie nods in my direction. "Nice to meet you too. And thanks for not being his type." She turns to help another customer who's flagging her down.

"Oh, wow... I did not see that one coming," I say honestly and lower my voice. "Are you sure she doesn't mind me being here with you?"

Thomas shrugs, taking a sip of his beer. "I explained there was nothing romantic between us. That we're just two people with overly controlling families finding solidarity in our shared misery."

Jamie hands me my beer. The bar is filling up fast—a Thursday night crowd of people who look refreshingly normal.

"God, that lunch was awkward," I say, returning to the main reason for our meeting.

Thomas groans and rolls his eyes. "Apparently, you're the full package—beauty, brains, and politically advantageous family connections."

"Fantastic," I mutter. "And here I thought my personality might be a factor."

"Oh, personality is optional in these arrangements," Thomas says with mock seriousness. "As long as you can smile on demand and produce at least two children—preferably boys—you've fulfilled your purpose."

I laugh, genuinely enjoying myself. There's something liberating about being with someone who understands the peculiar constraints of our world without judgment.

"So why can't you take Jamie home and introduce her?" I ask, even though I have an idea of the answer. "They'll get over the piercings and the tattoos eventually, right?"

Thomas sighs, tracing patterns in the condensation on his glass. "Jamie's not just a bartender, although if she were I'd like her just as much. She's also an international politics student. Getting her Master's at Georgetown. Brilliant, actually. Writing her thesis on authoritarian regimes and democratic erosion."

"But that's good, right? So what's the problem?"

Thomas hesitates, taking a long drink from his beer. "She's a Democrat," he says finally, his voice dropping slightly as if confessing something scandalous.

I stare at him for a moment, then burst into laughter. "Oh no, not a Democrat! How will your family survive the shame?"

"You laugh, but for the Cunninghams, it might as well be high treason," Thomas says, though he's smiling too. "My grandfather once disowned a cousin for voting for Carter." He shakes his head. "Almost a year together, and I've never brought her to a family event. Never posted a photo online. Never even mentioned her name." The shame in his voice is palpable. "I keep telling myself I'm working up to it, that I'll find the right moment, but..."

"You're afraid," I finish for him.

"Terrified," he admits. "Not only of their disapproval, but of what they might do. My father has connections that could make Jamie's academic career difficult. They wouldn't see it as vindictive—just 'protecting the family from poor decisions.'" He huffs. "Honestly? I'm worried about what they're capable of and I hate myself for that. For not being strong enough to stand up to them. For choosing the easy way."

I nod. "I get it. More than you know." I pause. "It must be nice having someone who knows the real you. Even if it's complicated."

Thomas looks at me curiously. "You speak from experience?"

I hesitate. "More like lack of it."

"Well, you're young, beautiful, and clearly smart as hell," he says. "What's stopping you?"

The question is deceptively simple yet impossibly complex. What's stopping me? Where would I even begin? With my father's political career? With my family name? With the expectations that have been heaped on me since birth? The fact that I'm well and truly gay to the core and currently sexually frustrated to the point that I can't think of much other than kissing women?

"It's complicated," I finally say, the understatement of the century.

"Well, in that case..." Thomas raises his glass. "To complicated lives and the bars where we escape them."

The moment I clink my glass against his, my phone buzzes in my pocket. I'm about to turn it to silent when I see Athena's name on the screen. My heart immediately jumps to my throat. Athena never calls—our communication is strictly limited to emergencies.

"I'm sorry," I tell Thomas, suddenly anxious. "I need to take this. It's important."

I hurry toward the door, pushing through the crowd, my mind racing through possibilities. Has there been a security breach? Has someone connected me to the club? Is my double life about to collapse?

I step onto the sidewalk, my hands shaking slightly as I answer. "Athena? Is everything okay? Please tell me I don't need to panic."

"Diane, calm down," Athena's voice instantly reassures me. "I'm sorry for alarming you. I should have texted first."

I lean against the brick exterior of the bar, my pulse gradually slowing. "You said you'd never call unless it's an emergency."

"Well, this isn't an emergency," she assures me. "It's a proposition I wanted to discuss with you."

I exhale slowly, relief washing over me. The kind of relief I didn't know existed until now. "A proposition?"

"That's right. I have a friend," Athena begins, "who would like to go on a date with a woman. Her first real date, actually. And... well, I thought of you. You're private, you don't do relationships, but you like to have a bit of fun now and then, nothing extreme..."

I frown, trying to process this unexpected turn. "Someone from the club?" I ask hesitantly. While I've had casual encounters with women I met at Athena's club, nothing has ever sparked enough to pursue anything more and why would she waste her time trying to set me up?

"No," Athena says. "She's not in the club. That's why I'm calling."

My guard immediately rises again. "Then I don't feel comfortable with it. You know I need discretion, Athena. Absolute discretion."

"I know. Do you trust me?" she asks simply.

The question catches me off guard. Do I trust her? Athena has been the guardian of my most dangerous secret for two years. She's created a space where I can be myself without fear. If anyone understands the importance of privacy and discretion, it's her.

"This is about as discreet as it gets," she continues before I can answer. "My friend isn't looking for anything serious either so maybe just say yes this once? If nothing else, you'll make an amazing new friend and I think she could really do with a friend. She's really cool, Diane."

I watch through the window as Thomas laughs at something Jamie has said, their easy intimacy visible even from a distance. "Who is she?" I ask, still hesitant but more curious now.

"Someone who understands discretion as well as you do," Athena replies cryptically. "Someone who has as much to lose as you, if not more."

I close my eyes, thinking of the dating app still hidden on my phone, of the conversations that never progress beyond words on a screen. Of Diana Peters, who exists in digital spaces but never gets to step into the real world. "Would I meet her in Vegas?"

"Yes, but not at the club," Athena says. "Next week, if you can make it. I know it's short notice."

A gust of wind sends trash skittering down the sidewalk. In the distance, a siren wails. I think about returning to my empty apartment tonight, about my meetings tomorrow, about the endless cycle of appearances and obligations stretching into my future.

"Why me?" I ask. "If she's not from the club, how do you even know we'd get along? And why not just make her a member?"

"I'm pretty sure you'll get along but I'm afraid I can't make her a member for reasons I can't disclose," Athena says. "That's why I'm proposing a blind date. If you're not interested that's completely fine; I can ask someone else. But you were my first choice."

I lean my head back against the rough brick wall. "I don't know, Athena. Blind dates aren't really my thing."

"It's not entirely blind," she counters. "It's me, introducing two people I care about who I think would enjoy each other's company. Nothing more, nothing less. I can't promise you'll click on a physical level; I'm not Cupid. But I can promise you discretion and a pleasant night. It's up to you."

I sigh, torn between the undeniable pull of possibility and the weight of caution that's governed my entire adult life. Looking through the window at the crowded bar, I realize I'm already having more fun tonight than I've had in months, just by stepping outside my usual boundaries. What's one more small deviation from the script?

"Okay," I say finally, the word escaping before I can overthink it. "I'll do it."

11

ZARA

I can't stop pacing. My body feels like a live wire, conducting anxiety from my fingertips to my toes. I'm tracing the same path I've been walking for days— from bedroom to living room to kitchen and back again.

This was supposed to be my week off. Seven days to decompress, to settle into my new surroundings, to breathe before the whirlwind of rehearsals and media preparations begins. Instead, I've filled every moment with noise and motion, terrified of what might happen if I allow myself to be still.

I called Mo, my choreographer, begging him to fly in early to rehearse in my suite.

"We need to refine the opening sequence," I told him, the lie slipping effortlessly from my lips. "I've been thinking about it, and we need more impact."

He arrived the next morning, confused but professional as always. For hours, he drove us through exhausting routines, tweaking movements long past the point of improvement. I pushed my body to the edge of exhaustion, hoping physical fatigue might quiet my mind. It didn't.

"I've never seen you this... intense during pre-production," he said yesterday, toweling sweat from his face after our fifth hour. "We haven't even started formal rehearsals."

I mumbled something about creative vision and Vegas expectations, but the truth burned in my chest: I'm terrified of tonight. Terrified and exhilarated in equal measure. My first real date with a woman. And I know absolutely nothing about who I'm meeting.

I stop in front of the windows, pressing my forehead against the cool glass. Below, Las Vegas sprawls like a circuit board, pulsing with neon veins. I close my eyes, trying to focus on my breathing the way my vocal coach taught me before big performances. Four counts in, hold for seven, exhale for eight. It isn't working.

Behind me, the bed is covered with discarded outfits—six different variations of "casual" that somehow all feel wrong. Too revealing. Too conservative. Too obviously trying. Too carelessly thrown together. Too me, or maybe not me enough.

What does "casual" even mean in this context? My date's version might be entirely different. There's no one to style me for this. No one to approve my choices. Just me, standing in a room full of clothes, feeling like I've forgotten how to dress myself.

I've tried to work through this anxiety. Last night, I sat at my Steinway for hours, fingers hovering over the keys, waiting for inspiration to strike. But every melody that came felt hollow, every lyric forced, and I couldn't concentrate long enough to finish a single phrase.

I glance at my phone. Only two hours before I have to be ready. Before I can think better of it, I video call Jess.

She answers on the third ring, her face filling my screen. She's in her kitchen, hair piled messily on top of her head.

"Zara? Hey! I didn't expect to hear from you so soon. How's Vegas?"

Seeing her familiar face calms me a little. "Vegas is..." I hesitate, unsure how to continue. "Honestly, I have no idea. I've just been up here in my suite, rehearsing with Mo. But there's an infinity pool on the terrace; you'll love it."

"Of course you have an infinity pool," she laughs. "I bet you have a rotating bed too."

"Not quite." I angle the camera to show the chaos on my bed. "I need help," I admit. "I have a... thing tonight and I'm completely overthinking what to wear."

Jess peers closer at her screen. "A 'thing'? What kind of thing requires six different outfits? And why are you asking me for fashion advice? I'm terrible at this kind of stuff. You have a stylist, right? Don't they dress you for formal events?"

"Yeah." I nod, unable to meet her eyes. "But it's not a formal event. It's a date."

Her brows shoot up, and she throws her head back and laughs. "Holy shit, Z. That's huge! Who's the lucky guy? Someone from the show?"

"Not a guy," I say. "And not someone from the show."

Jess blinks, processing. "Not a guy?"

"Do you remember Emma Walters?" I ask.

"Emma from NYU? The music theory girl with the crazy hair?" Jess tilts her head, confused by the sudden change in topic. "Yeah, of course I remember her. The one you made out with that time the heating broke in your dorm." She laughs. "Why are you bringing her up now?"

I twist a strand of hair around my finger. "And do you remember Rachel? From that bar in the East Village?"

Jess frowns, thinking. "Rachel... wait, the bartender with the tattoos? The one you kissed when we were celebrating your first gig? Of course I remember—you were drunk and kept saying she had the most beautiful eyes you'd ever seen. But—" Her expression shifts as she connects the dots. "Wait..." She stops mid-sentence, her eyes widening as realization dawns. For a moment, she stares at me through the screen. "Oh..."

"Uh-huh," I confirm, my heart hammering in my chest. "I'm going on a date with a woman tonight." I feel simultaneously lighter and more terrified than I have in years.

"Z..." Jess's voice is soft. "I had no idea you still... I mean, I thought college was purely experimentation. I didn't realize you still had those feelings."

I shake my head, a small, sad smile crossing my lips. "It doesn't just go away, Jess. It's not a phase that passed. I've had to ignore it because of my career." My voice cracks slightly. "But I need this. I really need this." Tears sting at my eyes and I wipe them away. "I'm sorry I didn't tell you."

"Hey, don't be sorry," Jess says. "It's a good thing, right? I'm just surprised. All these years, you never said anything. I wish you would have told me sooner," she continues. "Face to face, so I could give you a proper hug while we talked about this. Because you look like you could do with a hug right now."

I wipe at my eyes again, embarrassed. "I'm nervous and freaking out," I say, trying to laugh it off. "It's stupid. I've performed for crowds of thousands, but the thought of dinner with one woman has me falling apart."

"It's not stupid. This matters so of course you're nervous." She pauses. "Who is she? How did you meet?"

"That's the weird part," I admit. "I don't know who she is. It's a blind date. Athena—the casino owner—arranged it. Apparently she knows people who... value privacy as much as I do."

Jess raises an eyebrow. "A blind date? Seriously? Is that safe?"

"Athena vouches for her. And it's not like I'm going to some stranger's apartment. It's somewhere in this building, very private." I sigh, feeling some of the tension release. "I know it sounds crazy. But it's the only way I could do this. My management would have a collective stroke if they knew."

"Well, I'm proud of you," Jess says simply. "That takes guts. You're very brave."

"Or stupid," I mutter.

"No, Z. Brave. Thank you so much for trusting me with this." She smiles, then her expression shifts to concern. "Hey, take a deep breath. You look like you're about to have a panic attack."

I hadn't realized how shallow my breathing had become and inhale deeply, feeling light-headed.

"That's it," Jess encourages. "In through the nose, out through the mouth."

I follow her instructions, feeling my pulse gradually slow.

"Better?" she asks.

I nod, managing a weak smile. "Sorry. I don't know what's wrong with me."

"I do," Jess says. "You're finally doing something impulsive and real. It's scarier than the stage because there's no script." She tilts her head, studying me through the screen. "Now, you better clean up those mascara streaks from under your eyes before your date. As gorgeous as the raccoon look is, it might send the wrong message."

I laugh, wiping under my eyes. "Great, now I have to redo my makeup."

"That's not one of your outfit options, right?" She gestures to my current outfit—yoga pants and a T-shirt.

"No. Of course not. I just can't decide what to wear. Hence the fashion crisis call." I wince. "I know you're not my go-to person for that, but I don't want to explain myself to anyone else."

"Well, let's see what you've got, then."

I prop the phone against a pillow and begin holding up each outfit in turn: dark jeans with a silk blouse, a casual knit dress, leather pants with a simple tee, a black jumpsuit, a midi skirt with a cropped sweater, and black pants with a blazer.

Jess considers each one thoughtfully, her brow furrowed in concentration. "In my humble accountant opinion, the jumpsuit," she decides finally. "It looks comfortable but elegant, and it has pockets for nervous hands."

I lift the jumpsuit, examining it with new eyes. It's one of my favorites—something I bought for myself rather than for an appearance.

"With a simple necklace," Jess adds. "And flat sandals in case you need to make a quick getaway or in case she's much shorter than you." She winks, and I can't help but laugh again.

"Thanks, Jess," I say quietly.

"Anytime. That's what friends are for." She glances over her shoulder as a crash sounds from somewhere off-screen. "Shoot, Lucas is awake and apparently redecorating. I've got to run, but Z? Try to enjoy yourself tonight and let me know how it went, okay? And don't panic, it's going to be fine."

12

DIANE

*T*he baseball cap sits low over my eyes, the brim obscuring my features from wandering gazes. Dark sunglasses complete the disguise—a look that screams "trying not to be noticed" but feels necessary nonetheless. The jeans and white linen shirt are deliberately unremarkable, chosen to blend into any crowd. Not because I'm famous, but because the last thing I need is for someone from my parents' circles to spot Senator Washington's daughter in a casino. They might claim they never gamble, but I know better.

The security guard who met me at the entrance moves at a rushed pace, his bulk parting crowds like a ship cutting through water. He hasn't spoken since the initial greeting, just nodded when I confirmed my name. We weave through the casino floor, past rows of slot machines that chime and flash, around blackjack tables where players clutch their cards like they actually believe this hand will be the one.

My heart pounds with each step. The one and only time I attempted this—an actual date with a woman—I made it as far as the restaurant parking lot before panic seized me entirely. I stood outside, watching through the window as she waited at the bar, checking her phone, glancing toward the door. Bernie, her name was. A dentist from my dating app who'd seemed funny and intelligent in our messages. In person, through that glass, she'd looked kind. Patient. But I got back in my car and drove away without going inside.

The guilt from that night still bugs me, the memory of her final text—"I waited for an hour. I hope you're okay"—a reminder of my cowardice. I'd deleted the app the next day, then reinstalled it a week later, then deleted it again. The endless cycle of approach and retreat.

But tonight there's no backing out. Maybe it's the controlled environment, the fact that Athena has arranged this. Maybe it's simply that I've reached a breaking point with my own isolation, tired of digital conversations that lead nowhere and fantasies that remain safely locked in my head, occasionally satisfied by a fling with someone from the club.

The rational part of my brain catalogues all the ways this could go wrong but beneath the paranoia lies something I've buried for so long I almost don't recognize it: hope. Raw, desperate hope that tonight I might meet someone I have a spark with, even if it's casual and temporary.

We veer away from the main gaming floor and the guard uses a keycard to access a corridor marked "Authorized Personnel Only." The sounds of the casino fade as we move deeper into the building's inner workings, past laundry carts and cleaning supplies, the glamorous facade giving way to the practical machinery that keeps this place running.

An elevator at the end of the hall requires another swipe of his card. We ride in silence to what feels like the top of the building. My ears pop from the altitude change, and I grip the handrail as nervous energy courses through me.

The guard stares straight ahead, unreadable, giving no hint about what awaits me above.

When the doors open, we're in what's clearly private territory—shiny marble floors, tasteful artwork that looks like original pieces rather than hotel reproductions. The air here smells different too, clean and outdoorsy.

The guard leads me down a hallway lined with tall windows that offer glimpses of the gaming floor far below, and we stop at a door marked only with a small brass nameplate: "A. Stavros." He knocks twice before opening the door.

I frown as I step into what appears to be an office. This is curious in itself, but it's the transformation of the space that stops me short.

A dining table sits in the center of the room, set for two with white linens and flickering candles. Soft jazz plays, something sultry and atmospheric. The lighting has been dimmed to create pools of warm amber throughout the space and fresh flowers—white roses and baby's breath—sit in a simple glass vase at the table's center. Two place settings await, complete with multiple courses of silverware that suggest this won't be a simple meal, and a bottle of wine is chilling in an ice bucket nearby. A woman in black stands in a corner, hands folded in front of her. It's one of the waitresses from Athena's club.

Athena rises from behind her desk, dressed in white slacks and a white silk blouse.

"Diane. There you are."

"Hey, Athena. Thanks for arranging this..." I glance around again. "This date in your office." I'm unable to hide my amusement with a smirk.

"One of the most secure places in Vegas," she says, moving around the desk to greet me with a kiss on each cheek. "Sorry about the detour through the service areas. It was either that or go up in my private golden elevator which is the most prominently visible one in the building."

I gesture toward the transformed space. "Well, this is... this was clearly a lot of trouble. No pressure, huh?" I joke, a laugh escaping me.

Athena laughs along. "Please don't feel pressured. I just wanted you both to feel comfortable. My office seemed like the best option."

A fresh wave of curiosity stirs in me. Who is this woman that Athena would convert her own office into a romantic hideaway for? My imagination has been running wild since she first called, but this seems crazy.

"She'll be here any minute," Athena continues, heading toward her private elevator at the far end of the room. "Ally will take good care of you and security will be stationed outside all evening to escort you out whenever you're ready. Whatever happens, I think you'll enjoy each other's company."

And then she's gone, leaving me alone in her office-turned-restaurant. I take a seat at the table, my hands immediately gravitating to the cloth napkin as nervous energy demands an outlet. I fold and refold it as I try to process the bizarre turn my life has taken.

I stare at the door, my pulse quickening with each passing minute. When the door finally opens, I'm caught completely off guard.

I frown and swallow hard. I know this face. The whole world knows this face.

The door closes behind her and she approaches the table with an uncertain smile. When she extends her hand, I notice she's trembling—a detail that registers through my shock as both surprising and oddly comforting.

"Hi, I'm Zara."

As if I wouldn't know. As if her face hasn't graced the covers of magazines, billboards, and social media feeds for the better part of a decade. As if her voice hasn't sound-tracked countless moments of my life, playing from radios and playlists. As if she isn't one of the most recognizable and iconic people on the planet, standing in Athena's office, introducing herself to me like this is a perfectly normal occurrence. Most baffling of all, it seems Zara Nova is queer.

I should stand, I remind myself. I should greet her properly, say something welcoming and normal and polite. Instead, I remain frozen in my chair, staring like an absolute idiot as my brain struggles to process what's happening.

"Hi, I'm Diane," I say, finally snapping out of it. Somehow I manage to get up and shake her hand, and she leans in and kisses me on each cheek. "It's lovely to meet you. I, um..." I pause, trying to collect my thoughts. "I apologize for being a little out of sorts. I didn't know what to expect and then... well, then you walked in."

"I get it." She winces, nervously shuffling from one foot to another. "Do you still want to do this, or..."

"No, of course I do," I say quickly. My voice is caught somewhere between my throat and my chest, my mind reeling with the implications. The night just got even more surreal.

13

ZARA

I'm thrown when Diane pulls out my chair. The gesture is so unexpectedly gallant that it highlights just how foreign this entire situation is to me.

"Sorry," I say, settling into the seat while heat rushes to my cheeks. "I'm not used to..." I gesture vaguely between us. "I'm not used to any of this."

"Don't apologize," Diane says, taking her own seat across from me. "We're both figuring this out as we go."

The waitress approaches, and I watch her with the hyperfocus that anxiety brings as she fills our wine glasses. She places leather-bound menus in front of us, embossed with "Parthenon" in gold lettering.

"I'll give you a few minutes to look over the menu," she says, then heads out the door.

I stare after her, my paranoia kicking into overdrive. The rational part of my brain knows that Athena wouldn't have arranged this without considering security, but the part of me that's lived in the public eye for a decade immediately catalogues potential disasters.

One photo. One leaked story. One overheard conversation. My career hasn't prepared me for discretion in romantic contexts—quite the opposite. Every so-called relationship I've had has been performed for public consumption and maximum publicity benefit. The idea of genuine privacy, of authentic connection without cameras or contracts feels almost mythical.

I lean forward, lowering my voice. "Do you think we can trust the waitress?" The words tumble out before I can consider how they might sound. "How do we know she's not going to the tabloids?"

Even as I ask, I cringe internally at how I must appear— paranoid, narcissistic, unable to exist in the moment without calculating the potential fallout. But the fear is real, bred from years of having my privacy violated.

Diane follows my gaze to the now-closed door, then looks back at me. There's no judgment in her expression, no eye-rolling at my celebrity neuroses. Instead, she seems to understand the concern behind the question.

"We're safe," she says simply. "I know her."

Something in her tone makes me believe her, though she doesn't elaborate.

I reach for my wine glass, intending to take a civilized sip, and instead find myself downing half the contents in one desperate gulp. The wine is excellent but I barely register the taste through my nerves. The alcohol hits my empty stomach immediately, sending warmth through my limbs. Hopefully it will reach my frazzled mind soon.

"God," I say, setting the glass down too hard and laughing at myself. "I should probably apologize in advance. I'm... I'm not exactly myself right now."

"You're nervous?" Diane asks. Her smile is soft, encouraging, the kind that invites honesty.

"Terrified," I confess. Maybe it's the wine, or maybe it's the way she's looking at me. Curiously, now that the initial shock has worn off. "I might actually be undatable."

Diane laughs. "You're not undatable and for what it's worth, I'm scared too."

"Good. That makes me feel better. I'll be fine in a minute," I continue, trying to reclaim some semblance of dignity. "Going on a date with a woman was unthinkable to me until recently, let alone a blind date."

"I've never been on a blind date either," she says. "I've never even been in a relationship with a woman. And if I'm not your type, that's okay. We can just have a nice dinner. If you're uncomfortable, you can leave and I won't be offended."

I shake my head and hold up a hand. "No, I don't want to leave. Do you have any idea how much stress I went through to get here?" I laugh. "I've been a mess all week. I even cried today."

"I'm sorry." Diane reaches over the table and briefly touches my arm. "I can assure you this stays between these walls. I have a lot to lose too."

"Thank you," I say, and I mean it more than she could possibly know.

Now that the initial nerves are wearing off slightly, I really look at Diane for the first time. She's beautiful in a way that's both understated and striking—the kind of beauty that grows more compelling the longer you observe it. Thick, dark hair, big, dark eyes, intelligent and warm, framed by naturally long lashes. A strong jawline, pale skin, and a genuinely sweet smile.

Something about her presence, about the way she carries herself, suggests privilege and education, yet her clothes contradict that—dark jeans, a simple white linen shirt, and a baseball cap.

As if sensing my observation, she takes it off and runs a hand through her hair. "I know I must look like I didn't make any effort, but I was actually dressing down on purpose—trying to blend in, hoping no one would recognize me on the way here." She laughs. "Now that seems pretty silly, considering I'm having dinner with *you*."

I chuckle. "I think you look nice."

"So do you," she says. "You look beautiful."

"Thank you." My cheeks burn at the compliment, and I'm grateful for the dim lighting. "So are you from around here?" I ask. "Since you mentioned being worried people might recognize you?"

"Nowhere near," Diane says, rolling her eyes with a self-deprecating grin. "I'm from Washington. Just super paranoid, that's all. I can't begin to imagine how you must feel." She tilts her head as she studies me. "Forgive me for being forward, but I had no idea you were queer."

"No one knows," I admit. "It's something I want to explore, but it's not easy when you're in the public eye."

Something I want to explore. Such careful language for desires that have been burning inside me for years. Such diplomatic phrasing for the dreams that visit me in the small hours, for the way my pulse quickens when I catch a glimpse of a woman's collarbone or the curve of her smile. Such sanitized words for the fantasies swirling through me.

"It's a fundamental part of me, and it's time I recognize it," I continue. "I've been suppressing it for too long; it's not healthy and I'm getting to the point where my mind is consumed with what-ifs. What if I did explore this part of me? What if I don't? What if I never feel like I felt in college again? Those few times I made out with a girl... they're still such vivid memories. That must mean something, right?" I pause and meet her eyes. "Athena offered to set me up, so here I am."

"I'm flattered to be your first." Diane's eyes widen as she realizes what she's just said. "I mean—not your first *first*," she says quickly, stumbling over the words. "I don't expect us to... I mean, I'm not assuming anything about tonight or what you want or..." She stops herself, laughing as she brings a hand to her forehead. "God, I'm making this worse, aren't I? You know what I mean."

"Don't worry. I know what you mean." I'm grateful I'm not the only one nervous here, and lean back in my chair, wine warming my bloodstream and loosening the tight coil of anxiety.

"So, is Zara your real name?" she asks. "Or is that a stage name?"

"It's both, actually. My birth name is Zara Vilanova. When I signed with my label, they felt Vilanova wasn't catchy enough so they shortened it to Nova. And Zara with a 'Z' was my mom's idea from the start. Sara with an S is incredibly common in Colombia and my mom wanted something more unique." I shrug. "It worked out well for branding, I suppose. Easy to remember, looks good on a marquee."

"Zara Vilanova," Diane says, testing it out. "I like it."

"Thank you. Sometimes I miss hearing my full name. Only my mom still uses it, and only when she's scolding me." I laugh. "Everything else is just Zara Nova now—the brand, the business." I try to break the tension with a joke. "And is Diane your real name?"

Diane laughs. "Yes. Diane Washington. Born and bred."

"So, Diane Washington... Athena told me you weren't looking for anything serious. Is that right?"

"Yes," she says. "My situation... my life doesn't allow me to be openly gay, so it wouldn't be fair to anyone to become seriously involved with me."

I nod. "Why is that? Please tell me about yourself."

14

DIANE

"**S**o what's your type?" I ask, moving back in my chair as the waitress clears our empty plates. I'm finally starting to feel human again after my second glass of wine and the first two courses of Greek-inspired haute cuisine.

I still can't quite believe I'm sitting here having dinner with Zara Nova, and I'm even more baffled that she hasn't bolted after learning about my family's political affiliations. When I mentioned my father's senate career and the foundation's work with conservative donors, I watched her face carefully for signs of judgment or discomfort but found none.

There's nothing particularly interesting about me compared to her—I'm just another privileged political offspring managing family money and trying to stay out of scandals, while she's an international superstar adored by millions. Yet here she is, still engaged in our conversation, still seeming interested in my mundane existence.

We've actually had a lovely time so far. After the initial awkwardness, we've both relaxed considerably. Zara told me about her upcoming residency and how she's looking forward to having more creative control. She lit up when talking about her four-month-old godson, showing me photos on her phone. She also mentioned her mother, who still lives in a modest apartment in Brooklyn despite Zara's attempts to relocate her somewhere better.

In return, I've shared stories about the foundation's work, the challenges of balancing genuine philanthropy with political optics, and the satisfaction I find in seeing our education programs actually make a difference in students' lives. Both of us were shy and clumsy at first, but now our conversation is naturally drifting toward more personal territory—specifically, our dating lives, or rather, the lack thereof.

Zara considers my question. "Athena asked me the same thing but I have no idea what my type is," she says with a laugh. "I'm bisexual, I guess, though I hate labels. I've been in love with exactly two men in my life, but I've had fleeting crushes on dozens of women over the years."

She rolls her eyes and takes a sip of wine. "I think I generally develop a crush on any woman who pays me the slightest bit of attention. Pathetic, right?" She continues without waiting for an answer. "There was this dancer a few years ago who made one flirty comment during rehearsal, and I spent the entire tour analyzing every interaction we had. Then there was a friend of a friend who used to give me these cute nicknames when we'd hang out, and I convinced myself she was into me."

I watch her as she talks, noting the mix of embarrassment and amusement in her expression. There's something endearing about her vulnerability, the way she's willing to share these intimate details with someone she's just met. She's even more beautiful in person, which seems impossible given how stunning she appears in photographs. Her naturally curly hair catches the candlelight, dark waves framing her face in a way that's both wild and elegant.

"Oh, and my massage therapist," Zara says, shaking her head. "God, that was mortifying. I was so convinced she was flirting with me that I started booking three sessions a week instead of one. I was planning this whole romantic scenario where I'd finally work up the courage to ask her out. Then one day she showed up with a massive engagement ring, practically glowing with happiness as she told me all about her fiancé's proposal." She covers her face with her hands. "I'm the queen of misreading situations. It's honestly pathetic, and it's probably a good thing I never actually made a pass at any of them."

"You're not pathetic at all," I say, leaning forward. "I know how difficult it is to read those situations. When you're closeted or questioning, every friendly gesture feels loaded with possibility because you want so desperately for there to be something more."

"Yeah, exactly. You get it." Zara looks up at me. "I once spent three weeks convinced my yoga instructor was into me because she kept adjusting my poses. Turns out I just have terrible form. Wishful thinking is my nemesis."

I laugh, and she joins in.

"What about you?" Zara asks, turning my earlier question back on me. "What's your type?"

"I don't really have a type either," I admit. "I would consider myself lesbian. I don't date men; I've managed to avoid that despite my mother's increasingly creative attempts at matchmaking." The wine makes me bolder than usual. "I'm mainly that anonymous person on a dating app who talks to women and never actually meets up."

"Really?" Zara's eyebrows lift with genuine surprise. "So you never... I mean, you don't..."

"Have sex?" I finish for her, amused by her sudden shyness after her earlier candor. "I didn't say that," I reply with a mischievous smile. "I've met discreet women over the years, and we've had fun for a night or two. That was opportunity rather than real chemistry but still, it did the job. Stopped me from going entirely insane."

Zara laughs. She has a cute laugh; more like a short, high-pitched giggle. "We're quite the pair, aren't we?" she says. "Two adult women, afraid to..." she hesitates. "Do what we really want to do."

"Yeah. Sometimes I wonder if I'll ever have a normal relationship. Or even an abnormal one. At this point, I'd settle for abnormal."

"I'm with you." Zara shoots me a grin. "I'd settle for any kind of action."

I snort, almost spilling my wine. "I can help you with that."

Immediately I feel my face flame red. Fuck. What did I just say? It was meant as a flirtatious joke and came out more serious than I intended. If it were anyone else sitting across from me—literally anyone else in the world—I might have actually meant it. But this is Zara Nova. Global superstar. Billboard chart-topper. The idea of us together seems so preposterous that I can't even begin to take Athena's matchmaking attempt seriously. What was she thinking? It's like setting up a house cat with a leopard.

Thankfully, the waitress materializes, sliding plates in front of us, and I seize the distraction.

"Sea bass! Lovely!" I clap my hands together with the enthusiasm of someone discovering fire, my voice pitched several octaves higher than normal. The words bounce around the room with manic energy that makes me want to crawl under the table and hide until morning.

Why can't I behave like a functioning adult human being? Why does my mouth have a direct pipeline to the most inappropriate thoughts in my brain, bypassing all reasonable filters?

Zara's expression shifts through several phases—surprise, confusion, and what might be amusement—while I sit frozen.

"I mean," I stammer, desperately trying to backpedal, "obviously ignore what I said. That's... that was... you know... Because clearly this whole situation is just..." I gesture vaguely at the space between us, as if that explains anything at all.

The more I talk, the deeper I dig myself into this conversational grave, until Zara finally steps in.

"You really, really like sea bass, huh?" she says with a grin that's equal parts amused and merciful. "Should I be worried about competing with a fish for your attention?"

I let out a strangled laugh. "It's a tough choice," I manage weakly. "Me and my mouth. I hope I didn't make you feel uncomfortable."

"Not at all," Zara says. "I'll let you take the other comment back if that's what you want." She pauses, then shoots me a look that makes my pulse quicken. "Or not..."

15

ZARA

$\mathscr{T}$he conversation has shifted into that magical territory where time becomes irrelevant. We've shared stories about our mothers, debated the merits of various coffee brewing methods, and somehow ended up in a passionate discussion about whether pineapple belongs on pizza. The kind of meandering dialogue that only happens when two people genuinely enjoy each other's company.

Diane is full of enthusiasm; she gestures wildly when she's excited about something. And she listens—really listens—in a way that feels foreign after years of people nodding along with me. I'm used to agreement and this is refreshing.

"I can't believe I'm saying this," Diane says, setting down her wine glass, "but I actually have to head back soon."

"Oh God, I've kept you here way too long, haven't I?"

"No, not at all," she says quickly. "I could stay here all night talking to you, honestly. But I have a meeting back in Washington at ten AM tomorrow morning, and unfortunately I can't cancel it. It was hard enough to sneak out to Vegas unnoticed."

I check my phone and nearly choke on my wine. "It's two AM. We've been here for five hours."

"It doesn't feel that way, does it?" Something in Diane's tone makes my pulse quicken.

Five hours. How is that possible? I've sat through countless dinner meetings that felt like geological epochs, checking my watch every few minutes. Yet tonight disappeared like smoke, each moment flowing into the next without any awareness of time passing.

"And where are you staying?" Diane asks. "Do you live here?"

"Yeah. I'm in one of the VIP suites." I stare at her lips— something I've been doing with increasing frequency. They look soft and have a natural rosiness that makes me wonder what they'd feel like pressed against mine. When she smiles there's a hint of mischief that draws me in completely. The thought of kissing her sends waves of arousal through me, and I have to force myself to look away before she notices.

The problem is, I can't read her. Is she being polite, or is there genuine interest there? The flirtation from earlier— her offer to "help me with that"—made me blush, but Diane's so naturally warm and engaging that I can't tell if her attention is truly romantic. She's probably just being kind to the neurotic celebrity.

"Would you like to do this again?" I ask, holding my breath while I wait for her answer.

Diane looks surprised, as if she hadn't expected the question. "Yes," she says after a moment. "Would you?"

Relief floods through me, followed immediately by a flutter of nervous excitement. "Absolutely. I had a really wonderful time tonight."

She reaches into her purse and pulls out a business card. "I won't be offended if you don't call me, but I would like to see you again."

I take the card, our fingers brushing briefly in the exchange. The contact is electric, lasting only a second but leaving my skin tingling. "Washington Foundation," I read from the front. "Executive Director."

"My thrilling career in convincing rich people to give away their money for the privilege of having buildings named after them," she says with an eye roll, then stands and smooths down her shirt. "Sorry I have to leave. It was such short notice, and I wasn't able to rearrange my schedule in case I wanted to stay a little longer." She shrugs, but there's unmistakable flirtation flashing in her eyes as she adds, "You know, just to talk."

My pulse races at the way she says "talk," and I bite my lip, studying her, wondering if she's going to kiss me good-bye. How typical. Any hint of interest and I'm ready to fall at someone's feet.

I stand too, and immediately the easy flow of conversation gives way to awkwardness. The transition from sitting and talking to preparing to leave highlights the uncertainty of what comes next. Do we hug? Kiss? Is there some protocol for ending a first date between two women who barely know how to navigate this territory?

Diane looks like she's wrestling with the same questions as she pulls the baseball cap over her head. Now I can clearly see the internal debate playing out across her face—the same mixture of desire and uncertainty that's been building in me all evening.

The wine has definitely lowered my inhibitions. Four large glasses over five hours has left me feeling bold. And it's not just the alcohol that's making me brave, but watching her smile, listening to her laugh, feeling more naturally connected to someone new than I have in years.

But I don't know the rules here. With men, the expectations are clear. With Diane, everything feels uncharted. Who makes the first move? How do I know if she wants to be kissed? What if I misread the signals completely?

She takes a small step closer, and I catch a hint of her perfume. It makes me want to lean in and inhale deeply. Our eyes meet and hold.

"Thank you," she says softly, "for tonight. For being yourself. For making me feel like I could be myself too."

"Thank you for coming all the way here," I reply. "I would really love to see you again, but I know it's not easy for you and—"

"I'll make it happen." She interrupts me and steps closer, close enough that I can see the flecks of gold in her dark eyes. Then she takes my hand and the effect is immediate and overwhelming. Heat shoots up my arm, my breath catching in my throat.

The moment stretches and we stand there connected, her thumb brushing once across my knuckles. I search her face for some sign of what she's thinking, what she wants, but her expression is unreadable.

Just as I'm gathering the courage to lean forward, she drops my hand and steps back. The loss of contact is jarring.

"Call me," she says, her voice slightly hoarse, and then she moves toward the door with quick, decisive steps that suggest she's fleeing before she can change her mind.

I stand frozen in place, watching her disappear, my hand still tingling from her touch. I stare at the closed door for what feels like minutes, replaying every moment of the last few seconds, trying to decode what just happened.

Was that hesitation or rejection? Interest or politeness?

Now I'm second-guessing every smile, every glance. Maybe I imagined the chemistry. Maybe her warmth was good manners, her laughter courtesy. Maybe I've spent the evening projecting my own desperate hope onto someone who was simply being kind.

This feels messy and uncertain and terrifying in a way I didn't think was possible. I look down at the business card still clutched in my other hand, damp from the heat of my palm.

16

DIANE

*T*he Cunningham dining room could have been lifted from the pages of Architectural Digest with its cream silk wallpaper, ancestral portraits, and fresh white roses from their greenhouse in sterling silver vases placed at precise intervals down the length of the table.

I take another bite of my salmon, barely tasting it despite the chef's obvious skill. The conversation flows around me like background noise—something about patent legislation and its impact on research funding. Dad and Commissioner Cunningham are deep in their usual political strategizing, and Mom and Barbara have been exchanging glances since they noticed Thomas and I were genuinely pleased to see each other again.

If only they knew.

Thomas sits across from me, playing his part with admirable commitment. He asks thoughtful questions, compliments me on my looks, and maintains the right amount of eye contact to suggest interest without overplaying his hand. To our parents, we must look like a courtship proceeding exactly as planned.

I'm happy to let them believe I'm developing feelings for Thomas while my mind replays every moment of my date with Zara in excruciating detail. The way her eyes lit up when she laughed. The electricity when our fingers touched. The agonizing moment when I almost kissed her and instead fled because... Well, honestly, I have no idea why I fled. Insecurity, I suppose. Fear of rejection. Because why would someone like Zara Nova be interested in someone like me? Was she just being polite when she said she wanted to meet again?

I've been torturing myself for forty-eight hours, dissecting every second of our goodbye. I should have kissed her, the moment was there. What if she thinks I'm not interested now? What if she's changed her mind about seeing me again?

"Diane?" Mom's voice cuts through my spiral of self-doubt. "Barbara asked you something."

I blink, forcing myself back to the present. "I'm sorry, what was the question?"

Barbara Cunningham smiles indulgently, the expression of a woman accustomed to being the center of attention. "I was wondering if you'd consider co-chairing the Children's Hospital benefit with me next spring."

Great. She's already playing mother-in-law.

"Of course. I would love to," I reply before my mind wanders back to Vegas.

She didn't call yesterday. Or today. Maybe she never will. Maybe—

My purse vibrates against my leg, and my heart immediately leaps into my throat. I freeze mid-chew, fighting the urge to grab my phone immediately. It could be anyone—my assistant, a friend, a spam call...

But what if it's her?

The conversation continues without me, something about venue options. I nod at appropriate intervals while my entire nervous system fixates on my phone beneath the table. The temptation to check is almost unbearable, but pulling out my phone during dinner would be rude, especially here.

Still, I can't resist, and I bend down to find my phone, then angle it enough to see the screen without lifting it above the table's edge. It's a message from Zara.

Hi Diane. I'm sorry it took me so long to text you. I've been staring at my phone for two days trying to figure out what to say. Anyway, I'm just going to be honest: I haven't been able to stop thinking about our date. I really hope I didn't misread anything, because I would love to see you again. Now you have my number. X Zara

The words blur slightly as I read them again, then a third time, my pulse racing. She's been thinking about me. She really wants to see me again.

My hands are actually shaking as the reality sinks in. This isn't politeness or obligation. This is genuine interest.

"Don't you think so, Diane?"

I look up to find Barbara Cunningham watching me expectantly, along with everyone else at the table. Heat rushes to my face as I realize I have absolutely no idea what she's asked me yet again.

"I'm sorry?" I manage.

Barbara's penciled eyebrows lift in surprise. "I was saying that April would be the ideal time for the gala—after the winter doldrums but before everyone disappears for summer holidays. Don't you agree?"

"Yes," I say quickly, nodding with what I hope appears to be thoughtful consideration rather than complete distraction. "April sounds perfect." My phone slips from my trembling fingers and lands on the floor with a thud that sounds enormous in my paranoid state. I fumble to grab it, nearly knocking over my wine glass in the process.

"Oh!" I gasp, reaching out to steady the crystal glass. "I'm so sorry."

The commotion draws concerned glances from around the table. Dad frowns—he hates any disruption. Mom looks mildly embarrassed by my clumsiness and Barbara maintains her hostess smile.

"Are you feeling alright, dear?" Mom asks with the kind of pointed concern that really means 'pull yourself together.'

"I'm fine," I insist, carefully sliding my phone back into my purse with hands that refuse to stop shaking. "Just tired. It's been a long week." I've been using that excuse a lot lately, and it couldn't be farther from the truth. Since Vegas I've felt alive, buzzing.

Thomas shoots me a curious glance. He understands having secrets, having a life that can't be shared with the people in this room.

"Actually, Diane, I was hoping to get your advice on something work-related," he says, coming to my rescue. "Perhaps we could get together sometime? After you've gotten some rest, of course. I hear you; it's been a long week for me too."

"Sure. Anytime," I say, shooting him a grateful smile. "Drop by my office or we could meet up somewhere more casual, if you prefer?"

His commitment to the charade is admirable; if I didn't know better, I might actually believe he was interested.

The strange thing is, I don't feel guilty about the deception. For years, I've been living a lie and that's been exhausting. I deserve a break, to have something that is just for me. Let them think Thomas and I are interested in each other.

Let them focus on his charming smiles and my distracted responses, reading romance while we're hiding in plain sight.

As long as they're satisfied with the illusion of my interest in their chosen candidate, they won't look too closely at what else I might be up to. They won't question my travel schedule or wonder why I'm suddenly so distracted.

Mom practically glows with satisfaction, her wine glass suspended halfway to her lips as she processes our exchange. "Oh, how wonderful!" she exclaims, her voice pitched high. "You know, there's that lovely little coffee shop on M Street—very intimate." She turns to Barbara, who nods sagely.

"I'm sure we can manage to find a place to meet, Mom," I say dryly.

"Of course, dear," she replies. "You two work out all the details yourselves. I wouldn't dream of interfering!"

I catch Thomas's eyes again and see him fighting back laughter. I wonder if he'd be up for a trip to Vegas with me.

17

ZARA

*M*y fingers drift across the keys in no particular pattern, finding notes that feel right without conscious direction. There's a melody lurking somewhere in the back of my mind but every time I try to pin it down, it slips away like smoke.

I press middle C, let it ring, then add the fifth above it. The sound fills the living room of my suite, reverberating off the high ceilings and marble surfaces. Outside, Las Vegas glitters against the desert darkness, a constellation of artificial stars that never dims. The view from up here makes the city look ethereal, like a mirage that might vanish if I blink too hard. Neon signs pulse in rhythm with the traffic below, creating patterns of light that shift and flow like music made visible.

Apart from an interview for a lifestyle magazine, my schedule has been blissfully clear today, a rare gift that I'd planned to use for writing. I need new material, and I've been putting it off, distracted by rehearsals and settling in and—if I'm being honest—thoughts of a certain foundation director who hasn't texted me back yet.

It's been three hours since I sent that message. Three hours of checking my phone every few minutes, constructing scenarios for why she might not have replied.

I play a minor seventh chord, something melancholy that matches my uncertainty. The notes hang in the air like a question waiting for an answer. There's definitely a song here somewhere—something about waiting, about hope and uncertainty, about the way desire can make you feel simultaneously alive and afraid.

My right hand picks out a simple melody while my left maintains the chord progression. It's tentative, exploratory, like I'm having a conversation with the piano about what this song wants to become. "Maybe it starts here," I murmur to myself, playing it again with slight variations.

I hum along with the melody, letting my voice find its own path through the notes. A ghost of a lyric wants to emerge. Something about masks and truths, about the space between who we are and who we're allowed to be. But every time I reach for the words, my phone catches my eye from its spot on the piano bench beside me, and my concentration fractures.

This is ridiculous. I'm a professional songwriter. I've written dozens of hits, crafted melodies that have moved millions of people. I should be able to focus for more than five minutes without checking my phone like some obsessed fangirl.

I shift to a major key, trying to shake off the melancholy. The melody transforms, becoming lighter, more hopeful. This could work for the bridge, maybe—a moment of optimism. "Something about taking chances," I sing softly. "Something about... fuck, I don't know."

The words aren't coming. Usually, when I'm truly inspired, lyrics flow. I'll sit at this piano for hours, lost in the process of creation, until suddenly I have a complete song that feels like it was always supposed to exist.

"Come on," I mutter to myself. "Write something. Anything."

My phone buzzes against the piano bench and I nearly jump out of my skin, my hands hitting a discordant cluster of keys that rings through the room like an alarm. My heart hammers as I grab the phone, and when I see Diane's name on the screen, I smile so widely it actually hurts my cheeks. Thank God no one can see me right now—I must look like an absolute fool.

So nice to hear from you. I was at a dinner and couldn't reply earlier, but your message definitely made me smile. I was worried I might have messed things up the other night.

I read it three times, parsing every word for subtext. She was at dinner—that explains the delay. And my message made her smile, which has to be good, right? But then that last part catches my attention and I don't get it.

Why would you think you messed anything up? I hit send.

Her response comes quickly this time: *Because I didn't kiss you.*

I stare at the screen, my heart stopping completely before resuming at double speed. She's thinking about the same moment I've been replaying obsessively.

My hands are shaking as I type back: *So you wanted to?*

The phone buzzes again. *Did you want me to?*

I laugh out loud. *Yes. I really, really wanted you to kiss me.*

She responds: *I'm glad to hear that. I spent the entire ride back to my hotel kicking myself for not being braver.*

Heat spreads through me like I've swallowed sunshine. She wanted to kiss me.

This must be what everyone else gets to experience— this giddy, breathless anticipation over someone they're genuinely attracted to. I've never felt a flutter of excitement about seeing someone again, never had my pulse quicken over a text message from someone. Not to this extent.

I've almost forgotten what real desire feels like. The kind that starts in your chest and spreads outward, making your skin hypersensitive and your thoughts scatter. The kind that makes you want to press closer to someone because you can't help yourself.

This is what I've been missing all these years while playing at romance for the public. This is what I gave up when I decided my career was more important than my authentic self.

I slide off the piano bench and lie flat on my back on the Persian rug, staring up at the coffered ceiling. The phone rests on my chest, rising and falling with each breath as I process this information. She wanted to kiss me.

I hold my phone above my face and type: *Next time, let's both be braver.*

She replies: *That's a promise. So when is good for you?*

I grin at the ceiling, feeling giddy and light-headed. I'm so unfamiliar with this roller coaster of emotions over simple text exchanges, this complete inability to focus on anything else.

Anytime next week would be great, I type back. *After that, I'll be in rehearsals. I know you're busy too, so I can work around your schedule.*

Zara Nova is offering to work around my schedule? That's not something I ever expected to hear.

I laugh again, shaking my head at her teasing. Usually I'm the one juggling impossible timelines and making demands but this feels more important than any obligation.

Don't worry, I can make time next week, she adds. *And I'll make sure I won't have to rush home this time.*

I blink at the screen. What is she insinuating? A flash of heat shoots between my thighs and suddenly I'm very aware of my heartbeat and the way I'm lying on the floor of my suite grinning at my phone like a complete disaster of a human being.

Perfect, I type back, because my brain has apparently short-circuited and that's the only word I can manage.

The melody that was eluding me earlier starts to take shape now, floating through my mind with new clarity.

18

DIANE

A Friday crowd fills The Rundown with laughter and the click of pool balls. I spot Thomas, and Jamie is sitting next to him, her arm draped casually over the back of his chair.

"Diane!" Thomas stands as I approach, pulling me into a quick hug. "Good to see you again."

"Good to see you too," I say, then turn to Jamie and greet her. "And you, of course. Are you off tonight?"

"Yeah." Jamie grins, raising her beer bottle. "I have to keep an eye on him now that your parents think you two are crushing on each other. You might actually start falling for his charms, and I'm here as insurance against that disaster." She shoots Thomas an exaggerated suspicious look. "Can't have him running off with a senator's daughter, can I?"

I laugh, immediately warming to her dry sense of humor. "Your boyfriend is safe, I promise." I slide into the chair across from them, accepting the beer Thomas has already ordered for me. "How have you both been?"

"Can't complain," Thomas says. "Work's been crazy, but

at least I've had good company." He squeezes Jamie's shoulder.

"And I've had a break from drunk guys who think tipping me means I owe them my number," Jamie adds with an eye roll.

"The glamorous life of a bartender," Thomas says with mock sympathy. "We rarely see each other during daylight hours but Jamie has a week off to study, so we've been stealing moments and that's been a real treat."

"That sounds difficult," I say. "How do you make it work with such different schedules?"

"We're actually trying something new," Thomas says, glancing at Jamie. "She's moving in with me next month."

My eyebrows shoot up. "Really? So you're going to tell your parents?"

Thomas shakes his head. "No, they never come to my place. My mother thinks my apartment lacks proper entertaining space so they prefer to summon me to their house when they want to see me."

"Which works for us," Jamie adds. "I can exist in his space without ever crossing paths with the extended Cunningham family."

"It's really the only way we'll get to see each other more," Thomas continues. "Between her classes and work, and my ridiculous hours, we're like ships passing in the night. At least we'll wake up in the same bed."

"That's really sweet," I say, touched by their determination to make it work despite the obstacles. "Speaking of which, I actually had a favor to ask you both."

"Because borrowing my boyfriend isn't favor enough?" Jamie says with a hint of amusement.

I chuckle and take a sip of my beer. "It's a fun favor. I was wondering if you'd like to come to Vegas with me. Both of you, for a night. We'll fly out in the morning and back the next night."

Jamie nearly chokes on her drink. "I'm not really into threesomes," she then says with a perfectly straight face.

I laugh so hard I almost spill my beer. "No, God, no. I'm meeting someone there, and I need an excuse to go. If Thomas goes with me, my parents won't ask questions about why I'm always so interested in going to Vegas." I shrug. "I've been twice this month already and three times might be a stretch. I don't want them to think I have a gambling problem."

Thomas leans forward, his expression shifting to curiosity. "Does this by any chance have to do with whoever messaged you the other night during dinner? You seemed a little... flustered."

I grin goofily. "Correct."

"So who's the lucky guy?" he asks.

"I can't tell you that."

Jamie tilts her head, studying me. "Why not?"

I hesitate, choosing my words carefully. "My date is very private. Like, extremely private."

Jamie lets out a low whistle. "Who can be more private than you? You're literally sneaking around, borrowing my boyfriend just so you can go on a date. That sounds like a seriously complicated combination—the two of you."

If only she knew how complicated. I take another gulp of beer, using the moment to gather my thoughts. "I really can't tell you, but it would be my treat. You two can do whatever you want—spa, shows, casino, room service. We'll fly there and back together and stay in the same hotel. That's all I ask for."

Jamie's eyes light up with interest as she turns to Thomas. "A night in Vegas? On someone else's dime?" She grins. "I'm thinking those jacuzzi tubs you're always seeing in the movies. Maybe some actual room service instead of leftover pizza. A casino where I can lose twenty dollars and feel fancy about it."

Thomas laughs, wrapping his arm around her shoulders. "You had me at jacuzzi tub." He looks back at me. "When were you thinking?"

"The Cartwright Hotel where I'm staying has jacuzzis," I say, hoping that will seal the deal. "It's not on the Strip but it's close. Are you free this Friday? I know it's short notice, but—"

"I can make it work." Thomas grins and turns to his girl-friend. "Jamie?"

"I'm so in," she says without hesitation, then gives me a curious look. "Though I have to admit, I'm dying to know who this mystery person is. Someone important enough to make Diane Washington orchestrate a cover story. Are you two serious?"

"No, it's only our second date," I say. "We haven't even kissed yet."

Jamie frowns, setting down her beer. "You haven't kissed? That's... unusual." She tilts her head, studying me with the analytical gaze of someone who's witnessed countless first encounters from behind a bar. "I mean, either you kiss on the first date or you don't, right? And if you didn't, that usually means there's no chemistry there. So why go back for round two?"

I blush thinking of Zara. It's all still so bizarre. "There's definitely chemistry," I say. "I just... chickened out. We both did, I think."

"Ah," Jamie says. "But you don't strike me as the shy type. Interesting." She exchanges a glance with Thomas. "And why can't he come here? Wouldn't that make it much easier than flying to Vegas for a hook-up?"

"That's not an option," I say to Jamie. "If I could tell you more, I would. But I really can't."

"Fair enough," she concedes. "As long as there's a jacuzzi and room service involved, I'll stop with the questions."

Thomas raises his beer bottle. "I guess that's settled then. To Vegas and mysterious dates."

"And to secrets," Jamie adds with a wink.

"And to new friends who don't ask questions," I finish, clinking my bottle against theirs.

19

ZARA

"God, you look exhausted," I say, studying Jess's face through my phone screen. Dark circles ring her eyes, and her blonde hair is pulled back in a messy bun that suggests it hasn't been brushed in days.

"Thanks for the confidence boost," she says with a tired laugh, adjusting her position on her living room couch. "Sorry I haven't called you back sooner. Lucas has been sick and I haven't slept more than two hours at a stretch in four days."

My stomach immediately clenches with worry. "Oh no, what's wrong with him? Is he okay?"

"Just a really bad ear infection," Jess explains, rubbing her temples. "You know how it is with babies—they can't tell you what hurts, so they scream. And scream. And scream some more." She sighs heavily. "The pediatrician finally got him on antibiotics yesterday, so he's getting better. He's actually sleeping right now, which is why I'm calling you back."

"Poor little guy," I say, my heart aching for both of them. "And poor you. Are you getting any help?"

"My mom's still here, thank God. She's been a lifesaver, even if she does keep rearranging my kitchen and suggesting I move back to New York every five minutes." Jess shifts again, wincing slightly. "But enough about my sleep deprivation. Tell me about your date. I've been dying to know how it went."

I feel my face warming, and I can't suppress the smile that spreads. "It was... really good."

"Really good?" Jess's eyebrows shoot up. "That's it? Come on, Z. Details."

I laugh, settling back against the pillows on my bed. "Well, we talked for five hours. Five hours, Jess. I didn't even notice the time passing."

Jess whistles. "Okay, that's definitely a good sign. What did you talk about?"

"Everything. Her work, my music, our families, coffee preferences, whether pineapple belongs on pizza—"

"Please tell me she's team anti-pineapple," Jess interrupts with mock seriousness.

"She is, thankfully. Our relationship can continue." I grin, then catch myself. "Not that we have a relationship. I mean, it's—"

"Z," Jess says, her tired eyes suddenly more alert, "you're grinning like you have the world's biggest crush right now. It's so cute."

"I don't have a crush," I protest, though I can feel my cheeks burning. "I barely know her. But I do really want to see her again. We're going on a second date."

"That's great! Did you kiss?" Jess leans closer to her phone screen. "Is she a good kisser?"

"No, we didn't. But we've messaged since and both admitted we wanted to."

Jess places a hand over her heart with an exaggerated expression. "Oh my God, that's even cuter. You're like a couple of loved-up fourteen-year-olds passing notes in study hall."

"Fuck off." I roll my eyes and laugh.

"And when is this second date with the prospect of a kiss happening?"

"This Friday. She's flying back out to Vegas." Butterflies flutter in my stomach at the thought. We've been texting since that night, and each message makes me more eager to see her again.

"She's flying back out? From where?"

"Washington D.C." I hesitate, knowing how this is going to sound. "She works for a political foundation there."

Jess frowns. "What kind of political foundation?"

"A conservative one." I bite my lip. "Please keep this to yourself; I know I can trust you. Her father is actually senator of Virginia."

The silence stretches long enough that I wonder if our connection has frozen. Then Jess blinks slowly. "You're dating a conservative?"

"She's not—I mean, it's complicated," I stammer. "Just because her family is conservative doesn't mean she is."

"Zara," Jess says carefully, "they're against marriage equality."

My stomach drops. I knew Diane's family was political, but I hadn't really processed the implications. "That doesn't mean Diane agrees with him," I say weakly.

"Maybe not, but honey, you realize what this looks like, right? Zara Nova, gay rights advocate, secretly dating the daughter of one of the most anti-LGBTQ senators in Washington?" Jess runs a hand through her messy hair. "I'm not trying to be a buzzkill, but this could be a disaster if it ever got out."

"Well, it's not going to get out. We'll be careful." Jess has a point. How did I not think this through? I was so caught up in the excitement of connecting with someone that I completely ignored the not-so-minor details. "And anyway, all we both want is something casual, nothing more."

Jess sighs. "Look, I'm not saying don't see her again. I'm happy you've met someone you click with, and I can see how excited you are. I'm just saying be careful. Really careful."

I nod, even though part of me wants to rebel against the caution. When I'm texting with Diane, when I remember the way she looked at me across that candlelit table, politics feels irrelevant. But Jess is right—in the real world, everything counts when you're in the public eye.

"What's she like, though?" Jess asks, her voice softening. "Forget about her family for a minute. What's she actually like?"

"Smart," I say. "Really smart. And funny in this dry, unexpected way. She's got beautiful dark eyes and she's kind. You can tell she genuinely cares about the work her foundation does, even if she's frustrated by some of the constraints."

"Constraints?"

"Considering she's gay, she's not exactly free to be herself," I say. "Her family doesn't know, and she's playing a role most of the time, just like I am. Maybe that's part of why we connected."

Jess studies my face through the screen. "You really like her."

"I do," I admit quietly. "Is that crazy? After one date?"

"Honey, you've been performing relationships for years.

Of course you're going to feel overwhelmed when you meet someone you actually have chemistry with." She shifts, and I hear a soft whimper in the background that makes her tense. "Oh, please don't wake up yet," she whispers toward the other room.

"Go check on him," I say immediately. "We can talk more later."

"No, no, I think he's still sleeping. Fussing a little in his dreams." She turns back to the camera. "Look, Z, I'm happy you're exploring this side of yourself. I really am. Just... be smart about it, okay? Don't let your heart overrule your head completely."

"When do I ever do that?" I ask with mock indignation.

Jess gives me a look. "Do you want the chronological list or the alphabetical one?"

"Point taken," I laugh. "I'll be careful. I promise."

"Good. And maybe do a little research on dear old dad before you get in too deep. Know what you're potentially getting into."

A wail erupts from the other room and Jess sighs in exhausted resignation.

"And there he goes." She stands. "I've got to run, Z. But seriously—be careful, okay?"

"I will. Give Lucas a kiss from me."

The screen goes dark, leaving me alone with my thoughts and the distant hum of Vegas traffic. I set my phone aside and stare out at the city, Jess's warnings echoing in my mind.

It's going to be fine, I tell myself. This isn't some grand romance that's going to spiral out of control. We've both been clear about what we want—something casual, something private. A few stolen weekends, some texts, maybe a handful of dates before we both move on with our lives. No one will ever find out because there won't be anything serious enough to find out about.

I can compartmentalize this. I've managed my public image so far and this is just another boundary to maintain, a little secret to keep.

20

DIANE

I spot them in the business class lounge—Thomas in his usual casual chic attire, and Jamie all dolled up, looking slightly overwhelmed as she examines the complimentary wine selection at the bar behind their table. She's already holding a plate with snacks in one hand.

"This is all free?" she asks the attendant, gesturing at the spread of food and drinks. "Like, all of it?"

"Yes, ma'am," the woman replies patiently. "Please help yourself to anything you'd like."

Jamie turns to Thomas with wide eyes. "The drinks are free too, Thomas. Why didn't I know this?"

I smile as I approach their table. Jamie's wearing a pretty black dress and cowboy boots and her hair is styled in loose waves. She looks gorgeous and incredibly excited.

"Hey, there," I say, settling into the chair across from Thomas. "How are you both?"

"I'm fucking great. This is insane," Jamie says, setting down her plate loaded with what appears to be every appetizer available and a glass of chilled white wine. "I feel like I'm crashing someone else's life."

"I'm glad you're happy with the arrangement," I say with a smile. "And just so you know, I booked you guys into the honeymoon suite at the Cartwright."

Jamie nearly chokes on her wine as she takes a sip. "The honeymoon suite? Are you serious?"

"Totally serious. Complete with butler service."

"Oh my God," Jamie turns to Thomas with sparkling eyes. "Did you hear that? We're getting the full romantic treatment." She grins at me. "You're officially my new favorite person. Thank you!"

"Don't mention it. You have no idea what a favor you're doing me."

"I should probably go call my sister and brag about this before we take off," Jamie says, standing up and taking her wine glass. "Don't say anything interesting while I'm gone."

Thomas shoots her an endearing smile. When Jamie excuses herself, he leans forward.

"I know what this looks like. You probably think I never treat her," he says. "But the truth is, she's incredibly stubborn about not wanting my help financially. She insists on paying her own way for everything, even when it means we can't do things together because she can't afford them." He glances toward her, his expression fond. "The fact that you offered this trip was brilliant. She's perfectly happy to let you spoil us, just not me."

I nod, understanding the dynamic. Jamie's independence is admirable. "I'll sure she'll have the best time. Did your parents ask any questions about the trip?"

Thomas laughs. "None whatsoever. They were too busy planning their own weekend getaway to some spa resort. I don't think they even asked where we were going." He pauses. "Yours?"

"Same here," I say. "They were thrilled I was taking initiative with our 'courtship.'" I make air quotes, rolling my eyes.

I check my watch, then immediately check it again as if the time might have changed. I want to take off, make it to Vegas.

My phone buzzes with a text, and my heart leaps. It's become automatic at this point—any notification could be Zara. It's not though, just my assistant with a generic question. I answer her and sigh as I slip my phone into my purse.

"Are you okay?" Thomas asks. "You seem a little..."

"A little what?"

"Nervous. Fidgety."

He's right—I've been unconsciously shredding my napkin into small pieces, and my leg won't stop bouncing.

I take a deep breath. "I'm fine, but yes, definitely nervous. This is only our second date, and I..." I pause, unsure how to explain the magnitude of what I'm feeling without revealing too much. "I really like this person. More than I expected to."

"Where are you meeting him?" Thomas asks.

I hesitate. Zara and I have discussed the logistics extensively over text. Meeting in public was out of the question for obvious reasons, and a restaurant, even a private one, felt too exposed. Her suite seemed like the natural choice— completely private, secure, and comfortable. But explaining that to Thomas makes it sound more intimate than I'm ready to admit it might be.

"His place, actually," I finally say.

Thomas raises an eyebrow. "His place? Are you sure you'll be safe if you've only met him once before?"

"Yeah. Don't worry. I—"

Jamie returns, practically glowing with excitement. "They have a whole section of magazines I've never heard of, and the soaps and lotions in the bathroom smell amazing." She settles back into her chair, then notices Thomas's expression. "What did I miss?"

"Nothing," I say quickly, shooting Thomas a warning look. "Discussing the flight."

"Oh, don't even get me started on the flight," Jamie says, her eyes lighting up. "I've never flown business before. I've barely flown at all, actually."

I watch her enthusiasm and feel a pang of guilt. The cost of these business class tickets—three round-trip seats to Vegas—is probably more than Jamie makes in two months bartending. For me, it's nothing. The ease with which I can throw money at problems and jet across the country on a whim is a privilege I've never had to think about because I've never been without it.

My parents have always given me everything I needed and most of what I wanted. Private schools, college tuition, a car at sixteen, a trust fund. I've never applied for a position I wasn't guaranteed to get, never worried about rent or student loans or whether I could afford to take a sick day.

I often wonder what my life would look like without their support. If I'd been brave enough to come out as a teenager, would I still have access to any of this? Would they have cut me off entirely, or just made my life difficult enough that I'd learn to stay quiet? The questions have been nagging at me more lately, especially as I watch Jamie's excitement over things I take for granted. Part of me envies her independence, even if it means struggle. At least her life is authentically hers.

My phone buzzes with a text, and this time it's from Zara.

Can't wait to see you later. Safe travels.

Just reading her words makes my pulse quicken.

Tonight, I'll be in her suite, alone with her, with no time constraints or interruptions. I have to consciously remind myself to breathe normally. It's like anticipating the drop on a roller coaster—that suspended moment before gravity takes over.

"We're twenty minutes delayed," Thomas announces, checking the screen.

"Yay!" Jamie claps her hands together like a child on Christmas morning. "More time for smoked salmon and Chablis!"

I catch Thomas watching me curiously as I type a reply.

"Stop," I murmur.

"Stop what?"

"That inquisitive look. There's literally nothing I can tell you beyond what I already have."

21

ZARA

"Come in," I say, opening the door and stepping back to give Diane space. My voice sounds steadier than I feel, which is a minor miracle considering my heart is hammering against my ribs like it's trying to escape.

Diane stays in the doorway for a beat, and I drink in the sight of her. She's wearing a cream-colored linen suit and her hair is tied back. Fuck. She looks gorgeous.

I'm wearing my favorite little black dress. It's flattering and comes off easily.

"Hi," she says softly, handing me a bouquet of pink peonies. "These are for you."

"Thank you. They're beautiful." I smile as I take the flowers, shuffling on the spot. How are we supposed to greet each other? I should have asked Athena about this. If I were dating a man he would have no doubt kissed me after our first date, and I would have waited for him to take charge again. The old rules were clear to me, this is not. But I'm so, so happy Diane's not a man.

She gives me butterflies as we stand there for a beat, both of us caught in uncertainty. I see her eyes flick to my lips, then back to my eyes, and I wonder if she can hear my pulse because it's so loud in my own ears that it's drowning out rational thought.

Then something shifts in her expression—a decision being made in real time. The hesitation falls away from her face and she steps forward into my space and leans in close.

"We said we'd be braver this time," she murmurs, her voice low.

Before I can respond, before I can overthink or second-guess or retreat into my own head, her hands are on me. One slides around the back of my neck, fingers threading through my hair, while the other comes up to cup my chin while she gently nudges me back against the wall. And then she moves even closer, eliminating the last inches of space between us as she pushes herself against me.

Her lips meet mine, and all I can feel is that single point of contact. The kiss is soft and lingering, as if she's giving me the chance to pull away. But pulling away is the last thing on my mind and instead, I melt into her, my hands finding her waist and pulling her even closer.

She responds immediately, deepening the kiss with a confidence that makes my knees weak. Her lips are soft as they move against mine, sensually, longingly. It's been so long, I forgot what it was like to kiss a woman.

Diane grinds against me, her body a line of heat from my chest to my thighs. The hand in my hair tightens slightly, angling my head, and I let out a soft sound that gets lost somewhere between us. Every fantasy I've had, every dream that's visited me in the early hours, pales in comparison to this reality.

The flowers fall onto the floor as my hands start to wander, weaving through her hair, sliding down her back. She tastes warm and faintly sweet, and my body responds with an intensity that surprises me, arousal pooling low in my stomach as her tongue traces my bottom lip.

She inches back and I'm left gasping, my chest rising and falling rapidly as I stare at her in complete bewilderment. Her lips are shimmering, her hair is mussed from my fingers, and there's something wild in her dark eyes. I don't know what to do with my hands, with my body, with the sudden absence of her mouth on mine.

The flowers are still on the floor between us. I bend to pick them up, needing a second to catch my breath. "I should—" I start. "I'll put these in water."

She follows me to the kitchen and my fingers fumble with the flowers as I reach for a vase. But before I can turn on the tap, before I can even process what's happening, we're drawn together again—gravity or instinct or pure need pulling us back into each other's orbit. I think I'm the one who moves first, or maybe it's her, or maybe it's both of us in the same desperate moment, but her hands are in my hair again and I'm pressing her back against the kitchen counter, the flowers forgotten in the sink as we lose ourselves once more.

This time there's no hesitation, no careful exploration. The kiss is hungrier, more urgent. My hands slide under her blazer, fingertips finding the hem of her top, and when she arches into my touch, a soft sound escapes her throat that makes something inside me unravel. She shivers when I trace the line of her collarbone and gasps when my lips find a sensitive spot on her neck.

Her hands are everywhere, sliding down my sides, pulling at the hem of my dress, and never have I wanted anything more. Not just this kiss, not just this moment, but everything. I want to learn what makes her come undone, want to see her spread across my sheets, want to discover every sound she makes when she loses control.

Her hands still against my waist, and she pulls back, breathing hard. "Maybe we should wait," she says, though her voice wavers with effort.

"I don't want to wait," I whisper. My body is humming with want, crying out for her. "Unless you..."

"No." She shakes her head and smiles, then brushes her lips against mine. "I want you, Zara." She claims my mouth and slips a hand under my dress and between my thighs, cupping my sex while she grinds her hips into me.

I close my eyes and gasp, my head falling back. It's like she's found a switch and my body is suddenly turned up to maximum frequency. The sensation is overwhelming—her fingers pressed against the damp fabric of my panties, the heat of her body, the way she's looking at me like she wants so much more.

My hips buck involuntarily against her hand, seeking more pressure, and a needy whimper escapes me. I'm instantly, embarrassingly wet and if she doesn't stop, I think I might combust right here in my kitchen.

When I open my eyes again she's watching me, biting her lip, her eyes hazy. She knows the effect she has on me and she's enjoying every second. Gone is the hesitant woman who didn't have the courage to kiss me last week. In her place is someone who knows exactly what she wants and isn't afraid to take it.

"Bedroom?" she whispers against my ear while she pulls her hand away. "I don't want to rush this."

I nod, resisting the urge to chase her touch. I'm finally brave enough to claim what I've been circling.

22

DIANE

*T*he bedroom is dimly lit, the bed has been turned down, and the curtains are drawn. There are fresh roses on the nightstands and music plays softly from hidden speakers.

Zara watches me while I take it all in, and when I turn back to meet her gaze, she looks a little embarrassed.

"I may have called housekeeping and asked them to, you know, set the mood a little. Just in case." She shoots me a goofy grin. "Now I wish I hadn't. It looks presumptuous."

I pull her flush against me. "You can be presumptuous with me. I'm flattered."

She licks her lips, keeping her eyes locked on mine and we're drawn back together again in an all-consuming kiss. Now that I've started kissing her, I can't seem to stop and I don't want to. It's the first real thing I've felt in years. A physical pull that makes everything else in my life seem irrelevant.

Zara pushes my blazer off my shoulders and tugs at the hem of my T-shirt. I help her, desperate to feel her skin against mine. Her gaze wanders over my breasts and she traces a finger over the black lace edge of my bra.

"You're..." She swallows hard. "You're beautiful."

"So are you," I whisper, then kiss her again, deeper, my tongue tracing the seam of her lips until she opens for me with a soft sigh. There's a quality to her touch that speaks of discovery—fingertips that linger at the hollow of my throat, palms that smooth down my arms, learning another woman's body for the first time.

She unbuttons my trousers and the fabric slides down my legs. I step out of them, giving her time to absorb the sight of me in my bra and panties. Her eyes move over me, taking in each curve and line with genuine wonder. Her hands hover near my waist with the kind of exploration that suggests she's cataloguing differences—the softness, the way a woman's body yields and curves in places a man's would not.

"Your dress," I murmur against her lips. "I want to see you."

Zara smiles, reaching for the zipper at the back of her neck. I turn her, brushing her curls aside, and slowly work the zipper down. The black fabric parts to reveal her back, and I press my lips to the nape of her neck. She shivers at the contact.

The dress falls away and she turns back to face me. She's wearing matching creme lace and she's stunning—all curves and soft mahogany skin.

"You're perfect," I whisper, watching color bloom across her cheeks.

"I've..." She hesitates. "I've never done this before."

"I know. We don't have to do anything if you're uncomfortable..."

Zara shakes her head. "I want to." She unclips her bra and drops it to the floor.

I swallow hard and step close, running my hands over her shoulders, her breasts, her waist... She gasps and arches against me when I take a nipple in my mouth, her hands fisting in my hair.

"Fuck, Diane." She whimpers when my hand skims up her thigh and curls around to her behind. I squeeze her and pull her flush against me, trailing my mouth back up to her neck.

"Are you okay?" I whisper.

She nods, eyes hazy as I guide her backward toward the bed. Her legs hit the edge, and I ease her down, following her body with mine.

"Tell me what you like," I say with a teasing smile, hovering above her.

Zara hesitates. "I... I don't know," she admits.

"Then let's find out." I kiss my way down her body, taking my time, savoring each new sound she makes. Her breathing quickens when I reach her stomach, and I hook my fingers into the waistband of her lace underwear, looking up for permission.

"Yes," she breathes, lifting her hips so I can slide them down her legs.

I move back up to kiss her, sliding my hand up the inside of her thigh. When I finally touch her she cries out against my mouth, her nails digging into the skin of my back.

She's so warm, so wet, and the knowledge that I've done this to her, that she wants me this much, makes my own desire spike to almost unbearable levels. I explore her slowly, sliding my fingers through her wetness, circling her clit, learning what makes her gasp, what makes her buck against my hand.

When I slip one finger inside her, she groans in pleasure, tightening her grip on me.

"Oh my god," she breathes. "Yes..."

I add a second finger, moving slowly, watching her face for every reaction. I'm transfixed by the way her lips part, how her eyes flutter closed, the tension building in her body. I kiss her, grinding my hips into her while I fuck her, slowly and deeply, cherishing her moans that escape with each exhale as she surrenders to pleasure without reservation.

Her hands are everywhere—in my hair, clutching my shoulders, trailing down my back. I watch her face as pleasure builds, memorizing every expression, every gasp.

"I want to taste you," I whisper against her ear, and she moans louder, shivering at my breath tickling her ear.

I kiss my way down her body again, pausing to lavish attention on her breasts before continuing lower. When I settle between her thighs, I look up at her once more. Her chest rises and falls rapidly, her curls splayed across the pillow.

The first stroke of my tongue makes her cry out and tremble. I hold her steady, savoring her taste, her scent.

Her fingers grip the bedsheets, knuckles turning white as I explore her with my tongue. I find a rhythm that makes her thighs quiver, alternating between broad strokes and focused attention on her clit. Each sound she makes guides me, teaching me what her body craves.

"Diane," she gasps, one hand finding my hair. "Oh god, I—"

I look up without stopping, wanting to see her face as she climbs higher. Her eyes are squeezed shut, head thrown back, throat exposed. I slide my fingers back inside her as I continue to taste her, curling them forward to find that spot that makes her whole body jerk.

"Yes," she cries. "Fuck, yes!"

And then she falls. I hold her steady, gentling my touch as she rides out her orgasm, her thighs quivering against my cheeks. When she collapses back onto the mattress, I press kisses to her inner thigh before crawling up to lie beside her.

"Holy shit," she breathes, eyes still closed, chest heaving, hand covering her forehead. "That was..."

I grin, feeling a little smug as I trace circles on her stomach. "Okay?"

She laughs, a breathless, disbelieving sound. "Let's just say I'm currently having an internal debate about whether I wasted my twenties." She turns to face me, her expression softening as she studies my face. "Better late than never, I suppose. Will you stay the night?"

23

ZARA

I wake to unfamiliar sensations—the weight of an arm draped across my waist, the warmth of another person's breath against my shoulder, the scent of skin that isn't mine. I'm caught between sleep and consciousness, until the memories flood back in vivid detail.

Diane.

My eyes flutter open to find her face inches from mine, dark hair spilled across the white pillowcase, features soft with sleep.

I don't move and quietly absorb the reality of what happened—what I did, what we shared. The evidence is everywhere: in the tender soreness between my thighs, in the faint marks her mouth left on my breast, in the way my body still buzzes with the memory of her touch. We made love for hours, and I loved every moment of touching and tasting her in return.

This is what I've been missing. Not just the physical act —though that was beyond anything I'd imagined—but this. The intimacy of shared breath and tangled limbs. The profound quiet of waking beside someone who's seen you completely and stayed.

With previous lovers, mornings always felt performative. I'd wake wondering if my hair looked acceptable, if I should reach for lip gloss before they opened their eyes, if I was playing the role of satisfied lover convincingly enough. But lying here with Diane, I feel no urge to perform. She's seen me gasping and desperate, heard me whimper her name, watched me fall apart in her arms. There's nothing left to hide behind.

The vulnerability should terrify me. This woman could destroy me with a single photograph, a careless word to the wrong person. One leaked detail about last night would detonate my public image. Zara Nova, America's sweetheart, secretly gay and sleeping with a conservative senator's daughter? The headlines would write themselves.

But instead of fear, I feel something wonderful—peace. The constant noise in my head, the endless worries about image and appearance, has gone quiet. I'm exactly where I want to be, doing exactly what I want to do.

I study Diane's sleeping face, tracing the arch of her eyebrows with my gaze, the curve of her lips. She's beautiful in a way that becomes more compelling the longer I look— not the manufactured perfection of my industry, but something real and lived-in. There's a small scar near her hairline, barely visible, and freckles across the bridge of her nose that makeup usually conceals.

My fingers itch to touch her but I resist. This moment feels precious, stolen from the demands that will inevitably intrude. Soon she'll need to catch her flight back to Washington. Soon I'll return to rehearsals and interviews and the relentless machinery of my career.

But right now, I can pretend this is normal. That waking

up next to a woman I'm falling for is just another morning instead of the most significant shift in my understanding of myself.

Because I am falling for her. The thought sits in my chest like a small flame, warm and dangerous. I'm already imagining the next time I'll see her, planning how to carve out space in my schedule for stolen time. This was supposed to be casual exploration, a safe way to dip my toes into this side of myself without risking everything. Now I'm lying here wondering when I can see her again.

I've avoided emotional entanglements that could complicate my career, never allowed myself to want someone this much. But with Diane's arm around me, breathing in her heat, I can't bring myself to care about the complications.

She stirs, her arm tightening around my waist, and my pulse quickens. I wonder what she'll be like when she wakes up fully—whether she'll be shy or confident, whether she'll want to talk about what happened or pretend it's not a big deal.

The memory of her mouth between my thighs sends heat pooling low in my belly. I've never felt anything like the intensity of last night, the complete surrender to sensation and need.

I shift slightly, trying to ease the sweet ache between my thighs, and the movement causes Diane to murmur something unintelligible in her sleep. Her hand flexes against my hip, fingers pressing briefly into my skin before relaxing again.

It's so easy to imagine a different life—one where I could claim her openly, where we could build something real. But that's fantasy, not reality. We both have too much to lose and even if we wanted more than casual encounters—and I'm not sure she does—the obstacles are insurmountable. We're both trapped by expectations that leave little room for authentic desire. Maybe that's part of what draws us together.

Diane's eyes open slowly, blinking before focusing on me. For a moment, we simply look at each other, and I search her expression for any sign of regret or discomfort.

A slow, private smile spreads across her face. "Good morning," she whispers.

"Good morning," I say. "How did you sleep?"

"Better than I have in months." Her thumb brushes across my hip bone. "You?"

"Same." I pause, gathering courage. "No regrets?"

"None." Her answer is immediate and firm. "You?"

"No." I shake my head, relief flooding through me. "None whatsoever."

"Good." She leans in to press a soft kiss to my lips. "Because I'd really like to do this again."

"I'd like that too," I say, grinning. "I wish you didn't have to leave. Maybe I can cancel–"

"No, I don't want you to cancel your rehearsal for me." Diane glances at the clock on the nightstand, "But we still have two hours before I need to leave for the airport." Her eyes meet mine with unmistakable intent. "We can do a lot in two hours."

Before I can respond, she's rolling on top of me. Her hands capture both of mine, pressing them into the pillow above my head, and suddenly I'm pinned beneath her.

I gasp, my back arching. The sensation of being held down sends shockwaves through me that I didn't expect. My body responds instantly—pulse racing, skin flushing, an intense throbbing between my thighs.

"Oh," Diane says, her voice dropping to a husky register that makes my toes curl. "You like that, do you?"

She presses her mouth to mine, claiming me with a passion that makes last night seem tentative by comparison. This kiss is hungry, demanding, and when she shifts her weight, wedging her thigh between my legs, I nearly come undone from that contact alone.

I grind against her and every nerve ending in my body seems to have relocated to that single point of contact. I moan into her mouth, lost in the overwhelming sensation of our kiss combined with the delicious friction.

"I guess I do," I murmur against her lips.

Her smile is wicked as she releases my hands to trail her fingers down my body. When she reaches my breast, she doesn't hesitate—her mouth follows the path her hands have traced, and then she bites down on my nipple with enough pressure to make me cry out loud and desperate.

Diane lifts her head to look at me, her dark eyes gleaming with satisfaction. "I'm discovering a whole new side of you," she murmurs, her voice heavy with flirtation. "And I like what I'm finding."

She's right. This is a side of myself I never knew existed, desires I never allowed myself to explore, and when she bites me again I lace my fingers through her hair and grab hold tight. I like it when she takes charge.

"Turn around," Diane whispers. "I want to fuck you from behind."

I squirm at her words and obey without hesitation, rolling onto my stomach.

"Get on your hands and knees." Her hands smooth over my back, down to my waist, then lower as I shift position. "You're trembling. Are you okay?"

"Yes." I feel her shift behind me, her weight settling more

fully against my thighs, and I moan when she slides a finger between my legs and over my folds. I'm so wet. "I'm very, very okay."

And then her fingers are inside me, filling me. I grip the headboard, throwing my head back in ecstasy. I'm losing control, my body responding so quickly that I'm already close to the edge. She fucks me hard and fast, her moans suggesting she's really getting off on this too.

I arch my back, my breathing ragged as I press my forehead against the headboard. This is carnal. The kind of raw, animalistic pleasure that has always been so alien to me. Now, I want more. I want it all. I want to explore with her, to discover what makes me come apart at the seams.

Loud sounds are pouring out of me, each thrust of her fingers drawing another moan from my throat, and I don't care how desperate I sound. I want her to know what she's doing to me.

"You feel so good," she breathes behind me. "God, I love watching you like this."

My arms are starting to shake from holding myself up. "Diane," I pant, "I'm going to—"

"Let go," she commands, curling her fingers inside me as her other hand reaches around to circle my clit. "I want to feel you come."

The dual sensation is too much, and I shatter with a cry, my entire body convulsing. I collapse onto the mattress, my body still shaking from the aftershocks. Diane's hands are gentle now, soothing strokes along my back as I struggle to catch my breath. She settles beside me, pulling me against her chest, and I feel utterly boneless in her arms.

24

DIANE

*T*he Mayflower Hotel's ballroom buzzes with three hundred of Virginia's most influential conservatives. I stand beside my father near the silent auction tables, watching him work the room. He runs a hand through his silver hair as he leans in to shake hands with Donald and Ann Marshall.

"Senator Washington," Ann gushes, her diamond tennis bracelet sliding down her wrist as she gestures. "What a wonderful turnout for the Heritage Foundation auction. You must be so proud of the work your foundation is doing with Diane at the helm."

My mind drifts as the familiar pleasantries continue. I should be focusing but all I can think about is Zara.

It's been four days since Vegas, and I haven't been able to concentrate on anything. During yesterday's meeting, I caught myself staring out the window, replaying all the times she came undone in my arms. My assistant has started giving me concerned looks when I fail to respond to direct questions.

"—don't you think, Diane?" Ann's voice cuts through my reverie.

I blink, realizing they're all looking at me expectantly. Heat creeps up my neck as I scramble to piece together what I've missed. Something about traditional values...

"I'm sorry, could you repeat the question?" I ask, forcing a smile.

"I was just saying how important it is that organizations like yours continue to promote traditional family structures," Ann says. "With all this nonsense about redefining marriage, our children need strong role models who understand what real families look like."

My stomach drops. I've navigated this discussion countless times, nodding along while internally screaming. But tonight, with the memory of Zara's touch still burning on my skin, the casual dismissal of people like us feels more insulting than ever.

"The Supreme Court's decision was devastating," Donald adds, his face pinched with disapproval. "Allowing these people to marry undermines the very foundation of our society. What's next? Polygamy? Bestiality?"

Usually, I simply excuse myself or respond with careful neutrality, some version of "the foundation focuses on education rather than social policy." Safe, noncommittal. But tonight, something snaps.

"Actually," I say, "I think it's probably time we adjusted some of our views. They're becoming rather dated, don't you think?"

The silence that follows is deafening. Ann's eyebrows shoot up, and Donald's mouth opens slightly in shock. My father's gaze burns into me, but I press on. "Love is love, regardless of gender. Two people who want to build a life together, raise children, contribute to their communities—how is that threatening?"

Ann's expression shifts to something between pity and horror. "Oh, my dear, I think you've been spending too much time in the wrong company. It's not natural. These ideas go against everything God intended for families."

"This is exactly the kind of thinking that's destroying our country," Donald interjects. "First it's gay marriage, then it's transgender bathrooms, then they're coming after our children's education—"

I feel an intense urge to let rip on him, but before I get the chance, my father grabs hold of my arm.

"If you'll excuse us," he says, "I need to steal my daughter away for a moment. Thank you both for your continued support."

He guides me away from the Marshalls and we stop near a quieter corner of the ballroom, beside a towering floral arrangement that provides some privacy from the surrounding crowd. When he turns to face me, his expression is thunderous.

"What the hell was that?" he hisses. "Have you lost your mind?"

I straighten my spine, meeting his gaze directly. "I was expressing an opinion. Isn't that allowed?"

"Not *that* opinion. Not here. Not ever." He glances around to ensure we aren't being overheard. "Do you have any idea what you did? Donald Marshall sits on the board of three major conservative PACs. They control millions in donations."

"So we're supposed to compromise our principles for money?" I ask, though I immediately realize the irony—I've been compromising my principles my entire life.

"We're supposed to be smart," he snaps. "We're supposed

to understand that politics is about building coalitions, not alienating our base with liberal talking points."

I wonder what would happen if I simply walked away from all of this. If I resigned from the foundation, found work that didn't require me to smile and nod while people dismiss my very existence.

"Don't you think people should be able to marry who they want?" I ask. "Personally, I mean. Forget politics for a moment—what do *you* actually believe?"

Dad clenches his jaw as he considers his response. "Personally? I think the gay marriage stuff is nonsense—not because I care who sleeps with whom, but because it's a distraction from real issues. Do I give a damn if two men or two women want to play house and call it marriage? Not particularly. But it's not about what I want, Diane. It's about what our voters want. It's about maintaining the coalition that keeps us in power so we can work on issues that actually matter."

The comment about "playing house"—cuts deeper than his anger. This is how he sees people like me. As playing pretend, as fundamentally unserious. We don't matter.

"And what if someone in our family was gay?" I ask. "Would you still think it was nonsense then?"

His eyes narrow, studying me. "Is there something you need to tell me, Diane?"

My heart pounds hard and fast. This is it—I could tell him the truth, right here. But the words stick in my throat, held back by decades of conditioning and the very real fear of what would happen next. My foundation. My trust fund. Though maybe it was never really mine to begin with.

"I've always followed what our family stands for," I say finally, the coward's answer. "I've never really taken the time to figure out what *I* stand for. Maybe that's changing."

"You can have any values you want," he says in a patronizing tone, "as long as you don't voice them publicly. Your personal evolution is irrelevant if it threatens what we've built."

He adjusts his tie, his politician's mask sliding back into place as he prepares to return to the crowd. But then he pauses.

"Don't ever do that again," he adds. "People might start questioning whether you're 'that way' yourself. Understood?"

25

ZARA

*T*he Palestra stage feels enormous without an audience, just bare wood stretching toward empty rows of red velvet seats. I've been running through the opening sequence for three hours straight, working with Mo to perfect the choreography that will accompany "Electric Nights"—one of my biggest hits that will open the show. Without the band, without the costume changes, without the lighting design, it's only me, six dancers, and a backing track echoing through the cavernous space.

"From the top," Mo calls out.

I wipe sweat from my forehead and nod, moving back to my starting position center stage. The spotlights are brutal —white-hot beams that turn the stage into a furnace. My black leggings and tank top cling to my skin, and moisture drips down my spine.

The music starts again, and I launch into the routine. Step-touch-turn, arms up on the beat, move downstage during the verse while I sing along to the backing track into a muted microphone. The choreography is more subtle than my usual tour work—designed for a theater rather than a stadium. That doesn't mean it's easier. Every move has to be perfect because the audience will be close enough to see hesitation, to spot when I'm not fully committed.

I spin through the bridge, hitting my mark as the music swells. The song ends and I stand in the final pose, chest heaving. Mo makes notes on his tablet.

"Better," he says.

I nod, reaching for the towel I left on the monitor speaker. The fabric comes away damp as I press it to my face and neck. Three more songs to run through before we call it a day, and my legs are already protesting. I haven't done this level of physical work since my last tour ended.

"Let's take ten," Mo announces, heading toward the wings where his water bottle waits.

That's when I notice her. Athena sits in the back row, barely visible in the darkened auditorium. She begins to clap.

I walk to the edge of the stage, peering out into the darkness. "How long have you been sitting there?"

"About twenty minutes," she calls back. "Hope you don't mind. I was curious."

I laugh, jump down from the stage into the orchestra pit and make my way up the aisle toward her. As I get closer, she unwraps something that smells absolutely incredible— garlic and herbs and grilled meat.

"Gyros," she says, holding up a second wrapped package. "Figured you might want some fuel. Best Greek food in Vegas. That doesn't say much, but still, it's really good."

My stomach growls in response. I've been surviving on protein bars and coffee since this morning. "Thank you. You're a lifesaver." I gratefully accept the food and settle into the seat beside her.

The gyros is incredible—lamb, tzatziki, pickled vegetables and salad wrapped in warm pita. I close my eyes as I take the first bite.

"So?" Athena asks, taking a bite of her own meal. "How does it feel to be back in rehearsal mode?"

"Exhausting," I admit, wiping tzatziki from the corner of my mouth. "It's still hard to imagine the full production. Everything feels so bare-bones right now."

"Well, I happen to have a vivid imagination," Athena says with a grin. "What I saw up there was an excellent foundation. Once you add all the bells and whistles, it's going to be spectacular. I'm confident this residency will be everything we hoped for."

I smile, feeling some of the day's tension ease. Athena's confidence is reassuring.

"Next week we add the full band and all the technical elements," I explain. "That's when things get really complicated."

"And really exciting," she counters. "Speaking of exciting, how are things going with Diane?"

A goofy grin spreads across my face. Just hearing her name makes me giddy, a feeling I'm still getting used to. "Really well. She stayed over on Friday."

"Oh?" Athena returns my smile. "And?"

"And..." I pause, taking another bite to buy myself time. "I really like her. Way more than I expected to. Way more than I probably should."

"Fabulous. I was hoping you two would hit it off."

"You might be Cupid after all," I say with a chuckle. "But you've also sabotaged my residency. I'm completely distracted. I've been walking around in this weird haze, replaying conversations, checking my phone constantly."

"Don't worry about your performance; you're going to do

great. You might be distracted, but surely it makes you feel inspired too?"

"Yeah. I've started to write music again. It feels good. And I know it's complicated," I continue. "We both know it's complicated. Neither of us can be involved in anything serious—our lives don't allow for it. But we don't want to stop either." I set down my gyros, suddenly needing to use my hands as I talk. "It's like... being with her makes me feel whole. It makes so much sense."

"And Diane feels the same way?" she asks.

"I think so. She seems as surprised by the intensity of this as I am." I laugh, remembering our awkward goodbye, the way we both struggled to part. "It's all so new."

"That's sweet," Athena says. "You're getting to discover this together."

I lean back in my seat, staring up at the ornate ceiling of the theater. The Palestra is designed to evoke ancient Greece, with columns and classical motifs worked into the architecture. It's beautiful and timeless, but it also feels somewhat surreal.

"The timing is terrible," I admit. "I'm about to start my residency and she's dealing with family pressures in Washington. I don't know where it's going, or if it can go anywhere at all. But I'm finally excited about something that has nothing to do with my career."

"I'm so happy for you, Zara. Really. Don't overthink it. Enjoy it." Athena crumples up her gyros wrapper and stands. "I should let you get back to rehearsal. Would you like to come over for dinner at my house next week? I'll invite Diane too. You two can spend the night if you like."

My eyes widen in surprise. "Yes. I'd love to." Athena doesn't strike me as someone who casually invites people into her personal space. She's warm and generous in her professional capacity, but there's always been a careful boundary between her public persona and her private life, and I feel honored that she trusts me enough to let me in. "Will we meet your new love interest?"

"Yes, my partner. We're official." Athena pauses, a sweet expression crossing her features. "I'm sure she'll be delighted to meet you. She's a fan but don't tell her I told you that." She winks and heads toward the exit.

I remain in my seat, finishing my meal. From this vantage point in the back row, the stage looks dauntingly exposed. I try to imagine what I'll look like to an audience from here—vulnerable under those blazing lights. No matter how many times I've done this, the beginning of a new project always feels like standing at the edge of a cliff, unsure if I'll soar or fall.

There's something different this time, though. The Olympus is not just a workspace, but a sanctuary where honest conversations can happen, where I can admit to feelings I'm still learning to name. Strange that in Vegas, of all places, what happens offstage matters more than the performance itself.

26

DIANE

*M*y apartment looks like a high-end hotel suite that someone forgot to check out of. The Georgetown one-bedroom is pretty and functional—gray sofa, glass coffee table, abstract art in muted tones—but there's nothing personal about it. I never bothered making it feel like home because I don't spend enough time here to care.

I never invite people over, never host dinner parties or casual hangouts. When I meet friends, it's always at restaurants or bars downtown, and the idea of bringing a woman here has never even occurred to me as it's too risky.

The space reflects my priorities: efficient, presentable, emotionally vacant. I buy groceries maybe twice a month, mostly coffee and wine. The kitchen exists only for show.

I'm curled up in the corner of the sofa, phone in hand, talking to Zara. Her face fills the screen, hair damp, her piano and a portable clothes rack in the background. Even her hotel suite feels more lived-in than my apartment.

"I'm sorry you had to deal with that," she says, referring

to the story I've just finished telling her about my father's reaction at the Heritage Foundation event.

"Yeah, well." I shrug, trying to shake off the heaviness that settles over me whenever I think about that conversation. "I'm sure you're pretty stressed out with your rehearsals. How's all that going?"

Zara grins. "Busy, sure. And physically exhausting. But not stressful exactly. Every day is delightfully predictable in a way my life hasn't been in years."

I smile. "Predictable how?"

"Well, I wake up at seven," she begins, counting on her fingers with mock seriousness. "I have breakfast in my suite over a video call with Peter, my manager. I rehearse from ten to one with Mo and my dancers. I eat lunch, and then rehearse from three to six again, and at night I meet with my assistant, order room service, take a bath in that ridiculous marble tub, and call you."

I laugh. "That still sounds pretty full-on to me."

"It's fine," Zara says. "But next week Peter has thrown in a few photoshoots and interviews so it will be a little busier." Her eyes sparkle with flirtation. "When can you come back?" The question tumbles out of her and I watch her blush. "I mean, when you have time. No pressure. I know you're busy."

"I've been thinking about that constantly," I admit. "Next weekend maybe? I know it's not easy for you to plan around—"

"I'll make it work," she interrupts. "Whatever day, whatever time. I'll figure out the logistics. Oh, and Athena has invited us over for dinner. She said she'd call you too. We can spend the night there."

"That sounds fun. I can't wait to see you." I bite my lip, considering the complications. "I'll see if Thomas and his girlfriend can join me again. Having Thomas in Vegas makes it easier to explain my absence."

"And if they can't?" Zara asks.

"Then I'm still coming." I blow her a kiss. Three weeks ago, I would never have considered taking such a risk but I've stopped caring as much.

"Really?" Zara's smile is radiant, and I wish I could reach through the screen to touch her face. She's so beautiful, so entirely herself when she talks to me. I sometimes forget who she is. "Athena stopped by to watch the rehearsal," she says. "Brought me the most incredible gyros and we talked about..." She pauses. "About us, actually."

"About us?" Now it's my turn to blush. I like the word 'us.' "What did you tell her?"

"That you're distracting me from my work," she says with a laugh.

"I can relate to that." My smile widens as I settle deeper into the sofa. "And I miss you," I say quietly.

"I miss you too." Zara shakes her head. "Which is crazy, right? We've only met up twice." She looks away for a beat, like her mind is going elsewhere.

"What are you thinking about?"

Her expression turns mischievous. "Wouldn't you like to know?"

"Tell me."

"Oh, you're being bossy again now, are you?" she asks in a teasing tone.

"Only if you like me being bossy."

"I do. I like it when you take control." Zara's voice drops to a whisper, her eyes darkening. "In all honesty, I was thinking about the last morning we spent together. The way you... you know... took charge."

A twitch shoots between my thighs. I've never been one

to push sexual partners toward submission unless they brought it up first. It's something I love, something that feels natural to me, but I've rarely explored it. At the club, sex wasn't on my mind. What mattered there was just catching up and talking freely, feeling like I could be myself. And if I clicked with someone, we'd meet up somewhere private. I'm not into public displays but behind closed doors, with the right person, the dynamic can be incredible. "Go on," I say.

She bites her lower lip, looking a little shy. "I've never wanted anyone to have that kind of power over me before. But with you... God, Diane, I crave it."

My breath hitches and the heat in her eyes makes my pulse race. I shift on the sofa, crossing my legs as desire builds. "I kind of love being dominant in bed." Bringing the phone closer to my face, I ask, "Is that something you'd like to explore?"

Zara's eyes flutter closed for a moment. "Yes. I've been touching myself every night, reliving that morning."

My free hand grips the arm of the sofa as I picture her alone in that massive hotel suite, her hands moving over her body while she thinks of me. "Jesus, Zara."

"It's true," she whispers. "You make me lose control."

"Next weekend," I say, my tone leaving no room for argument, "I'm going to spend hours learning what you need, and I'm going to push every boundary you'll let me push."

The silence that follows is thick. I watch her process my words, see the moment they land. Her hand moves off-screen, and I don't need to guess where it's going.

27

ZARA

*T*he address Athena gave me leads to a gated community in The Ridges, where multi-million-dollar homes line the streets behind tall gates and greenery. Reaching a beautiful contemporary house, I'm nervous in a way I haven't been since my first Grammy performance.

I'm going to have dinner with Athena and her girlfriend Ruby, and Diane will be there too. My Diane. It's such an ordinary thing—couples meeting up, socializing over food. The kind of casual double date that happens in living rooms and restaurants across the world every single day.

But for me, this is revolutionary.

I've never been able to sit around a table where I could reach for a woman's hand. Never experienced the simple pleasure of being part of a couple in a social setting where I don't have to perform or pretend.

Athena knows exactly who I am, who Diane is, and what we're navigating. There's no pretense required and for once, I can just exist as myself—a woman falling for another woman, giddy and nervous and completely out of my depth in the most wonderful way.

Pulling through the gates, I take a deep breath and remind myself that this is what I've dreamed of—the chance to be real, to be seen, to stop living my life in fragments for a while.

The front door opens before I can knock, revealing Athena in white jeans, a white linen shirt, and her signature fedora.

"Zara, welcome," she says, pulling me into a warm hug. "I'm so glad you could make it."

"Thank you for having me."

She leads me through a foyer and living room with soaring ceilings toward the back of the house, and we step onto a terrace that overlooks the pool and the desert landscape beyond. The view is spectacular with the setting sun, but it's not the scenery that makes me stop short. It's Diane, rising from a chair at the outdoor dining table.

I practically run toward her, and Diane meets me halfway. We fall into each other's arms like we've been apart for months instead of days. She smells like the perfume I've been missing, and when she kisses me—soft and lingering and completely unconscious of our audience—the world narrows to this moment.

"I love it when a plan comes together," Athena says with obvious satisfaction, and we break apart laughing. "Ruby, come meet Zara."

A woman emerges from the house carrying a tray of drinks, and I'm immediately struck by how beautiful she is —tall and elegant with auburn hair, dressed in black shorts and a simple black top. She sets down the tray and extends her hand with a warm smile.

"Zara! Wow... I have to confess, I'm a bit of a fan," she says. "I've been so excited to meet you."

"The pleasure is all mine," I reply, pulling her into a hug instead.

The terrace is set for an intimate dinner—the table dressed with white linens and candles, cushioned chairs arranged to take advantage of the view.

"This is incredible," I say, gesturing toward the house and grounds. "Athena, you have a beautiful home."

"Actually," Athena says, glancing at Ruby, "this is Ruby's house. My place is next door."

"Next door?" I ask, settling into the chair beside Diane. "That's convenient."

"Very," Ruby agrees, pouring wine into our glasses. "We sleep next door but tend to entertain here. It's more..." She hesitates. "Private."

I glance toward the neighboring house and can see the roof peeking out over the wall and the palm trees in her yard. I'm about to comment on the fact that next door looks pretty private too, but Athena stands before I get the chance.

"I should check on the lamb," she announces. "Babe, would you mind helping me with the sides?"

The moment they're gone, I turn to face Diane, my heart hammering. The butterflies that have been fluttering in my stomach all day intensify under her gaze. She looks beautiful in the golden hour light, her dark hair pulled back. Her navy top gives me a glimpse of her cleavage and a silver necklace graces her neck.

"Hi," I whisper.

"Hi yourself," she says, reaching for my hand. "I missed you."

"I missed you too." I lean toward her and our lips touch in a soft kiss. When we part, I rest my forehead against hers. "I can't believe you're actually here. Did Thomas and his girlfriend manage to join you?"

Diane shakes her head. "They couldn't make it so I told my parents I wasn't feeling well and turned my phone off for the weekend. They think I'm home in bed with the flu."

I roll my eyes humorously. "Look at us—I'm sneaking around Vegas like I'm having an affair, and you're faking illness to avoid your parents. We're like teenagers again, except with better credit scores and significantly higher stakes."

We hear laughter from inside the house and Athena and Ruby emerge with the food. They serve a Mediterranean feast—grilled lamb with herbs from her garden, colorful salads and dips, roasted vegetables, and fresh bread, warm from the oven.

"Did you make all this yourself?" I ask incredulously.

"I made the lamb—my mother's recipe from back home," Athena says. "Ruby makes the best salads. Everything else came from the Olympus kitchen because we know our limits. We're not trying to pretend we're domestic goddesses, but we refuse to serve bad food."

The conversation flows easily as we eat, touching on everything from my upcoming residency to travel stories to Ruby's work as an M&A lawyer.

What strikes me most is how natural this feels already. Sitting beside Diane, her hand occasionally brushing mine as she reaches for her wine glass, listening to her laugh...

The sun has fully set now, and the terrace is lit by the warm glow of candles and string lights woven through the olive trees scattered throughout the yard. I notice lights flickering on in the yard next door—Athena's house—and then I hear the distinct sound of a car pulling into a driveway.

"Were you expecting company?" I ask, glancing toward the neighboring property.

Athena follows my gaze and something uneasy flickers across her expression. She hesitates for a moment, exchanging a look with Ruby.

"Zara," she says finally, "I consider you a friend now, so I want to tell you something in confidence, and I need you to swear this goes no further."

I raise an eyebrow, intrigued by her serious tone. "Hey, you hold my biggest secret in your hands. I think you know you can trust me."

Athena glances at Diane and Ruby, who nod. "I run an underground club from my home," she says. "For people like us. Powerful women who like women. It would be too risky to have you over there at night when members arrive. If paparazzi followed you, they might see things they're not supposed to see."

The revelation clicks several pieces into place—the careful way Athena manages introductions, the level of discretion that surrounds everything in her orbit.

"I don't want you to feel like you're not welcome in my home, and I hate keeping secrets from friends. That's why I'm telling you," she continues. "But the truth is, while all my members are prominent in their fields—successful, high-profile women—none of them operate at your level of public recognition. The risk calculation changes completely with someone of your visibility. Even with the best security, I'm not certain I could guarantee the level of protection you'd need. And more than that, I'm not sure the other members would feel comfortable. It's not about you personally—it's about what your presence would mean for their safety."

"Trust me, I understand," I say. Athena's right to be cautious. Even when I think I've shaken them, paparazzi have a way of finding me—lurking in parking garages, tipped off by hotel staff, tracking my movements through social media posts from fans who spot me. I've learned to live with the constant surveillance, but bringing that level of scrutiny anywhere near private gatherings would be reckless.

The casual way Athena refers to me as a friend means more than she probably realizes. It's almost impossible to make genuine friends when you're a global superstar—at least not real friends who like you for your company instead of just wanting to be seen with you or gain something from the association, and I'm touched. "Thank you for trusting me with that. And I feel the same way—I consider you a friend too. And you, Ruby," I add, turning to her with a smile. "Thank you so much for your hospitality and for letting us stay here tonight."

Ruby's face lights up with genuine delight. "Are you kidding me? Zara Nova, my new friend, sleeping at my house? I'm never washing the guest sheets again." She laughs. "But seriously, you're always welcome here. And not because I'm a fan; you know that, right? You're lovely, and Athena speaks so highly of you. Plus, anyone who can make Diane Washington blush deserves a medal. Or at least a guest room."

28

DIANE

*T*he night has been perfect—great conversation flowing as easily as the wine, which we've consumed in copious amounts. The candles have burned low, and I feel totally relaxed. Maybe it's the wine, or maybe it's being in a space where I can hold Zara's hand without looking over my shoulder, but the tension I've been carrying lately has finally loosened.

Ruby refills our glasses with the last of the third bottle, her cheeks flushed from laughter and alcohol.

"I know we've met a few times at the club," she says, settling back in her chair and turning to me, "but we've never really talked about your work. You run the Washington Foundation, right?"

My stomach immediately clenches as I force a smile and reach for my wine glass. "I do. Please don't judge me." It was meant to sound like a joke but it didn't come out that way.

Ruby's expression softens with concern. "I'm not, I promise. But I'm curious. You do a lot of fundraising, right? How are you finding it?"

I flinch involuntarily at the question. Even here, in this

safe space with people who understand the value of secrets, talking about my professional life feels like stepping on broken glass. Ruby notices my reaction immediately.

"We don't have to talk about it if it makes you feel uncomfortable."

"No, it's fine," I say, taking a sip of wine. "It's just that lately, I feel like a complete fraud. I work my ass off raising money for people who don't think people like us should have the right to get married. Hell, half of them probably don't think we should exist at all."

Zara's hand finds mine under the table, her thumb brushing across my knuckles in silent support.

"I mean, it was always just my life, you know?" I add. "All I'd ever known. You grow up in a certain world with certain expectations, and you don't question it because questioning would mean admitting that everything you've built your identity around might be wrong." I laugh, but there's no humor in it. "But I've recently started questioning what the hell I'm doing with my life. And it's about time. I feel ashamed it took me so long."

Athena leans forward. "I'm sorry. That can't be easy."

"It's not." I shake my head. "I'm not sure what I'm going to do, but I can't keep living like this. I can't keep smiling and nodding while people discuss how to limit the rights of people like us. I can't keep writing grant proposals for organizations that might dismiss me if they knew who I really was."

Zara leans into me. "This is recent?" she asks softly. "This feeling about your work?"

I meet her eyes. "It's been building for a while, but it's become impossible to ignore recently." I glance around the table, then back to her. "Once you meet someone you really click with, everything becomes so much clearer. Suddenly you realize what you're sacrificing to maintain a life that isn't even yours."

The truth of that statement settles over me like a heavy weight. Before I met Zara, I could compartmentalize. I could separate my weekend escapes to Vegas from my weekday existence in Washington. I could tell myself that my job was just a job, that my personal life was irrelevant to my professional duties. But now, with her hand in mine, the cognitive dissonance has become unbearable.

"I spent years telling myself I was doing good work," I continue, eager to get it all out now that I've started opening up. "Education initiatives, scholarship programs, literacy campaigns—that stuff matters, right? But it's all funded by people who would be horrified if they knew their money was being managed by a lesbian. The irony is suffocating." I pause, taking another sip of wine as the full scope of my professional compromise crystallizes. "And since recently, these same donors want to control what's taught in schools. They're funding initiatives to remove books from libraries, to dictate what teachers can say about history, to ensure that kids like I never learn that people like us even exist. I'm helping them erase us from education while pretending it's about academic excellence."

Ruby nods. "I can imagine. It must feel like you're betraying yourself every day."

"Yeah." I'm grateful she understands without judgment. "And the worst part is, I'm good at it. I'm really good at convincing wealthy conservatives to write big checks. I know how to speak their language, how to frame initiatives in ways that appeal to their values."

"What would you do instead?" Zara asks. "If you could walk away?"

"I don't know," I say honestly. "I haven't allowed myself to think that far ahead. Walking away would mean giving up everything—my salary, my trust fund, possibly my family. It would mean starting over at thirty with nothing but my education." I shrug. "I suppose I could forget about the money altogether and maybe find work with an organization that actually aligns with my values. Somewhere I could use my fundraising skills for causes I believe in."

"Those organizations would be lucky to have you," Athena says. "Your experience, your connections, your track record—that's incredibly valuable, regardless of which side you've been working for."

I laugh ruefully. "My connections might not be as valuable if I'm openly gay. Half the people in my contacts would refuse to take my calls."

"Then you'd build new connections," Ruby says firmly. "Better ones. People who see you as an asset because of who you are, not in spite of it."

The conversation has taken on a weight I didn't expect when the evening began. These three women are seeing me grapple with questions I've been avoiding for years, watching me admit that the life I've built is fundamentally incompatible with who I am.

"I'm sorry," I say, suddenly self-conscious. "I didn't mean to turn this into a therapy session."

"Don't apologize," Zara says immediately. "This is important."

Athena stands abruptly and heads inside. When she returns, she's carrying a bottle of whiskey and four crystal tumblers. She sets our half-full wine glasses aside and replaces them with the whiskey, pouring generous measures for each of us.

"I always say, 'wine for pleasantries, scotch for truth,'" she announces. "And I think you deserve a stiff drink after that admission." She raises her glass toward me. "You know, I spent years thinking I would follow in my father's footsteps. I was practically groomed to do so even though I had no interest in shipping. My father was a tough man. He would have never accepted me if I came out to him." She swallows hard and I catch a glimpse of pain behind her controlled facade. "And then he passed away. I still miss him every day, but I don't know what was easier: living with him or living without him. I know one thing though. Security isn't worth much if it comes at the cost of your soul."

29

ZARA

*W*e close the bedroom door behind us, and finally we're alone. The scotch has left me feeling bold and uninhibited, and I'm fueled with an urgent need to feel Diane's skin against mine.

I press her against the door and kiss her, my hands already working at the buttons of her shirt. The fabric parts under my fingers and I push it off her shoulders.

"You're still pretty lively after all that alcohol," Diane says with a chuckle, her hands finding my waist.

I shoot her a mischievous smile. "You remember what we talked about, right?"

Diane's hands still for a beat. "Oh, you're still up for that?" she asks, her voice dropping to that husky register that makes my knees weak.

"If you are," I mumble against her lips.

Watching her being vulnerable tonight, hearing her speak her truth about work and family—it only made her more irresistible. There's something incredibly sexy about a woman who's brave enough to question everything she's been taught.

Diane turns us around, backing me toward the bed. "Well, it's your lucky night. I asked Athena to put some toys in the room before we arrived."

My eyes widen and I feel heat rush to my cheeks. "You told Athena?"

Diane smiles and shrugs. "Relax. Athena is the most open-minded person I know. She wouldn't have flinched. There are things going on next door that you don't know about, but trust me, this is nothing."

I frown, processing this information. "Have you been next door?"

"Yes. Many times. That's how I know Athena."

"Oh..." I pause. "Do you go there to have sex?"

"No, I go there to socialize. But I've met sexual partners there in the past. Nothing serious." Diane's tone is matter-of-fact, but she's closely paying attention to my reaction.

"Do you still go there?" The question reveals an insecurity I wasn't aware of.

Diane's eyes lock with mine as she cups my cheek. "I probably will at some point, to catch up with friends. But right now, I have better things to do in Vegas. Also, do you really think I still see other women? How could I possibly ever want anyone but you?" Her confident expression wavers and she bites her lip as she takes a small step back. "Sorry, is that too much? I know this is supposed to be casual and I don't want to claim you or anything. I just meant—"

"No," I interrupt, taking her hand and kissing it. "It's not too much. Actually, I've been wanting to talk about this. I want to be exclusive."

Her eyebrows lift in surprise. "Really?"

"Yeah. I know we agreed to keep things light, but the truth is, I only want you too. I can't stand the thought of you being with someone else."

"Neither can I," she says. "So we're doing this, huh?" When she kisses me again, it feels possessive. She takes the hem of my dress and lifts it over my head, then tosses it behind her. Her eyes move over my body with appreciation and desire, and I feel beautiful under her gaze.

"You're so gorgeous," she murmurs, her fingers tracing the lace edge of my bra. "I can't believe you're mine."

"Show me," I whisper. "Show me I'm yours."

Something primal flickers in her gaze, and then her hands are everywhere—unclasping my bra, sliding my panties down my legs, guiding me toward the bed.

"Lie down," she commands, and I obey without hesitation.

The sheets are cool against my heated skin as I settle onto the mattress. Diane moves to the nightstand and opens the drawer. I can't see what's inside it but part of me doesn't even want to know. I just want to surrender, to let things happen.

She picks out a black satin tie and dangles it in front of me. When she joins me on the bed, I reach for her, but she catches my wrists.

"No," she says firmly. "I'm going to tie your wrists together. May I?"

I nod, my heart pounding wildly.

She positions herself above me, her thighs straddling my hips as she ties my hands together over my head. When she leans down to kiss me, it's deep and possessive, her tongue exploring my mouth like she owns it. Her lips move to my neck, finding a spot that makes me gasp and arch beneath her. She bites down gently, then soothes the mark with her tongue.

"I love how responsive you are," she murmurs in my ear.

"Every sound you make, the way you move—it drives me crazy."

Her mouth continues its journey down my body, pausing to lavish attention on my breasts. When she takes one nipple between her teeth and bites down with just enough pressure to make me cry out, I squirm in pleasure.

I want to touch her, but when I move my hands, she pins them back down over my head. She's in complete control and every sensation feels even more intense tonight.

"Please," I breathe, not even sure what I'm asking for.

Diane smiles, a predatory expression that makes my pulse race. "There's no need to beg, Zara. I'm going to give you exactly what you need." She brings her mouth close to my ear and whispers, "I'm going to make you come so hard you'll forget your own name."

She moves lower, her hands spreading my thighs apart. The anticipation is almost unbearable—every nerve ending in my body feels electrified. When she finally touches me, I arch off the bed with a sharp gasp.

"Mmm... You're already so wet for me. Don't move, stay in position," she murmurs before she reaches into the drawer again and shows me a pair of nipple clamps connected by a delicate silver chain. "Have you ever worn something like this before?" Diane asks.

I shake my head and swallow hard.

"Don't be afraid. They'll pinch at first, but then the sensation becomes... intoxicating." She leans down and takes my nipple in her mouth again, swirling her tongue around it until it's hard and sensitive. "At any point when you want me to stop, say 'abort,' okay? I'll take them off and untie you immediately. Can you repeat that for me?"

"Abort." I hesitate. "Do we really need a safe word?"

"Always. But I won't hurt you. Do you trust me?"

"Yes," I whisper, shivering as I'm eyeing the clamps.

The first one makes me suck in a quick breath—the feeling is sharper than I expected, but not painful. More like an intense pressure that sends strange but pleasant sensations to my core. The second one draws a moan from my lips, and when Diane gently tugs on the chain connecting them, I cry out and squeeze my thighs together.

"Nuh-uh," she says, sitting up and parting them again. "I told you to stay in position, didn't I?"

"Yes," I stammer, fighting the urge to close my legs. I feel more exposed than ever and the pinch of the clamps sends waves of arousal to my already throbbing pussy.

Diane trails her fingers down my stomach, teasing, never quite touching where I need her most. When she finally dips between my thighs and pulls at the chain simultaneously, I squeeze my eyes shut and gasp at the contradicting sensations of pleasure and pain.

"You like that?" she asks, though she clearly knows the answer from the way I'm writhing beneath her.

"Yes," I pant.

"Good," she says, finding more items in the nightstand. A riding crop and a vibrator. "Pleasure and pain. A match made in heaven." She holds them up, giving me time to process what's happening. "Are you okay with this?"

Licking my lips, I nod, and she smiles, clearly pleased.

"I'll start slow. Tell me if it's too much."

The first stroke of the crop against my inner thigh is so light it almost tickles. The second has more weight behind it, creating a warm sting that spreads across my skin. Diane watches my face carefully, gauging my reactions as she alternates between gentle strokes and firmer ones, moving higher and higher up my thighs.

The pinch of the clamps and the soft sting of the crop

feels delicious and when she turns on the vibrator, my body tenses in anticipation. Diane traces it slowly up my inner thigh, watching my face as I writhe beneath her. When she finally presses it against my pussy and tugs at the chain, I moan so loudly I'm startled by my own noise.

"That feels good, doesn't it?" she murmurs.

I'm in no state to answer. My breathing becomes erratic and my wrists pull against the restraints. I'm so close but she turns off the vibrator and goes back to flogging me, harder now.

Every nerve ending in my body is on fire with pleasure and sweet pain. When I think I can't take any more, Diane leans down and devours my pussy with her mouth. Her tongue is relentless, circling, flicking, sucking until I barely know what to do with myself.

"Fuck!" I yell, my bound hands clenching into fists above my head.

And then she stops again. I want to beg her to continue but I'm still catching my breath. I'm throbbing and I know that if I close my thighs now, I'll come.

As if reading my mind, Diane shifts back and takes hold of my ankles. "Don't move." She stares at me with such intensity that I melt under her gaze. "Has anyone ever fucked you with a strap-on before? I assume not?"

A soft moan leaves my lips as I shake my head.

"Would you like that?"

My mouth goes dry as I nod, still unable to form words. "Yes," I finally manage. "I want that."

Diane's eyes darken as she smiles. "Good girl."

She releases my ankles and moves away from the bed. I watch, transfixed, as she sheds her clothes. Her body is magnificent—all smooth curves and lean muscle. When she opens another drawer and pulls out a harness and dildo, my eyes widen at the sight. I realize I'm way more innocent than I thought, and I can't take my eyes off her as she straps it on and adjusts the toy.

Grabbing the flogger, Diane returns to the bed and positions herself between my legs, spreading her knees to prevent me from moving. She teases and tickles me first, then flogs me harder, moving higher and higher. I suck in quick breaths between moans, clenching my jaw at the occasional sharp sting of pain. My nipples are throbbing, and I'm desperate for release.

Diane bites her lower lip as she regards me with a mischievous look, and I hold my breath as I know what's coming. She brings the flogger down hard and it hits my pussy. I arch off the bed, crying out so loudly I'm worried Athena and Ruby will hear me in the house next door.

When she throws the flogger on the floor, I'm panting and wincing, my eyes shut tightly at the burn between my legs.

"Look at me," she commands, and when I meet her gaze, I see pure hunger reflected back at me. She positions the tip of the dildo at my entrance, not pushing in yet, just letting me feel its presence. "I'm going to fuck you now, Zara. Tell me you want it."

"Please fuck me," I beg, my hips instinctively tilting toward her. "I need you."

She pushes in slowly, giving me time to adjust to the unfamiliar sensation. It's bigger than her fingers, fuller, and I feel myself stretching to accommodate the intrusion. A low moan escapes my throat as she slides deeper.

"Let go," she breathes, her voice strained with arousal as she moves into me. The fullness is overwhelming in the best possible way, and I can feel every inch as my body adjusts.

She starts thrusting slowly, pulling almost all the way

out before sliding back in. Each thrust sends shockwaves through my already oversensitive body, and the chain connecting the nipple clamps sways with our movement, adding another layer of sensation that makes me dizzy with pleasure.

"More," I gasp, my bound hands flexing helplessly above my head. "Please, harder."

Diane's control seems to crack at my plea. Her thrusts become deeper, more forceful, and the sound of our bodies coming together fills the room, punctuated by my increasingly desperate moans.

She releases the clamps, and the sudden rush of blood back into my nipples makes me cry out, the throbbing so intense it borders on pain. But before I can recover, she leans down and takes one into her mouth, soothing the sensitivity with her tongue while she continues to fuck me.

Draping herself over me, she takes my bound hands in hers and kisses me hard. It's the most wonderful thing I've ever felt, like all of her is pouring into me. Everywhere all at once. The weight of her body against mine, the feeling of being completely surrounded by her and filled by her is mind-blowing.

Diane's pace quickens, and tension builds rapidly low in my belly, spreading outward like molten heat. My legs wrap around her waist, pulling her deeper, needing more of this connection that's rewiring me.

She grinds into me, harder and harder, moaning at the friction of the harness, and I know she's close too.

"Come with me," she whispers. "I want to fall apart together."

Her words push me over the edge and the orgasm crashes through me with devastating intensity, starting deep in my core and radiating outward until every limb is on fire. It's so powerful and doesn't seem to stop.

Diane moans against my lips, her body shuddering. We move together through the aftershocks, neither of us able to stop the small thrusts and movements that prolong the sensation.

Finally, she collapses on top of me, both of us panting and covered in a sheen of sweat. I feel so utterly spent, so completely satisfied. I can barely catch my breath as Diane carefully pulls out, making me gasp.

She unties my wrists, massaging them tenderly where the satin has left faint marks on my skin.

30

DIANE

a tear rolls down Zara's cheek as I hold her against my chest, both of us still breathing hard.

"Are you okay?" I ask softly, brushing the tear away with my thumb.

She lets out a shaky chuckle. "Yes. God, yes. It was just... very, very intense." She takes a deep breath, her voice unsteady. "My emotions are all over the place right now. Good emotions," she adds, tilting her head up to meet my eyes.

I press a soft kiss to her forehead and she tilts her head back to face me. "Where on earth did you learn to do that?" she asks. "In Athena's club?"

I shake my head. "No, as I told you, I don't have sex there." I pause, feeling heat creep up my neck as I realize I'm about to share something I've never told anyone. "It was my cello teacher, actually. A long time ago."

Zara's eyebrows shoot up, and she scoots closer, her naked body pressing against mine. "Please elaborate, because this sounds like a juicy story," she says in a teasing tone. "How old were you?"

"Eighteen," I admit. "I started taking lessons when I was seventeen. My mother insisted."

Zara props herself up on her elbow, giving me her full attention. "So you play cello? I had no idea you were musical."

"I don't," I say. "I mean, I don't anymore. I had zero talent for it—I was absolutely terrible. The only reason I kept going back was because I had the most enormous crush on my teacher."

Zara grins. "Of course you did. What was she like?"

"Her name was Victoria and she was in her late thirties, an elegant woman with long dark hair and graceful fingers. She had this way of standing behind me to adjust my bow hold that made it impossible to concentrate on anything musical."

"I can imagine," Zara murmurs. "So you were a terrible student because you were too busy fantasizing about your teacher?"

"Yeah. I was hopeless. Absolutely hopeless. I couldn't read music to save my life, my bow sounded like I was torturing cats, and I think I spent more time watching her demonstrate technique than actually attempting it myself."

"That's adorable," Zara says with a laugh. "How long did this tragic musical charade go on?"

"Almost two years. Victoria was endlessly patient, probably because my mother was paying her very well, but I could tell she was mystified by my complete lack of progress." I pause, remembering my sexual frustration during those lessons. "I'd practice for hours before each session, but the moment she walked into the room, everything I'd learned would evaporate. She could have been teaching a brick wall for all the musical progress I made."

"So what happened? How did cello lessons turn into... well, what you just did to me?"

"I showed up on the wrong day by accident. I'd gotten my dates mixed up, and when Victoria opened the door, she was clearly expecting someone else," I say. "She was dressed in leather. Head to toe black leather—corset, hot pants, thigh-high boots, the works. And she looked just as startled to see me as I was to see her. We both stood there for a moment, completely frozen."

Zara's eyes widen. "Oh my God."

"I turned about fifteen different shades of red and started apologizing profusely for getting the day wrong," I continue. "We were both talking over each other until she finally invited me in for tea instead of sending me away. I think she was worried I'd pass out on her doorstep from embarrassment."

"And then what happened?"

"Nothing, that day. We sat in her kitchen drinking tea and making incredibly awkward small talk about the weather while I tried not to stare at her outfit. She called to cancel whoever she'd been expecting, said something had come up, and I left after an hour or so."

"I bet your concentration was even worse during your next lesson."

"Are you kidding? I was a complete mess. Finally, Victoria set down her bow and asked if I had questions about her personal life. She said she could tell I was curious, not just shocked or scandalized. I'd never encountered anything like that before. BDSM wasn't something I'd been exposed to in my sheltered upbringing. I asked her if it hurt, if it was safe, what it felt like, and Victoria was incredibly open about it all. Told me about the community she was part of, the club she attended on weekends, what it meant to her. She explained that it was about power exchange and trust, not just sex. That it was consensual and careful and actually quite beautiful when done right."

"And then she propositioned you?"

"Something like that," I say, remembering the careful way Victoria had approached the subject. "She said something like 'You seem genuinely interested in this. Is it something you might want to explore?' I admitted that I did but she made me think about it first." I chuckle. "When I came back the next week, she didn't even get the cello out and during the five months that followed I didn't play a single song during my lessons."

"Five months?" Zara's voice has gone husky again. "Were you in a relationship?"

"No. We only saw each other during my weekly allocated timeslot."

Zara throws her head back and laughs. "Imagine if your mother knew what she was paying for."

"Yeah. Thank God she never found out." I shoot her a goofy grin. "Anyway, I was submissive at first. Or I tried to be. But Victoria said I was like a CEO trying to be an intern —it didn't fit. So, we switched roles, and suddenly everything clicked. I think I liked it because my own life was so decided for me. It felt like I was taking back some control."

"What happened with Victoria?" Zara asks. "Why did you stop seeing her?"

"She got engaged. She said we had to stop, that it wouldn't be fair to him."

"That must have been devastating."

"It was. I was completely infatuated with her, but I got over her eventually."

"Did you ever see her again?" Zara asks. "Have you ever thought about looking her up?"

"No, I never saw her again and I prefer to leave the past in the past."

Zara grins. "Well, if you do ever see her again, let me know so I can send her flowers. I owe that woman for teaching you." She shifts and drapes herself over me. "Now, maybe it's time you give me another lesson. I'm an eager student, and I want to know what *you* like."

Her lips find mine before I can respond, and I'm lost again in the taste of her, in the way she fits against me like she was made for this. Made for me.

31

ZARA

*T*he morning air carries a desert coolness that won't last much longer. Ruby's housekeeper has made us breakfast—fresh fruit, pastries that smell like they came from a Parisian bakery, and strong coffee. We sit on the terrace wrapped in silk robes we found in our room, enjoying the view. The pool reflects the early sunlight in rippling patterns and it's blissfully quiet.

I tear apart a croissant with my fingers, completely unselfconscious about eating with my hands for once.

Diane stares at me over her coffee cup, and I catch her looking.

"What are you thinking about?" I ask, though the flush on her cheeks gives me a pretty good idea.

"Nothing," she lies, taking a sip of coffee to hide her blush.

I grin, completely charmed by how transparent she is.

Last night was a revelation. Not just the incredible sex—though that was mind-blowing—but the intimacy that came after. We stayed up talking until three in the morning, wrapped in each other's arms in Ruby's guest room. The conversation meandered through everything from childhood fears to career dreams.

"What would you like to do today?" I ask, reaching across the table to steal a piece of pineapple from her plate.

"What do you mean? We'll have to stay here, right?" she says, gesturing toward the privacy walls that surround Ruby's property.

"Not necessarily," I say with a chuckle. "You think I never go out in the wild? I'm pretty good at disguises and I'm sure Ruby has something I can borrow." I lean forward, excited by the possibility that's forming in my mind. "How about we take a drive into the desert? I came here in my rental car because I needed a break from my security team."

Diane looks genuinely surprised. The idea that I might have strategies for moving through the world semi-normally from time to time clearly hasn't occurred to her.

"Unless you're uncomfortable with that?" I continue quickly. "I totally understand if—"

"No," she interrupts, reaching for my hand. "But what if someone sees us?"

"As long as we behave and act like we're friends, it should be fine, right?" I shrug. "I'm allowed to have friends, and so are you. What's the worst thing that can happen? Someone sells a picture of us hanging out to the tabloids? Unless you're worried your parents might find out you weren't really in bed with the flu."

Diane waves a hand. "What are they going to do? Ground me?" She laughs. "No, let's do this while we can."

The phrase "while we can" leaves me a little sad. She's right, of course—opportunities like this are rare and precious in our complicated lives. We need to grab these moments of freedom when they present themselves.

The truth is, I'm desperate for some semblance of

normalcy with Diane. I want to be out in the world with her, even if we have to pretend we're just friends.

"In that case, we should probably get ready if we're going to beat the heat," I say. "Athena took me out for a drive last week, so I know my way around a little." I stand and stretch. The robe shifts, and I catch Diane's gaze at the flash of skin revealed. The knowledge that I have this effect on her, that she wants me as desperately as I want her, is turning me on all over again.

Diane gets up and walks toward me, her eyes dark with intent. She slides her hands inside my robe, her palms warm against my ribs as she pulls me close and kisses me.

I giggle against her lips, nudging her hands away when they trail up to my breasts. "Not here," I whisper, glancing toward the house. "The housekeeper might see us."

"Don't worry about the housekeeper," comes a voice from behind us, and we jump apart to find Ruby standing in the doorway, arms crossed with an amused expression on her face. "She sees nothing and hears nothing. Discretion is part of her job description."

Ruby shoots us a wink. "Sorry to interrupt your morning, ladies. I was just checking to see if you have everything you need. Athena had to go to the Olympus—there was something she needed to deal with, so she apologizes for not being here to say good morning."

"Ruby, hi..." I quickly close my robe, mortified at being caught. "We were—"

"Being adorable," she finishes with a laugh. "Don't be embarrassed, it's cute."

"Good morning, Ruby." Diane steps back with an equally embarrassed grin. "We were actually discussing venturing out today," she says, recovering faster than I am. "Zara wants to drive into the desert."

"That sounds lovely." Ruby smiles and thanks her house-keeper who hands her a cappuccino. She's clearly dressed in her Sunday casual attire: slippers and a linen kaftan. From the state of her hair, she looks like she's just woken up. "Is there anything you need? I can arrange a packed lunch for you?"

"Thank you, but we've just had breakfast," I say. "But do you happen to have anything that could pass as a disguise?"

Ruby chuckles. "What kind of disguise are we talking?"

"Anything, really. Something that would make me look less like me."

"Okay... I think I might have something," she says, frowning as she sips her coffee. "My niece came to Vegas for a bachelorette party last month and left behind a wig. And I've got oversized sunglasses too. Would that work?"

"That sounds perfect." I walk up to her and give her a hug. "Thank you for everything, Ruby. I really appreciate all of this, and we had so much fun last night."

"So did we. Please come over any time, you know where to find us." Ruby steps back and squeezes my shoulder. "Give me ten minutes and I'll go find you some stuff upstairs."

As she disappears inside, I turn to Diane, who's watching me with a mixture of amusement and affection.

"Embarrassed?" she whispers, closing the distance between us again.

"Totally," I admit. "You?"

"Same. Though honestly, the prospect of seeing you in whatever ridiculous wig Ruby's niece left behind is completely worth getting caught."

32

DIANE

Zara's rented convertible hums along the desert highway, wind whipping through my hair. I glance over at her behind the wheel, and I have to bite back laughter. The wig is outrageous—a bright blue bob with sharp bangs that looks like it belongs in a nightclub. Combined with oversized sunglasses that cover half her features and a flowing white shirtdress that billows in the wind, she looks like she's starring in a music video.

"Stop staring at me," she says without taking her eyes off the road, though I can see her trying not to smile.

"I can't help it. You look absolutely ridiculous."

"Thanks," she says dryly. "Really boosting my confidence here."

"Ridiculously amazing," I amend, reaching over to touch one of the electric blue strands. "I never would have pictured you as a blue-haired rebel, but somehow you're pulling it off."

The landscape unfolds around us in waves of rust and gold—rock formations carved by wind and time into fluid shapes. The mountains rise in the distance, purple shadows against the horizon, while closer ridges reveal layers of geological history in stripes of red sandstone and limestone.

"You're kind of sexy when you're driving," I say.

She glances over with a grin. "Only when I'm driving? I need to step up my game the rest of the time."

"Trust me, your game is fine."

We've been driving for half an hour, leaving The Ridges behind as we venture deeper into the Mojave. It's so peaceful—no traffic, no construction, just the wind and the engine and the occasional cry of a hawk circling overhead.

"I think I remember," Zara says, downshifting as we approach a turn. The blue bob shifts slightly with the movement, and she absently pushes the bangs out of her eyes. "Athena showed me a lookout point somewhere around here. It's completely off the tourist trail."

We bump and jostle over rocky terrain, the car's suspension working overtime as we climb steadily upward. Just when I'm starting to wonder if we're lost, the track opens onto a flat outcropping of rock that offers a panoramic view of the valley below.

Zara parks and kills the engine, and suddenly we're surrounded by absolute silence. There are no signs of human presence anywhere in the vast landscape spread before us, and the quiet is so complete it feels sacred.

"Wow," I breathe, stepping out of the car and walking to the edge of the rocky platform.

Las Vegas is visible in the distance, a small cluster of buildings shimmering in the heat haze like a mirage. The mountains stretch in every direction, their peaks worn smooth by millions of years of erosion.

Zara comes up behind me, pulling off the garish blue wig with obvious relief and shaking out her dark hair. "God, that thing is itchy," she says, tossing it into the car before sliding her arms around my waist and pressing her body against my back. "What do you think?"

"It's beautiful." I lean into her warmth.

"I thought I'd feel trapped surrounded by all this emptiness," she says, her chin resting on my shoulder. "But it's been calming in a way I wasn't expecting." She pauses. "I have a small strip of private beach behind my home in Malibu, but even there I sometimes spot paparazzi at a distance, so I'm always aware I'm being watched if I go out for a walk or a swim."

I turn in her arms, studying her face. Her hair is messy from the wig, the curls that her stylists usually tame into submission now wild and frizzy. Without makeup and with the desert sun bringing out the golden undertones in her skin, she looks breathtaking.

"Do you ever get used to it?" I ask. "Being in the spotlight constantly?"

"No, I don't." Her honesty is immediate and unguarded. "Some days it feels normal, like background noise I've learned to ignore. Other days it's suffocating." She looks out at the empty landscape. "But I'm grateful for everything that's happened to me, for everything I have. I know how lucky I am."

"It didn't just happen to you," I say. "You're very talented. You write your own music, you're an amazing performer... Though I have to admit, I've never actually seen you live."

"Maybe it's time we change that." She smiles. "How about front row seats for my opening night? For you and Thomas and Jamie, if they'd like to come too. It would be nice to meet them, even if they don't know about us."

"I have no doubt they'd love that. Are you sure?"

"Yeah. I want you there. I want to look out into the audience and see you." Zara takes my hand and leads me away from the edge of the plateau toward a formation of red rocks.

"Come on," she says, her fingers intertwined with mine. "Let's go higher."

We climb carefully, our feet finding purchase on the weathered stone. At the top, the rock formation creates a natural bowl—a smooth depression that's partially shaded by an overhanging cliff. It's like a private amphitheater carved by nature, hidden from view of anyone below.

"This is awesome," I say, settling onto the smooth stone.

Zara sits between my legs and leans back against me, her body fitting so well in the curve of my arms. I hold her close and breathe in the scent of her hair, feeling completely peaceful and happy.

"We should try to get out here more often," she says. "I like being in nature with you." She tilts her head back to look at me. "When I was little my mom would take me to Prospect Park in Brooklyn on Sunday afternoons. We'd find a quiet spot under a tree and just sit, watching people walk by. I'd forgotten what that felt like until—" She breaks off with a sharp intake of breath, her body going rigid against mine.

"Zara? What's wrong?"

"Ouch!" She pulls her left foot toward her, wincing as she moves. "Something stung me. Or bit me. Shit, that really hurts."

I shift so I can see her ankle, and my stomach drops. There's a small puncture wound above her sneaker, and already I can see swelling beginning to form around it. Then my eyes are drawn to movement. A small, pale scorpion scuttles away from us and disappears into a crevice in the rock.

"Scorpion," I say, trying to remain calm. "We need to get you down from here right now."

"A scorpion? That's bad, isn't it?"

Zara groans in pain as I help her to her feet. The swelling is spreading rapidly.

"Can you make it down?" I ask, positioning myself to support her weight.

"I think so," she says, but she's breathing hard and beads of sweat are already forming on her forehead.

We make our way down the rock formation slowly, Zara leaning heavily on me as we navigate each natural step. By the time we reach the bottom, she's trembling and the swelling has spread up her calf.

"Diane," she says, and there's fear in her voice now. "I can't feel my foot."

My blood runs cold. I help her to the car and get her settled in the passenger seat, then grab my phone to call 911. The screen shows no bars—no service out here in the middle of nowhere.

"Fuck," I mutter, then look at Zara. We're at least forty minutes from the nearest hospital, maybe more if I can't remember the route back to the main road. But staying here and hoping for cell service isn't an option.

"I'm getting you to a hospital," I say, moving around to the driver's side. "Right now."

My hands are shaking as I start the engine. "Drink some water and stay with me," I tell her, putting the car in gear and heading back down the rough track as fast as I can. "Keep talking to me."

"I'm okay," she says weakly. "Just hurts. A lot."

The car bounces and lurches over the uneven ground. Every jolt makes Zara wince, but I can't afford to go slower. When we finally reach the paved road, I floor the accelerator, pushing the convertible to its limits as we race toward the city.

"Zara, can you hear me?" I glance over at her. She's slumped against the passenger door, her skin clammy.

"Yeah," she mumbles. "Please hurry. It's bad."

33

ZARA

"You're going to be fine," Dr. Snow says, pulling off her latex gloves and dropping them in the biohazard bin. "The antivenom worked quickly, and your vital signs have stabilized. You got lucky—bark scorpions can be nasty, but we caught this on time."

Relief floods through me so intensely that tears spring to my eyes. The past four hours feel like a nightmare I'm finally waking up from. One moment I was lying peacefully in Diane's arms watching the desert sky, the next I was struggling to breathe as she raced me toward the city.

I remember fragments: Diane's voice desperately trying to keep me present, screeching into the emergency room parking lot and then Diane getting out of the car and shouting for help. The medical staff swarming around me, asking rapid-fire questions about my symptoms while they hooked me up to monitors and started an IV.

The pain was excruciating—a burning, electric sensation that radiated up my entire leg. Then came the nausea and dizziness, my heart racing so fast I thought it might explode. When my vision started to blur and my speech became slurred, I genuinely thought I might die in that hospital bed.

"How long do I need to stay?" I ask Dr. Snow, trying to sit up straighter.

"We'll keep you for observation overnight, just to be safe. Scorpion envenomation can have delayed effects, but you should be okay to go by tomorrow morning. Make sure not to put too much weight on that leg for the coming week to prevent more swelling."

"Thank you." I hesitate. "Did anyone... Do you think anyone saw me come in?"

Dr. Snow gives me a sympathetic smile. "Honestly, yes. I believe people are aware you're here and there's nothing we can do about that unfortunately. We've notified Peter Ward as he was your emergency contact. He's on his way and he's sent over a security detail who's currently outside making sure no one will disturb you."

I nod. "As long as my friend can come in. Is she still here?"

"I'm right here and I'm not going anywhere." Diane lets herself in with a coffee and a bottle of water and Doctor Snow leaves the room to give us privacy. Diane looks like she's aged five years in the past four hours. Her face is pale and her hands are trembling slightly as she approaches my bed and hands me the bottle. "How are you feeling?"

"Still sore, but immensely happy to be breathing." I reach for her hand, needing the contact. "Thank you. You saved my life."

"I was so worried," she says, squeezing my hand. "You kept closing your eyes and became unresponsive. I thought..." She looks away, and I can see her struggling with emotion. "I thought I was going to lose you."

Our moment is interrupted by Peter striding in, his

usual polished appearance slightly disheveled, his green tortoiseshell glasses askew.

"Zara, thank God," he says, rushing to my bedside. "When the hospital called me, I thought—" He stops himself, taking in the monitors and IV line. "How are you feeling? What did the doctors say?"

"I'm going to be fine," I assure him. "They gave me antivenom, and the worst is over. I'll have to take it easy during the rehearsals next week though."

"Don't worry about the rehearsals. As long as you're okay." Peter gives me a small smile and leans in to kiss my forehead. "I'm glad I flew in a few days earlier. I literally just landed today and saw the missed calls from the hospital. Why on earth did you go out into the desert without a security detail? You know better than this, Z."

"I wanted some privacy," I say quietly, feeling like a scolded child. "Real privacy."

"Well, your privacy is out the window now." He runs a hand through his hair. "I saw paparazzi parked outside when I arrived. They've set up camp in the parking lot."

"Fuck," I say, my stomach dropping. I turn to Diane. "I'm so sorry. Maybe it's best that you leave so you won't get seen with me."

"No," Diane says firmly, her hand tightening around mine. "You have nothing to be sorry about and I'm staying. I want to make sure you're okay. I'm a nobody. They're not going to care about me."

Peter turns to look at Diane properly for the first time, his manager instincts clearly cataloging everything—her expensive clothes, her educated accent, the way she's holding my hand like she has every right to be here.

Diane notices his stare and pulls her hand back.

"Peter, this is Diane," I say. "Diane, my manager, Peter. Diane is a good friend. She saved my life."

Peter extends his hand to Diane. "Thank you. For getting her here safely."

"Of course," Diane replies. "Can I get you a coffee?"

"Actually, that would be wonderful." Peter wipes his fore-head. "Can you make it a double shot? I need to prepare a short press statement, just to get the press off our backs for now."

"What about me?" I pout, making Diane chuckle. "I'm dying for a coffee."

"I'll check with the doctor to see if you're allowed caffeine." She shoots me a wink. "And Athena and Ruby are on their way. Athena is bringing food; she said hospital food is a crime against humanity and she's not letting you suffer through it."

"That sounds like Athena." I smile, imagining her marching through the hospital corridors with takeout containers like she's on a rescue mission.

"You've made friends," Peter observes when Diane leaves to get coffee. "You two seem close."

"Yeah, we're very close. Actually, I want you to add Diane to my inner circle."

Peter's eyebrows lift in surprise. My inner circle is sacred territory—a small group of people who have permanent access to me, no questions asked. Security knows to let them through immediately, venues prepare separate entrances for them, and they can reach me even when I'm in complete lockdown mode. Right now there are just four people on that list: my mother, Jess, Peter, and Mei. Adding someone new isn't a decision I make lightly.

"That's... significant," Peter says carefully. "You've known her for what, a few weeks?"

"A month. But she drove me to the hospital when I was dying," I point out. "That's the kind of person I want in my life."

Peter nods, processing this. He knows better than to question my judgment about people—I've learned to be incredibly selective about who I trust, and when I do decide to trust someone, it's usually for good reason.

"Of course. What's her last name?"

"Washington," I say, then add, "She's very private. Please make a note of that."

34

DIANE

I wrap my arm around Zara's waist as we exit the hospital through a side door, her weight pressing against me as she favors her uninjured leg. Peter walks ahead of us with Zara's security detail, phone pressed to his ear as he coordinates our departure.

"The limo should be right around the corner," he says over his shoulder. "Athena arranged for it to pick us up at the service entrance."

My heart hammers against my ribs. The plan seemed simple enough when Peter outlined it—slip out the back, into the waiting car, and away from the photographers who've been camping at the main entrance since the news of Zara's hospital visit broke. I'm exhausted after spending the night curled in the chair next to Zara's bed, my neck stiff and my eyes gritty from too little sleep. Every time she stirred or made a sound, I was instantly awake, checking her breathing, making sure she was okay. The nurses assured me she was stable, but I couldn't bring myself to leave.

"Are you okay?" Zara asks.

"I'm fine, but I'm worried about *you*."

She squeezes my arm. "I'm alright. Really. Just sore."

We round the corner and I spot the black car idling near the loading dock, its windows tinted. The driver steps out, scanning the area before opening the rear door.

But as we approach the vehicle, a figure emerges from behind a maintenance shed. The photographer moves in front of us, his camera raised as he fires off shot after shot.

"No pictures," the security detail says, immediately positioning himself between the photographer and us. "Please back off."

Another photographer appears and starts shouting questions.

"Zara! How are you feeling?"

"Was it really a scorpion sting?"

"Will you be able to perform on your opening night?"

I instinctively turn my face away from the cameras but it's too late.

"Get in the car," Peter says urgently.

I hesitate for a split second, knowing I should step back and let Zara go. I'm supposed to head for the airport in my own taxi but the photographers are closing in and without thinking, I slip into the back seat beside her, my protective instincts overriding rational thought. Besides, it's better to hide in the car than stand exposed in the parking lot while they document every angle of my face.

"Shit," Zara says as Peter climbs in after us and slams the door. The photographers immediately swarm the vehicle. "Diane, I'm so sorry. I didn't think they'd be waiting back here."

"Don't be sorry," I say, trying to keep my voice steady even as my pulse races. "It's not your fault."

The driver pulls away slowly, forced to navigate around the photographers who seem determined to get one more shot. Through the windshield, I see cars pulling up behind us—the paparazzi convoy preparing to follow us.

"I might have to come with you to the Olympus now," I say, watching the photographers give chase. "They can't follow us into the private parking garage, right? I can stay for an hour and slip into a taxi from there."

"But you're going to miss your flight," Zara says, her hand instinctively reaching for mine.

The gesture is so natural, so unconscious, that neither of us realizes what she's done until Peter's gaze drops to our intertwined fingers. His expression doesn't change, but I see the moment of calculation, the manager's brain filing away this new piece of information.

Zara quickly pulls her hand away, color flooding her cheeks.

The silence in the limo becomes thick and awkward. I stare out the tinted window, watching the city blur past. Behind us, three cars maintain pursuit, their drivers weaving through traffic.

"This is what it's like to spend time with me," Zara says quietly. "Welcome to my world."

I turn to her, noting the tension in her jaw, the way her hands are clenched in her lap. This isn't just an inconvenience for her—it's a prison she carries everywhere.

"I can't imagine what it must be like for you," I say. "Living like this all the time."

"It's not constant," she replies, glancing at the cars trailing us in the side mirror. "Only when something happens, when there's something to report. A scorpion bite isn't exactly front-page news. Tomorrow it'll be old news and they'll leave me alone again for a while. At least until opening night."

The driver takes an unexpected turn, and I watch the

pursuing cars scramble to keep up. One of them cuts off a taxi, earning an angry honk.

"Have you ever been able to lose them?" I ask.

"Sometimes. My driver in LA knows all the tricks. Back alleys, service roads, parking garages with multiple exits. But usually it's easier to let them get their shots and politely ask them to leave." Zara shrugs. "Fighting them only makes them more persistent."

The Olympus lies ahead of us, and we turn into what looks like a maintenance entrance, using a keycard to access a private roadway that curves around the back of the building. The pursuing cars slow at the gate, unable to follow without authorization.

Descending into an underground parking garage restricted to VIPs, we let out a collective sigh.

"Safe," the driver announces, putting the car in park.

"Great. Thank you." Peter immediately pulls out his phone. "Zara, if you're up for it, we need to go through your schedule for the coming week. Since you need to take it easy with your leg, we might need to swap some of the rehearsals for media commitments."

Zara glances at me, then back at Peter, a silent negotiation passing between them.

"Could you give us some time?" she asks. "Maybe an hour? Then I'm all yours."

Peter's eyebrows lift slightly, but he nods. "Of course. Call me when you're ready." He climbs out of the limo and disappears toward the elevator bank, leaving us alone in the cavernous garage.

"An hour," Zara says, turning to face me fully. "That's not much time."

"It's enough," I reply, though I'm not sure what I mean by that. Enough for what? To process what just happened? To figure out how to handle the inevitable fallout when those photographs surface?

But looking at her and taking in the exhaustion around her eyes, I realize that none of that matters right now. What matters is that she's safe, that the antivenom worked, that we made it through something that could have been much worse.

"Come on," I say, helping her out of the car. "Let's get you upstairs."

35

ZARA

*P*eter and I have spent the afternoon reorganizing my schedule, moving interviews and photo shoots, and fielding calls from concerned industry contacts. He was all business, his efficiency cranked up as he worked to contain any potential damage. But I caught him curiously glancing at me several times. He knows something.

The way Diane and I look at each other, the unconscious intimacy in the limo, the need for privacy before she left for the airport—it's hard to hide and Peter's too smart and too experienced not to recognize the signs.

Saying goodbye to Diane left me sad and I keep thinking about those photographs from the hospital—paparazzi shots that will probably show us as nothing more than friends, but still. I don't want to drag her into my media circus. She has enough complications in her life without adding my baggage to the mix.

I pour myself a generous glass of Cabernet from the wine fridge. My ankle is throbbing with a dull ache as I settle onto the bench behind the piano.

The melody that's been haunting me lately emerges again. It only existed in fragments. A chord progression here, a melody line there, scraps of lyrics scribbled in my notebook. But now, with the taste of fear still sharp in my mouth and the memory of Diane's fierce protectiveness, the pieces finally click into place.

I start with the verse, singing along softly.

Baseball cap pulled low, your secrets taste like wine. From lips that hide the truth beneath the vine. Golden elevators rise above the noise where money talks and silences our voice.

The words flow like water, finding their voice as I continue into the chorus, the second verse, and the chorus again.

Both of us performers in our different ways. You smile through the small talk, I live on the stage. You speak their language, I wear their disguise but when alone, our performance dies.

Silk against my wrists, shadows on the wall. Whispers in the darkness, a touch that makes me fall. Morning light reveals the marks left on my skin and silence is the only way we win.

Both of us performers in our different ways. You smile through the small talk, I live on the stage. You speak their language, I wear their disguise but when alone, our performance dies.

My left hand hits the bass line while my right picks out the melody, the harmonies weaving together in ways that feel inevitable. As I build toward the bridge, my voice grows stronger.

Desert winds can't cool the fire you ignite. In the stolen hours we escape the light. I've sung of love forever but never felt it burn until you taught my heart how to return.

I love you. I love you. That's the truth I can't deny. Though loving you means learning how to lie.

I think about the hospital room, about Diane curled in that uncomfortable chair, refusing to leave even when the nurses assured her I was stable. I think about the way she held my hand, how she kissed me and gave me the longest hug before she left.

Both of us performers in our different ways. You smile through the small talk, I live on the stage. You speak their language, I wear their disguise but when alone, our performance dies. When alone, our performance dies. When alone, our performance dies.

After the final chord fades, I sit in the silence for a while, my heart pounding. This song is dangerous—too honest, too revealing. *I love you.* Fuck. I just sang that, and I meant it. A jumble of emotions makes me choke up, and my eyes well up. Fear, excitement, love, and a bone-deep terror at how vulnerable I've become. And underneath it all, a fierce protectiveness—not just of Diane, but of this fragile thing between us that feels too precious to survive the harsh light of scrutiny.

I've revealed my feelings for her in a song. A good song. No. Possibly a great song.

I play it through again, this time recording it on my phone so I won't lose the arrangement because the bones are solid.

Listening back to the recording, I hear there's a rawness in my voice. It reminds me of the demos I recorded in my bedroom at seventeen, before I learned to sand down all the rough edges, before every note had to justify its existence to a room full of executives. My vocal coach would tell me that breath before the bridge is audible, that the vibrato wavers on the final chorus. But those imperfections feel essential, like scars that prove the song lived through something.

This isn't how I usually write. Normally, I start with a

concept, a hook that will resonate with a broad audience. I think about radio play, streaming numbers, what will translate well in a stadium. My team weighs in—Peter with his market analysis, my producers with their commercial instincts. We craft songs like architects designing buildings, each element considered for maximum impact. But this song wrote itself. The question now is what to do with it. Do I add it to my residency setlist?

Of course, I can never tell the world who inspired it. Diane will have to remain my beautiful secret. But knowing she exists, knowing what we have together—even if it's complicated and potentially temporary—has unlocked something in my creativity that I thought fame had killed.

I pick up my phone and scroll through my contacts until I find Athena's number. I may not be able to tell the world, but I have friends I can trust, and I trust Athena's judgment.

"Zara? How are you feeling?" she asks. "Do you need anything? Anything at all?"

"I'm okay," I say, nervous about what I'm about to ask. "Still sore, but okay. Can I ask you for a big favor?"

"As I said, anything."

"Well... It's kind of personal. I've written a new song and I'd love your opinion."

There's a pause, and then Athena's voice comes through warm. "That's not a favor, Zara. That's a privilege. I'll be right there."

36

DIANE

*T*he taxi smells like stale cigarettes and air freshener, a combination that makes my already queasy stomach churn. I slump against the seat as we pull away from Reagan National, exhaustion weighing down my limbs like lead. My body aches from sleeping in that hospital chair, and my mind keeps replaying the moment those photographers appeared from nowhere. Has my picture been published? Too tired to care, I can't bring myself to check.

My phone buzzes incessantly in my purse. I've been ignoring it since landing, but the persistent vibrations are impossible to tune out. With a heavy sigh, I fish it out and see five missed calls from Dad and seven missed calls from Mom, along with a string of increasingly urgent text messages from Mom.

Diane, please call me back. We need to talk immediately. This cannot wait until tomorrow. Call me now, Diane.

My thumb hovers over her contact. All I want is to go home, take a hot shower, fall into bed, and ignore whatever crisis has Mom in a panic right now. She doesn't read gossip columns so it's unlikely the news has already reached her.

I press call and lean my head against the cool window as the phone rings.

"Diane, finally." Mom's voice is sharp, clipped. No pleasantries, no asking how I'm feeling. "We need to talk. Right now."

"Hi, Mom. I'm still not feeling well, and I really just want to—"

"Nonsense," she cuts me off. "I know you're not sick."

I close my eyes and blow out my cheeks. "Okay..."

"You were in Vegas. Don't deny it."

Great. That didn't take long.

"The daughter of a friend saw your picture in a gossip column," Mom continues. "At a hospital. With Zara Nova. Even I know who Zara Nova is." Her voice drops to that tone she uses when she's furious but trying to maintain composure. "I have it right here. She sent it to me. Your picture is right here, Diane. What on earth is going on?"

The taxi hits a pothole and I wince. "You're right, I'm not sick. I'm sorry I lied to you, Mom. But can we please talk about this tomorrow? I'm really, really tired."

"No. Tomorrow we're having dinner with the Cunninghams."

I frown. "That dinner is tomorrow?" With everything that's been going on, it completely slipped my mind.

She sighs, the sound heavy with exasperation. "Yes, don't you remember? Don't you dare bail on us again, Diane. Does Thomas even know you went to Vegas? Barbara told me she saw him yesterday. Did you lie to him too? What were you doing there? And since when are you friends with celebrities?"

The questions come rapid-fire, each one hitting my brain like a small explosion. I need a moment to gather my thoughts, to figure out how to navigate this minefield.

"Thomas has nothing to do with what I get up to on my weekends," I say. "And yes, Zara and I are friends. We met through a mutual friend in Vegas."

"But you don't have friends in Vegas," Mom says as if it's her God-given right to know every detail about my life.

I've had enough. The exhaustion, the panic from yesterday, the emotional intensity surrounding my secret relationship with Zara—it all coalesces into a wall of resistance.

"Mom, as I said, I'm tired and I'm going home now. I'll see you tomorrow. I'm sorry I lied about being sick, but there's really nothing to discuss."

"Don't be ridiculous, Diane. This isn't just about lying—this is about your reputation, our family's reputation. It's one thing that you stopped going to church with us, but this is a whole new level of questionable behavior. Do you have any idea what people will think when they see this photograph?"

"What people, Mom? I really don't care what anyone thinks anymore."

"Don't you take that tone with me. First you're spouting nonsense at that charity auction and now you're gallivanting around Las Vegas, gambling with pop stars—"

"I wasn't gambling or gallivanting anywhere," I protest. "We were driving through the desert. Zara was hurt and I helped her get to a hospital. That's what decent people do."

"Decent people don't lie to their families and disappear to another state without explanation. I excused you from the Bellevue event last night. I told them you were sick and now you're making me look like a fool. How long has this been going on? How many times have you lied to us about Vegas? Do you have a gambling problem? Is that what this is?"

The taxi turns onto my street and I feel a desperate need to end this conversation before it spirals further out of control. "Mom, I'm almost home. Can we please—"

"No, we cannot. Your father is going to be furious when he sees this. He's been trying to call you all day. He was genuinely worried about you, and meanwhile you're off living some secret life we know nothing about."

The mention of my father makes my stomach clench with anxiety, but I push through it. "I'm an adult, and if I want to make friends in Vegas or anywhere else, that's my business."

"But it's not just your business, Diane!" Mom's voice rises several octaves. "Your picture is in a tabloid with one of the most famous women in the world and you owe us an explanation. You know, there are treatment centers. Residential facilities in places like Arizona and Nevada where people go when they can't control their addiction. If that's what you need we can talk about that, but you need to tell me the truth."

I roll my eyes and shake my head, staring out at the familiar Georgetown streetscape. If she only knew the truth —that I'm gay, that I've been sneaking off to an underground lesbian club, that I'm falling head over heels for a woman—gambling would be the least of her worries.

The taxi stops outside my building. I pay the driver, grab my bag, and step out onto the sidewalk, looking up at the elegant red brick townhouse converted into condominiums. The doorman nods as he holds open the heavy glass door framed in polished brass.

"I have to go," I say, my thumb moving toward the end call button. "I'll see you tomorrow night."

I hang up before she can respond and immediately turn off my phone. I've never hung up on my mother. Never refused to discuss something she deemed important, and the small act of rebellion feels liberating.

37

ZARA

"Look at you, getting so big!" I coo, adjusting Lucas in my arms as he grabs at the necklace draped around my neck. His chubby fingers are surprisingly strong as they wrap around the chain. He's definitely showing signs of his mother's stubborn streak, and he's so much more alert than the last time I saw him.

"I can't believe you're both here," I say, using my free arm to pull Jess into a tight hug while balancing Lucas against my hip. "He's growing so fast and look at those little teeth coming in!"

Jess squeezes me and kisses my cheek. She insisted on coming sooner after I called her from the hospital last week. She pulls back to study my face, then glances down at my bare feet. "Ouch, that looks painful," she says, pointing to my left ankle.

I follow her gaze to where the swelling is still visible. The skin has taken on a mottled purple-yellow color that looks worse than it feels. "It's much better already. I can actually walk on it, so that's progress."

"Are you sure you should be rehearsing at all?" Jess asks, her mom voice kicking in.

"The doctor cleared me as long as I don't do anything too strenuous. I should be okay for opening night." I bounce Lucas gently, earning a delighted giggle. "I'm going to be fine. Promise."

Jess finally takes a moment to look around the suite, whistling through her teeth as she takes in the soaring ceilings, the marble surfaces, the floor-to-ceiling windows that frame the Vegas skyline. "Holy shit, Z. This place is incredible."

"Language," I say with mock sternness, covering Lucas's ears theatrically. "There are innocent babies present."

"Sorry, little guy." Jess kisses her son's forehead. "Mommy forgot her manners."

I lead her toward the terrace doors, eager to show off the outdoor space. "I took the liberty of booking a nanny who'll be here all day while you work. She comes highly recommended."

"Zara, you didn't have to—" Jess starts, but I cut her off with a wave.

"Of course I did. I'm so happy you came all the way here. The least I can do is make sure you can actually focus on your work."

When I slide open the terrace doors, Jess steps outside and stops dead in her tracks at the sight of the infinity pool.

"This will be a whole new level of working from home for the next few weeks," she says. "I might never want to leave."

We settle onto the cushioned seating area with a jug of fresh lemonade, Lucas content to play with the fabric tassels on the throw pillows while we catch up.

"Mom will be joining us next week," I tell her,

adjusting a pillow behind my back. "She's flying in two days before opening night and she's got a room on the same floor."

"Great." Jess's face brightens. "I haven't seen Isabella in forever. Not since she last visited you in L.A. How is she?"

"Still trying to convince me to move back to Brooklyn and give her grandchildren." I laugh and shake my head. "She's going to spoil Lucas rotten when she gets here."

"I'm sure he wouldn't mind some spoiling," Jess says, watching her son attempt to stuff an entire throw pillow into his mouth. Raising Lucas alone has been harder than she admits, though she'd never complain, and having her here for a few weeks will be good for both of us. "So, any plans for today?" she asks.

"I actually have an interview at six." I check the time on my phone. "But after that, I thought maybe we could have a quiet dinner up here? Catch up properly?"

"We definitely need to catch up." Jess shoots me a knowing look. "I want to hear all about this woman you've been dating. I saw her picture in the article. She's kind of hot."

"Yeah, the picture... I wish that hadn't happened. Even Peter wasn't able to contain it from going viral but luckily everyone will assume we're just friends." I shift Lucas to my other knee. "We went for a drive out into the desert, trying to have some normal time together away from all this." I vaguely gesture toward the city. "I got stung and she raced me back to the hospital. She probably saved my life and stayed with me all night."

Jess studies my face. "You're falling for her, aren't you?"

"Yeah," I admit. "I really am."

"And she feels the same way?"

"Yes. I'm sure it's mutual." I run my fingers through

Lucas's soft hair, finding comfort in his innocent presence. "It's complicated though. Her family situation, my career..."

"But you're happy," Jess observes. "Even with a swollen ankle and paparazzi drama."

She's right. Despite the chaos of the past few days, despite the complications and the very real risks we're taking, I feel more like myself than I have in a very long time.

The sliding door opens behind us, and Peter appears with his tablet. "Zara, the Entertainment Weekly team is here. They're setting up in the living room."

I nod and hold up a hand. "Can you give me ten more minutes? I want to help Jess get settled."

"Five minutes. No more," Peter negotiates. "They're on a tight schedule." He gives Jess a wave. "Hi, Jess! Nice to see you again and welcome to Vegas."

Jess returns his wave. "Thank you and likewise!" When he disappears back inside, she lowers her shades to the tip of her nose and mimics Peter's clipped tone perfectly. "Five minutes. No more."

I burst out laughing. Jess has met Peter a handful of times over the years—at album release parties, award shows, that disastrous Thanksgiving in L.A. when he called me six times during dinner and then showed up unannounced because I didn't pick up—and she's never missed an opportunity to tease him. His voicemail greeting says, "Leave a message. Keep it under ten seconds," and Jess has admitted to prank calling him multiple times just to leave rambling three-minute messages about absolutely nothing.

"Stop it," I say, still laughing. "He's going to hear you."

"Please. The man lives in noise-canceling headphones half the time." She adjusts her sunglasses back into place.

"But I'll behave. Go do your interview. Lucas and I will be right here soaking up this ridiculous luxury."

"Sorry. Welcome to my world. Constant interruptions and someone always waiting."

"It's okay," she says, standing and reaching for Lucas. "We'll be fine. Go be fabulous for the cameras, we'll catch up later."

I kiss Lucas's forehead, breathing in his sweet baby smell one more time before heading inside to transform back into Zara Nova, pop star. But the transition no longer feels like putting on armor. It feels like wearing a costume I'll get to take off again soon, returning to the woman I'm finally learning to be.

38

DIANE

*T*he pre-dinner ritual plays out around us in the Washington family dining room—drinks are poured and pleasantries exchanged. While our parents catch up, Thomas practically drags me to a corner near the French doors that lead to the backyard.

"What the fuck, Diane?" he whispers, his eyes wide. "Is it true? Are you really friends with Zara Nova? Jamie sent me a link and I couldn't believe it when I saw you two together. I haven't told anyone, I swear."

I smile, trying to appear nonchalant despite my racing pulse. "We know each other, yes. Mom knows and I can only assume everyone will soon but for now, please keep it quiet."

"That's so cool," he says, leaning closer. "How do you know her? Is it through that guy you're seeing in Vegas? He must be some big shot to have connections like that."

"Something like that." I glance toward our parents, who are deep in conversation. "But keep your voice down. Mom is livid. I told her I was sick and went to Vegas, and now she thinks I have a gambling problem."

Thomas throws his head back and laughs, quickly

covering his mouth when both our mothers turn to look at us. "Maybe that's not a bad thing, considering how desperate you are to keep your affair quiet."

"Are you kidding me? I don't know what's worse. She keeps mentioning this facility in Arizona. She's determined to send me there, no matter how many times I deny having a problem." I shrug. "Luckily, she can't force me."

"I don't know about that," Thomas says dryly. "It's your mother, after all. Anyway, what's Zara like? Is she going to be okay?"

My mind flashes to Zara, curled against me in bed, her face free of makeup, hair tousled from sleep. She's stunning on magazine covers and red carpets, but that polished version pales in comparison to the woman I held in my arms.

"Yes, she'll be okay and regarding your other question, why don't you find out for yourself? Would you and Jamie like to come to the opening night with me? I have front row tickets."

Thomas's jaw drops as he stares at me. He grabs my arm, his grip tight enough to leave marks. "Are you serious? Front row seats to Zara Nova's Vegas residency?" His voice cracks slightly on the last word, and I have to bite back a laugh at how eager he sounds.

"Dead serious." I pause, watching his expression cycle through various stages of disbelief and excitement. "Do you think Jamie would be up for it?"

"Oh my God, she's going to scream. Literally scream." He runs a hand through his hair, bouncing on the spot. "She plays Zara's music while studying all the time. Diane, this is incredible. Thank you."

"Don't thank me yet. You'll have to sit through dinner with our parents pretending to be smitten with me first." I glance back at where our mothers are in conversation. "So, has Jamie moved in with you?"

"Yeah, and it's been great," he admits. "Coming home to her every night, waking up together, sharing normal domestic stuff like grocery shopping and arguing about who's going to take out the trash... But I wish I could just make her part of my life. My whole life, you know? It's ridiculous that I can't tell my parents."

"I know. I get your frustration," I say. At least Thomas gets to share a living space with Jamie, but he can't introduce her to his colleagues, can't bring her to family events, can't post photos of their weekend adventures on social media. It's a half-life, better than nothing but still fundamentally incomplete.

"And how's your thing going?" Thomas asks, turning the question back to me. "I assume it's going well since he's introduced you to his celebrity friend?" He gasps suddenly as he connects dots that lead nowhere near the truth. "Wait... he's a celebrity himself, isn't he? An actor? A singer?" He grabs my arm again. "That's how you know Zara Nova— you're dating someone in the industry."

"Again, you know I can't tell you anything more," I say. "But it's going really well."

The truth is, I want to tell him everything. He's my friend and I trust him. But even Thomas might not be ready for the reality that his fake girlfriend is actually gay and falling hard for one of the most famous women in the world.

From across the room, I catch my mother's gaze lingering on us. She nudges Barbara, who turns to observe our private interaction with delight. I can practically hear their commentary—how close we're standing, the way I'm smiling as I speak to him.

"They're watching us," I murmur to Thomas, maintaining my smile while speaking through clenched teeth.

"I know. My mother looks like she's already planning our wedding," Thomas says with a grin. "I'm grateful to them for one thing though."

I chuckle and shoot him a skeptical look. "Oh yeah? What's that?"

"I made a great new friend," he says. "I only met you once before they started their matchmaking attempts, and I never came along to their dinners. But now I'm happily joining, knowing you'll be there." He shrugs. "I like how honest we can be with each other. Well, I know you can't be entirely honest, but for now, I'll take it."

"I will some time soon, I promise," I say, touched by his sincerity. And I'm grateful I met you too." I hug him, not because of our audience, but because I want to and immediately I hear a delighted squeal from across the room. Our mothers hurry over, drawn by the display of affection like moths to a flame.

"Well, well," my mother says, her earlier irritation temporarily forgotten in favor of matchmaking triumph. "What's brought on this lovely moment?"

I think quickly and decide to tell the truth for once. "I just told Thomas I'm taking him to Zara Nova's opening night of her residency in Vegas."

Worry creeps into Mom's expression at the mention of Vegas. But Barbara Cunningham claps her hands together in delight.

"Oh, how wonderful! Isn't it nice when young people share their musical interests?" She turns to Thomas. "I remember the first time your father took me to a concert. It was Lawrence Welk at the Kennedy Center—such a gentleman, such beautiful music. It was the most wonderful, romantic evening."

Mom forces a smile, clearly trying to reconcile Barbara's enthusiasm with her own concerns. "Yes, it's wonderful," she says. Then, as if deciding to embrace Barbara's excitement rather than fight it, she adds, "Did you know Diane is friends with her?"

I suspect Mom's sudden shift comes from recognizing Barbara's genuine delight and realizing that fighting it would only draw more attention to her concerns. Knowing Barbara will discover the connection sooner or later anyway, she continues, "Diane was actually visiting with her this weekend when Zara got a nasty scorpion bite. Fortunately, Diane was able to get her to the hospital in time."

I watch this performance with fascination. My mother is being a complete hypocrite—spinning the very Vegas trip she was furious about into a heroic rescue story because it plays well to her audience. I suppose I can now at least be open about going to Vegas.

Barbara gasps, pressing a hand to her chest. "Oh my goodness, how terrifying! A scorpion bite? That must have been so frightening, dear."

"It was pretty scary," I admit, which is entirely true. "But Zara's going to be fine."

Barbara links her arm through Thomas's, beaming at both of us. "You know, Thomas, a woman with connections like this is a rare find. Mark my words, if you two end up together, you'll never have trouble getting concert tickets again." She leans in conspiratorially, stage-whispering loud enough for everyone to hear. "And imagine the wedding entertainment! Though I suppose Zara Nova would be a bit above our budget."

39

ZARA

*T*he Palestra stage clears as we wrap up our final full run-through for today. Backup dancers towel off in the wings, the band packs up their instruments while sound technicians coil cables and lighting designers make last-minute adjustments to cue sheets. After a month of intensive rehearsals, we've finally hit that sweet spot where everything clicks—the choreography flows seamlessly, the band is tight, and I'm confident this show is going to be good.

My voice feels strong, my leg is fine, and the costumes look fantastic. More importantly, I'm not nervous anymore.

"Everyone, can I have your attention for a moment?" I call out. Conversations stop, heads turn.

I scan the assembled group—forty-three people who've worked tirelessly to bring this production to life. Mo wipes sweat from his forehead, still breathing hard from the final dance number. The backing dancers return to the stage, the backup singers cluster together near the piano, and sound and lighting crews come closer.

"I know we're locked and loaded for opening night," I

begin, "but I've written some new material over the past few weeks, and I'd like to add one song to the show."

The reaction is immediate and visible. Mo's eyebrows shoot up in alarm. Sarah, our production manager, actually takes a step backward like I've announced we're scrapping the entire show. The lighting designer looks like he might faint.

"Zara," Sarah says carefully, "we open in four days. The technical elements alone—"

"It won't need choreography or musicians," I interrupt, holding up a hand. "Just one song, only me and the piano. We can do it as an encore, keep it simple."

I can see Sarah mentally calculating all the moving pieces this would require. Even a "simple" addition means adjusting lighting plots, sound levels, stage positioning, and the delicate timing that governs live theater. Her smile is strained as she forces enthusiasm into her voice.

"That sounds... fabulous. Really. We can absolutely make that work."

"I know it's last-minute," I continue, addressing the room but keeping my eyes on Sarah, "and I apologize for the added complexity. But this isn't up for discussion. We're doing it." Admittedly, I should have proposed this sooner, but I couldn't decide whether it was a good idea to add the song or not. Today, however, my gut is telling me I should.

A silence follows. The kind of silence that happens when a roomful of professionals realizes their plan has just been upended by creative inspiration. I've been in this industry long enough to recognize the look—equal parts frustration and resignation that comes with working for someone who can make unilateral decisions.

Peter emerges from the wings where he's been observing. He's been busy all week, juggling photo shoots and interviews between rehearsals and liaising with my team. I can read the tension in his shoulders as he approaches.

"What kind of song are we talking about?" he asks.

"Ballad. Piano-driven. Very intimate." I turn to address him more directly. "Actually, I've written quite a bit of new material lately. Almost enough for a full album. This would be a perfect way to give the audiences a preview of what's coming next."

His eyebrows lift with interest, his mind shifting from logistics to marketing opportunities. "New work during the residency launch? That could generate significant buzz."

The creative burst has surprised me as much as anyone. I've filled two notebooks with lyrics, recorded voice memos at three in the morning when a chord progression won't let me sleep, spent hours at the piano in my suite exploring emotional territory I've never had access to before. I have something to write about now, something that demands to be expressed through music, and the songs practically write themselves.

"The song is strong," I tell Peter, knowing he needs more than artistic enthusiasm to sell this to the team. "Different from my previous work, but in a good way. I'd be happy to play it for you right now. It's called 'Performers'."

I haven't told Peter about any of this before now. The songs have felt too private, too raw, born from experiences and emotions I couldn't explain without revealing too much. Late-night sessions at my piano have produced melodies that feel like confessions, lyrics that cut so close to the bone I sometimes have to stop playing mid-song to catch my breath.

But these songs deserve to reach the world. They're the most honest work I've ever created, even if no one will know they're about falling in love for the first time, about the terror and exhilaration of finally living authentically, about discovering new parts of myself. The emotions are universal enough that they'll resonate.

Diane deserves to hear them too. She's unlocked something in me that I thought fame had killed forever—the ability to transform personal truth into art without sanitizing it for mass consumption.

Peter's expression shifts as he processes what I've revealed—not just the new song, but the fact that I've been writing an album's worth of material without telling him. I briefly see a flicker of hurt cross his features. We've worked together for a long time, shared the highs and lows of my career, and I've just admitted to keeping something significant from him.

I step closer and continue in a private whisper. "I'm sorry. I should have told you sooner, but it all felt so personal."

He nods slowly, and I can see him working through his feelings—the manager part of him excited by the prospect of new material, the friend part wounded by my secrecy. Peter knows me better than anyone in my professional life. He's witnessed every creative phase, every breakdown, every artistic evolution, every moment of doubt and triumph.

And he definitely knows about Diane. Perhaps when he hears this song, he'll understand why I needed to keep these songs close until now. And I know he'll carry my secret with the same discretion he's always shown.

"'Performers,'" he repeats. "Okay, I'm certainly curious. Let's hear it."

I walk across the stage to the grand piano and settle onto the bench, shifting my position until I find the right angle to the keys.

The overhead spot is adjusted to eliminate the harsh shadows across the piano. Sarah pulls out her tablet, ready to take notes, and the sound engineer approaches with a microphone stand, testing levels and positioning it to capture both my voice and the piano without feedback.

Mo settles into a seat in the front row, arms crossed, and the backup singers have found spots scattered throughout the theater, some sitting on the edge of the stage, others claiming seats in the orchestra section. There's an expectant hush as everyone waits.

The weight of what I'm about to do hits me. Once I play this song for Peter and the team, it stops being mine alone. It becomes part of Zara Nova's catalog, subject to analysis and interpretation.

There's no taking it back when it's out there. The song will live in the world independent of its origins, carrying pieces of my heart to strangers.

But maybe that's exactly why it needs to be heard. Maybe the whole point of art is to take something impossibly personal and make it universal, to transform private pain and joy into something that can touch other people's lives. Standing here in this empty theater, surrounded by the machinery of performance, I realize I need to start showing people who I actually am.

40

DIANE

*T*he cursor blinks in the search bar: "nonprofit development director jobs." I've been staring at this screen for twenty minutes, my coffee going cold while I construct justifications for what I'm doing. This is research, I tell myself. Due diligence. Market analysis of potential career pivots.

But my browser history tells a different story. The Ford Foundation, Doctors Without Borders, Environmental Defense Fund, United Way—organizations focused on causes I care about.

A position at a Los Angeles-based nonprofit catches my attention: Director of Development and External Affairs. The salary isn't great—roughly a quarter of what I make now, but I like the description. "Lead comprehensive fundraising strategy to advance LGBTQ+ rights and expand support services for queer youth. Partner with donors who share our commitment to building safe, affirming communities where LGBTQ+ individuals can thrive."

I lean back in my chair, letting myself indulge in the fantasy for a moment. L.A. Sunshine almost every day instead of D.C.'s gray winters and humid summers. I could have a balcony with plants that thrive year-round, wear sunglasses and sandals.

And distance. Three thousand miles between me and my parents. I could visit them—fly back for holidays, major events. But they wouldn't be constantly in my space, monitoring my schedule, questioning my choices. The thought of that breathing room delights me. I could build a life that's actually mine, not just an extension of theirs.

Zara would be close. Not that proximity solves anything, but the possibility of spontaneous visits makes me smile. We could grab coffee on a random Tuesday morning. I could watch her work in the studio. She could come over after a long day and we'd order takeout and fall asleep on my couch like normal people do.

It's too early to think about any of this seriously—we haven't known each other long enough. But the dream feels so vivid I can almost taste the salt air from the Pacific, feel the warmth soaking into my skin. In L.A., I could be someone who goes to the farmer's market and spends time on the beach. Someone who hikes on weekends.

I'm getting ahead of myself. Way ahead. But I'm starting to consider a future other than my predetermined path stretching endlessly in one direction.

My phone buzzes with a text from Zara: *Rehearsal went well today. Added something special to the show that I can't wait for you to hear. Miss you.*

Miss you too! I'm so excited to hear it! I reply, smiling despite my spiraling anxiety. Opening night is in four days, and I'll be there with Thomas and Jamie, watching from the front row as Zara claims the stage.

If our relationship ever became public, would I survive professionally? Probably not in my circles. The Washington

Foundation board would want me removed. My father's political career would suffer collateral damage from having a gay daughter, especially one involved with someone so high-profile. My parents built their careers on traditional values and their only child being gay would shatter more than personal expectations; it would threaten their political and social infrastructure.

The rational part of my brain argues they wouldn't disown me entirely. I'm their daughter. Surely that counts for something. But the more I consider Dad's reaction to my mild defense of marriage equality, the less certain I become. The life I've built, precarious as it feels lately, rests entirely on their continued approval of choices I'm increasingly unable to make.

The L.A. position description mentions comprehensive benefits and relocation assistance. I click through to the organization's website, scrolling through photos of staff at pride events, testimonials from LGBTQ+ youth who found support through their programs. These people wake up every morning knowing their work matters.

My office door opens after a single knock—my assistant's way of announcing something urgent.

"Your mother called," she says. "She wants to know if you're free for lunch on Thursday."

"Tell her I already have plans." Changing my mind, I hold up a hand. "Actually, let me call her back."

My assistant retreats and I stare at my phone. What if I just told her? What if I simply said: Mom, I'm gay. I'm in love with a woman, and I'm tired of pretending otherwise for everyone's comfort? The mental image of her reaction makes me nauseous.

"Diane?" Mom always picks up on the second ring, like she's been waiting by the phone.

"Hi, Mom. I got your message about lunch on Thursday. I won't be able to make it—I'm going to Vegas." I pause and correct myself. "Thomas and I are going to Vegas."

"But the concert isn't until Friday, right?"

"Yes, but we decided to go a day early. Make the most of it, you know?" The lie comes too easily now. What I can't tell her is that Zara asked me to come earlier, that I'll be meeting her mother and her best friend before opening night.

"Right." Mom clears her throat and concern creeps into her voice. "What do you mean by 'making the most of it'? Are you sure you're not gambling? Does Thomas gamble? Did he get you into this? Because if he did, you need to tell me, Diane. You can both get help. Barbara and I will figure something out and—"

"Please, not the gambling speech again!" I close my eyes and let out a groan of frustration, repeatedly stabbing my pen into my mousepad. "I'm not having this conversation again. How many times do I have to tell you—I don't have a gambling problem. Neither does Thomas."

"Then what is it about Vegas that keeps drawing you back? Three times in two months, Diane. That's not normal behavior for someone who doesn't gamble."

"We want to get away for a little while," I say. "Have some time to ourselves. Is that so hard to understand?"

The silence on the other end stretches too long—she's trying to decide whether to push harder or back off, weighing maternal concern against the risk of driving me further away.

"Very well," she says finally. "I won't mention it again." Another pause. "You and Thomas have a nice time together."

I hate the way she says "together" and I'm desperate to shatter her illusion. But I'm not ready for that explosion yet.

41

ZARA

*M*ei's voice carries across the suite before I see her, talking through her Bluetooth headset.

"Peter, I need you to resend Zara's schedule for the week —the full version with travel times, not the abbreviated one. It's my first day back so I'm catching up." She appears in the living room area, balancing two take-out coffees and her tablet. "Perfect, thank you. I appreciate it."

She ends the call and fixes me with an assessing look. "Hi! You look good," she says, handing me my coffee "Rested."

I'm sitting at the piano in my pajamas and a robe. I've been composing since dawn.

"Mei, welcome back!" I say, closing my notebook. I get up to greet her. "How was Hawaii?"

Mei sets down her coffee and tablet, then holds up her left hand, wiggling it in front of me. A simple solitaire gleams on her finger.

"Jun proposed," she says with a beaming smile. "On the beach at sunset. It was so perfect and romantic."

"Mei!" I gasp and pull her into a tight hug. "That's wonderful! Congratulations!"

When I pull back, tears are gathering in her eyes. She laughs and dabs at them with the back of her hand. "Sorry, I keep doing this. I cry every time I tell someone."

"Don't apologize," I say, taking her hand to look at the ring more closely. "This is beautiful. Tell me everything."

Mei settles onto the couch, and I sit beside her, tucking my legs under me as she launches into the story.

"We'd been on the beach all afternoon, swimming and reading. Nothing special planned—or so I thought. When the sun started going down, Jun suggested we take a walk along the water." She smiles at the memory. "We were barefoot, holding hands, and he kept stopping to point out shells or crabs. I thought he was being unusually nerdy about marine life."

I laugh. "Stalling."

"Exactly. Then we reached this spot where someone had built a little cairn—you know, those stacked rocks? Jun stopped and said his grandmother used to tell him that if you make a wish and balance a stone on top without it falling, the wish comes true." Mei's eyes shine. "He handed me a smooth black stone. I put it on top and it stayed so he told me to close my eyes and make a wish. I wished that we'd always be this happy together."

"Oh, Mei."

"And when I opened my eyes, Jun was on one knee in the sand, holding the ring box." She wipes at her eyes again. "He said, 'I already made my wish three years ago when I met you.'"

"That's so sweet," I say, feeling my own eyes prickle.

"I ugly-cried," Mei admits. "Full sobbing. I couldn't even say yes at first—I just nodded like a maniac while tears and snot went everywhere. So romantic." She laughs. "But eventually I managed to say yes, and he slipped the ring on, and we sat there in the sand watching the sun disappear."

"I'm so happy for you both," I say, squeezing her hand. "He's the one, huh?"

"Yeah. He really is."

She takes a breath and looks at me. "Anyway, enough about me. How's your foot? How are you feeling? I thought about coming back sooner, but you kept insisting you were fine and Peter said you were managing okay, but if you needed me I would have—"

"Stop," I interrupt, squeezing her hand. "I've been great and my ankle has healed."

"Good. I'm glad to hear that." She smiles, wiping her eyes. "You were lucky," Mei says. "This friend who drove you to the hospital... the one you added to your inner circle..."

"Diane," I supply with a grin. I can't help it; my face does this happy thing every time I say her name.

"Right. Diane Washington." Mei picks up her coffee and takes a sip. "I looked her up."

"Of course you did." I shrug. "And before you say anything, Diane is not her job. She's not her family or her last name or the foundation she works for. She's her own person."

Mei nods and before the conversation can go any further, the guest room door opens and Jess appears in yoga pants and an oversized sweatshirt, bouncing a fussy Lucas against her shoulder. His face is red and scrunched up, little fists waving in protest.

"Morning," Jess says over his whimpering. "Someone's having a rough morning. Teething is not his favorite activity." She turns to Mei. "Hey! It's lovely to see you again."

243

"Morning, Jess. Guess what? Mei got engaged!" I announce, grateful for the interruption.

"What?" Jess's face lights up. "Mei, that's amazing!" She shifts Lucas to one arm so she can hug Mei with the other. "Congratulations! When did this happen?"

"Thank you! He asked me last week in Hawaii," Mei says, showing her the ring.

"It's gorgeous." Jess peers closer at it. "It seems like love is in the air lately." She shoots me a teasing look and I respond with a sharp warning glance that makes her bite back a chuckle.

"Can I?" Mei asks, reaching for Lucas. Jess hands him over and Mei settles him against her shoulder. Lucas's whimpers quiet almost immediately. "Hey, little man. You're not so tough, are you? All that crying and you just needed a new person to hold you."

"Show-off," Jess mutters. "He's been fussing for an hour with me."

"It's the fresh arms phenomenon," Mei explains, swaying him. "Babies always calm down for someone new. Give me ten minutes and he'll remember he's unhappy."

"Natural though," Jess observes. "Do you and Jun want kids?"

Mei gazes down at Lucas. "Yeah," she says. "We've talked about it. Maybe not right away but someday." She traces a finger along Lucas's cheek, and he grabs it with his fist, his crying completely forgotten now. "Look at these little fingers."

My phone pings with a message, and I glance down to see Diane's name on the screen. A grin spreads across my face as I pick up the phone to type a reply. When I look up again, Mei is studying me with an amused expression.

"You look giddy," she says, her eyebrows lifting. "What's got you smiling like that?" Heat rushes to my cheeks.

"Just a funny meme," I mumble, flipping my phone face-down on the coffee table a little too quickly. The smack of it hitting the glass makes Lucas jolt. His face scrunches up again in preparation for another crying session.

Mei quickly hands him back to Jess. "Okay, we can have more cuddles later, but I should probably get to work." She turns to me. "Your mom arrives today, right?"

"Yes, around three."

"I'll go check on her room right now. Make sure she has Coke and salted pretzels." Mei picks up her tablet and coffee. "And I'll coordinate with the front desk about her arrival. Do you want me to arrange a car to pick her up from the airport?"

"I already offered, but you know Mom. She insisted on taking a regular taxi. Said she's not some diva who needs a private car service."

"Of course she said that." Mei laughs. "Okay, I'll be back in an hour to take you to dress rehearsal. Please be showered and dressed by then?"

42

DIANE

*J*amie's sprawled in the chair next to mine in the business class lounge, one leg hooked over the armrest, flipping through a magazine she grabbed from the rack behind her. Thomas is at the bar ordering us drinks.

"Listen to this," she says, reading aloud. "'Ten essential oils to enhance your meditation practice.' Number seven is frankincense. Costs four hundred dollars an ounce." She looks up at me. "Four hundred dollars. For tree sap."

I snort, and Jamie grins before tossing the magazine on the table. She watches Thomas for a moment. "You know, when Thomas first told me about you, I was convinced you were going to be a problem."

The shift in conversation surprises me. "A problem?"

"Yeah." She glances at me. "I kept thinking about how you must look on paper. Senator's daughter, runs a foundation, probably went to some fancy school—all the boxes his parents have been trying to get him to check off since he could walk. Deep down, I was scared of losing him to you."

I smile and shake my head. "That is one thing I can honestly promise you will never happen."

"I know that now," she says. "I trust you."

Leaning in, I squeeze her hand briefly. I didn't realize how much I wanted her approval, her friendship even. "I trust you too. And thank you for this—for coming along."

Jamie gives me an amused look. "You're thanking *me*? You're thanking me for bringing me to Zara Nova's opening night in Vegas, front row seats, all expenses paid?"

"With a meet and greet," I add with a wink.

Jamie actually squeals—a sound I didn't think she was capable of making. "I still can't believe that's happening. Like, we're actually going to meet her. Talk to her. I don't even know what I'm going to say."

"You'll think of something," I assure her. "You're getting a master's degree in international politics. I'm sure you can handle a conversation with a musician."

"That's different," she protests. "I can debate foreign policy all day, but meeting someone I've admired for years? That's terrifying."

I take in the full sleeve of tattoos on her left arm—intricate designs that look like they tell a story. The multiple piercings in her ears, the edgy haircut. Her style is so different from the polished, conservative aesthetic of Thomas's world. "I didn't take you for a Zara Nova fan. You seem more—please forgive me for making assumptions—a heavy metal fan?"

Jamie laughs. "Yeah, I like heavy metal music. But Zara... That woman stands for everything I believe in. She's used her platform for actual good and I admire that. Do you know how rare that is?" She pauses, then adds with a mischievous smile, "Frankly, I'm surprised she even wants to be associated with you. No offense."

"None taken," I say, laughing along.

"Seriously though, thank you, Diane," she says. "These Vegas weekends are a real treat for me. I was gutted I couldn't come last time because of my exams. I had a paper due that week and I was drowning in research, but part of me wanted to say fuck it and come anyway."

"You made the right call. Missing one weekend in Vegas isn't the end of the world, but tanking a paper you worked that hard on would've been." I pause. "But Jamie, it's okay to let Thomas spoil you now and then. He knows you're not with him for the money."

Jamie sighs. "I know. But I'm a feminist, and I don't want to let a man bankroll my lifestyle. I've worked so hard to be financially independent, to get to where I am." She looks up at me. "My mom was completely dependent on my dad, and when he left, she had nothing. No job skills, no savings of her own. We had to move in with her sister and she worked double shifts at Walmart to get by. We were even in a shelter for a few months. I swore I'd never be in that position."

"That must have been hard," I say.

"Yeah. It was terrifying. I was sixteen, and suddenly everything I thought was stable just... collapsed. That's why I work so hard. It's why I'm stubborn about paying my own way. The idea of depending on someone else, even Thomas..." She trails off. "It feels wrong."

"Is it really about the money," I ask, "or is it about staying in control of your own life?"

"Maybe both? I don't know. It's complicated. But you know what? It's actually going really well between us, and I'm slowly starting to trust that this might be the real deal. That maybe letting him do nice things for me doesn't make me weak or dependent. That I can accept his generosity without losing myself."

"Thomas already thinks it is," I say. "The real deal, I mean. He's completely gone for you."

Jamie's cheeks flush, and I catch a glimpse of the softer side she usually keeps hidden. "He said that?"

"Thomas said what?" Thomas arrives with three champagne flutes and Jamie and I exchange quick glances.

"That Zara's music is awesome," Jamie says smoothly, accepting a glass from him.

"Obviously," Thomas agrees, settling into the chair opposite us. "So, Diane, do you have insider information about the show?"

"I don't know anything more than you do. But Zara mentioned she's added something new to the setlist. Something special that she's been working on."

"New material?" Jamie asks.

"I think so. She's been writing a lot lately."

"God, I still can't believe you know her," Jamie says, leaning forward. "Like, actually know her well enough that you hang out and she gives you front row tickets. How does that even happen? How the hell did you meet?"

"We met through a mutual friend," I say. "We hit it off, started talking, discovered we had more in common than expected."

"What could you possibly have in common with Zara Nova?" Thomas asks, not unkindly. "I mean, your worlds are completely opposite and I know that more than anyone because I live in your world."

He has no idea how right he is, or how wrong. Yes, our worlds are opposite in almost every way that matters publicly, but privately, we're both trapped in a life we can't escape.

"She's more than her public image," I say. "Underneath

all the fame, she's just a person, like me, trying to figure things out."

43

ZARA

"*Mija*," Mom says, wrapping me in her arms.

"Mom." I squeeze her tightly. "I missed you."

"Five months," she says, pulling back to look at me properly. Her hands grip my shoulders as she studies my face. "Five months since you came to visit."

As always, the guilt hits me. "I'm sorry. My schedule was—"

"I know, I know." She waves a hand. "You're busy. Famous. Important."

"Mom—"

"I'm teasing." She cups my face with both hands, and I notice the new lines around her eyes, the gray streaking through her dark hair more prominently than last time. "You look good though. My beautiful girl. How's that ankle?"

I'm barefoot, wearing the ratty NYU sweatshirt she bought me freshman year and I'm not wearing any makeup. I always dress down for Mom; it makes her happy. "It's good, Mom. All back to normal."

Jess joins us with Lucas and Mom squeals in pleasure.

"There you are! Finally I get to meet you!" She reaches for Lucas, who goes to her willingly. "Look how big you are already! And those teeth coming in—ay, Dios mío, you're going to be a heartbreaker."

"Hi, Isabella." Jess hugs her. "So good to see you again."

"You too, honey. How have you been? This one keeping you up at night?" Mom bounces Lucas, cooing at him, and he giggles.

"He's been vocal for sure," Jess confirms. "Teething is not for the weak. But Zara hired a nanny so I've been able to work which has been amazing."

"A nanny?" Mom turns to me. "Well, you can tell her not to come in while I'm here. I didn't fly all this way to sit around while someone else takes care of this little one."

I'm about to protest but she ignores me completely, making faces at Lucas. "Look at him—he already loves me more than anyone."

Jess and I settle on the couch and Mom sits in the armchair with Lucas. I pour Mom's Coke over ice how she likes it and grab a bag of salted pretzels, then pour a glass of red wine for myself and Jess.

"So you found your room okay?" I ask, handing Mom her drink.

Mom takes a long sip before responding. "Yes, the concierge took me there personally. And Zara, honey, that room was completely unnecessary. It's too much. People would pay months of rent for two weeks I'm staying there."

"It's free, Mom," I lie smoothly. "It's on the Olympus. They're sponsoring the residency, so they're covering every-thing. Just take it."

She gives me a look that says she knows I'm not being entirely truthful, but she doesn't push. "If you say so.

Though I'm not sure what I'm supposed to do with a bath that big. I could fit three of me in there."

"Enjoy it while it lasts," Jess says with a grin. "That's what I'm doing. The gym, the pool, the room service..." She looks up. "Gift from heaven."

Mom shakes her head, smiling. "You two. Living in a different world now." She settles Lucas more comfortably in her lap. "So, tell me everything. How's the show coming together? Are they treating you well? You eating enough?"

"The show is good. Really good, actually. We had final dress rehearsal this morning and it went smoothly." I take a sip of wine. "And yes, I'm eating. Probably too much, honestly."

"I doubt that. You could use a few more pounds." Mom eyes me critically. "You were too skinny on that last magazine cover. Bones showing." She huffs. "Fashion people. No sense."

Jess catches my eye. She's heard this rant before.

"How's the apartment?" I ask, redirecting. "Did you get that leak fixed? The one you insisted you didn't need my help with?"

"Finally. Took the landlord three weeks and me threatening to call the city, but yes, it's fixed." She breaks open the pretzel bag. "Mrs. Bellamy from 3B asked about you. Wanted to know when you're coming to visit."

"As soon as my residency ends." Another pang of guilt. "Until then, there's always a room for you here. You can stay as long as you want."

"That's nice but I prefer it when you come to me," she says. "This is your world. When you come to Brooklyn, you're just my daughter again." Lucas has fallen asleep in Mom's arms, his head resting against her shoulder.

"I'm still me, Mom."

"I know. But it's healthy to take breaks from all this glitz and glamour. To remind yourself that it's not normal. To eat Cocoa Puffs straight from the box and have coffee in your pajamas on the fire escape in the morning."

I nod, though the picture she's painting isn't quite accurate anymore. Even when I visit her in Brooklyn, there's at least one security detail stationed outside her building. I can have coffee on the fire escape, but my team needs to sweep the area first. I can chat with the neighbors, but they all treat me differently than they used to. The normal life she remembers me having disappeared years ago, but I don't have the heart to tell her that the gap between her world and mine has grown wider than she realizes.

"I met someone," I tell her. It's not an excuse to change the subject. I've been waiting to tell her in person.

Mom's eyebrows lift. "Oh?"

"It's new. Only a couple of months. But it's..." I trail off. "It's really good. I'm happy."

"That's wonderful, mija." Mom's expression softens. "What's his name?"

"Her name," I correct, gauging her reaction.

Mom doesn't react the way most mothers might. No shock, no concern, no questions about whether I'm sure. She just nods.

"Like Sofia," she says.

I smile. Sofia—the woman Mom dated briefly when I was in high school. I remember her clearly: warm laugh, kind eyes, the way she looked at my mother like she hung the moon. They were together for about eight months before Sofia moved to Seattle for work, and Mom still talks about her sometimes with this wistful fondness she never showed for my father.

"Yeah," I say. "Like Sofia."

"Tell me about her. Is it the woman from the articles? The one who took you to hospital?"

"Yes. Her name is Diane and she's beautiful and smart. Really smart. And funny in a dry way." I swirl the wine in my glass. "She's dealing with her own stuff and our situation is complicated, but when we're together it feels... easy. I can be myself with her."

"That's important," Mom says. "If she makes you happy that's all that matters. When can I meet her?"

"Tomorrow. She just landed in Vegas and she's spending the evening with friends so you and I can catch up but I invited her over for dinner tomorrow."

"Great. I'm looking forward to it." Mom shifts topics with the ease of someone who's said what needs saying. "Now tell me about this show. What should I wear? I brought that nice black dress, the one I wore to your Grammy party. Or is that too fancy?"

44

DIANE

"You're here," Zara breathes, and before I can respond, she throws her arms around my neck and kisses me deeply in the doorway.

I kiss her back instinctively, my body responding to her. But something makes me pull back—voices in the background. "Wait... Is that your mom? Does she know about us?"

"Yeah. I told her." Zara frowns. "You said it was okay, right?"

"Yes, of course." I take her hand and squeeze it. "It's your mom and your best friend. If you can't tell them..." Following Zara into the living area, I'm faced with two women, one holding a baby on her hip. They're both watching us curiously.

"Diane," Zara says, "I'd like you to meet Jess, my best friend, and this is my mom, Isabella. And this little guy is Lucas, my godson."

The blonde woman—Jess—steps forward with a grin that's equal parts mischievous and welcoming. "I'm so excited to meet you," she says, bouncing the baby. "Zara's been practically glowing since she started seeing you."

"It's lovely to meet you too," I manage, accepting her offered embrace while Lucas grabs my hair. "And you..." Inching back, I chuckle as I release my hair from his fist. "What a handsome little man you are."

Zara's mother approaches with a warm smile. She's smaller than I expected, probably in her early sixties, with silver-streaked hair pulled back in a practical bun. There's nothing flashy about her appearance—simple black pants, a white blouse, but she carries herself with quiet dignity.

"I'm Isabella," she says, hugging me. "Thank you for saving my daughter's life." She squeezes me hard. When she pulls back, her expression turns stern. "I'm still angry with her for keeping it from me until she was discharged from the hospital. Can you imagine? Finding out your daughter nearly died?" She takes my hand. "Please promise me you'll call me if anything like that ever happens again, okay? I'll give you my number before I leave. Someone needs to keep me informed since this one thinks she's protecting me by hiding things."

"Mom," Zara starts. "The doctor said I was going to be fine and I didn't want to worry you and—"

"No." Isabella holds up a hand. "You don't get to 'Mom' me on this. It's unacceptable and I'm having a word with Peter when I see him."

I have a feeling Peter is about to face the maternal reckoning of his life and I don't envy him one bit.

"Now, let's sit," Isabella says, patting my back. "The food is almost ready."

"It smells amazing," I say, glancing toward the kitchen where I can see pots on the stove. "Did you cook?" It hadn't occurred to me that anyone staying in a suite at the

Olympus would actually use the kitchen. The dining table has been laid out elegantly, set for four with fresh flowers and candles.

"Of course I cooked," Isabella says, as if the question itself is absurd. "Hotel prices are ridiculous; I don't care how wealthy my daughter is. Besides, room service never gets the seasoning right. Americans are afraid of flavor. Zara, come help me, will you? Jess, you pour the wine. I'll have a Coke."

"Can I help?" I ask.

"Absolutely not. You sit." Isabella points at the table with the same authoritative tone one might use to command a golden retriever. I find myself obeying before I've consciously decided to move.

Zara catches my eye and gives me an amused shrug as she follows her mother. "How are Thomas and Jamie?"

"They're great," I say, settling at the table next to Jess, who's opening a bottle of red. "All lovey-dovey, enjoying each other's company and super excited for tomorrow. Especially Jamie. She's been talking about it nonstop."

"Do they know?" Zara calls from the kitchen. "About us?"

"No, I haven't told anyone."

Zara returns with Isabella and they set down an impressive spread—salad, rice, beans, chorizo, and chicharrón, topped with fried eggs. "Maybe you should tell them," she says. "I told Jess and Mom so it's only fair that you can tell your friends. You trust them, right?"

"Yeah, I trust them." I consider this, taking a sip of the wine Jess hands me. "Maybe I will."

Isabella heads back to the kitchen to retrieve two more dishes—golden fried plantains and sliced avocado. She shakes her head. "All this sneaking around is silly if you ask me. So what if you're two women? What's the big deal? You love each other, you tell people. Simple. I was in a relationship with a woman when Zara was younger. That was the best time of my life."

"Really?" I can't help but laugh. "I wish my parents had your perspective."

"I know, right?" Jess chips in. "Zara is lucky to have such an open-minded mom. And Isabella doesn't sugarcoat anything. She tells it exactly how it is."

Isabella settles into her chair. "Well, it's true. Your parents are not the ones who have to live your life." She points her fork at me. "You only get one life, mija. Don't waste it."

"I'm trying not to do that anymore," I say as she plates for me. "How long will you be in Vegas?"

"Two weeks. It's the longest I've ever been away from home. I prefer my own apartment with my own things." She waves her hand dismissively at the opulent suite around us. "All this luxury is nice, but it's not for me. I like my small kitchen where I know where everything is, my neighbors, my routine. I told Zara I could sleep on the couch in her suite, but she insisted on putting me in my own fancy room."

"You deserve to be spoiled a little," Zara responds. "I want you to be comfortable."

Lucas babbles from his high chair, dropping pieces of his dinner onto the floor with obvious delight.

I take my first bite and the flavors are incredible—rich, well seasoned. Real, simple home-cooked food. "This is delicious, Isabella. Really amazing."

"See?" Isabella looks triumphantly at Zara. "Diane appreciates good cooking."

"I appreciate it too," Zara protests through a mouthful. "I miss your food."

"Then why do you always tell me not to cook when I visit?" Isabella demands. "You say 'Mom, don't worry about it, we'll order in,' and then when there's actual food on the table, you eat like you haven't seen a home-cooked meal in years."

"Because you're supposed to be relaxing, not working— ow!" Zara yelps as Isabella reaches over and pinches her bicep.

"Look at this arm. Skinny like a chicken wing. These should be the size of my thigh, at least. All that money for personal trainers and fancy gyms, and my daughter still looks like the wind could blow her away."

Zara swats her mother's hand away, laughing. "I'm a healthy weight, Mom. The doctor said so."

"Doctors." Isabella shakes her head. "What do they know? I'm your mother. I know when you need to eat more."

Zara shoots me a humorous grin that clearly says *I can't win with her.*

I watch the easy back-and-forth between them—the teasing, the obvious affection, the lack of pretense—and wonder what it would have been like growing up with a mother like Isabella. Less wealth, certainly, but also less performance. Just straightforward love without conditions or negotiations attached. My mother has never pinched my arm and told me to eat more.

45

ZARA

*T*he dressing room finally falls quiet after I dismiss the last of the makeup and costume team. I need a moment alone to ground myself, to find some calm in the storm of pre-show chaos. My hands won't stop shaking as I stare at my reflection in the mirror, watching my fingers tremble over the makeup brushes they've left behind.

The face looking back at me is prepared for stage—flawless foundation, dramatic eyes, lips painted in deep red—but underneath the artistry, panic is building like a storm.

I drop into a forward fold, letting my arms hang loose while I try to stretch out the knots between my shoulder blades. When I roll back up slowly, vertebra by vertebra, my throat still feels constricted, even after my vocal warm-up.

"Twenty minutes to places," comes the voice through the intercom.

I feel like I'm on a roller coaster. This shouldn't be happening. I've performed for stadium crowds, headlined festivals, sung for presidents and royalty. The Palestra holds only two and a half thousand people.

A knock interrupts my spiral. "Come in."

Athena enters, elegant as always in a white suit, carrying two crystal tumblers and a bottle of scotch. She pauses in the doorway, taking in my obvious distress.

"Am I interrupting?"

"No," I say, spotting the scotch. "I could do with some liquid courage."

She steps inside and closes the door behind her, setting everything down on the vanity beside my makeup kit. "You look like you're about to faint."

"I might." I press my palm to my stomach, where butterflies have transformed into something with claws. "I don't know what's wrong with me. This is just another show."

"Is it because Diane will be there?" Athena pours a small amount of scotch into each tumbler.

"I don't know." I take a sip, letting the warmth burn down my throat. The alcohol does help marginally with the trembling, though my heart is still hammering against my ribs. "What if they hate my new song?"

"Are you kidding me?" Athena settles into a chair. "When you sang 'Performers' for me, it brought a lump to my throat." She grins. "And you know I don't easily get emotional."

I pace the room. "The whole team thinks I've lost my mind for adding it in so late in the schedule."

"Have you?" She arches a brow. "Lost your mind?"

"Maybe." I laugh. "It's so—"

"I know. It's very personal." Athena's tone stops my movement.

"Yeah. What if I get too emotional? What if I can't make it through?"

"Then you take a breath and keep going. Emotion is beauty. Beauty is art." Athena downs her scotch and pours herself another. "You and Diane have something special."

Her dark eyes lock onto mine. "So show her what she means to you. She'll know, you'll know. That's all that matters." She steps closer and cups my cheek. "You're not nervous because the song is bad, Zara. You're nervous because you know it's good. And you're worried about what people will read into it."

The observation lands with uncomfortable accuracy. I take another sip of scotch.

"Here's the thing about truth," she continues. "Once you put it out there, you lose control of how people interpret it. That's what makes it scary. Not the exposure itself—the loss of control over the narrative."

"Exactly. What if someone figures it out?" The question I've been avoiding all week finally surfaces.

"Figures out that you wrote a love song?" Athena raises an eyebrow. "You've written dozens of love songs. That's literally your job."

"But what if Diane hears it and realizes—" I stop myself.

"Realizes that you're in love with her?" Athena shrugs. "Isn't that the point? Besides, I think she already knows that." She downs her scotch again and sets down the tumbler. "You know what matters tonight? Not what two thousand strangers think. Not what critics will write. Not even what ends up on social media. What matters is that when you sit at that piano, you're going to sing from the heart. And the woman you love is going to be in the front row, and she's going to hear it."

She heads for the door, then pauses. "Stop trying to control what people think. Do what you do best and enjoy it. Good luck, Zara."

She leaves just as Sarah comes in.

"You're on," Sarah says, running her gaze over me. "You good?"

I take one last look in the mirror, then turn to face her. "Yeah. I'm good."

"Great. Let's go make some magic." She holds the door open and I put in my earpiece as I follow her into the backstage area.

Dancers stretch in every available space, running through sequences one final time. The backup singers huddle near the piano and technical crew members take their place.

Sarah hands me my mic for the opening number.

"Sound check," the audio engineer calls through my earpiece. I sing a few bars of "Electric Nights" while technicians make final adjustments in the booth.

"Level," comes the voice in my ear. "You're ready."

Through a gap in the backdrop, I catch my first glimpse of the audience. Faces turned toward the stage, programs rustling like leaves, conversations gradually fading as the house lights begin their slow fade. In the front row, I spot the shapes I've been looking for—Mom in her black dress, Jess in the sparkling jumpsuit she borrowed from me, what I assume are Thomas and Jamie, and next to them, Diane.

Even from this distance, even in the growing darkness, she draws my attention like true north. She's wearing a midnight blue jumpsuit, her hair is pulled back and God, she's so beautiful.

Something shifts in my chest as I watch her lean over to say something to my mother, who laughs and touches her arm. Last night wasn't just dinner. It was Diane fitting into the spaces between the people I love most.

Maybe we can actually do this. Something that lasts beyond stolen weekends.

The house lights fade to black and the crowd roars.

"Places, everyone. This is places," Sarah calls.

Dancers take their positions in the wings, musicians settle at their instruments. Mo gives me an encouraging smile from his position stage right. The stage manager performs a final check—mic levels, earpiece.

The backdrop begins to rise, revealing the darkened stage. In thirty seconds, I'll step into a pool of light.

The music begins—a single piano note held in the darkness, soon joined by strings. The opening chord progression of "Electric Nights" builds slowly, giving the audience time to prepare for the journey I'm about to take them on.

I step onto the stage and the spotlight finds me. Then, adrenaline takes over and everything else disappears.

46

DIANE

*T*he entire theater erupts as Zara takes her final bow, over two thousand people on their feet in thunderous appreciation. The standing ovation rolls on and on, wave after wave of applause. I clap until my palms sting, my heart swelling with pride so intense it borders on painful.

She was magnificent. For ninety minutes, I watched her command that stage with a confidence and vulnerability I've never seen before. Every song felt like an intimate conversation between her and the audience. Her voice soared through ballads and drove hard through the dance numbers, never wavering, never faltering.

The opening number was amazing. "Electric Nights" with its pulsing beat and intricate choreography had the entire audience on their feet within the first thirty seconds. But it was the quieter moments that truly showcased her artistry. When she stripped down to just her voice and a single spotlight, everyone held their breath.

"Holy shit," Jamie gushes beside me. "She's incredible. I

mean, I knew she was talented from her albums, but seeing her live—that was something else entirely."

"Transcendent," Thomas finishes, shaking his head in amazement. "She made it feel like she was singing directly to each person in the audience. How does she do that?"

I nod, glowing as I watch Zara in her element. Seeing her joy and power and artistry on full display has left me emotionally overwhelmed.

Zara straightens from her bow and scans the audience, her smile radiant under the stage lights. When her eyes find mine in the front row, that smile becomes something more personal, more intimate. She looks directly at me for a moment that feels suspended in time.

Without thinking, I blow her a kiss. The gesture is small, barely noticeable in the chaos of applause, but Zara catches it and responds with a subtle wink.

The applause begins to fade as Zara and her dancers take one final bow together. The backup singers join them center stage, all of them beaming with the satisfaction of a flawless show. Her lead dancer pulls her into a quick hug before gesturing for her to take a solo bow. The audience responds with renewed enthusiasm.

I expect the house lights to come up now, for the audience to begin the slow shuffle toward exits, but instead Zara holds up a hand. The theater falls silent with surprising speed, that kind of attentive quiet that happens when an audience senses something special is about to occur.

Zara dismisses her dancers with hugs and thanks, sending them into the wings. The backup singers follow, each of them stopping to kiss her cheek or squeeze her hand before disappearing. Soon she's alone on the vast stage, looking smaller without the energy of the full production surrounding her.

She kicks off her heels and walks to the grand piano positioned stage left. When she settles onto the bench and adjusts her position, I feel a flutter of anticipation. For the first time since she stepped on stage, Zara looks nervous. She takes a deep breath, her hands hovering over the keys for a moment before she looks up at the audience.

"If you can put up with me for another five minutes," she jokes, "this is a new song. I hope you like it."

She begins with a simple chord progression and when she starts to sing, the lyrics wash over me with the force of recognition. This is about us.

The specificity of the details makes my skin flush hot. Anyone could interpret these as metaphors about hidden relationships, but I know exactly which moments inspired each line and tears begin to roll down my cheeks as the full meaning of the song becomes clear.

The audience is completely silent, hanging on every word. Even without knowing the personal context, they can sense the raw honesty in her performance. Zara has stripped away every layer of protection and offered her truth to a room full of strangers.

I'm vaguely aware of Thomas staring at me, probably because I'm crying. But I can't focus on his reaction, can't think about anything except Zara's voice filling this space with our story.

The melody builds as she moves into the bridge, her voice growing stronger with each line. I can see her confidence returning as she loses herself in the song, as the initial nervousness gives way to the power of the music itself.

Desert winds can't cool the fire you ignite. In the stolen hours we escape the light. I've sung of love forever but never felt it burn. Until you taught my heart how to return

When she sings the next lines, her eyes find mine across the darkened theater, and I feel like she's speaking directly to me:

I love you. That's the truth I can't deny. Though loving you means learning how to lie.

My hands are shaking as I grip the armrests of my seat. She loves me.

Zara's voice breaks and she's barely holding it together as the song continues. I wasn't prepared for this—for the enormity of being loved so publicly while remaining invisible. For a confession on stage. I want to climb onto that stage and take her in my arms, tell her that I love her too as a hand finds mine in the darkness.

Isabella's fingers, warm and steady, lace through my own. She doesn't look at me, keeps her eyes on her daughter at the piano, but the squeeze she gives me says everything. *I know.*

Both of us performers in our different ways. You smile through the small talk, I live on the stage. You speak their language I wear their disguise.

The accuracy is almost unbearable as Zara blinks tears.

But when alone, our performance dies.

The last note hangs in the air, Zara's hands still on the keys. The silence that follows is absolute and sacred. Nobody moves. Nobody breathes.

Then the applause and cheering begins again. Reverent. The sound of the crowd acknowledging they've just witnessed something rare.

Isabella releases my hand to stand and clap, and I follow, my legs unsteady. Thomas, Jamie, and Jess are on their feet too, though Thomas is staring at me instead of Zara. Questions, probably. Realizations, maybe.

But I can't think about that now. Can't think about

anything except Zara taking her bow, her eyes locked with mine. She wipes away a tear and smiles at me.

I press my palm to my chest, to the place where my heart is doing wild things. This is real, messy, and terrifying. She's brave, and she makes me want to be brave too.

The lights begin their fade to black but even in the darkness, I can still feel her. And I've never felt closer to anyone.

47

ZARA

I sink into the plush velvet couch in my dressing room, my legs finally giving out after carrying me through my performance and one devastating encore. The door is locked—I made sure of that before collapsing here. My team knows better than to interrupt when I need five minutes of solitude after a show, especially one like tonight.

The dressing room feels like a cocoon after the vastness of the stage. Mei has placed flowers from well-wishers on every available surface and the air is thick with their competing fragrances, sweet and cloying in the aftermath of my emotional breakdown.

I reach for the bottle of whiskey Athena left on the coffee table and pour myself a generous measure. I take a sip, lean back against the cushions, and blow out my cheeks, letting the alcohol work its way through my system.

Tonight went well until the encore. Until I sat down at that piano and opened my chest for everyone to see inside. I've never broken down during a concert. I've been emotional; that's to be expected when thousands of people give you a standing ovation. But crying to the point that I'm having trouble singing? Never. The audience loved that song. I could feel it in the silence that followed, in the quality of their applause.

The moment plays back in my mind like a film loop I can't turn off. Have I done the right thing? Did I scare Diane? Was it too much?

The whiskey is helping, warming my blood and slowing the frantic pace of my thoughts. I pour another small measure, not enough to impair me but sufficient to take the edge off the emotional whiplash.

A soft knock interrupts my spiral of thoughts. "Zara? It's Peter."

I walk to the door to unlock it, and Peter steps inside, taking in my disheveled appearance.

He immediately pulls me into a long hug, the kind that says more than words ever could. His embrace is tight and for a moment, I let myself be held by him.

"That was extraordinary," he says when he finally releases me, moving his hands to my shoulders. "I've never seen you perform like that, Z. The entire show was flawless, but that encore... I understand now why you insisted on adding it."

His approval means more than any critic's review. Peter has seen me at my best and worst, has witnessed every creative breakthrough and professional crisis. When he says something was extraordinary, he means it.

"The audience was completely captivated," he continues. "During the song, you could have heard a pin drop. And the response afterward—I've never seen anything quite like it. Everyone was crying. Even *I* was crying."

He pauses to remove his glasses and cleans them with the cloth from his pocket. "Are you okay?"

"Yeah." I smile and nod, though I'm not entirely sure it's

true. The adrenaline is fading, leaving behind a strange mixture of elation and exhaustion.

Peter replaces his glasses and studies me. "That song," he says finally. "It's very..." He trails off, searching for the right word. "Specific. Was it Diane? Did she inspire all of this?"

I could deflect, laugh it off. But after what I did on that stage, lying feels ridiculous, especially to Peter.

"Yes," I say simply.

Peter nods. "How long?"

"A few months. Since I got here, really. I couldn't tell you. It's complicated, Peter. Not just for my career but for Diane too."

"I know it's complicated." He turns to face me. "But Zara, I've spent ten years protecting you. Building your brand, managing your image, making sure every public relationship fit the narrative we created. And I've watched you be lonely through most of it."

I blink, surprised by his bluntness.

"Look, we'll have to navigate this if it becomes public. But it won't destroy your career." He shakes his head. "You deserve to be happy and if Diane makes you happy, then we'll figure out the rest."

Staring at him, relief washes through me. "Thank you." I pull him into another long, sweaty hug. His arms tighten around me and his chin rests briefly on top of my head. When we pull apart, I see his eyes are a little teary behind his glasses.

"I didn't think you'd be so chilled about this," I say quietly. "You know... sponsors and all that."

Peter's eyebrows lift. "You think I became a manager to make money? That's a slim chance and I got lucky with you. No. I became your manager because I love music. And tonight, you were truly amazing."

My throat tightens. "I've never heard you talk like this."

"Well, we're also friends, aren't we? Or at least, I hope we are."

"We are," I say, and mean it. "I'm sorry I didn't trust you with this sooner."

"Don't apologize. It's your business." He stands and buries his hands in his pockets. "Do you need some alone time?"

"No, I'm fine now. Are my mom, Diane, and Jess backstage? And Diane's friends—are they on the VIP list?" I ask.

"Yes, Mei just picked them up. They're on their way down now." Peter glances at the whiskey bottle and I chuckle, handing him Athena's tumbler. I suspect he might need a drink too. "Help yourself."

Another knock, and the door opens to reveal my mother, her face radiant.

"Mija," she says, her accent thicker than usual the way it gets when she's emotional. "You were incredible. I have never been more proud of you."

The tears in her eyes threaten to start mine flowing again. Mom has seen me perform hundreds of times, but tonight there's a recognition that what she witnessed was more than entertainment.

"Thank you, Mom."

"I wouldn't have missed it for the world." She reaches up to smooth a strand of hair away from my face. "That song at the end—it was beautiful. So beautiful and brave."

Jess appears behind her to hug me, and Mei materializes shortly after, congratulating me and organizing more vases for the flowers Mom and Jess have brought. Then I see Diane in the doorway, and the room full of people might as well be empty.

Her makeup has run in dark streaks down her cheeks

and as our eyes meet, I watch her face open. Not a smile, not tears, just this complete unguarding. Like every wall she's ever built has been dismantled.

I can't move. My legs are still trembling from the performance, from breaking down at that piano, from singing words I've never admitted aloud.

She takes one step forward, then another, and I see her hands shaking. She's usually so composed, but right now she looks like she's been turned inside out.

When she reaches me, her mouth opens like she's going to say something, but nothing comes out. I watch her throat work as she swallows, watch her eyes fill with fresh tears that she doesn't bother to hide.

She wraps her arms around me, holding me tighter than she ever has. Her body melts against mine, and when she whispers, "I love you too", everything settles into place and I'm finally calm.

48

DIANE

*T*he dinner table in Zara's suite would give my mother an aneurism. Chinese takeout containers crowd the surface—lo mein noodles spilling from cardboard boxes, sweet and sour chicken glistening under the crystal chandelier, spring rolls scattered beside shrimp and broccoli. It's past midnight, and the mismatched elegance of expensive furnishings hosting cheap food feels oddly perfect.

Zara and Jess are both wearing silk robes, their hair still damp. Zara picks at her broccoli with chopsticks, occasionally feeding bites to Lucas, who has woken up and sits in Jess's lap making appreciative baby noises.

I sit beside Zara and Isabella occupies the chair to the other side of her daughter. She's traded her dress for comfortable clothes—leggings and a sweatshirt.

Thomas and Jamie sit across from me, still appearing somewhat dazed by their surroundings. When I suggested they join us for dinner, I doubt they expected to end up in Zara Nova's private suite sharing takeout with her inner circle. Thomas keeps glancing around the space while Jamie seems torn between starstruck wonder and the natural ease that comes with good wine and food and casual conversation.

Peter holds court at one head of the table, his shirt wrinkled now, tie loosened, sleeves rolled up while he entertains us with bloopers from Zara's career, and Mei is seated at the other end.

The contrast with my family dinners is stark. Where Washington meals serve as venues for strategic and social reasons, this feels genuinely nourishing. People speak without hidden agendas, laugh without measuring the appropriateness of their responses, exist without performing for anyone's benefit.

Thomas catches my eye and raises his eyebrows slightly, a silent question about what he's witnessing between Zara and me. Throughout the evening, I've noticed him and Jamie exchanging glances, clearly puzzling over dynamics they're observing.

The signs must be fairly obvious. The way Zara's fingers brush mine when passing dishes, how we sit closer than typical friends, the comfortable way we anticipate each other's needs.

"That encore," Thomas says. "It was beautiful. Will it be on your next album?"

"I hope so," Zara replies, her hand finding mine under the table. "It's part of new material I've been developing. I've been feeling inspired lately." She looks at me and I'm unable to wipe the wide grin from my face as she leans in to whisper in my ear, "Let's tell them. Peter knows, and I want Mei to know too if you're okay with that."

It's time, I decide. I'm happy tonight, and I want to share my happiness. "Can you keep a secret?" I ask, looking between Thomas, Jamie, and Mei, who I only met for the first time tonight.

Thomas nods. "Of course. What's going on?"

Jamie leans forward slightly, her earlier starstruck wonder replaced with genuine concern. "Sure. Are you okay?"

Mei nods, but the way she looks at Zara makes me think she's already figured it out.

"I'm fine. Better than fine, actually." I take a breath. "I just hate lying to you and so I wanted to tell you that Zara and I have been dating."

Exhaling, I watch the information land. Thomas's mouth opens, closes, then opens again. Jamie's wine glass stops halfway to her lips, suspended in mid-air as her eyes widen.

"Wait," Thomas says finally. "When you said you were seeing someone in Vegas, you meant—" He gestures between Zara and me, his hand moving back and forth. "You meant Zara. Zara Nova. You've been dating Zara Nova."

"Yes," I say simply.

Jamie lets out a breathless laugh that's half disbelief, half delight. "Holy shit. I mean—sorry, I—" She looks at Thomas, then back at me. "We kind of suspected something was going on between you two tonight. The way you were looking at each other during that encore, but I thought maybe I was reading too much into it because I wanted it to be true, you know? Like, representation and all that." She's talking faster now. "But actually dating? Like, for real dating?"

"For real dating," Zara confirms, leaning into me.

Mei clears her throat from the end of the table. "Okay, I definitely did not see this coming." She blinks slowly, processing, her mouth slightly open like someone just told her gravity works backwards on Tuesdays. "I mean, I knew something was different when I got back. You had this glow about you, kept smiling at your phone, seemed weirdly excited about being in Vegas." She shakes her head. "I thought maybe you'd finally found a good therapist or started meditating or something. But this? Clearly I missed all the interesting developments while I was away."

Zara shrugs with a sheepish smile. "Well... surprise?"

"Surprise is an understatement," Mei says. "Though now that new song makes a lot more sense."

Thomas runs both hands through his hair. "This is... wow. Diane, I had no idea you were—I mean, I never would have guessed you were—"

"Gay?" I finish for him.

"Yeah. Does your family know?"

"No. And they can't, for obvious reasons. Which is why I'm asking for your discretion."

"Of course," Thomas says immediately. "We won't say anything." He glances at Jamie, who nods vigorously.

"Not a word," Jamie confirms. "I swear. But—" She turns her attention to Zara. "I don't understand why you would trust us with this. You don't know us at all."

"Diane trusts you," Zara replies. "That's enough for me so please keep this quiet until we've figured out what we're doing next. We're still navigating this ourselves." She smiles and adds with a wink, "Until then, I'm sure I'll see you both around, so I'm looking forward to getting to know the people helping Diane maintain her double life. Any tips on how to keep her parents off the scent would be greatly appreciated."

Thomas laughs, some of the tension breaking. "Well, our current strategy seems to be working. Though I have to say, this explains a lot about Diane's eternal singleton status."

"What? They call me a spinster already?" I joke. "Don't even answer that; I have a suspicion some do. And thank you, Thomas. You have no idea how much pressure you've taken off me. My mother thinks I'm finally settling down with an appropriate man. Meanwhile, I'm—" I gesture toward Zara.

"Settling down with a completely inappropriate woman," Zara finishes with a laugh.

Isabella snorts into her wine. "My daughter, always making the simple choice."

Lucas reaches for my wine glass, and I gently redirect his chubby fingers toward a piece of banana Jess has chopped up instead. He looks at me with serious dark eyes, as if considering whether this substitution is acceptable, then breaks into a gummy grin that makes everyone at the table laugh.

"I can't believe this is real," Jamie says, shaking her head. "Like, I'm sitting here eating Chinese food with Zara Nova, who's dating my boyfriend's fake girlfriend. This is officially the weirdest night of my life."

"Get used to it," Jess says jokingly from across the table. "Everything about Zara's life is weird and wonderful."

"I don't think I'll ever get used to it," Jamie admits. "But I'm honored you trust us, both of you. And Diane—" She meets my eyes. "I'm really happy for you. You deserve this."

49

ZARA

*E*NTERTAINMENT WEEKLY EXCLUSIVE
Zara Nova's Vegas Residency Opens with Stunning Performance—And a Tearful Encore That Has Everyone Talking

By Darius Clarke

LAS VEGAS — Zara Nova's residency at the Olympus Casino launched Friday night to a sold-out crowd, delivering a spectacular 90-minute show that showcased why she's one of pop's biggest stars. But it was the encore that stole the night.

After dismissing her dancers and band, Nova sat alone at a grand piano and performed an unreleased ballad titled "Performers." The stripped-down track left both Nova and much of the audience visibly emotional.

By Sunday, #Performers was trending worldwide. Fans have been dissecting the lyrics, which deal with hidden relationships and the tension between public image and private truth.

Amateur footage shows Nova appearing to direct the performance toward someone in the front row. Among the VIP attendees was Diane Washington, daughter of Virginia Senator Richard Washington and executive director of the Washington Foundation. Washington was photographed with Nova at a Las Vegas hospital last month after the singer suffered a scorpion sting during a desert excursion.

Nova, who has previously been linked to actors and musicians including Jake Morrison and indie rocker Dean Phillips, could barely finish the song without breaking down. The combination of the song's intimate lyrics and the captured moment between Nova and Washington has sparked speculation on social media about whether their relationship extends beyond friendship.

Representatives for Nova declined to comment on the song's inspiration, but her management confirmed it will appear on her upcoming album and represents "exciting new creative territory" for the artist.

I stare at the tablet screen until the words blur together, then set it down on the coffee table like it might explode. The entertainment blog headline sits there mocking me, accompanied by a photo that captured the exact moment I locked eyes with Diane during "Performers."

Peter sits across from me in my suite's living room. He arrived twenty minutes ago with what I hoped would be a celebratory stack of Monday reviews from opening night—glowing write-ups in Variety, Rolling Stone, and The New York Times that should have been the focus of our morning meeting. The reviews were glowing indeed, but instead of riding the high, we're dealing with this.

Diane and I spent all of Sunday in bed—ignoring the world, ordering room service, existing in our own bubble. No phones, no social media, just us. After she left for the airport this morning, I finally turned my phone back on to find seventeen missed calls from Peter and a string of increasingly urgent texts. I knew something was wrong before I even opened the first one.

"When was this published?" I ask.

"Saturday. It's been shared over half a million times since then." Peter's voice carries an undercurrent of concern that tells me he's worried this won't be the end of it. "Three more entertainment blogs have picked up the story, and I've had calls from TMZ, People, and Entertainment Tonight."

I rub my face with both hands, pressing my palms against my closed eyes until I see stars. The pressure helps momentarily, then reality crashes back with full force. "Okay... what do we do? Can I get away with ignoring it altogether?"

"I doubt it. They won't let this go." Peter shrugs. "Honestly, I'm not surprised. It was pretty obvious to me."

"Fuck." I think about Diane, who's probably read it too by now, and I feel sick with guilt. This is my fault. I brought this upon us.

"What do you want to do?" Peter asks. "Even if you don't comment or make a statement, you're going to get questions in interviews. It's a matter of time."

I stand and walk to the windows. The view from up here usually calms me, but today it feels like looking down from a precipice.

"I don't know," I admit, my breath fogging the glass. "I need to speak to Diane."

"Yes, you do," he says. "Whatever decision you make now will have consequences, so I suggest you discuss this together before either of you speaks to the press. I'll postpone that interview with Billboard today, and meanwhile, you talk to Diane."

The practical nature of his response steadies me slightly.

This is Peter at his best—not panicking, not making assumptions, just creating space for me to figure out what I actually want rather than simply reacting to circumstances.

"We should probably deny it," I say, the words coming out automatically. It's the obvious response, the safe one. The entertainment industry playbook for this situation is well-established: issue a statement clarifying that we're just friends, maybe make a joke about media speculation, move on.

"That would be the obvious thing to do," Peter agrees, settling into one of the armchairs near the window. "But honestly? For you, it wouldn't be as much of a scandal as it would be for Diane. Your fans will probably accept it—they might even embrace it. You've been an ally for years, so coming out would feel authentic to your brand. But Diane..." He shakes his head. "Her world may not be as forgiving as yours."

"So denial makes sense," I say, though something inside me rebels against the idea.

"It might work for a while," Peter continues. "But not forever. And you can't hide forever, Zara. No one can."

I think about last night, about the courage it took to sing "Performers," about the way it felt to finally put myself out there. My audience responded to that honesty, felt the truth in my song.

"Diane's not ready for that," I say. "Her whole life would implode."

"Perhaps." Peter follows my gaze out of the window. "But you pay me to represent you, not Diane. I've watched you struggle with this for years. The secrecy, the isolation, the way you've had to compartmentalize everything. And for you, this could be an opportunity rather than a crisis. Please keep that in mind."

I turn to stare at him. In all our years working together, we've never had this conversation directly. "You knew I was into women?"

"I had my suspicions," he says. "Little things over the years—the way you talked about certain people, relationships that never quite rang true, the distance you kept from anyone who got too close. I notice things."

"Why didn't you say something?"

"Why didn't you?" He turns the question back on me. "You know you can talk to me about anything."

"I didn't see the point. There was never anyone special in my life and I wasn't sure..." I pause. "I needed to explore this part of myself." Returning to the couch, I pick up the tablet again, scrolling through the comments under the article. They range from supportive speculation to harsh criticism about publicity stunts. The internet has already decided we're either deeply in love or that I'm faking my sexuality for career advancement.

"Listen to this," I say, reading aloud. "'Classic publicity stunt. Pop star dates conservative politician's daughter right before her Vegas residency. So transparent.' Or this one: 'Finally! We all knew Zara was gay. About time she stopped pretending.'"

"People will have opinions regardless of what you do," Peter says. "The question is whether you want to live your life according to those opinions or despite them. That counts for both of you."

I read the comments section and it's a digital battlefield of speculation and judgment. Fans and haters dissecting the few photos of me and Diane, trying to piece together a timeline.

"If you decide to deny the relationship, we need a statement soon, before this gains more traction," Peter says.

"Something that clarifies your friendship with Diane while shutting down romantic speculation."

"And if we don't deny it?"

"Then we need a different strategy entirely. We'd have to control the narrative, choose how and when to confirm the relationship rather than letting speculation run wild. An interview with someone sympathetic, where you can tell your story on your terms."

He sighs, thinking through the implications. "We need to prepare for backlash—both political and cultural. Some of your fans will be thrilled, others will feel betrayed or confused. Conservative media will have a field day with the political angle. Liberal media will want to know how you reconcile being with someone from that family."

I nod. This isn't about my comfort level—it's about Diane's future. Coming out isn't just a personal choice when you're the daughter of a conservative senator. It's a political minefield.

"There's something else to consider," Peter adds. "If you deny this now and your relationship continues, there will be more opportunities for exposure. Paparazzi will be watching more closely, looking for any sign that contradicts your statement. Eventually, the truth tends to come out anyway."

"I know." I think about the constant vigilance required to maintain a lie, the way it would poison even private moments with the fear of discovery.

"I'll leave you to call Diane and think about this." Peter stands, straightening his jacket. "Let me know what you decide."

50

DIANE

I'm nearly out of breath by the time I slip into the conference room twenty minutes late.

"I'm so sorry," I say, setting my purse down. "My flight was delayed. I came straight from the airport."

No one responds. Margaret Henley examines her nails. Others clear their throats and shuffle papers. David McGourty, who usually greets me with questions about my weekend, won't meet my eyes. My father, who occupies his position at the head of the table, gives me a brief nod.

"Is everything okay?" I glance around. "What did I miss?"

Dad's jaw tightens, and he exchanges a look with Margaret. "I suppose you haven't seen what's been circulating online over the weekend?"

My stomach drops. "No, I've been traveling. I went to that concert in Vegas, remember? Why? What's going on?"

Without a word, Dad slides his phone across the table surface. The screen shows an entertainment blog article with a headline that makes me gasp: *Zara Nova's Mystery Woman: More Than Just a Friend?*

"What... How?" My heart pounds so hard I can hear it in my ears, and sweat breaks out across my forehead.

"That's just one of the many articles," Dad says.

"Fuck," I mutter. "Fuck, fuck, fuck."

Margaret Henley's eyebrows shoot up at my language, but Dad ignores my cursing. "I've already explained to the board that my daughter is not of that persuasion," he says. "That you are, in fact, dating Thomas Cunningham. However, given the speculation, we feel it's necessary that you make a public statement immediately and cut all ties with Miss Nova. We cannot have our donors—or voters—thinking you might be..."

I look around the room, taking in the faces of people I've known since childhood. Margaret Henley, who used to give me candy when I was little, now regards me with suspicious concern. Robert Cunningham studies his hands, clearly uncomfortable with the entire situation. Board member Patricia Mills, who has always been kind to me, looks at me like I'm a stranger.

"Look, I know this might be inconvenient right now, but I'm not going to cut ties with a friend because of a few articles. What kind of nonsense is that?"

"I'm afraid it's non-negotiable, Diane." Dad taps the table. "This foundation represents traditional family values. We cannot afford any association that might suggest otherwise."

The room feels like it's closing in on me. These people have known me my entire life and they're treating me like a liability to be managed.

"Your father is right. The Washington Foundation has a reputation to maintain," Margaret adds. "Perception matters in our world, dear. Surely you understand that."

"What I understand," I say, "is that you're asking me to abandon a friendship because of gossip and speculation."

"It's much bigger than that," Robert Cunningham interjects, speaking for the first time since I arrived. "It's about the foundation's mission and your father's political future. This kind of controversy affects others, including my son. He's not picking up his phone; I imagine he's upset."

What Robert doesn't know is that Thomas and Jamie decided to stay in Vegas for another night. He's not sitting around moping because of that article. He's having fun with Jamie. His real girlfriend. The woman he loves.

Board member James Harrison, who owns the largest construction company in the state, nods in agreement. "We've already had three major donors call this morning asking about the article. They're concerned."

I huff. These same donors have no problem with the foundation's male board members having affairs or drinking problems, but the suggestion that I might be gay sends them into panic mode.

"So what exactly are you proposing?" I ask, though I'm not sure I want to hear the answer.

Dad pulls out a prepared statement from his briefcase and hands it to me. "A simple clarification. You'll state that Miss Nova is a vague acquaintance whose life you helped save, nothing more. You'll confirm your relationship with Thomas Cunningham and express disappointment that a charitable act has been misconstrued by the media. And, of course, you are never to be seen with Miss Nova again."

I scan the statement, noting the careful language. The urge to throw it back in Dad's face is overwhelming but I hold back. "And if I refuse?"

Dad's expression doesn't change, but something shifts in

his eyes—a hardness I've seen on a few occasions. He's never directed it at me.

"Then we'll have to reconsider your position here," Margaret says quietly. The threat is delivered with polite gentleness, but it's a threat nonetheless.

"I see." I push the statement away.

"We're simply asking you to clarify a misunderstanding," Dad says. "Nothing more."

But it's much more than that. This is the moment I've feared my entire adult life—being forced to choose between authenticity and family, between truth and security. The balance I've created is crumbling, and there's no middle ground left to occupy.

I think about Zara, probably sitting in her Vegas suite right now, dealing with her own version of this crisis. I think about that song, the courage it took to sing something so personal. I think about the way she looked at me, like I was the only person in the world who mattered.

Then I look around the conference room and know I have to choose. And whatever I decide, it's all or nothing.

My phone buzzes with a text from Zara: *Call me when you can. We need to talk.*

All or nothing. A little voice in the back of my mind tells me to think before I say something I'll regret but that voice sounds suspiciously like my mother's so I push it away. I get up, leaving the statement on the table. "Fire me, I don't care," I say. "I can't do this anymore."

51

ZARA

"Have you read all the articles?" I ask, watching Diane's face on my screen.

She sighs. "I read a few but I stopped once I realized some blogs have started referring to me as the Capitol Hill Closet Case."

"You're joking."

"I wish I were." She shakes her head. "And apparently they've decided I'm the villain in this story."

"That's ridiculous."

"That's the internet." She glances out the taxi window. "At least they're creative, I guess."

She looks down, her eyes narrowing. "My mother is calling me again." Her thumb moves across the screen. "And again." She stabs at her phone repeatedly. "She won't stop."

"Maybe you should—"

"No. Not right now."

Despite everything, Diane is oddly calm on our video call. I'd expected panic when she finally called, the kind of meltdown that comes with having your private life splashed across entertainment blogs without warning. Instead, she looks and sounds composed, almost resigned, like she's been preparing for this moment longer than I have.

"And you went to work this morning?" I ask.

"Briefly. I walked out after ten minutes." She sighs. "They cornered me in a board meeting. Wanted me to issue a statement denying everything, clarifying that you're just a 'vague acquaintance.'" She lets out a bitter laugh. "And they told me I couldn't see you anymore. Like I'm sixteen and they're grounding me for missing curfew. Like I don't have agency over my own life. I'm an adult for God's sake."

My stomach twists. "Diane—"

"So I walked out," she continues. "Told them to do whatever they felt they needed to do."

"Wait, you just—" I stand up from the couch and walk to the terrace doors, needing to move. "Diane, please don't do anything you'll regret. I don't want to be the reason you blow up your entire life."

"You're not the reason," she says firmly. "They are. This whole system is. I've been complicit in it for too long, and I'm done."

Through the glass, I see Mom and Jess in the pool with Lucas. My mother doesn't understand how complex this is. She even rolled her eyes when I told her about the articles and mumbled something about people having nothing better to do than gossip. But those very people can make or break careers. "But your job, your family..." Diane shifts and opens the window. "Where are you heading?" I ask.

"I'm going home for now and after that..." She hesitates. "Well, frankly I have no idea what happens next. But that's okay. I'm okay. I'm keeping it together. How are you?"

"I'm coping." I turn and pace the length of my suite's living room. "Peter will do his best to manage the situation, but he needs to know where we stand."

"Of course," she says. "What do you want? Tell me honestly what *you* want, Zara."

The question stops my pacing mid-stride and the answer comes without hesitation.

"In an ideal world, I want to be myself," I say. "I want to live authentically, to be honest about who I love. So much has changed lately and I'm not sure I can go back. I don't want to go back." I pause, gathering my thoughts. "I'm proud to be with you, Diane."

Diane smiles. "I feel proud to be with you too." She takes a moment to look at me. "God, you're so beautiful."

"You're beautiful. You're... amazing. You're everything." I return her smile. "Look, I know I can do this, but I don't expect you to be on board. I understand your position, and you'll never get any judgment from me for not wanting to come out. We'll have to keep some distance for a while."

"Thank you," Diane says quietly. "But I don't want to stop seeing you. Not for a few months until this blows over, not ever." She shifts the phone, and I catch a glimpse of George-town architecture sliding past the taxi window. When she looks back at the screen, her jaw is set. "My whole life, I've been making choices based on what other people need from me," she says. "What my father needs for his career. What my mother needs to make her look good for her friends..." She touches her finger to the screen, tracing where my image must be on her end. "And then I met you, and for the first time I made a choice just because it felt right."

The taxi makes a turn and she braces herself against the movement, but her eyes don't leave mine. "So no, I'm not going to hide. Not anymore."

My pulse hammers in my throat. Diane, my love, has just told me she's done hiding. Through the window, I see Mom lifting Lucas above the water while he squeals with delight, and the normalcy of it—the simple joy—calms me. Everything is about to change. Not only for me, but for both of us. We're stepping into a version of our lives we've only imagined in private moments.

Diane gives the driver directions and turns back to me. "Give me twenty-four hours," she says. "To get my head straight, to think through all the implications clearly. If we're going to do this—really do this—I need to talk to my family first. They should hear it from me before they read it in a statement or press release."

"Okay." I'm buzzing with adrenaline, still trying to fathom that this might actually happen. "Take your time."

I sink onto the couch, processing what she's just said. Two months ago, this conversation would have been unthinkable. Two months ago, I was dreading my first date with a woman.

"When did we get so brave?" I ask.

"I don't think we did," Diane says. "I think we just got tired of being afraid."

52

DIANE

*M*y key slides into the lock of my parents' front door and a strange sense of detachment settles over me. It's like I'm floating outside my own body, watching myself go through the motions of what might be the last normal moment I have with my family. The sensation isn't alarming—it's more like the eerie stillness that comes before a thunderstorm, when the air pressure drops and everything goes quiet.

"Hi," I say, standing in the doorway of the living room where my parents sit in their usual chairs, both with a scotch in hand.

They look up at me. Mom's face is composed, but her knuckles are white where she grips her glass, and Dad's jaw is set in a rigid line.

I pour myself a measure of scotch from the decanter on the side table and down it, then pour myself another one.

"Okay, we need to talk," I say, settling into the chair across from them.

The color drains from Mom's face.

"We certainly do," Dad says. Unlike Mom, his face turns

red. "That was uncalled for, storming out of the meeting yesterday. The board was trying to help you, work with you to resolve this, and you embarrassed all of us."

Mom doesn't say anything. "Is it true?" she asks finally. "It's not, is it? It can't be true. You and Thomas looked so happy together. I saw how you smiled at each other."

My heart pounds as I look at these two people who raised me, who've shaped every aspect of my life for thirty years. In this moment, I feel simultaneously like their little girl and like a stranger about to shatter their world.

"Yes," I say. One syllable. Such enormous consequences. "Yes, it's true. Zara and I are together. I love her and she loves me."

Mom makes a weird sound, her hand flying to her stomach as if she's about to be sick. "But—" she starts, then stops, her mouth opening and closing without words.

"Yes, I'm gay," I repeat. "I always have been. I just couldn't tell you."

Dad's face settles on a dangerous purple. "That's ridiculous and you'll have to deny it," he says. "Immediately. Tonight. Can you even begin to understand what this means for us?"

The political calculation in his response shouldn't surprise me, but it still stings. Even now, facing his only child coming out to him, his first thought is about damage control and public image.

"No," I say, meeting his gaze. "I will not deny it. I won't deny who I am any longer. I'm tired of pretending to be someone else for your comfort."

Dad's chair creaks as he leans forward, his eyes blazing with anger. "Then you'll have to step down from the board. Immediately. We cannot have someone in leadership who refuses to uphold our values."

"I know," I say simply. The acceptance in my voice seems to surprise him. "I thought I already made that clear in the meeting."

Mom clears her throat. "Diane, we have to talk about how we're going to handle this. What we're going to tell people." Her eyes have a little crazy in them now, like she's in full-on panic mode.

I sigh and set down my scotch, the burn in my throat nothing compared to the distress I feel. "We can talk all you want, but that's not going to change the fact that I'm gay. No amount of strategy sessions or damage control is going to make me straight."

Mom flinches at the word 'gay' like I've slapped her. "Our only child," she whispers, her voice breaking. "What did we do wrong to make you turn out this way? Was it letting you have too much independence? Where did we fail you?"

Now it's my turn to flinch. Mom's not just disappointed —she's grief-stricken, mourning the daughter she thought she had.

"You didn't do anything wrong," I say, anger building. "This isn't something that happened to me or something you caused. This is who I am. I was gay when I was five years old and playing house with my dolls, I was gay when I was nineteen and sleeping with my cello teacher, and I'm still gay now. The only thing that's changed is that I've had enough of hiding it. I'm gay, period."

"Stop saying that word," Mom says sharply. "Not in this house." I note she's completely skipped over the cello teacher revelation. Selective hearing must be a survival mechanism.

"What word? Gay?" I stand up, frustration finally boiling over. "It's not a dirty word, Mom. It's my reality."

Dad slams his glass down so hard I'm surprised it

LISE GOLD & MADELEINE TAYLOR

doesn't shatter. "Your reality is that you're a Washington. You can't just decide to throw all of that away for some phase you're going through."

A sarcastic laugh escapes me. "The only phase I've been going through is pretending to be straight for your political convenience."

"Watch your tone," he warns, pointing a finger at me. "I am still your father, and you are still living off the family name and family money. If you want to continue doing so, you'll find a way to make this problem disappear."

The threat is implicit but clear: conform or be cut off.

"I see," I say. "So my choice is to live a lie forever or lose my family."

"Your choice," he says. "Think about someone other than yourself for once. Think about the example you're setting."

I raise a brow and huff. "Oh? You mean refusing to be ashamed of who I love? Yeah, that would be a terrible message." I look from Mom to Dad and back. "So what about *my* life? What about *my* happiness? Does any of that even matter to you?"

Mom lifts her chin. "Thomas is a good man from a good family. You could be happy with him."

I stare at Mom and wonder how we're even related. She doesn't understand me at all.

"I think we're done here," I say. "This is pointless."

53

ZARA

"How long can you stay?" I trace patterns on Diane's bare shoulder as we lie tangled in the silk sheets.

"As long as you want me to." Diane gives me a sad smile. "There's not much to get back to; I'm in no rush."

"I'm sorry."

"Don't be. I'm okay." She sighs. "I just need to figure out what I'm going to do next. Leaving was the right thing to do. Maybe my parents will come around and maybe I'll be able to have some sort of relationship with them again in future. I saw I had a missed call from Mom when I landed, which is a good thing, I suppose. But I messaged her and told her to leave me alone for a while. I need distance from them to focus on my future."

"Do you think they've told anyone else?" I ask.

"I don't think so. Not yet. But the news will spread, so if we're going to go public, we shouldn't wait too long."

"I know." I brush my lips against Diane's. "This is going to be a wild ride in the coming weeks. I hope you're ready."

"Are *you* ready?" Diane cups my cheek. "It will be worse

for you." Her hand is warm against my skin, and I bring it to my lips.

"Don't worry about me. We'll figure this out together." I pause, propping myself up on my elbow. "So you're going to look for a job? What kind of work are you thinking?"

She considers the question. "I'm pretty open-minded about potential roles as long as it's something that aligns with my values. I know I'll have to take a hit on salary and that's okay."

"You could do incredible work in LGBTQ+ advocacy," I suggest. "Your fundraising skills, your understanding of how these networks operate."

"I know. I've applied for a few vacancies where I could use everything I learned in my father's world to tear down the barriers they've built." Diane chuckles. "There's something poetic about that." She rolls onto her back, staring up at the ceiling. "I don't know if anyone will have me; I might be tainted after the media storm dies down. But I saw a vacancy in LA..."

"Really?" I find her hand in the darkness. "You'd consider moving to LA?"

"I would if I can get a job there," Diane says. "Sun, sea..." She turns back to me and kisses my jawline down to my throat. "You... What's not to love?" Then she laughs and hastily adds, "Don't worry; I wasn't suggesting moving in with you or anything. Just being in the same city so we can see each other more would be nice."

My grin spreads so wide it almost hurts. "I'd love to have you close." Tangling a hand in her hair, I pull her against me. "But I have to admit, I do like the idea of you moving in with me..."

Diane's eyes lock with mine, and she chuckles again, shyly this time. "Isn't it a little soon for that?"

"Maybe, but it feels right. And I'm still stuck in Vegas for another nine months, so it wouldn't be right away. We have plenty of time to talk about it and you'll have plenty of time to look for a job."

"True." Diane arches a brow at me. "I bet you have a nice house."

"Beautiful. It's right on the beach. And you know what would make it even nicer?" I pause for effect, stroking her hair. "Having the most amazing woman in the world to share it with. I never even considered that to be a possibility, but now... It's within reach. Everything I ever wanted is within reach."

"Yeah. I never dared to dream like that either." Diane's eyes well up like the realization has just hit her. "I don't know what I was so terrified of. The worst thing I thought could happen, happened, and the world hasn't ended. And now I'm here with you and we're talking about a future together." She sniffs. "I love you."

"I love you too," I whisper through my own tears. "And I genuinely believe we can handle anything together. Whatever happens in the coming days, weeks, months... I think we can—"

Diane silences me with a kiss and I taste her salty tears on her lips. Kissing her erases my thoughts, reduces me to nothing but this delicious friction of mouths and breath. Her tongue traces my bottom lip and I open for her, letting her take what she needs. There's a desperation in the way she holds me, fingers pressing into my ribs.

I roll her beneath me and she gasps, her legs parting to make space for my hips. The sound she makes when I settle my weight against her is half-sob, half-plea. I kiss the tears from her cheeks, then her eyelids, then back to her mouth.

Her hands slide down my spine and grip my ass, pulling me harder against her.

My mouth finds her neck, tracing the pulse point beneath her jaw. Her skin is warm, a feverish heat rising from her body as I taste the sweetness there. She lets out a trembling sigh that vibrates against my lips, her hands still gripping me, urging me on.

I raise myself enough to look at her face. Her eyes are dark pools, her cheeks flushed and damp with tears. She shivers, muscles tensing under my touch as I trace slow circles over her breasts, watching her eyelids flutter as her breathing quickens.

Lowering my hand between her thighs, I gasp at how wet she is. The slick heat of her makes me dizzy with want, and I circle her entrance with light, teasing touches, watching her face contort with pleasure before I slide a finger up to her clit.

"Zara," she breathes, arching into my hand. "I need you inside me."

As much as I love Diane's dominant side, watching her surrender to me slays me. In this moment, she's all mine and I've never felt closer to her.

Sliding two fingers inside her, I feel her clench around me as a low moan escapes her throat. Her hips rise to meet my hand, demanding more, and I add another finger, stretching her, filling her. I lower my head to capture one of her nipples between my lips, sucking gently as I continue to work my fingers inside her.

The sensation is intoxicating and I curl my fingers forward, finding that spot that makes her gasp and tremble.

"Look at me," I command gently, and her eyes flutter open, focusing on mine with such raw vulnerability that I almost choke up. "I want to see you."

She nods, struggling to keep her eyes open as I increase my pace. Her thighs begin to tremble, her breathing becomes ragged and uneven.

"God, Zara," she gasps, her back arching off the mattress. "Don't stop. Please don't stop."

I lower my mouth to her breast again, taking a nipple between my lips as my thumb finds her clit. The dual sensation makes her cry out, one hand flying to tangle in my hair, holding me against her. I suck harder, matching the rhythm of my fingers, feeling her inner walls beginning to pulse around me.

"I've got you," I murmur against her skin. "Let go."

Her body tenses beneath me, suspended in that exquisite moment just before release. I curl my fingers once more, pressing firmly, and she shatters, her inner muscles clamping down on my fingers as she comes.

I love this woman. I love her in ways that make everything before feel like practice.

Easing my fingers out, she whimpers at the loss. I pull her against me, tucking her head beneath my chin. We don't speak. There's nothing left to say that our bodies haven't already articulated.

54

DIANE

*T*he sound of crying—high-pitched and insistent —cuts through the quiet. Zara stirs against me, her body warm where we're pressed together, my arm draped over her waist and her back tucked against my chest.

Zara chuckles, her hand finding mine where it rests on her stomach. She brings it to her lips and kisses my knuckles before reaching for her phone on the nightstand.

"Six AM," she murmurs, her voice rough with sleep. "Right on schedule."

Through the wall, I hear Jess's muffled voice: "Seriously, Lucas? Can't you let Mommy sleep a little longer for once?"

"He's already a morning person," Zara says. "Just like his godmother." She shifts in my arms, turning to face me. Her hair is a wild mass of curls and she looks more beautiful than ever. "As nice as it is being in bed with you, I should probably give Jess a break."

She starts to pull away but I tighten my hold on her, not quite ready to let go. "I'll come with you."

"You don't have to," she says, brushing a strand of hair

from my face. "Go back to sleep. You've had a rough few days."

"So have you." I kiss her softly. "Besides, I'm awake now. I'll make coffee if you get Lucas."

I put on a robe and head for the kitchen. Through the suite, I hear Jess's door open and Zara's voice, then Lucas's cries beginning to subside.

"You're a saint!" Jess calls out. "I love you so much right now!"

I'm making coffee when Zara appears with Lucas on her hip. His little face is red and blotchy from crying, his eyes still heavy with sleep and confusion. Fat tears cling to his lashes, but he's calming now, his whimpers becoming occasional hiccups as he rests his head against Zara's shoulder.

Zara looks so natural with him, so utterly maternal in a way I wouldn't have expected from her. The way she unconsciously sways, the gentle circles her hand traces on his back, the soft murmuring sounds she makes to soothe him —it's instinctive, tender, and so sweet.

"Okay, little man," she coos, bouncing him. "You're smelly. Let's get you changed and then we'll find you something to eat, okay?"

She disappears down the hallway, and I turn my attention back to the kitchen where I find bread, eggs, and butter. Isabella must have bought them because I know Zara lives on room service and takeout.

I crack eggs into a bowl and whisk them, then melt butter in a pan and put the bread in the toaster. For some reason, the simple domesticity of making breakfast for us feels more surreal than anything we've been through.

Zara returns with Lucas, his diaper changed and his mood significantly improved. He's making babbling sounds, his chubby hands reaching for everything within his limited grasp.

"Babe, you didn't need to do that," Zara says when she spots the breakfast I'm plating. "But my God, it smells good and I'm hungry."

She leans against the kitchen counter and takes that first sip of her coffee, a small sound of contentment escaping her throat.

Lucas immediately reaches for the mug, grasping even as Zara pulls it away. We both laugh, and I take him from Zara so she can enjoy a few more sips of coffee without the threat of a scalding disaster.

"Thank you," she says. "This is nice."

Lucas squirms in my arms, his attention already shifting to the next interesting thing—in this case, my hair. His fingers tangle in the strands and I extract myself before he can get a good grip.

"Let's take breakfast outside," Zara suggests, nodding toward the terrace. "It's still cool out there and it won't last long." She opens a cupboard and retrieves a jar of baby food. "And you, sir, need to eat too."

We settle at the outdoor table with Lucas in the baby chair, the city spread below us still relatively quiet. I feel calm. Happy, even. Which seems strange given that I walked away from my family three days ago, that my entire life has imploded, that I'm facing an uncertain future without the safety net I've relied on. But sitting here with Zara and Lucas, eating scrambled eggs as the sun rises over Las Vegas, I feel truly at peace.

Zara catches me looking at her and smiles. She looks happy too.

"Can I ask you something?" I say, setting down my fork.

"Of course."

"Do you want kids?" The question surprises me as much as it probably surprises her. I hadn't planned to ask it, but watching her with Lucas this morning, I'm curious.

Zara blushes and shakes her head. "I don't know," she admits. "Like so many other things, I never really considered it." She pauses, smiling lovingly at Lucas. "But I love kids. And I guess I'm open to it now. Maybe not right away, but someday." She meets my eyes. "What about you?"

"Same," I say. "They're cute. I don't know many babies, though. Most of my old friends in Washington have nannies, so when we meet up they rarely bring their children. And I'm an only child, so no nieces or nephews." I reach over and touch Lucas's soft cheek. "But you're pretty cute, aren't you?"

Lucas watches a spoonful of baby food approach with intense focus, his mouth opening like a bird. But as soon as the food touches his tongue, his face screws up in the most dramatic expression of betrayal I've ever seen. His nose wrinkles, his eyebrows furrow, and his whole body shudders with disgust. Then he spits it out, the orange mush dribbling down his chin and onto his bib.

Zara and I both burst out laughing. Lucas looks affronted by our reaction, his bottom lip trembling like he might cry again, but instead he lets out an indignant squeal that only makes us laugh harder.

"It seems he's not a fan of sweet potato," Zara manages between giggles. "Maybe we should start the day with pureed fruit instead."

"Clearly not a fan," I agree, wiping his chin with the bib, which makes him squirm and protest with more squeals.

I look at Zara, at the smile that hasn't left her face since we woke up. I think about the life ahead of us—uncertain and unconventional, but entirely ours. No more pretending. Just this: scrambled eggs on the terrace, a baby who hates sweet potato, and the woman I love beside me as we figure out what comes next.

55

ZARA

*P*eter spreads a folder of printouts across the coffee table in my suite. It's three in the afternoon, and we've ordered room service—sandwiches and coffee that sit mostly untouched while we face reality.

"Alright," he says, settling into the armchair across from where Diane and I sit on the couch. "Let's start with the good news, because there is some. Your streaming numbers are up forty percent since the story broke. A video of 'Performers' recorded by an influencer has been viewed over three million times in the past three days. Your social media following has grown by four hundred thousand across all platforms." He shows me a chart on his tablet with a clear spike in engagement. "People are paying attention, and a significant portion of that attention is positive on platforms that skew younger—Instagram, TikTok—you're getting about eighty-twenty positive to negative responses." He pauses. "On Facebook and X, it's more like seventy-thirty, but that's actually better than I expected given the political angle."

I study the numbers, trying to process what they mean.

"So the fans like the song and they accept the idea that I might be involved with a woman?"

"Absolutely," Peter says. "Your core audience—eighteen to forty-five, urban, progressive—they're supportive."

"That's great news," Diane says.

"It is. But now let's talk about the more complicated responses." Peter pulls out another stack of papers. "Conservative media has been predictably brutal." He slides a printed article toward me. The headline reads: "Zara Nova's Calculated Coming Out: Jumping on the Queer Trend?"

"They're questioning the timing," Peter continues. "Suggesting that you came out specifically to generate buzz for the residency. There's also commentary about the number of female artists who've come out as queer in the past few years. Some outlets are framing you as just jumping on the bandwagon for attention."

I roll my eyes and huff. "That's ridiculous."

"Of course," Peter says. "But from the outside, the timing does look convenient. Major artist comes out during the launch of a new residency, right when being queer is more commercially acceptable in pop music than ever before. I'm not saying those artists calculated it, but I understand why some people see it that way."

Diane shifts beside me. "What are they saying about me specifically?"

Peter tilts his head from side to side. "That's where things get a little messy. Progressive outlets are divided. Some are celebrating what they're calling your courage for potentially being with Zara despite your conservative background. Others are questioning why you worked for an organization that actively opposed LGBTQ+ rights if the speculation about you is true." He pauses. "Of course, since neither of you has confirmed anything, it's all still conjecture. But the narrative is forming."

"That was to be expected," Diane mumbles.

He hands her an article. "Zara Nova's new flame: Hypocrite or Victim?"

"The Washington Foundation itself hasn't issued an official response yet," Peter continues. "I think they're holding off until Diane has either confirmed or denied her relationship with you. Right now it's all speculation, but the moment either of you speaks publicly, that changes everything. They'll be forced to respond."

Diane's hand finds mine. "I expected this," she says. "None of it surprises me."

"I agree." Peter nods. "But I need you both to understand the scope of what we're dealing with. This isn't just entertainment news anymore—it's cultural, a referendum on family values in politics, LGBTQ+ rights and generational change. You've become symbols whether you want to be or not." He pauses. "The question now is how do you want to proceed?"

"We want to come out," I say, glancing at Diane.

She nods. "Yes. We're ready to confirm our relationship publicly."

"Very well. I fully support that decision." Peter looks from me to Diane and back. "I suggest you give a major prime-time interview. Live with someone like Robin West or Anderson Marhabi, someone trusted who can ask hard questions but give you space to answer honestly. You control the story by telling it yourselves, addressing the criticism directly instead of hiding from it."

"How quickly could you arrange something like that?" Diane asks.

"Within the week," Peter replies. "These outlets have

been calling constantly since the story broke. They'd clear their schedules for this but it has to be on a night Zara's not performing." He taps his tablet. "I'll suggest Wednesday as that's one of your nights off. We need to prep extensively. They'll ask about your father, Diane. About the foundation's positions on LGBTQ+ issues. About how you reconciled working there while being gay yourself."

"I know," Diane says quietly. "I've been thinking about how to answer those questions."

Peter nods. "I'll hire a media consultant to prep you beforehand. And Zara, they'll want to know about 'Performers'—whether it's about Diane, when you knew you were queer, why you've dated men publicly but never women. They'll ask if you were ashamed or in denial." He clears his throat. "As your manager, I wouldn't normally advise this, but in your case, I think it's best to be completely honest and transparent."

"I know," I say. "We agree."

"Good. Honesty is your best weapon here." Peter stands. "I'll reach out to Robin West's team first—she's done excellent work with similar stories. Don't engage with media. Don't respond to negative comments on social media— that's what they want, and it never ends well. And don't post anything online. Everything is ammunition now."

56

DIANE

*F*lying to LA in a private jet feels both luxurious and surreal. I'm seated in one of the cream leather chairs that look like they belong in a high-end living room rather than an aircraft. Across from me, Zara stares out the window, her chin resting on her hand, lost in thought. Peter sits further back, absorbed in his laptop.

The interior of the chartered aircraft is stunning. Polished wood accents, a small galley where a flight attendant prepared coffee earlier, windows that frame the clouds sliding past at thirty-five thousand feet. I still haven't adjusted to this being normal for Zara. The casual way she boards these flights, how she kicks off her shoes and curls into the seat like it's her couch at home.

I call Thomas and he immediately picks up.

"Diane, hey. How are you holding up?"

"I'm okay." I glance at Zara, who turns from the window at the sound of my voice. "Listen, I wanted to give you a heads-up. We're doing an interview tonight. Live television with Robin West."

A pause. "So you're really doing this?"

"Yes. Tonight at eight." I take a breath. "You might get some questions afterward. I wanted you to know it was coming."

"Thank you for the warning." His voice carries something warm. "I'm proud of you, Diane."

"Thank you." My throat tightens. "That means a lot actually."

"I heard you resigned from the foundation," he continues. "Or did they fire you? The rumors are all over the place."

"They didn't give me much of a choice, but it was the right thing to do regardless." I watch the clouds through the window, their tops bright white against the blue. "I feel good about it. My parents are a different story, but I'll try to talk to them in a few weeks. They need time to let this sink in and frankly, I'm too angry and disappointed with them to face them right now."

"That's fair. So you're coping?"

I almost laugh. "Thomas, I'm on a private jet to Los Angeles and about to come out on live television to millions of people. I've walked away from my family, my career, everything I've known for thirty years. But you know what? Somehow I'm keeping it together. Does that make any sense?"

"Not really." He laughs. "But if you say so."

"What are you going to tell your parents?" I ask. "After they see the interview. Do they still think we're dating?"

"I'm not sure what rumors have reached them but I'm going to tell them the truth. That we were just pretending to be interested in each other to get them off our backs, and that we've become close friends." He pauses. "And I might even tell them about Jamie. If you're brave enough to do something this enormous, I shouldn't think twice about coming clean either."

"Thomas, I'm sorry if this caused you—"

"No, it's fine. You're about to go on national television and tell the world you're in love with Zara Nova. My coming out is significantly less dramatic."

I chuckle. "When you put it that way."

"Are you nervous?" he asks. "About tonight?"

"Nervous?" I look across at Zara, who shoots me a humorous smile. I let out a shaky laugh. "Thomas, I'm absolutely terrified. This is the most frightening thing I've ever done in my life. But neither has Zara, and we're doing it together. That helps."

Zara reaches across the space between us and takes my hand.

"You're going to be great," Thomas says. "Jamie and I will be watching. She's already informed me that we're ordering pizza and making an event of it."

"Tell her I said thank you. For everything."

"I will. And Diane? Good luck. Go be brave."

The call ends and I set my phone down. The flight attendant appears, offering drinks. Zara declines, but I accept another coffee. The jet begins its descent, and through the window, Los Angeles lies below in an endless sprawl of buildings and freeways, the Pacific glittering in the distance.

I take a sip, watching Zara over the rim of my cup. "Where's your house? You live in Malibu, right? Can you see it from here?"

"I think so." Zara looks out of the window and squints. "Okay, see that pier? That's the Malibu Pier. Now follow the coast north—see where it curves and there's that big stretch of beach? That's Zuma. My place is between the two, closer to the pier." She traces the coastline with her finger against the window. "See those mountains coming right down to meet the water? Those houses tucked along that narrow strip? I'm in there somewhere."

I follow where she's describing, piecing together the geography. The Pacific stretches endless and blue, waves creating white lines against the sand. The mountains rise dramatically behind the narrow strip of development, and I can make out the ribbon of Pacific Coast Highway winding along the shore.

"It looks like a gorgeous place to live."

"It is." Zara smiles. "It's a shame we won't have time to go there since we're flying back right after the interview. But next time."

I stare at the city taking shape beneath us, trying to imagine myself living there. Waking up to that California light every morning. Finding my favorite coffee shop. Going for hikes on weekends. This could be my city. My fresh start.

Somewhere down there is a television studio where, in eight hours, the version of myself I've been performing for thirty years will cease to exist.

57

ZARA

*T*he dressing room at the CBS studios in Los Angeles has stark white walls and feels too bright. I can't stop fidgeting with the hem of my dress while a makeup artist does final touch-ups on my face.

"Try not to move," she says, holding a powder brush near my nose.

Diane sits in a chair beside me, looking great in a navy pantsuit and white shirt. We've spent the afternoon in a nearby hotel suite reviewing talking points with a team of advisors Peter hired, and now we're about to go live.

Peter stands nearby, watching us while he polishes his glasses. We've spent the past forty-eight hours in crisis management mode—coordinating with publicists and a media strategist, preparing for every possible question.

"Five minutes," calls the assistant director.

Robin West enters the room. She's known for asking tough questions without being hostile, for creating space for honest conversation rather than confrontation. Her interview with a prominent athlete involved in a doping scandal

LISE GOLD & MADELEINE TAYLOR

two years ago became the gold standard for how to handle these moments.

"Zara, Diane, thank you for doing this," Robin says, shaking our hands. She's smaller than she appears on television, her dark hair styled in a sleek bob. "I know this hasn't been an easy week for either of you."

"That's an understatement," I reply. "But we're glad to be here."

Robin smiles. "We're going to have a real conversation. Not a puff piece, not a hit job. I don't want to know anything up front. Just honest questions and honest answers. Sound good?"

Diane and I exchange glances. "Sounds good," Diane says.

An assistant leads us onto the set, and the studio audience begins to applaud as we enter. The lights are even brighter out here, and I feel hundreds of eyes on us as we take our seats on the sofa. Robin settles into her chair across from us, and someone adjusts our microphones.

The production assistant counts down from five, and then we're live as the audience is given the cue to applaud again.

"Good evening. I'm Robin West, and tonight we have an exclusive interview that many of you have been waiting for. I'm joined by Grammy-winning artist Zara Nova and Diane Washington, Washington Foundation director and daughter of Virginia Senator Richard Washington. For the past week, speculation has been swirling about the nature of their relationship following a performance at the opening night of Zara's Vegas residency. Tonight, they're here to set the record straight."

She turns to us. "Zara, Diane, thank you both for being here."

"Thank you for having us," I say, and Diane smiles and nods.

Robin looks at us directly. "Let's dive right in and address what everyone wants to know. Is there any truth to the rumors? Are you two in a relationship?"

I take Diane's hand, right there on camera where millions can see. "Yes," I say. "Diane and I are together. We're in love."

The studio audience reacts—some applaud and cheer, some gasp. Robin lets the moment breathe before continuing.

"Wow," she says, her eyebrows lifting with genuine surprise. "That's—I'm happy for you. I have to say, this is not the pairing anyone expected." She leans forward slightly. "How did you two even meet? You come from such different worlds."

Diane and I exchange a glance, and I can see the hint of a smile playing at her lips.

"We were set up," Diane says. "On a blind date, actually. We have a mutual friend in Vegas who thought we might get along."

"A blind date? With Zara Nova? That must have been quite the reveal."

"I panicked," Diane says with a laugh. "I recognized Zara immediately, obviously, and my brain stopped working. Then I spent the first ten minutes convinced she'd want to leave."

"It was just as scary for me," I admit. "I showed up not knowing who I was meeting, and when Diane walked in, I was so nervous and paranoid I made a complete fool out of myself."

Robin shakes her head and grins, clearly charmed by

the story. "So where was this blind date? I imagine finding a private spot for someone of your profile isn't easy, Zara."

"True," I say. "We actually had our date in our friend's office which she set up like a dining space. It sounds strange, but it was honestly one of the most secure, private places in the entire city. Very romantic, right? Office lighting, a desk in the corner..."

The audience laughs, and Diane laughs along. "All joking aside, it was impressive, actually. Candles, flowers, an incredible meal. It felt more like a private restaurant."

"And we forgot about the rest of the world for a few hours," I add, squeezing Diane's hand.

Robin sits back, a smile on her face. "That's actually incredibly romantic. And clearly something clicked, because here you are." Her expression grows more serious. "But both of you had to know this would be complicated. Diane, your father is Senator Washington, known for his conservative positions. Zara, you've been in the public eye for many years. What made you both decide it was worth it?"

I look at Diane, and she nods for me to go first.

"Honestly? I was tired of living half a life," I say. "I've spent my entire career being whoever people needed me to be. The pop star, the public figure. And I was lonely, even surrounded by people all the time." I pause, feeling emotion rise in my throat. "Then I met Diane, and I felt like I could be myself with her. And once I had that, I couldn't go back to pretending."

Robin turns to Diane. "And you? You had to know this would affect your father's career, your own career. Our sources tell us you walked away from the Washington Foundation five days ago."

Diane nods slowly. "I did. And yes, I knew the risks but I

guess I never thought it would turn into anything serious. That was our mindset going into the first date." She takes a breath. "Like Zara, I've spent years making choices based on what other people needed from me. And when I met her, I realized that life wasn't for me anymore."

The audience is completely silent now, hanging on every word.

"Zara, you've been an outspoken ally for the LGBTQ+ community for years—performing at Pride events, supporting advocacy organizations, speaking out for equality. But you've never publicly identified as queer yourself. Why is that?"

The question I knew was coming still makes me uneasy. "I was afraid," I admit. "I built my career on being accessible, on letting fans project their fantasies onto me. Coming out meant potentially losing that, losing people who'd supported me from the beginning."

"But you were comfortable accepting ally awards, speaking at events as a straight supporter rather than as a member of the community yourself?"

I lean back and sigh. "Looking back, that was cowardly, hiding the most fundamental truth about myself. I'd never really had the chance to explore my sexuality until I met Diane, but admittedly, I always knew I was queer. Representation matters, especially as a public figure, and although some people think I should have come out sooner, I wasn't ready. It was my personal choice to do it now. Not just because of the rumors but because I have Diane in my life and the time is right."

Diane turns to me and smiles. She's not performing for the cameras; I recognize that smile–the one that's just for me.

Robin nods before turning to Diane. "Diane, you served

as executive director of the Washington Foundation, an organization that has historically supported politicians and causes opposed to LGBTQ+ rights. How do you reconcile that with your own identity?"

Diane takes a moment before she answers. Her hand trembles in mine and all I want to do is take her into my arms. "Honestly, I can't reconcile it," she finally says. "I told myself I was working within the system to create change, that I could be a moderating influence. The truth is I was prioritizing my family's approval and my own financial security over my integrity."

Robin seems surprised by her honesty, and she too, needs a moment before she asks the next question. "Your father, Senator Richard Washington, has voted against same-sex marriage protections. Did you ever confront him about that?"

"No." Diane shakes her head. "At least not until recently. I stayed silent because speaking up would have meant revealing myself, and I wasn't ready for that. But now that we are where we are, I'm ashamed it took me so long."

"And how is your relationship with your family now?" Robin asks.

"I'm not sure what the future brings but currently it's best if we keep some distance." Diane sighs. "I can't speak for them; I can only speak for myself. They're my parents and I'll always love them, even though we're worlds apart and fundamentally disagree on just about everything. And of course, I hope that one day, we can have a relationship again. One based on mutual respect for each other's choices."

"Thank you, Diane." Robin gives Diane a sympathetic look before she turns back to me. "Zara, you wrote a song called 'Performers' that's gone viral this week. Can you talk about writing that song?"

I welcome the shift to something I can speak about more easily. "Yes, the rumors are true. I wrote that song for Diane. In fact, she inspired me to write a lot of new material. I think the lyrics speak for themselves. We've both been performers in our own lives and I sang it for her because I wanted her to know—really know—how I felt." I pause and add with a rueful smile, "Though I have to admit, I didn't expect the entire world to be onto me."

Robin chuckles. "Well, speaking of that..." She gestures to the screen behind us, where a photo appears—the now-infamous shot from opening night. In it, I'm looking down from the piano, tears streaming down my face, while Diane stares up at me from the front row, her hand pressed to her chest.

The audience erupts in a mixture of laughter and sympathetic "awws."

"I mean," Robin says with a hint of amusement in her voice, "for two people trying to keep a relationship secret, you both have truly terrible poker faces."

Diane covers her face with her free hand, laughing despite her obvious embarrassment.

Robin nods while the audience claps and cheers. "Well, I think it's safe to say the secret was out the moment that photo hit the internet."

I feel some of the weight I've been carrying lift from my shoulders. This is awkward and uncomfortable, but it's also freeing. Just us, messy and real and in love.

"So..." Robin points at the screen again and reads out an article quote. "This has been circulating online. 'Is Zara Nova's alleged relationship with the senator's daughter a publicity stunt to generate attention for her Vegas residency?'"

The words sting even though I knew they were coming.

"How do you respond to accusations that this is a publicity stunt?" Robin asks.

"Well, I've been in love with Diane for months," I say. "Long before anyone was watching, long before any specu-lation. The idea that we would fake a relationship and endure what we've endured this week—all for publicity—is absurd. Besides, what would be in it for Diane? I don't see why she would even consider being part of this as a publicity stunt. She's lost everything."

"You have a point." Robin lets the weight of that sink in. "Now, having just come out on prime-time TV, what would you say to people watching this who are struggling with their own identities? Diane?"

Diane considers the question carefully. "I would say that living in fear of exposure is its own kind of death." She pauses. "There's a quote by Anaïs Nin: 'And the day came when the risk to remain tight in a bud was more painful than the risk it took to blossom.' That's where I was. The pain of hiding had become greater than my fear of being seen."

I lean into Diane as she continues. "I'm not going to pretend this is easy, or that coming out is always safe for everyone. I have privilege—a home, education, options that many people don't have. And even with all that, I'm scared." She looks directly at the camera. "But I also want people to know that the freedom on the other side of that fear is real. Yes, I did lose things. But what I gained was myself and—" She turns to look at me, her eyes shimmering. "... love. And that's worth more than anything I left behind."

There's total silence as Robin swallows hard. "That's

beautiful, Diane. Truly." She turns to me. "Zara, what about you? What would you say to your fans who might be struggling?"

I think about all the messages I've received over the years from fans who saw themselves in my music but never knew I was one of them. "I would say that you don't owe anyone your truth before you're ready to give it. Coming out isn't a moral obligation—it's a personal journey, and only you know when the time is right." I pause. "But I also want to acknowledge that I had the luxury of waiting until I felt safe, and not everyone has that. So if you're watching this and you're scared, please know that there are people who will love you exactly as you are. Find those people. Build your chosen family. And remember that you deserve to take up space in this world as your authentic self."

Robin claps her hands together and holds them in a prayer-like gesture of gratitude. "That's powerful. Thank you both." She glances at her notes, then back at us. "We're going to take a quick break, and when we come back, I want to talk about what's next for both of you—your careers, your relationship, and how you plan to navigate this new chapter together."

The camera cuts, and immediately a production assistant appears with water bottles. Diane and I exhale simultaneously, the adrenaline draining from our bodies as the studio lights dim. Diane's hand is sweaty in mine, or maybe that's my hand—I can't tell anymore.

58

DIANE

"*W*hat on earth are we doing in Athena's library?" Zara asks, studying the leather-bound books surrounding us.

I can't help but laugh at her confusion. "Athena thought we might need some distraction after the interview," I say, taking her hand. "She and Ruby are away visiting Ruby's parents, but she wanted to do something special for us."

Zara glances around again. "A library tour?"

"Not exactly. Remember when Athena told you about her club? The sanctuary for women like us?"

"Yes..."

"This is it," I say. "This is where I've been coming for two years. My refuge. I know Athena explained why you can't come here when it's open—the security risk, the other members' privacy. But she didn't want you to feel excluded from this part of my life, so she arranged something special as the club is closed tonight. It's just for us."

"Aww... That's so sweet. But this is..." Zara she still looks confused.

I pull her along to the far end of the library where Robert, Athena's head of security, gives me a nod.

"Ms. Washington. Ms. Nova." He puts his hand on a particular leather volume and the entire bookcase swings open with a soft click, revealing a staircase.

Zara's mouth falls open. "You're kidding me."

"I'm really not." I gesture toward the stairs. "After you?"

She laughs, that delighted sound I love, and steps through the opening. I follow her down the stairs and music rises to meet us—something slow and sensual, the kind of soundtrack that promises decadence.

The club unfolds before us as we reach the bottom of the staircase, and I watch Zara take it all in—the deep red walls, the velvet divans, the Moroccan lanterns casting patterns across the floor. I remember my own first time descending these stairs, the way this space felt like stepping into a dream. The vibe is entirely different now – we're the only ones here, but it's no less fascinating.

Zara stops in the center of the room, slowly turning to take it all in. "What the..." She shakes her head. "Okay. This is not what I expected when you told me we were going for a private dinner."

"My home away from home," I say. "For the past two years, this was the only place I could be myself."

Movement catches my attention, and I see Ally emerging from behind the bar—the same woman who served us dinner on our first date in Athena's office. She's carrying a tray with two sake cups and a ceramic bottle.

Zara laughs again when recognition dawns. "Wait—I know you!"

Ally smiles, setting the tray down on one of the low tables. "Good to see you again, Ms. Nova. Under less nerve-wracking circumstances, I hope."

"Certainly. Right, now I get it." She turns to me. "When I asked if we could trust the waitress on our first date, you said we were safe because you knew her. This is why you were so confident."

"Ally has worked here since the club opened," I explain. "No one who works here would ever betray Athena's trust."

"Or yours," Ally adds warmly. She gestures toward one of the seating nooks where low cushions surround a brass table. "Diane told me you like sushi. I hope you're hungry."

We settle into the nook, and as we sip our sake, Ally fills the table with beautiful sushi platters. Delicate rolls arranged like art, sashimi fanned across slate plates, edamame dusted with sea salt. There's also miso soup in lacquered bowls, seaweed salad, and gyoza.

"This is so indulgent," Zara says, picking up her chopsticks. "Like, seriously indulgent."

"We refer to this space as Hedonism," I say, topping up our sake. "It's where women who can't normally let themselves go in public come to indulge in every single way—as long as it's legal. No judgment, no consequences, just freedom to be whoever you need to be for a night."

"And you came here to..."

"To breathe," I finish. "To have conversations where I didn't have to watch every word. To be around women who understood what it was like to live a double life." I pause, meeting her eyes. "And sometimes, to flirt and find sexual partners. But that part is over."

Zara winks. "You bet it is. You're mine now." She takes a piece of tuna sashimi, closing her eyes as she tastes it. "Okay, this is possibly the best sushi I've ever had. Where did this come from?"

"Athena has a chef on call. The club always serves excellent food. Part of the luxury is that everything is taken care of. You never have to think about the details."

I watch Zara relax, the tension from the interview slowly leaving her shoulders. She reaches for her sake cup and makes a face. "This stuff is strong."

I shrug. "I thought you might need some liquid courage before I show you the rest of the club."

Her eyebrows lift with interest. "There's more?"

"Oh, there's definitely more. The main room is the social space but beyond those curtains—" I gesture toward the velvet archways, "—are the private chambers."

Zara leans forward, her curiosity clearly piqued. "What kind of private chambers?"

"Various kinds." My heart is beating faster now. "The club isn't called Hedonism as some cheap marketing gimmick, in fact, it doesn't have an official name at all and as far as the world is concerned, it doesn't even exist. But, as you probably know, Hedonism is an ancient Greek philosophy. The belief that pleasure is the highest good."

Zara sets down her chopsticks, giving me her full attention.

"Here, women indulge in everything," I continue. "Exceptional food and drink, substances that are legal but help shed inhibitions—cannabis, certain psychedelics in controlled doses. And yes, sex. All of it without judgment and consequence. It's about pursuing pleasure in its truest, most holistic sense."

"So the private chambers are..."

"Different spaces for different desires," I say, my gaze lowering to her mouth.

I notice the shift in Zara's body language—the way she leans slightly forward, the unconscious parting of her lips. The rising heat between us is tangible, and I reach across the table to take her hand, bringing it to my lips for a brief kiss.

"But first," I say, "we finish this incredible meal. After that, I'll give you the grand tour of the chambers, and then —" I meet her eyes, "—we can do whatever you want."

59

ZARA

*D*ark walls absorb the soft lighting, making the space feel both intimate and infinite. My eyes are drawn to the padded cuffs hanging from the ceiling, the hooks mounted at various heights on the back wall, the beautiful armchair, the chest of drawers in a corner and above it, a selection of floggers and riding crops, and the multiple full-length mirrors reflecting my own wide-eyed expression back at me. Everything is immaculate, elegant—this isn't some crude dungeon fantasy. This is luxury with intention.

"Oh," I breathe.

Diane joins me and leaves the door open. She's watching me with that controlled intensity I've come to recognize—the look that says she's already three steps ahead and has anticipated my reaction.

"You okay?" she asks.

"Yes. Just... taking it in."

She moves closer but doesn't touch me. "We can have some fun if you want. Or—" she pauses, "—we can head home. No pressure, Zara."

My heart is racing, and there's a heat low in my belly. "I don't want to go home," I say. "I want to play."

"Are you sure?"

When I nod, Diane wraps her arms around my waist. "Okay. Your safe word is still 'abort,'" she says. "The moment you say it, everything stops. No questions. Do you understand?"

"I understand."

Diane's gaze travels down my body and lingers on my shoes. "God, I love these stiletto heels on you."

Color rises to my cheeks. "Yeah?"

"Uh-huh. Keep them on." Her voice has dropped half an octave, and there's no question mark at the end of that sentence.

She takes a step back, and suddenly there's a gulf between us. The woman who laughed with me over sake twenty minutes ago has been replaced by someone I've only glimpsed once before— the version of Diane who doesn't ask permission.

"Arms up," she says, guiding me to the center of the room.

I do, and she pulls down the cuffs and fastens them around my wrists. She checks the fit carefully, sliding two fingers between the cuff and my wrist.

"Too tight?"

"No. It's good."

Diane nods, then moves to the wall where a small control panel is mounted. She presses a button, and I hear a soft mechanical whir. The chains begin to retract upward, lifting my arms higher until I'm forced onto my tiptoes, balanced precariously in my stilettos.

My breath comes faster. The position is challenging— not painful, but enough to make me acutely aware of every muscle in my body, the strain in my calves, the way I'm stretched and exposed.

My heart hammers against my ribs.

"Breathe," Diane murmurs, circling around me slowly. I feel her presence behind me, then beside me, then in front again. She's studying me from every angle, and I'm hyper-aware of every inch of my body—the way my dress clings to my curves, the rise and fall of my chest, the trembling I can't quite suppress.

"You look incredible," she says. "Do you have any idea how beautiful you are?"

I can't form words. My mouth has gone dry.

Diane steps closer, and I feel the heat of her body against my back. She wraps her arms around me and trails one finger along my collarbone, down to the bandeau neck-line of my dress, then back up to my jaw. Her other hand is on my breast, skimming my nipple. The lightness of her touch is maddening.

"I'm going to take my time with you," she says. "And you're going to let me. Aren't you?"

"Yes," I whisper.

She pulls down the zipper of my strapless dress, and the slow descent of it raises goosebumps on my skin.

"We just came out on national television," she whispers, her breath warm against my neck. "We told the whole world about us. And now you're here, in the most secret place I know, trusting me like no one's ever trusted me. Thank you."

Diane pulls the dress down, and it falls around my feet. I'm left in my lingerie and heels, restrained and exposed. She presses her body against my back, her lips at my ear. "I'm going to show you how much that means to me."

"By spanking me?" I ask in a flirty tone.

Diane goes still behind me. Then she steps away, and she circles around to face me.

My pulse spikes and I brace myself, waiting for her response—for punishment, for that edge in her voice that tells me I shouldn't speak up unless I'm told to.

But when she meets my eyes, there's something warmer, almost amused.

"No," she says simply, cupping my chin. Her thumb traces my lower lip. "Not tonight. Tonight, I have other plans for you."

She reaches around me and unhooks my bra. The band releases and the elastic relaxes, causing the whole thing to shift upward. My breasts are exposed beneath it, the bra bunched uselessly above them.

Diane slides her hands down my sides to my hips, then hooks her fingers into the waistband of my panties and slowly draws them down my legs and takes them off.

"Look at yourself," she says, gesturing to the mirrors.

I catch my reflection—then another, and another. The room's design means I can see myself from every angle: front, back, both sides. My body stretched upward, stark naked, arms overhead, balanced on the balls of my feet. The flush spreading across my chest. The way my breasts lift with each quick breath. The shadows and highlights playing across my skin.

It's obscene and sensual, almost artistic.

"You're stunning," Diane murmurs, standing behind me. "Keep watching yourself."

Her hands slide up to cup my breasts, and I watch in the mirror as she touches me—her fingers tracing circles, thumbs brushing over my nipples. She presses her lips to the side of my neck, then lower, along my shoulder, and I can see everything: the way my body responds to her touch, the arch of my back, the way my eyes flutter closed before I force them open again. It's voyeuristic and intimate watching us like this. Multiple reflections, an infinity of our bodies together.

Diane's gaze meets mine in the mirror, studying our reflection with the same fascination.

Coming to face me, she kisses me fiercely before she dips her head to my breasts. Her lips wrap around one of my nipples and she swirls her tongue around it, causing me to gasp in pleasure. Her hand slides between my thighs, her fingers caressing my pussy and finding me slick and ready. Her touch is light, teasing, and I can't help but moan, straining against the cuffs.

"Stay still," she commands.

I try, but it's nearly impossible when her fingers start to circle my clit. My hips want to move, to chase the sensation, but the restraints and my precarious balance make it difficult.

"God," I gasp, watching her mouth on my breast and her hand work between my legs in the mirror. It's profoundly erotic and I'm completely consumed by sensation.

"Do you like watching yourself?" Diane asks in a low purr.

"Yes," I manage.

Her fingers slide inside me then, and my legs nearly buckle. She supports me with her other arm around my waist, holding me steady as she kisses me hard. The pressure builds as her fingers curl.

Just when I'm balancing on the edge, Diane pulls out of me, steps back and her hand slides up to my throat, not squeezing but resting there, a reminder of her control.

"No..." A frustrated sound escapes me. "Please don't..."

"Wait," she says with a wicked smile. "I need to get something. Don't move."

I let out a strangled laugh. "Move? I can barely stand."

Diane ignores my comment as she walks to the chest of drawers and opens them until she finds what she's looking for. "I've had this fantasy," she says. "To do something in this mirrored room. But there are always people in the club and I'm not into public sex." She takes out a harness and dildo to show me before she strips down to her underwear and puts it on. "But now that we're alone..."

I stare, transfixed by the sight of her wearing the strap-on. The black silicone stands out against her pale skin. She runs her hands over the harness, adjusting it, then approaches me, the gleam in her eyes almost predatory. My body trembles with need.

She presses the panel on the wall to lower me back to my feet. "This strap-on is special," she says, coming up to me and running a hand up my thigh. Her mouth is almost on mine, but she doesn't kiss me. Maybe she's teasing me. Or maybe she wants to watch me. She's holding a small remote and when I glance at it, she smiles. "It vibrates and it feels really, really good, for both of us."

"Oh?" My voice is high-pitched, strangled. I want her to fuck me so badly.

"Mhmm." Diane slides the remote into her bra so her hands are free. She cups my pussy again and I gasp. "See? You're so wet. I think our fantasies might be aligned. Am I right?"

I moan loudly, throwing my head back.

"Look at me," she says. "Look at us. Am I right?"

"Yes." I try to chase her lips but she pulls back a little, leaving me frustrated and yearning for her touch. "I want you to fuck me."

She licks her lips, her eyes never leaving mine. And then, she grabs my behind and lifts me up.

The cuffs at my wrists support me as my legs wrap around her and I'm hanging in the air. I can feel the dildo pressing against me and whimper with anticipation. She's right; this would have been my fantasy if I'd ever considered it being a possibility. I don't have time to analyze that thought though, because she's positioning herself, guiding the silicone shaft to my pussy.

It makes me gasp and she pauses there, teasing me, watching my face.

"Please," I whisper.

She pushes forward slowly, filling me inch by inch. The stretch is delicious, and I moan as she slides all the way in. For a moment, we're frozen like that—me suspended from the ceiling, wrapped around her.

Then she begins to move.

The mirrors multiply the experience exponentially. I can see every angle of our bodies—the way Diane's muscled back flexes with each thrust, the curve of her ass tightening as she drives into me, my own face contorted in pleasure. It's like watching the most intimate pornography starring ourselves, and it's unbearably arousing.

She reaches into her bra and presses the remote. The dildo comes alive, vibrating inside me and against her, and we both cry out.

My entire body is shuddering and I feel like I'm going to explode. The vibrations pulsate through us, creating a feedback loop of pleasure that draws loud moans from my lips. Diane moans too, her body tensing against mine.

"Fuck," she mutters, her rhythm faltering for a moment before she regains control.

"Diane," I gasp, clinging to her with my legs. My arms

349

feel tired but the vibrations send waves of pleasure radiating through my core.

Diane holds me securely, her arms supporting my weight as she drives into me with powerful thrusts. The chains above rattle slightly with our movement, adding a metallic soundtrack to our ragged breathing.

"I want to watch you when you come," she whispers against my ear. "I want to see it in every mirror."

I'm beyond speech now, reduced to primal sounds as the dual sensations of fullness and vibration push me toward the edge. My heels dig into her back as I lock my ankles behind her, pulling her deeper.

"That's it," she whispers, her pace increasing. "Come with me, Zara."

My muscles clench around the shaft as my orgasm crashes through me. My vision blurs, and a cry tears from my throat that I barely recognize as my own. Diane moans and holds me tight through it, witnessing every tremor and spasm that wracks my body. She's climaxing too; I can tell from the way her body shudders against mine, from how her rhythm falters and her jaw clenches..

For a moment, we're suspended in time, locked together in pleasure as we pulse in unison. I'm flushed, disheveled, and utterly wrecked.

Diane fumbles for the remote and switches it off. She's breathing hard, her forehead pressed against mine, our bodies still joined. Her arms tremble slightly with the effort of holding me.

"God, you're beautiful," she whispers.

I catch glimpses of us in the mirrors—my legs wrapped around her waist, her face flushed with exertion. It's primal and raw and perfect.

When the last aftershocks subside, she carefully pulls

out and lowers me until my feet touch the ground again. My legs are wobbly, and I'm grateful for the cuffs holding me upright.

Diane quickly reaches up to release the cuffs, supporting my weight as my wrists come free. Blood rushes back to my arms, and I wince at the tingling sensation.

"Come here," she murmurs, settling into the armchair and reaching for me. I climb onto her lap, still catching my breath, and she pulls a soft blanket over us both. I curl against her chest and she wraps her arms around me.

My body feels heavy, sated, like I could fall asleep right here.

"You okay?" she asks.

I nod against her chest, too content to form words. Her breathing steadies beneath my cheek. Mine matches hers without trying.

60

DIANE

"So," Ruby says with a knowing smile, cutting into her fish. "How was the other night? Athena told me she set you two up at the club."

I take a sip of the white wine she ordered for us—something Greek that pairs well with the feta and sun-dried tomatoes on top of the whole grilled sea bass we're sharing. The Pantheon's private booth wraps around us, muting the restaurant's noise.

"It was... great. Thank you for sharing your space with us."

Ruby laughs. "Oh, don't thank me—it was all Athena's idea. Though judging by that blush, I'm guessing you made good use of the facilities?"

"Ruby!"

"What? I'm just saying, that mirrored room is something else. Trust me, I know." She arches a brow at me, clearly enjoying my discomfort. "Anyway, the interview—I thought you both handled it beautifully."

"It went as well as it could have," I say, grateful for the

subject change. "Though it's strange to suddenly be in the public eye like this. I'll need some time to adjust."

Ruby's expression softens. "Are you struggling?"

I push a piece of fish around my plate. "I'm starting to understand how Zara lives her life now. I've barely left the Olympus since we got back from LA. There's always press around, photographers waiting. It's hard to... exist. Going to a store, taking a walk—things I never thought twice about before."

"That must be overwhelming."

"It is. And I'd be lying if I said I wasn't stressed. It's been a lot for both of us. There's been some bad press, mostly directed at me. The hypocrite angle, you know—working for my father's foundation while secretly being gay. Which is understandable." I shake my head. "But there's also been incredible support. Messages from people saying we gave them courage, that our story mattered to them. That makes it worth it."

I pause, then correct myself. "No, what am I saying? Even with only bad press, it would have been worth it. We get to be together now. Openly. And that's been really special." I smile, thinking about the past weeks. "I've gotten to know Isabella and Jess better and that time together has been priceless. They've decided to stay for a little longer, which is nice."

"Good." Ruby reaches across the table and squeezes my hand briefly. "But Diane, it's okay not to be okay. This can't be easy for you."

"It hasn't been," I say. "It's not just the press. My entire life has been structured around work, around purpose. And now I'm drifting, I suppose. I've been applying for jobs but haven't heard back from anyone yet. I'm not sure if it's because of the publicity or if I simply need to be patient."

I take a bite of fish, grateful for Ruby's presence. She doesn't rush to fill the silence, just nods and regards me.

"How are you and Athena doing?" I ask. "Did you have a nice time at your parents?"

"Yeah, it was lovely, actually," Ruby says. "Athena's been busy today, of course—she always is, and so am I—but she'll join us later." She breaks off a piece of bread. "We took the afternoon off so we could spend time with you. We figured you might need some distraction from everything."

Warmth spreads through me as I look at this woman who I'm grateful to call my friend now. "Thank you. I really appreciate it."

"That's what friends are for."

"You know," I say, "somehow, despite everything being uncertain and stressful, I'm happier now. Having lunch with a friend, knowing I'll share a bed with my partner tonight..." I laugh. "My partner. I still can't believe I get to say that."

Ruby grins. "How is Zara handling everything?"

"Zara's been amazing. Busier than ever—performing, interviews, appearances—but she always makes time for us." I think about this morning, how she kissed me goodbye before rushing off to an interview. "Even though this has been a lot, the residency is everything she hoped it would be, and I love watching her thrive."

"And you'll thrive too," Ruby says. "Give it time. The right opportunity will come along."

I want to believe her. I do believe her, mostly. But there's a voice in the back of my mind that wonders if I've made myself unemployable, if the Washington name has become a liability rather than an asset in this new phase in my life.

"The worst part is the waiting," I say. "I've sent out probably twenty applications in the past week. Good positions, too—ones I'm qualified for, where my experience should count for something. But I keep refreshing my email and there's nothing. Not even a rejection."

"Be patient," Ruby says.

"I know. But when you're used to being busy every second of every day, having nothing to do is torture." I drain my wine glass and Ruby refills it without asking. "Isabella and I have been helping with Lucas, and Jess lets me assist her with her accounting work, which probably says enough about how desperate I am for purpose."

Ruby laughs. "You're helping with taxes for fun?"

"Yeah. Believe it or not, I..." My phone buzzes in my purse. I ignore it at first, but it buzzes again. And again.

"You should check that," Ruby says. "Might be important."

I pull out my phone and stare at the screen. The caller ID shows a 213 area code—Los Angeles.

"Sorry, I have to take this," I say, standing quickly.

Ruby waves me away and I weave through the tables toward a quiet corner near the restrooms.

"This is Diane."

"Ms. Washington, this is Sarah Moreno from The Center LA. Do you have a few minutes to talk?"

I lean against the wall, trying to steady my breathing. The Center LA. I submitted my application for their Director of Development position—a role overseeing fundraising for one of the largest LGBTQ+ community organizations on the West Coast. They provide mental health services, housing assistance, youth programs, and advocacy work, all funded through individual donors, corporate sponsorships, and foundation grants.

"Yes, absolutely. Thank you for calling."

"I wanted to reach out personally rather than email you," Sarah says. "I've reviewed your application and have had several conversations with my team about your candidacy. I have to be direct with you—your current public profile presents both advantages and challenges for us."

My stomach tightens. Here it comes—the polite rejection wrapped in corporate language.

"I understand," I say quietly.

"Let me finish," she continues. "The challenges are obvious. You've worked for organizations that opposed LGBTQ rights. Your family connections are to conservative politics that have actively undermined our community. Some of our staff, donors, and the people we serve will question whether you're genuinely committed to our mission or simply looking for career rehabilitation after a public scandal."

I close my eyes, the words landing exactly as I expected them to. This is the conversation I've been dreading—the acknowledgment that my past makes me unemployable in the spaces where I want to work.

"However," Sarah continues, and I hear the shift in her tone, "your fundraising track record speaks for itself. In the past five years as executive director of the Washington Foundation, you increased annual donations by two hundred percent. You cultivated relationships with donors across the political spectrum, and you did it all while navigating one of the most complicated donor networks in the country. Those are not small accomplishments."

"That's kind of you to say."

"I'm not being kind, I'm being accurate. We've done our research, Ms. Washington. Your former colleagues—the ones willing to talk to us, anyway—consistently described you as strategic, organized, pleasant, and exceptionally good at building relationships. Those are exactly the skills we need and frankly, your recent coming out—while controversial—demonstrates something we value: the courage to choose integrity over comfort."

Hope flickers in my chest, cautious and uncertain.

"We're looking for someone who can expand our donor base beyond our traditional progressive supporters," Sarah explains. "Someone who understands how to talk to people with money. Your background gives you credibility."

"I'd be honored to be considered for the job," I say carefully.

"I want to be clear about what this would entail," she continues. "This is a high-profile position. You'd be managing our entire development strategy—major gifts, corporate partnerships, foundation grants, special events. You'd oversee a team of twenty and be responsible for raising about forty million dollars annually. You'd also serve as a public face for the organization. That means speaking engagements and media interviews."

"I have no problem with that," I say.

"There would also be internal pushback to work through," Sarah says. "Some of our staff and community members may be uncomfortable with the idea of hiring someone like you. You'd need to prove through your actions that your commitment is genuine, not performative."

The assessment is fair, even if it stings. "I wouldn't expect anything less. I have a lot to prove, and I know that."

"Good. Because if we move forward with this, you'll be under a microscope." Sarah pauses. "I also need to be honest about compensation. We're a nonprofit with limited resources. The salary for this position is one hundred and forty thousand, which I realize is significantly less than what someone with your background and experience would typically command. We can't compete with what you were likely making at the Washington Foundation."

One hundred and forty thousand. It's less than half. But it's also more than enough to live on, more than what most people make.

"That's not a concern," I say honestly. "I'm not looking to maintain my previous lifestyle. I'm looking to do work that matters."

"I appreciate that. Are you prepared for the level of scrutiny that may come with this role?"

I think about the past few weeks—the media attention, the way photographers follow Zara and me now. The constant awareness that people are watching, judging, analyzing every move we make.

"I'm learning to handle scrutiny," I say. "And let's face it; I doubt it can get any worse than it is now."

"Fair." Sarah chuckles. "Alright, here's what I'd like to propose. Come to Los Angeles for an interview. You'll meet with me, with our Deputy Director, and our head of programs."

I do a small fist pump against my leg where no one can see, grinning like an idiot. "My schedule has never been more open," I say, and Sarah laughs again.

"Excellent. I'll ask HR to set up a date with you and we'll talk more when we meet."

After we hang up I stand there for a moment, letting the conversation sink in. I have an interview. It's a chance.

When I return to the table, Ruby looks up expectantly, her fork paused halfway to her mouth. "Everything okay? You look like you're either going to cry or burst into song."

Before I can answer, Athena appears beside our table. She pulls out the empty chair and settles in, signaling a waiter for another wine glass.

"Hello, ladies. What did I miss?"

I can't keep the smile off my face. "I have a job interview."

61

ZARA

"That's a wrap," Claudette calls out, lowering her camera. "We got everything we need. Beautiful work, Zara."

I roll my shoulders after holding poses for two hours. The conference suite at the Ariel has been transformed into a makeshift studio—lighting equipment everywhere, racks of designer clothes, a hair and makeup team set up in the back.

"Thank you, it was a pleasure," I say, kicking off my stiletto heels. An assistant zips me out of my dress and I put on the pair of leggings, T-shirt, and sneakers I arrived in. "When will these run?"

"September issue." Claudette packs up her camera and equipment. "I'll send the selects by end of week."

I glance across the room to where Diane sits curled in an armchair, scrolling through her phone. When she catches my eye, she smiles.

"Sorry that took so long," I say, walking up to her.

"Are you kidding me? That was fascinating to watch." She gets up and kisses my cheek. "I love seeing you at work."

Around us, the crew packs up. I catch the quick glances —the makeup artist's eyes flicking toward us before she looks away, the stylist pretending to focus on hanging clothes. They're trying not to stare, but three days ago we came out on national television and everyone in this room watched it happen.

Peter appears, pocketing his phone. "There are photographers outside," he says.

I meet his eyes and blow out my cheeks. "How bad?" I gather my things and stuff them into my carry-all.

"Bad enough. Car's waiting at the entrance. Are you ready?"

We nod and he gestures toward the door. "Stay close, keep moving, don't stop."

Diane takes my hand and we take the elevator down. Peter makes a call on the way, liaising with security. When the doors open to the lobby, two of Zara's security guards are waiting.

"We'll walk you out," one of them says.

The lobby is crowded with tourists and gamblers, slot machines chiming. No one notices us as we cross toward the main entrance. But through the glass doors, I can see them —a cluster of men with cameras, a few more near the valet stand.

I don't mind fans. I love fans, actually because those encounters are genuine. They're nervous, excited, sometimes crying. They tell me what my music means to them, and I get to thank them for supporting my career. Those moments remind me why I do this.

But the paparazzi are not here because they love my music or want to connect. They're here for the shot that sells, the angle that generates clicks. Predatory. Relentless. And right now, they're waiting for us.

"Fuck," I mutter.

"Face down," Peter says. "Straight to the car."

Peter and the security guards position themselves around us and we push through the doors. Immediately, the shouting starts.

"Zara!"

"Over here!"

"Diane!"

They move fast, closing the distance. Our big, beefy protectors try to keep them back, but the photographers are darting around, cutting off angles, cameras firing. One man with a video camera walks backward in front of us, blocking our path to the SUV idling at the curb.

"Move," Peter barks, but the photographer ignores him.

"Zara, just one shot! Look up!"

"Diane, how's Senator Washington handling this?"

Another photographer comes in from the side, his lens inches from Diane's face. She flinches, turning into me, but he moves with her, still shooting.

"Back off," I say sharply.

He doesn't. None of them do. They're a tight pack now, circling, cutting off our route to the car. Every time a security guard pushes one back, another fills the gap.

"Is it true you're engaged?"

"Zara, smile for us!"

"Diane, are you moving to LA?"

Diane's panting beside me. Her hand in mine is slick with sweat.

We're maybe ten feet from the car when someone pushes in too close from behind. Diane stumbles forward and I catch her waist, steadying her. The cameras explode—everyone shouting, surging in, the space collapsing around us.

"Watch it!" One of the security guards snaps, getting between us and them.

But they don't watch it. A photographer to my right leans over Diane's shoulder, his camera so close I can hear the mechanical click of the shutter next to her ear. She makes a small, frightened sound.

"Get away from her," I snap.

"Just doing my job, Zara."

"Your job?" I turn to look at him—middle-aged, khaki vest, press badge hanging around his neck. "Back off!"

We stumble forward and I push Diane into the car, then climb in after her.

Peter slams the door shut and gets in on the other side while one of Zara's security guards slides into the front. The other stays behind, blocking the drive so other cars can't follow. The driver pulls away and we turn onto the street and finally lose them.

Diane sits rigid beside me, staring straight ahead. Her jaw is clenched so tight I can see the muscle jumping. She's not crying. She's not speaking. She's barely breathing.

"Diane," I say softly.

She doesn't respond so I touch her arm and she flinches, then seems to realize it's me.

"Is it always like that?"

"Sometimes," I say.

She looks away, back out the window. We're driving down the Strip now—tourists on the sidewalk, couples holding hands, people taking photos of the hotels. Normal people doing normal things.

"How do you cope?" she asks. "Every day. Every time you go anywhere."

I want to tell her it gets easier. I want to say she'll get used to it. But I can't lie to her; I'm still shaking myself.

"It's not easy. But you learn to live with it."

62

DIANE

"Thank God for The Olympus and its VIP entrance," I say, finally dropping my guard.

Zara puts her arm around me and pulls me close. I rest my head against her shoulder, cherishing the quiet and safety of her suite. Suddenly I'm crying, tears sliding down my face that I can't seem to stop.

"Sorry," I say, wiping at my eyes. "I don't mean to be dramatic. That was just a lot."

"You're not being dramatic. That was intense for me too."

I pull back to look at her. The heavy makeup from the shoot is still on her face, foundation and contouring that looks surreal in natural light. But underneath it, I see the exhaustion in her eyes, the tightness around her mouth.

"I'm slowly starting to understand," I whisper. "A little bit. What your life is actually like."

She nods but doesn't say anything.

"The way they—they don't even see you as a person. They see content. Something to sell."

"True."

"And you deal with that enough that you've learned to

live smaller. To avoid going places, doing things, existing in normal spaces." I touch her face. "I get it now. Why you rarely leave here unless you have to."

Zara takes my hand. "This life isn't for everyone, Diane. You should consider that." She sighs. "Now that everything has changed, it will be hard for you to leave The Olympus without being recognized. That must feel suffocating."

"Stop." I squeeze her hand. "You warned me about all of this. I made my choice. I don't care how hard it is—it's much easier to be with you than without you."

Zara's eyes fill with tears too, and she pulls me close again and kisses the top of my head.

"I love you," she says quietly. "We'll figure it out." She pauses. "And there are ways to make it easier."

"Oh, yeah?" I manage a small laugh. "What's that? Blue wigs?"

"Well, yes, that can work sometimes." She gives me a small smile. "But I'm talking about my nice big home in LA with ocean views. Secret escapes to private resorts. Restaurants and clubs where privacy is respected and protected." She tucks a strand of hair behind my ear. "Money *can* buy privacy, so how about we go away for a couple of days? Somewhere quiet. Just us."

I shake my head. "I'll be fine, really. I'm just a little shaken up. And you have to be here for your residency."

"I get the occasional break," Zara says. "I have three days off next week—no shows, no rehearsals. "Let's go somewhere nobody can find us."

I think about it—three days without cameras, without strangers shouting questions, without having to stay indoors. Three days of being together.

"Okay," I say. "That would be really nice."

She leans in and kisses me. Softly at first, then deeper,

her hands coming up to cup my face. I kiss her back, feverishly, and all I want to do is escape to the warmth of her bed.

The sound of the door opening makes us both jump.

"Zara? Diane?" Isabella calls out. "We're back!"

We break apart just as Isabella rounds the corner with Lucas and Jess trailing behind her.

"Oh!" Isabella stops short, taking in the scene—Zara and me standing very close, my face probably still tear-stained, Zara's photo shoot makeup smudged too. "Sorry, we didn't mean to interrupt."

"You're not interrupting," Zara says, stepping back.

"We definitely interrupted," Jess says, looking at me. "Are you okay? You've been crying."

"I'm fine."

"She's not," Zara says. "We got ambushed by paparazzi leaving my photoshoot. It was bad."

Isabella winces and hands Lucas to Jess. "Oh, honey, come here," she says, pulling me into a hug.

"I'm fine, really." I try to smile. "I'll get used to it."

"You shouldn't have to." Isabella points to the couch. "Sit," she orders. "Both of you. I'm making lunch."

"Mom, you don't need to—" Zara starts.

"Lunch," Isabella repeats firmly, heading toward the kitchen. "Jess, make them tea."

"On it, boss." Jess deposits Lucas into my arms before I can protest. "Hold him for a minute."

I settle onto the couch with Lucas, Zara dropping down beside me. He's warm and solid, wearing tiny jeans and a shirt with a giraffe on it. He looks up at me with wide eyes, studying my face with the intense concentration only babies can manage. Then, apparently satisfied with his assessment, he reaches up and grabs my nose.

"Ow," I say, laughing.

He giggles—an infectious, burbling sound—and does it again.

Zara leans over to kiss his cheek. "He likes you."

Lucas lets go of my nose and immediately lunges for Zara's face, his chubby hands patting her cheeks. When his palm hits the thick layer of foundation, he pulls back, confused, then tentatively touches her face again like he's trying to figure out what's wrong with it.

"Yeah, buddy, I know," Zara says. "It's a little sticky."

He makes a questioning baby sound—"Bah?"—and pokes her cheek one more time for good measure.

I can't help it—I laugh. Actually laugh. Some of my tension drains away as I watch this tiny human investigate Zara's face like it's the most fascinating mystery. I have to give it to him; her face truly is fascinating. It's the most beautiful face in the world.

63

ZARA

*T*hree whole days. No interviews, no performances, no meetings. Just Diane and me and seventy-two hours of privacy.

The helicopter waits on the rooftop helipad of the Olympus, its rotors spinning lazily in the pre-dawn air. The pilot—a woman named Adele—gives us a quick safety briefing before helping us into the back seats. Diane settles in beside me, her hand finding mine as Adele gives us headsets to communicate over the engine noise.

"Ready?" Adele's voice comes through. "Can you hear me?"

"Yes," Diane calls.

"All clear," I confirm.

The helicopter lifts, and my stomach drops as we rise above the rooftop.

"I've never been in a helicopter," Diane says through the headset, her grip on my hand tightening as we bank slightly to the right. "I'm a little nervous." She manages a smile. "Where are we going again?"

"Amangiri. It's a resort in southern Utah, near the Arizona border. About an hour flight from here."

The helicopter climbs higher, leaving Vegas behind as we head northeast. Below us, the development gives way to desert—stretches of tan and rust-colored earth punctuated by scrubby vegetation. The rising sun paints everything in shades of gold and amber, shadows still long across the landscape.

"It's built into the desert landscape near Canyon Point," I continue. "The whole philosophy is about privacy and connection to nature. Individual pavilions instead of hotel rooms, no other buildings visible from your suite. The kind of place where celebrities go to disappear for a while. It's been recommended to me by a few people."

The flight settles into a steady rhythm, the helicopter eating up miles of desert. Diane gradually relaxes.

"It's beautiful," she says, watching the sun continue its ascent. "So much empty space."

We pass over a dry riverbed cutting through the landscape, its banks lined with darker vegetation that marks where water flows during rare rains. In the distance, I can see the beginnings of red rock formations.

"Do you ever go on vacation?" Diane asks.

"Rarely," I say. "I've always been non-stop. When I do have time off, I usually visit my mom for a few days. That's about it." I glance at Diane. "What about you? Did you take vacations before all this?"

"Not really. I think because I never had anyone to go with," she says. "My old friends in Washington are all married with kids. We'd meet for lunch occasionally, but we were never close—not really. They didn't know my biggest secret." She pauses. "I wonder if they even want to be associated with me now."

I squeeze her hand. "If they don't, they were never friends to begin with."

"True." She smiles. "And it's nice to have someone to travel with now. Someone I actually want to be with all the time."

The red rock formations grow more dramatic—towering mesas and deep canyons, and the landscape shifts to something more sculptural.

"I think we both needed this break," I say. "I know you haven't been working these past two weeks, but between dealing with the press and sending out applications, you haven't had time to rest. And I've been busy since the residency started..." I trail off, watching a shadow move across a canyon wall below us. "Do you feel ready for your interview next week?"

"I think so." Diane shifts to look at me. "I'm trying not to get my hopes up, but I really want this job, Zara."

"You'd be great," I say. "They'd be lucky to have you."

"We'll see. There's a lot of skepticism to overcome." She gestures at the desert below. "But I don't want to think about that now. Let's just have an amazing time together."

Adele's voice comes through the headset. "We're about ten minutes from descent. You can see Amangiri ahead—that cluster of low buildings at two o'clock."

I lean forward, following her direction. The resort emerges from the landscape like it grew there—sand-colored pavilions scattered across the terrain, each with its own private pool carved into the rock. A large geometric pool at the center, flanked by desert palms, reflects the morning sky. Paths wind between the buildings like dry riverbeds, ensuring each sanctuary remains invisible to the others.

The helicopter touches down on a helipad set back from

the main buildings. Adele cuts the engine, and as the rotors slow, the desert quiet rushes in.

A man in casual linen resort attire approaches with a luggage trolley as we climb out. "Ms. Nova, Ms. Washington, welcome to Amangiri. I'm Marcus, and I'll be your personal concierge during your stay."

He leads us along a path that winds through the landscape, pointing out amenities. "The resort has six suites, spaced to ensure complete privacy. Your pavilion is in a particularly secluded section. All meals can be delivered directly to your suite if you prefer, the spa is available by appointment. Our restaurant by the main pool is open twenty-four-seven."

"Perfect," I say. "But I think we'll eat here."

"Understood. The phone in your pavilion goes directly through to me. Call me anytime, day or night. Otherwise, we'll leave you to enjoy your stay undisturbed."

Our pavilion comes into view—a low, modern structure that looks out over a private terrace with an infinity pool overlooking the desert. The interior is rustic and decorated with natural materials: pale stone, weathered wood, textiles in desert tones.

Marcus shows us the essentials—the outdoor shower with views of the mesa, the meditation area, the stocked bar and welcome canapés and champagne, the ridiculous bathroom with its stone soaking tub—and then, blessedly, he leaves.

Diane walks to the windows, taking in the view. "This is incredible. You weren't kidding when you said it was secluded."

I come up behind her, wrapping my arms around her waist. "Three days."

"Just us," she says, leaning back against me.

We stand there in silence, watching the morning light shift across the landscape. The exhaustion I've been carrying for weeks begins to loosen its grip. Here, in this desert sanctuary, I don't have to be Zara Nova. The desert doesn't care who I am.

64

DIANE

*T*he sun lowers toward the horizon, turning the desert into layers of burnt orange and violet. We've spent most of the day doing nothing—and I mean nothing in the most luxurious sense of the word. Massages, reading on the terrace, making love and napping in the enormous bed, and feasting on a delicious lunch.

Standing on the terrace with a glass of wine and classical music playing, we're watching the light shift across the landscape. Zara's barefoot, wearing linen pants and a loose tank top, her dark curls piled messily on top of her head.

"How about a dip in the pool?" I say, shooting her a mischievous wink. "A skinny dip."

Zara stares at me like I've suggested something outrageous. "A skinny dip..."

I spread my arms. "Is there an echo out here?"

She laughs, shaking her head. "We're outside, Diane. Outside."

"But it's so private. Look around—there's nothing but desert for miles."

"I know that logically," she says, moving to stand beside me. "But you know it goes against every instinct I have."

She grins but I can see the internal battle playing out—years of always being watched, of never letting her guard down where anyone might see. Even here, in the middle of nowhere, those instincts run deep. She bites her lip, looking out at the endless expanse of sand and rock. "You're crazy."

I press a kiss to her shoulder and release her hand. "Well, I'm going in with or without you."

I set down my wine glass and reach for the hem of my t-shirt, but instead of pulling it off, I pause. A flirty smile spreads across my face as I sway my hips to the music, slowly inching the fabric up my stomach.

"What are you doing?" Zara asks, but there's already laughter threatening at the edges of her voice.

"What does it look like? I'm stripping." I bat my eyelashes and lift the Tshirt over my head, revealing my bra. "This is very serious business." I turn around and glance at her over my shoulder, wiggling my eyebrows before twirling the T-shirt above my head like a lasso and tossing it dramatically in her direction.

It lands on her shoulder, and she catches it with one hand.

"There's more where that came from," I announce, striking a pose with one hand on my hip. The air feels great against my skin, warm and alive. I hook my thumbs into the waistband of my shorts, shimmy them down to my thighs, and do an exaggerated wiggle to get them off. I step out of them one leg at a time, nearly losing my balance and making Zara laugh.

I take off my bra and toss it toward her. Then I hook my thumbs into my underwear and turn around, looking back at her as I slowly, so slowly, start to slide them down over my hips. I make a show of it, swaying and humming along to the music.

Standing fully naked, arms spread wide like I'm about to take a bow, the look on Zara's face makes every second of my theatrical performance worth it. She's not tense anymore. She's just looking at me, and the expression in her eyes has shifted from amusement to something that looks much more like arousal.

Her eyes roam over my body. "Diane, you're killing me."

Letting my arms drop, I walk toward her, slower now, no longer playing, and stop right in front of her, close enough that I could touch her but don't. "Still think this is a terrible idea?"

She swallows hard, her gaze traveling from my face down my body and back up again. "I think... I think you're making it very difficult to think at all."

"Good." I reach out and tug at the hem of her tank top. "Your turn."

She chuckles nervously, then pulls it over her head. She's not wearing a bra and the golden light catches on her mahogany skin. When she pushes down her pants and panties in one go, I forget how to breathe.

The curve of her hip, the softness of her stomach, her full breasts and the way she covers parts of herself with her arms, protecting herself against her own vulnerability. She's always beautiful, but tonight she's ravishing.

I take her hand again, threading our fingers together. My free hand comes up to cup her jaw, thumb tracing the line of her cheekbone as I lean in and brush my lips against her cheek. I trail soft kisses along her cheekbone to her temple, then down to the hinge of her jaw. When I reach her ear, I pause, letting my breath ghost across the sensitive skin there.

She shivers and I press my lips just below her ear, then move up to whisper against the shell of her ear. "How does it feel?"

"Scary. Liberating. Both at once." She pulls me toward the pool and we walk down the pool stairs and immerse ourselves.

The water envelops us, fresh against my skin, and we move toward the deep end where the edge of the pool disappears into the landscape. Our feet find purchase on tiptoe, the water reaching our shoulders.

Beyond the vanishing edge of the infinity pool, the landscape is formed by waves of rock, now painted in shades of violet and indigo as the sun sinks lower. The mountains are dark cutouts against a sky that's turned the color of crushed plums and fire, streaks of orange and pink bleeding across clouds that look like they've been set ablaze.

Zara's dark curls have come loose, falling and floating around her shoulders.

She wraps her arms around my waist and mine go around her neck, pulling her close until there's no space left between us, only skin against skin and the water cradling us. Our bodies press together, soft and yielding, and Zara kisses me.

She makes a soft sound against my mouth, one hand coming up to tangle in my hair, the other splayed across my lower back.

"This is..." She trails off, shaking her head.

"Yeah," I agree, because I know what she means. There aren't really words for this—for standing naked in a pool in the middle of the desert as the sun sets and turns everything to gold and fire, for feeling the air on your skin, for being so completely alone with someone that the rest of the world ceases to exist.

I watch her tilt her face toward the sky, eyes closed, breathing deeply like she just surfaced. I suppose, in a way, she has.

65

ZARA

*O*ur table is set with white linens, crystal, delicate china, and candles. The sun has just set, leaving the sky dark and star-filled. The stars are so bright here, in dense clusters that blur together.

Diane sits across from me and we're both wearing the plush resort dressing gowns. We realized we didn't have to dress for dinner and decided to stay comfortable. We've been lazy, indulging, relaxing. It's been decadent in the best way, existing in this space where time moves slowly and obligations don't exist. We've slept in, taken walks at dawn when the air was still cool, chilled in the pool naked, taken long baths, eaten whenever we felt like it rather than by any schedule. This morning we went back to bed after our walk and stayed there until nearly midday, dozing and talking and making love, and now we're having a midnight dinner.

"This is so delicious," Diane says. "My appetite is through the roof, I haven't eaten this much in weeks." We've had seared scallops with truffle beurre blanc, and a delicate lobster risotto that melted on my tongue. Now we're feasting on wagyu steak, roasted heirloom vegetables drizzled with aged balsamic and celeriac mash.

"Well," I say, cutting into my steak, "we've been burning a lot of calories. All that... exercise."

Diane raises an eyebrow. "You mean sexercise?" She smirks. "My favorite kind of cardio. I could get used to being spoiled like this."

"You deserve to be spoiled," I say, locking my eyes with hers. "In every way. It's time to be selfish for once."

I love seeing Diane so happy and free. Distracted from her old life pressing down on her—the job she lost, the parents who rejected her, the constant worry about the press. She deserves everything and more.

I've felt the shift in myself too. The exhaustion I've been carrying since the residency started has melted away. My shoulders don't ache from tension, and I haven't had a single stress headache.

"What are you thinking about?" Diane asks, studying my face in the candlelight.

"How much I don't want to leave tomorrow."

Diane sets down her fork and reaches for her wine glass. "Me neither. It feels like we've been in a bubble here." She smiles. "It's nice to have you all to myself."

"I know," I say, and then pause, choosing my words carefully. "But we'll never really be alone like this when you're with me. In our home, sure, but as you've experienced, there's always someone watching."

Diane's expression doesn't falter. "I can handle it."

"Are you sure? Because you'll never get used to it. I'm still not used to it, even after all these years. The constant scrutiny, the lack of privacy, people forming opinions about you based on a single photograph or a ten-second video clip. It's relentless."

Diane tilts her head, narrowing her eyes. "Are you trying to put me off? Get rid of me?"

"Of course not," I say quickly. "I just don't want to be the reason your life gets impossibly complicated. I need you to understand what you're getting into."

Diane stands and comes around the table. When I scoot back my chair, she settles onto my lap and wraps her arms around my neck.

"My life is already complicated, Zara. And I'm happy." She kisses me softly, her lips warm and tasting faintly of wine. When she pulls back, she looks serious. "I really am."

I rest my forehead against hers, breathing her in.

"Do you ever wish you weren't famous?" she asks.

"No. I love to perform and I'm incredibly grateful that I get to make a living making music. I do sometimes wish I could turn fame off, though. Be anonymous for a day. Walk down a street or get a coffee without being recognized."

I run my hands up and down her back. "But we can do this more often in future. Go away together. We've gotten a taste of what it's like to escape and now we know it's possible. We could plan trips. Romantic getaways where no one knows us or cares who we are. After my residency ends, I'll have more flexibility so we could make it a regular thing." I pause, suddenly aware that I'm making plans. "I mean, if you want that. I don't want to be presumptuous and – "

"Stop," Diane interrupts, pressing a finger against my lips. She pulls back to look at me fully. "I want to move to LA. Whether I get this job or not, I want to be there. With you. LA is a big city. I'll find something."

"You're sure?" A lump rises in my throat and I swallow it down.

"I'm sure. And I like it when you use the word 'future.'" She kisses me softly. "That reminds me, I should probably start thinking about the interview. I haven't reviewed my talking points in days."

"Don't put too much pressure on yourself. You're passionate, driven, experienced, and you care about the cause. That comes through when you talk about it. They'll see that." I pause. "When are you flying to LA?"

"Tomorrow night. I want to be there the day before so I won't have to stress about delays." She sighs. "And at some point I'll have to head to Washington for a night or two. Pick up my post, maybe meet with Mom. She's still calling and messaging me. She really wants to talk."

"That's good, right?" I say.

"We'll see." She shifts slightly on my lap, her gaze drifting upward. "Oh my god—look."

I follow her eyes to the sky just as a streak of light blazes across the darkness. Then another. And another. Shooting stars, three of them in quick succession, brilliant and fleeting against the vast expanse of stars.

"Make a wish," Diane whispers. We sit there wrapped in each other, watching the sky, and I don't need to make a wish because everything I want is already here. When the last streak of light fades, Diane turns back to me, and I know she feels it too.

66

DIANE

*T*he Center LA occupies two floors of a modest office building in Silver Lake, the kind of neighborhood where vintage shops sit next to vegan cafes and rainbow flags hang from apartment windows. The building is clean and functional but far from flashy.

I sit across from Sarah Moreno and two other members of the hiring committee—Marcus Liu, the Deputy Director, and Elena Gomez, who heads their youth programs.

Sarah adjusts her glasses and smiles warmly. "Thank you for flying out, Diane. Did you come in from Washington this morning?"

"No, actually. I flew in from Vegas last night. I'm staying there with my partner." I meet each of their gazes with a polite smile. "As you know, I'm in a relationship with Zara Nova and she has a residency there."

There's a brief pause. Marcus and Elena exchange a quick glance, but Sarah just nods.

"Yes," Sarah says. "We watched your interview with Robin West. It was brave."

"Thank you." My hands rest in my lap, fingers laced

together to keep them from fidgeting. I'm wearing black pants and a cream silk blouse—professional but not stuffy.

"We've reviewed your application thoroughly," Sarah continues. "Your experience in development is impressive— the fundraising numbers you achieved at the Washington Foundation speak for themselves. Twenty-three million in one year is remarkable for an organization of that size."

"I had a strong team," I say. "And we were strategic about donor cultivation."

"No doubt." Marcus leans forward. "But let's address the obvious concern. Some of our donors will be skeptical. They'll see you as a liability—someone whose past associations could damage our reputation. How would you respond to that?"

I've been preparing for this question but I still need a moment before I answer. "I'd argue that my experience gives me unique insight into how conservative donors think, how they operate. I know their language, their priorities, their objections. That knowledge could be valuable in building bridges with moderate donors who might not otherwise engage with your work."

"Bridges?" Elena raises an eyebrow. "Why would we want bridges to people who've opposed our rights?"

"Because change happens at the margins," I say. "The people who are already committed to your mission will keep supporting you regardless. But there's a whole segment of potential donors—moderate conservatives, business leaders, people who've never considered LGBTQ+ issues a priority—who might be persuaded if approached correctly. I know how to talk to those people. I know what motivates them, what their objections will be before they voice them, and how to address those concerns without compromising your mission."

Sarah tilts her head thoughtfully. "Can you give us an example?"

"Sure. Corporate donors often worry about backlash from conservative customers or shareholders. They want to support LGBTQ+ causes, but they need political cover. I'd help them frame their support as an investment in workplace diversity and employee retention—business issues rather than social issues. It's the same outcome, just a different entry point."

Marcus exchanges a glance with Sarah. "That's pragmatic. Maybe cynical, but pragmatic."

"I prefer to think of it as strategic," I say with a slight smile. "The goal is to increase your funding base and your impact. How we get there matters less than the results."

"Tell us about your vision for this role," Elena says. "What would success look like?"

This is where I feel most confident. "First, diversify your funding base. You're heavily reliant on individual donors, which makes you vulnerable during economic downturns. I'd focus on corporate sponsorships and foundation grants to create stability. Second, implement a major donor cultivation program with personalized engagement strategies. People give more when they feel personally connected to the mission—when they meet the youth you serve, hear their stories, see the direct impact of their contributions."

I pause, gathering my thoughts. "Third, I'd create giving circles for different donor segments. Young professionals who can't write the biggest checks but want to be involved. Corporate partners who need structured programs they can showcase to employees. Legacy donors who want to ensure long-term support. Each group needs different engagement strategies."

"And how would you handle the media attention?"

Marcus asks. "You're dating one of the biggest pop stars in the world. That comes with scrutiny."

"It does," I acknowledge. "But visibility also creates opportunity. I'd be strategic about it—keep the focus on the work rather than my personal life. But I won't pretend that my relationship with Zara couldn't benefit your organization. She's been a vocal advocate for LGBTQ+ rights for years. Her association, even indirectly through me, could bring attention and support from people who might not otherwise engage with your work."

Sarah's eyes widen slightly. "You have a point."

"A starting point," I counter. "But I want to be clear—I'm not interested in being a figurehead who trades on her girlfriend's fame. I want to do actual work. I want to build systems, cultivate relationships, and increase your capacity to serve more people. The media attention is a tool, not the job itself."

Elena, who has been quiet until now, asks her first question. "What do you know about The Center's programs?"

"You provide mental health services to LGBTQ+ individuals, with a focus on youth who face disproportionate barriers to care. Your emergency housing program serves LGBTQ+ youth experiencing homelessness—one of the most vulnerable populations. Your advocacy work has been instrumental in pushing for inclusive policies at the state level, particularly around school protections and healthcare access. And your community center serves as a gathering space for people who might not have safe places elsewhere."

"That's our mission in a nutshell," Sarah says, and then she pauses, studying me. "But you could work anywhere, Diane. Why The Center specifically?"

I take a breath, feeling the weight of the question. "I'm thirty years old. I just told my parents I was gay a few weeks ago." I pause, aware of how that sounds. "In my world, being gay wasn't an option. It wasn't something you could be and still remain part of the family. So I didn't tell anyone. For thirty years, I just... didn't."

I look at each of them in turn. "And I had every advantage that made hiding possible. Money, education, security. A career where I could perform the role I was supposed to play. I could have stayed in that closet for the rest of my life. Probably would have, if I hadn't fallen in love."

My throat tightens, but I push through. "So when I think about a sixteen-year-old kid who gets thrown out of their home for being gay or trans—no money, no safety net, nowhere to go—I realize they don't get the choice I had. They can't hide. They don't have the resources to build a life in the closet. They're just... out there. Surviving. Trying to figure out who they are with nothing."

The room is silent.

"The work you do here keeps those kids alive," I say. "You give them a chance to become who they're meant to be when the world has taken everything else away from them. And I want to be part of that.

Sarah blinks, and I notice Elena has gone very still. Marcus clears his throat.

"That's—" Sarah starts, then stops. She glances at her colleagues before turning back to me. "That's exactly why we do this work."

Marcus nods slowly. "You're very passionate about this."

"I am. This isn't just about finding a new job for me—it's about aligning my career with my values for the first time in my life. I'm not going to waste your time or mine if I don't think I can make a real difference here."

Sarah closes her folder and exchanges looks with Marcus and Elena before turning back to me.

"Thank you for your candor, Diane. We have a few more interviews scheduled, but I'd like to give you a tour of the building today so you can meet some of the staff and get a sense of whether this is somewhere you'd actually want to be every day."

67

ZARA

*T*he restaurant is tucked into a quiet corner of the Ariel Casino. With its dark wood paneling and soft lighting, it's the kind of place where the menus don't list prices and the waiters appear exactly when you need them and vanish the moment you don't.

This is our last meal together before Mom and Jess fly out this afternoon—Mom back to Brooklyn, Jess and Lucas back to LA. We're seated at a table with a view of the gardens, privacy screens discreetly positioned to keep us invisible to the rest of the dining room. Mom sits across from me, looking simultaneously impressed and slightly uncomfortable in her navy cardigan and slacks. Diane is beside me, one hand resting on my knee under the table. Jess tries to distract Lucas in his high chair from making grabby hands at the table cloth.

"I have to say," Jess announces, reaching for her water glass, "These past weeks have been such a treat. The pool, the concierge, the room service, laundry service, help with Lucas, and seeing my bestie everyday... I've actually been able to catch up on work while having a great time." She grins at Diane. "And thank you for helping me organize my spreadsheets. I don't know what possessed you to volunteer for that level of tedium, but my reports have never looked better."

"I needed something to do," Diane says with a humorous shrug. "Besides, color-coding expense categories is my guilty pleasure."

"I'm so glad you've enjoyed yourself," I say to Jess. "And I'm going to miss having you around." I turn to Mom. "And you too, Mom."

"I'll miss you too, honey." Mom squeezes my hand. "But I'm also looking forward to getting back to my normal routine. My little kitchen, catching up with the tenants in the laundry room, and my Tuesday bingo nights…"

"Her bingo nights are sacred," Jess says solemnly. "Isabella told me she won forty-three dollars last time."

"Forty-seven," Mom corrects. "And I would have won more if Doris hadn't stolen my lucky seat."

Our food arrives—Mom ordered the sea bass, I went with the lamb, Diane has mushroom and truffle risotto, and Jess has ordered lobster thermidor.

Another waiter appears with a small bowl and sets it in front of Lucas with complete seriousness. "Butternut squash puree for the young gentleman," he announces. "Organic, locally sourced, with a touch of Madagascar cinnamon."

Lucas stares at him, mouth open, a string of drool descending toward the tablecloth.

The waiter maintains his composure. "Bon appétit, sir."

The moment he steps away, Lucas smashes both hands directly into the puree, sending orange specks flying across the white tablecloth.

"Oh my god," Jess mutters, grabbing for napkins. "Lucas, no—"

But it's too late. Lucas is gleefully finger-painting with his lunch, squealing with delight as he discovers he can make the orange stuff go everywhere. He looks up at us with a grin that shows off two tiny teeth poking through his gums.

We all lose it, and even Jess, who is mortified, bursts out in laughter.

"A hands-on approach to dining," Diane observes. "Very avant-garde."

"He's an artist," I say, watching my godson create abstract expressionism on the table, the floor, and himself.

Jess wrestles the bowl away from him and loads up a spoon. "Okay, buddy, let's try this the civilized way."

She guides the spoon to his mouth, and Lucas's eyes go wide. For a split second he goes completely still, then his mouth opens and he practically inhales the puree. He stares at the empty spoon, going slightly cross-eyed, his whole body leaning forward like he's trying to will more food onto it.

"More?" Jess asks, and Lucas makes an impatient squeaking sound, bouncing in his seat.

The next spoonful disappears just as fast, and suddenly all his finger-painting energy is redirected into the singular mission of eating as much squash as humanly possible.

"At least when he's eating, he's not redecorating," Jess mutters, loading up another spoon.

The rest of lunch passes without food flying around, the conversation flowing easily. Mom asks Diane about the interview, and Diane gives her a condensed version of the organization and what the role would involve. I watch

Mom's face as Diane talks, the way she nods and seems genuinely interested.

"So you'll be moving out there if you get the job?" Mom asks.

"That's the plan," Diane says. "I'd be based in LA, but Zara's here until next year, so I'd probably split my time between both cities initially, coming here on weekends."

"Good." Mom takes a sip of her Coke. "Zara needs someone looking after her. God knows she won't do it herself."

"Mom—"

"Don't 'Mom' me. You know it's true." She turns to Diane. "This one will work herself into the ground if you let her."

"I'll take care of her," Diane says, patting her arm. "I promise."

Mom smiles. "I know you will."

The moment feels significant. Mom's protective of me, always has been, and her approval of Diane is important to me. I look around the table—at Mom smiling at Diane with genuine warmth, at Jess wiping squash off Lucas's chin while he babbles contentedly, at Diane's hand coming to rest on my knee again. These are the people who matter most.

"Can we all get a picture together?" I ask, pulling out my phone to take a group selfie.

Lucas grins at the camera, his face a masterpiece of orange streaks. Jess makes a face of mock horror beside him, pointing at the mess he's made. Diane leans in at the last second and plants a kiss on my cheek, catching me mid-laugh so I look completely goofy, eyes half-closed and mouth open. Mom, meanwhile, sits up straight with her hands folded in front of her like she's posing for a passport photo.

The picture is a disaster—ridiculous and chaotic and better than any red carpet shot.

"This is definitely going on the fridge," I say, making it my phone background.

68

DIANE

I arrive at The Rundown fifteen minutes early because I want to be here first, settled in my seat with a drink in front of me when Mom walks in. I want her to be the one entering *my* new space, uncertain and out of place, instead of the other way around for once in my life.

Jamie is behind the bar, and she gives me a wave when I walk in, already grabbing me a beer. The television above the bar is playing a basketball game with the sound off, a handful of afternoon regulars are scattered across the space, and a couple is playing pool.

As I take a seat at my regular table, my phone buzzes with a text from Zara: *How are you doing?*

About to find out, I type back, then add: *I'll call you after.*

She sends back a heart emoji and I pocket my phone just as Mom walks in.

I watch her pause in the doorway like she's stumbled into another dimension. She's wearing a cream-colored blazer over a silk blouse, pressed slacks, and her pearl neck-lace. Her hair is styled in the way she always wears it, not a strand out of place, firmly secured with a whole lot of hairspray. She looks like she's about to have lunch at the country club.

Her eyes scan the space with a frown. She clearly thinks she's in the wrong place but then her eyes land on me. I raise my hand, and she walks toward my table, her purse clutched in front of her chest, perhaps worried she might get robbed. I watch her take in the sticky floors, the neon signs, the bartender with full sleeve tattoos, the pool table in the corner with its torn felt.

She slides into the chair across from me, setting her purse on her lap.

"Diane," she says.

"Mom."

We stare at each other and I take a sip of my drink to have something to do with my hands.

Jamie appears at our table.

"Hey, Jamie." I gesture to my mother. "This is my mom. Mom, this is Jamie, a good friend of mine."

Jamie extends her hand, and my mother takes it automatically, her decades of social conditioning kicking in even here. "Pleasure to meet you, Mrs. Washington."

"Likewise," my mother says, eyeing her tattoos.

"Can I get you something to drink?" Jamie asks.

My mother glances at my beer, then at the beer taps behind the bar, clearly out of her depth. "Do you have wine?"

"We've got house red or house white."

"White, please."

"Sure thing." Jamie shoots me a look that asks, *you okay?* I give her a small nod, and she disappears back to the bar.

Mom looks around the space again, processing everything, filing it away to examine later. A man at the bar laughs too loudly. Someone feeds quarters into the jukebox and a rock song starts playing.

"Is this where you..." Her voice trails off.

"Where I hang out?" I finish for her. "Sometimes. Mainly with Thomas."

"With Thomas? Really?"

"Yeah." I don't elaborate. I don't mention that Thomas and Jamie are together, that this place has become something close to a refuge, that the people here know me as just Diane, not as Senator Washington's daughter. Those details aren't hers to know.

Jamie returns with a glass of white wine that my mother accepts with a polite smile. When Jamie walks away, she takes a careful sip and winces slightly at the taste.

She takes a deep breath like she's bracing herself, and then her voice cracks. "I've missed you," she says. "I thought I'd lost you after you walked out."

I stare at her, at the way she starts to crumble, the way her eyes fill with tears she's trying desperately to hold back. I've never seen Mom like this, and instinctively, I reach out to take her hand.

"But you're ashamed of me," I say.

She flinches like I've slapped her, and a tear escapes down her cheek. She wipes it away quickly, glancing around to see if anyone noticed. Old habits.

"Honey, I'm your mother and I love you. Nothing will ever change that. Nothing, do you hear me?" She squeezes my hand. "When you walked out that night, I wanted to stop you. I wanted to run after you and tell you to come back, that we'd figure it out together." She's crying openly now, not bothering to hide it anymore.

"But you didn't..."

"No, I didn't and that was wrong."

My mother stands up, comes around to my side and pulls me into a hug. A real hug. Even as a kid, she rarely hugged me. Her arms wrap around me tight, and she's crying into my shoulder.

"I'm so sorry," she whispers against my hair. "I'm so, so sorry."

I'm crying too as I let myself sink into her embrace, and we stay like that for a long moment, a mother and daughter crying in a dive bar while rock music plays on the jukebox and strangers pretend not to notice.

When we pull apart, we're both a mess. My mother's mascara is smudged, her composure shattered. She pulls tissues from her handbag and hands one to me, and we both laugh a little at the absurdity of it all.

"Does Dad know you're here?" I ask, though I already know the answer.

"No." She dabs at her eyes. "He doesn't."

"Will you tell him?"

She fiddles with her tissue. "I don't know. Things between your father and me are... complicated right now."

I watch her twist her wedding ring around her finger, a nervous gesture I've seen a thousand times but never really paid attention to.

"He's angry and shocked about you and Zara," she continues. "About the publicity, about what it means for his career." She looks up at me, and there's something broken in her gaze. "But I'm tired of his career being more important than family."

"Mom—"

"I mean it," she interrupts me. "I've let too many things slide for too long. I've prioritized the wrong things, protected the wrong person." She takes a shaky breath. "I'm not saying

I'm going to leave him or make some grand gesture. I don't know what I'm going to do. But I needed you to know that I love you. That I'm proud of you and I think you're brave and remarkable. I watched the interview, and you were just so... authentic. And now I wish I'd know you like that."

Her words break me. I've spent thirty years waiting to hear them, and now that they're here, I don't know how to hold them.

"Thank you, Mom," I say. "My life is complicated right now and I'm sorry for the mess I've created for you. But I know one thing. I'm happy."

Mom sits down and takes my hand again. "I'm glad you're happy, Diane." She gives me a genuine smile. "And I hope that we can get to the point where we can all be together again as a family. You, me, Dad..."

"I'm moving to LA," I say.

She goes still, her hand freezing in mine. "What?"

"I've been offered a job there. Director of Development for an LGBTQ+ advocacy organization. I'm taking it."

"When?"

"Soon. In a few weeks, maybe. I want to be closer to Zara. I want to build a life with her. A real life, not just stolen moments between her work schedule and mine."

Mom sits back in her chair, processing.

"I'm going to get my own place at first," I continue. "Take some time to settle in. When Zara finishes her residency next year, we'll figure out what comes next. I'll probably move in with her."

"Wow." She blinks. "Okay. You're really going to be together."

"Yes, Mom." I meet her eyes. "I love her and she loves me."

Mom's eyes well up once more. "Will I ever see you again?".

Her vulnerability catches me off guard. I've always felt like a piece on her chessboard—the daughter who opened doors, who made the right connections, who reflected well on the family name. But she loves me. Somewhere deep down, I was never really sure if she were capable of true motherly feelings, but I see it now.

"Of course you will," I say quietly. "You can visit us in LA whenever you want. And if Dad comes around, I can come back to visit you both." I pause. "I just won't be involved in your lives the way I used to be. I need to be my own person, Mom. With my own values, my own career. I can't be an extension of you and Dad anymore."

She nods, dabbing at her eyes with the crumpled tissue. "I understand."

We sit in silence for a while and around us, The Rundown continues its afternoon rhythm. The jukebox switches to a different song. Someone breaks on the pool table. Jamie catches my eye from behind the bar and gives me a small, encouraging smile.

"I should probably go," Mom says, brushing her blouse, trying to compose herself. "Your father will be expecting me."

"Okay."

She stands, gathering her purse, putting her armor back on piece by piece. "Call me when you get back to Vegas? Let me know you're safe?"

"I will."

She leans down and kisses the top of my head. "I love you, Diane."

"I love you too, Mom."

She walks toward the door, and I watch her go, this

woman who gave me life and then made it her mission to shape me into something I could never be. At the door, she pauses and looks back. We hold each other's gaze for a moment, and I see it all there—her fear, her love, her regret, her hope.

Then she's gone.

EPILOGUE
DIANE (1 YEAR LATER)

*T*he front door closes behind me with a soft click, and I pause in the entryway to slip off my shoes. My feet meet with the cool marble, and I exhale deeply. Coming home always feels good.

Through the open floor plan, I can see straight through to the living room where Zara sits at the piano, her back to me. She's wearing shorts and a white shirt she stole from my wardrobe, and her hair is pulled into a messy knot at the base of her neck. Her fingers move across the keys effortlessly. She's in her element.

I don't announce myself. Instead, I let the music wash over me—a melody I haven't heard before, something new taking shape in real time. Her voice follows, quieter than when she performs, more intimate. The lyrics are about coming home, about finding solid ground. About learning to be still.

Her creativity has been soaring. Ten months in Vegas gave her the space to rediscover what making music felt like when it wasn't a product to be delivered on deadline, and over these past months living here together she's been finishing what she started.

She hits a chord progression that doesn't quite work, stops, tries it again differently. Better. She nods to herself and makes a note on the paper scattered across the piano's music rack.

I'm watching a master at work, and the knowledge that I get to witness these private moments—these raw, unfiltered creative processes that most people only experience from a concert seat—is still hard to believe sometimes. I'm sharing my life with the woman I love, and the life we've built together looks nothing like anything I'd imagined and everything I'd hoped for once I finally admitted the truth.

Zara reaches the bridge of the song and her voice opens up, filling the space with a power that makes me shiver. Not with the theatrical grandeur of her stage presence, but with something immensely vulnerable.

The song ends and she sits there, hands resting on the keys. I've been holding my breath and exhale.

"Are you just going to stand there or are you coming to say hello?" she asks without turning around.

I smile. "How long have you known I was here?"

"Since you walked in." Now she turns, and her face does something that still, after all these months, makes everything else around me fade away. "You have a way of trying to close the front door quietly but I can always hear you coming in." She smiles as I walk up to her. "How was your day?"

"Hectic," I say. She stands and kisses me and I forget all about the budget reports and the complicated logistics of planning a charity. When we break apart, Zara keeps her arms locked around my waist, and I let my forehead rest against hers. "But good. One week to go until the concert."

"I know, I'm excited," she says. "And ready. I'm so ready."

Her charity concert for The Center next week is completely sold out—the Forum, fifteen thousand people, all proceeds going directly to our organization. When I first mentioned the idea months ago, she didn't even need to think about it. "Of course," she'd said, like it was the most obvious thing in the world. Now we're looking at raising close to two million dollars in one night. Two million dollars for services that will change lives.

I chuckle at her confidence and shoot her a teasing look. "What about tonight though? Are you ready for tonight?"

"That, I feel less confident about." Zara rolls her eyes humorously and kisses me again. "But this isn't about me. How do *you* feel about seeing your dad again? It's been a year."

How am I feeling about it? That's the question I've been asking myself since Dad called three weeks ago. Not through Mom, not through an email, but an actual phone call in which he asked if it would be all right if he came with Mom to visit.

"Is that okay? I mean, would you be okay with having me over as well as Mom?" he'd asked clumsily like he was speaking a language he'd never quite learned. "Would I be... welcome?"

I'd been so surprised I'd nearly dropped my phone. Senator Richard Washington never asks for permission. He issues statements, makes declarations, expects compliance. But this person on the other end of the line sounded uncertain and afraid.

"I'm nervous," I admit. "It's been manageable having Mom here occasionally. We're finding our way. But Dad..."

"He's a wildcard." Zara takes my hand and leads me to

the couch, pulling me down beside her. "Have you spoken to your mom today?"

"Yeah. She called be before they left. Said he still genuinely wants to come. And that he's been different lately." I lean back into the cushions, and Zara tucks herself against my side, her head on my shoulder. It's a position we've perfected with countless evenings spent exactly like this. "Quieter. More withdrawn. Talking about retirement."

Thomas and Mom have kept me informed about what's been happening back in Washington. Thomas finally told his parents about Jamie—it didn't go well at first, but they're slowly coming around. Dad's career survived my coming out, technically, but he lost a lot of credibility. Although he's still Senator Washington, he's no longer the Senator Washington who mattered. Most days, I don't let myself feel guilty about not being on his political side anymore.

Zara's hand finds mine, our fingers interlacing. "Maybe that means he's waking up," she says quietly.

I turn to look at her. "You really think people can change like that?"

"I think people can surprise you," she says. "Look at us. We were both deeply closeted and after coming out to the world, we're living together and we're about to host your parents for dinner."

She's right. A few weeks after Zara and I came out on the Robin West Show I'd expected complete rejection from my father. What I got instead was more complicated.

He eventually released a statement through his press office. Brief, formal, saying that while he and I disagreed on matters of policy, I remained his daughter and he wished me well. It wasn't acceptance, but it wasn't total rejection either.

"I'm glad you're home early," Zara continues. "You can help me finish dinner."

"That was the idea..." I let out a long sigh and shake my head. "I don't think I'm ready but it's too late to cancel. Mom and Dan will have probably be on their way here from the airport by now."

"True. So let's get this dinner on the way." She pats my thigh. "The table's already been laid out. I just need you to dress the salad while I lay the final touches on the starter. You're good at dressing."

"Starter?" I shoot her an amused smile as she gets up and pulls me along. "Does that mean we're having multiple courses? Since when are you a kitchen princess? I told you we could just order takeout."

"We can't get takeout," Zara says with mock indignation. "This is a special occasion. It's the first time I'm meeting your dad and I want to give your parents a proper home-cooked meal."

I follow her into the kitchen and stop short. The marble counter looks like something out of a cooking show. There's a lasagna ready to go in the oven, fresh garlic bread, a caprese salad, a green salad, and a beautiful tiramisu sitting on the side.

I turn to Zara, genuinely amazed. "You made all this?"

She giggles, that guilty little laugh I adore. "Okay, so Daria did most of the work. But I helped! I... supervised. And I'm going to plate the vitello tonnato myself." She opens the fridge and takes out a platter of thinly sliced veal and a bowl of tuna sauce. "See? I know what it's called and everything."

"You supervised our housekeeper," I repeat, trying not to laugh.

"Very closely." Zara winks. "I also tasted everything. Multiple times. For quality control."

"Of course you did." The intercom buzzes and every

muscle in my body goes rigid. "They're early," I say, checking my phone. "They're not supposed to be here for another half hour."

Zara looks down at her stolen shirt and bare feet. "I need to change—"

"You look beautiful," I say quickly, though my own heart is hammering. "Don't worry about it."

But I'm worrying about everything. The salad isn't dressed. The bread isn't warmed. I'm still in my work clothes. Except I know it's not about any of that. It's about facing my father for the first time in a year.

I walk to the intercom panel by the door and buzz them in. Through the window, I watch a car pull up the driveway. It stops, and two figures emerge. Mom's unmistakable silhouette, and beside her, taller, broader—Dad.

I open the front door and step into the entryway.

He's aged and he looks tired. That's the first thing I notice. His hair is grayer, the lines around his eyes deeper.

We stare at each other across the threshold. A year of silence, of distance, of everything said and unsaid.

Then he steps forward and pulls me into a hug. Not the perfunctory, one-armed political embrace I'm familiar with, but a real one. His arms wrap around me tight and he holds on like he's afraid to let go.

"I'm sorry," he whispers against my hair. "Diane, I'm so sorry."

I close my eyes and let myself be held by my father. I can feel him shaking and neither of us lets go.

When I finally pull back, Mom is crying and Zara is standing in the doorway with her hand pressed to her mouth. Dad's eyes are wet too, and he doesn't bother hiding it.

"Come in," I say, moving back to make room.
And they do.

AFTERWORD

I hope you've loved reading The Residency as much as I've loved writing it. If you've enjoyed this book, would you consider rating it and reviewing it? Reviews are very important to authors and I'd be really grateful!

ABOUT THE AUTHOR

Lise Gold is an author of lesbian romance. Her romantic attitude, enthusiasm for travel and love for feel good stories form the heartland of her writing. Born in London to a Norwegian mother and English father, and growing up between the UK, Norway, Zambia and the Netherlands, she feels at home pretty much everywhere and has an unending curiosity for new destinations. She goes by 'write what you know' and is often found in exotic locations doing research or getting inspired for her next novel.

Working as a designer for fifteen years and singing semi-professionally, Lise has always been a creative at heart. Her novels are the result of a quest for a new passion after resigning from her design job in 2018.

When not writing from her kitchen table in London, Lise can be found cooking or singing her heart out some-where, preferably country or blues.

ALSO BY LISE GOLD

Lily's Fire

Beyond the Skyline

The Cruise

French Summer

Fireflies

Northern Lights

Southern Roots

Eastern Nights

Western Shores

Northern Vows

Living

The Scent of Rome

Blue

The Next Life

In The Mirror

Christmas In Heaven

Welcome to Paradise

After Sunset

Paradise Pride

Cupid Is A Cat

Members Only

Along The Mystic River

In Dreams

Chance Encounters

Songbirds of Sedona

Red Rock Ranch

Mistletoe Motel

The Turning Tides of Us

Hedonism

Midnight Wine

Stormy Waters

Erotica under the pen name Madeleine Taylor

The Good Girl

Online

Masquerade

Santa's Favorite